PRAISE FOR
A BLOODY FIELD BY SHREWSBURY

"Outstanding...a tale compounded of romance, stirring adventure, and subtle psychological insight."

—Publishers Weekly

"Chivalry, treachery, conflict of loyalties...are the rich threads in the tapestry...the clash of wills is as stirring as the clash of steel."

—Observer

"A vivid portrait of Hotspur...one of the last knights-errant of the age."

—Sunday Telegraph

A

BLOODY FIELD

BY SHREWSBURY

A BLOODY FIELD
BY SHREWSBURY

A KING, A PRINCE, *and the* KNIGHT WHO BETRAYED THEIR DYNASTY

EDITH PARGETER

Published by Sourcebooks Landmark, an imprint of Sourcebooks, Inc.
P.O. Box 4410, Naperville, Illinois 60567-4410
(630) 961-3900
Fax: (630) 961-2168
www.sourcebooks.com

Originally published in 1972 by Macmillan London Limited.

Library of Congress Cataloging-in-Publication Data

Pargeter, Edith.
Bloody field by Shrewsbury : a king, a prince, and the knight who betrayed their dynasty / by Edith Pargeter.
    p. cm.
1. Percy, Henry, Sir, 1364-1403—Fiction. 2. Great Britain—History—
Henry IV, 1399-1413—Fiction. 3. Nobility—Great Britain—Fiction.
4. Middle Ages—Fiction. I. Title.
PR6031.A49B57 2010
823'.912—dc22

2010014387

Printed and bound in the United States of America.
VP 10 9 8 7 6 5 4 3 2 1

ALSO BY EDITH PARGETER

The Brothers of Gwynedd

Prologue

SEPTEMBER 1399 TO MARCH 1400

I

SEPTEMBER TO OCTOBER 1399

The boy was not yet two months past his twelfth birthday, but tall and well-grown for his age, with long, slender bones, a lofty carriage, and the light, gawky, mettlesome gait of a high-bred colt. The burnished hair that curved in a close-fitting cap about his head was a rich chestnut, and the eyes that stared guardedly out of his solemn oval face were hazel, coloured like sunlit water over variegated pebbles, and like running water, inscrutable and inapprehensible. His chin was firm, and strongly cleft, a chin to be reckoned with, even while he walked unsteadily on English earth after his long adjustment to the vagaries of the Irish sea, and looked about him like one lost and uncertain of his ground, thus abruptly restored to the arms of a father he knew but very imperfectly, and released from the durance of a king he had known intimately and affectionately, and without whom he was lame and at a loss.

They had sent a ship from Chester to fetch him out of his captivity—for they insisted that he had been a captive—along with his fellow-hostage, sickly cousin Humphrey of Gloucester, and the trappings of King Richard's chapel, left behind with the boys when the tocsin sounded. He remembered the voyage now as one remembers the last dream before waking, the turmoil of his own mind, the uncertainty that lay before him, the fury of the seas, which by contrast hardly troubled his long agile legs, and never his stomach, the dogged advances that were beaten back for so many days, as though the elements willed to fulfil his own suppressed half-longing to be back in Ireland on the old terms. But there was no going back; he knew already that there is never any going back.

Humphrey had died on the crossing, and it had meant almost nothing to him, the withdrawal of so pale a presence that he hardly noted its extinction. They had never had anything in common. He had been sorry about it, as one should be sorry when a relative dies; a formal acknowledgement, like the sign of the cross. But then they had limped successfully into Chester at last, and only when he had stepped ashore into a world of ceremony had he felt the sea turning his head into a weathercock and his legs to willow wands.

He had everything to learn again in a new way. For he had seen at once, by the deference paid him, by the adulation that surrounded him, that he was now, whether they dared yet utter it or not, the king's son. And he learned quickly, for all the look of blank in-comprehension that kept his face stony and mute so many days and weeks, for all the custody he kept of his tongue, speaking dutifully and low, and of his eyes, veiled and lonely. He could not choose but learn quickly what seduced him so irresistibly. For he had within him a deep, insatiable appetite for glory.

So he embraced his father, kissed the hand that fondled him, answered all questions with circumspection, and so far as he could truthfully, walled up within him all the doubts no one had time to answer, took his place with determination a pace ahead of his brother Thomas, who was little more than a year his junior but still a child, and lived from day to day and hour to hour, looking no further ahead than nightfall.

He made only one mistake, and that came late, after he had lowered his guard. Throughout that strange parliament of September 30th— if it was a parliament, for the king who had issued the writs for it had resigned his throne, so they were told, the day before it assembled, and every official and every magnate scrupulously avoided the use of the committed, the legal word, and spoke rather of a gathering of the estates of the realm—throughout that extraordinary meeting, whatever its true title, he had stepped delicately, looked austerely, and held his peace, never setting a foot astray. Though the sight of the empty throne, draped with its cloth of gold, had caused his heart to turn within him, and his eyes to sketch in there involuntarily the familiar slight figure that was missing, with its fair hair and fair face, clean-shaven, sensitive and melancholy in repose. But Richard was in the Tower. A commission of the estates had visited him there the previous day, and he had declared himself willing and ready to resign the crown, and yielded up his signet ring to Henry of Bolingbroke. "For if it rest with me," so they had reported him, "I could wish that my cousin should be my successor."

The record of his renunciation had been read aloud in Latin and in English by Archbishop Scrope, and then, to better the legality of the occasion, they had added a long catalogue of the articles charged against Richard's mismanagement of the kingdom, thirty-two items in all. And by acclamation the estates had accepted his abdication, and set up instantly a commission to carry out the formal deposition, which they had done in all solemnity, standing before the vacant throne and declaring it as empty of majesty as the boy's practical eyes had already seen it to be. He had been afraid that he would have to enter into Richard's presence. He should have been afraid rather, if he had had more experience, of this glaring absence and loud silence. He should have been afraid of what he felt now in his bones, that he would never see Richard again. His charm was too well known, his following still too great, his eloquence too persuasive; neither then nor at any future time would Richard be allowed to walk into Westminster Hall and speak in his own defence.

And then Henry of Bolingbroke, duke of Lancaster, had risen in his place, and laid claim in good English to the realm and crown of England, by his direct descent from King Henry the Third, by the grace of God which had plainly stood by him and approved him in giving England into his hand, and by the need the country had of right governance by a strong man. And the estates had declared their acceptance of him as king, witnessed the testimony of Richard's signet ring, and set him on the throne.

The boy had been unable to suppress the glow of excitement within him as he saw his father seated in state; but this, too, he had contained, keeping a magisterial face and a still tongue, a magnate among magnates, grave when they consulted him, saying little but when he had an inner certainty what to say. All through the conferences of state that followed, while the offices of power were prudently filled with trusted Lancaster retainers, while Northumberland and Westmorland, those inveterate allies and rivals, were wisely invested with equal honours as constable and marshal of England respectively, and silly little Thomas was set up exultantly as steward of England, and put to work allotting rights and roles in the coronation ceremonies, with the earl of Worcester to hold his hand when he got frightened, the boy carried himself royally and unobtrusively, knowing well in his burning dreams that there was something greater in reserve for him.

And then, after all his care, he had to make his one mistake; for by nature and inclination he was open, impulsive and warm, quick in affection and direct in speech, and it was only by early and wincing experience that he had learned circumspection. So when King Henry declared his intention of knighting all his sons at the Tower on the eve of his coronation, the boy looked with tolerant disdain on the jubilant excitement of his three younger brothers, and said at once: "I am a knight already."

"Are you so!" said the king, sharply but softly. "And where did this befall, and who knighted you?"

"The king," said the boy without a thought, "in Ireland."

He could have bitten out his tongue the moment it was said. He held his breath, but there was no outburst and no protest, only a frozen stillness that arrested the very stirring of the blood in his father's florid cheeks, and the motion of his long hand in the folds of his gown. The full brown eyes, which had been fixed upon the boy's face, lengthened their focus upon something far beyond, piercing through his flesh like needles so fine that he felt no pain. And then the youngest boy, Humphrey, began to clamour gaily about Sunday's great ceremony, and the stillness warmed and moved again, and they two moved with it, each with infinite caution and gentleness, not to startle and confound the other. And strangely this impulse of ruth, of mutual consideration and regret, drew them closer together for a moment, so that there was no bitterness in it when the king said: "Then you need no ministrations of mine!" even though his smile was wry.

"Sir," said the boy, low-voiced and with aching care, "I need always your example and your grace."

Nevertheless, he took good heed that there should be no second such slip on his part.

They gave him the sword of justice, the unsheathed Curtana, to carry at his father's coronation. Long before the ceremony in the abbey was over he had learned one of the basic lessons of his life, that justice is a burden heavy to bear.

His wrists ached maintaining the Curtana upright and unmoving all through the long processional walk and throughout the consecration. His head swam a little with the smoke of torches and cressets, and the dazzle of so much gold and scarlet and silk and miniver and jewellery, and the scent of incense and oil, and the chanting, and the monotone of the archbishop's voice. Now that his hands were free, and the sword girded about his father's loins, he could stand back, his duty done, and marvel at what he saw, the royal head crowned and anointed, the royal hand gripping the sceptre, with an assertion of possession that expected now no challenge.

That is England he is holding, the boy thought. It is his now. And I am his firstborn son, and what is his will some day be mine. And all the while he could not shake out from his heart the conviction that it was still Richard's.

Richard had done impermissible things, they said, things which undid the good governance of the state, and made him unfit to rule. As the powers of life and death must be kept out of the hands of children and madmen, so they had had no choice but to take them out of Richard's hands, for the saving of his realm and his people, and give them to a responsible man of the blood royal, capable of restoring order, peace, and justice. The word recurred wherever he turned his mind, like the sword at the gate of the garden closing every way.

He could not quarrel with their condemnation of Richard, for who had known him better? There had been impositions never sanctioned by law, extortions, extravagances, he knew all that. He knew how his own father had been exiled without cause—a year ago this very day he had left England, the day of St. Edward the Confessor. Was that why he had chosen this same day for his triumph? And when Grandfather of Lancaster had died, last February, Richard had revoked the license of his heir's attorneys to receive the inheritance, and declared him perpetually banished, and all the possessions of the house of Lancaster forfeit to the crown. Which was rankest robbery, not to be borne by any nobleman of spirit, not to be tolerated by any of his peers. The crime was gross and open; he had known it for what it was even then, hedged about as he was from the worst buffetings of fortune by the indulgence and luxury of his place at court. For no sooner had his father quitted England than Richard had taken the son into his own household, and used him as a son, and a favourite son at that. Richard had no children. And he had loved his first queen out of all measure, and for any child of hers would have laid down his life and his kingdom and all, without a qualm. He had kept the borrowed boy always about him, lavished gifts on him, ridden with him, played with him—when had his real father ever found time or inclination to play?—and prophesied great things of him, taking such delight in his wisdom and his prowess that the boy grew like a nursed sapling during the year Richard had charge of him. A whole year! When had he ever had so much of his own father's time and interest? He peered back through the mist of smoke and gold into his infancy, and what he saw of his father was an eternal departing, once for a year of crusading in the north of Europe with the Teutonic Knights, often for some diplomatic mission into France, once on a whole year's pilgrimage to the Holy Land. Always busy, always abstracted, always grave, his father had been a distant and revered figure, almost without features for him. After his mother's death—of her he remembered warm arms and a silken lap, but a wan, worn face at once childlike and old—he had been brought up by a series of careful tutors in the houses of noble kinswomen, and surely his father had always made his arrangements for his children with the most loving care—but distantly. Richard had been always near, always accessible, always playful and attentive. The boy had no illusions; he had seen that comely face distorted with anger and hatred, but never towards him, had heard that mellifluous voice raised in vituperation, but never against him. More, he well remembered the year when Richard's Anne had died in June, and his own mother in July. He had been only six years old, but he remembered the dry, formal mourning in his father's household, the mild sadness and the marshalling of life into its new shape without her. And he remembered Richard's appalling grief as a cataclysm like the end of the world. He had climbed into his lap to hug and comfort him, when none but the children dared go near, and he had not been repulsed even then, but gentled and reassured, and Richard's tears had been stemmed to put away his tears.

Now they told him—and he did not argue the issue—that he had been taken into the king's household, and borne away with him to Ireland when he sailed to quell the rebellion there, as a useful hostage to compel his father's quiescence. Yet if that was truth, why had not Richard ever made use of him as a bargaining counter? They said he had been left behind in Trim for the same reason, when Richard got word of his cousin's landing in England to claim

his inheritance—a prisoner and a hostage. But still no ill use had ever
been made of him. Richard could have threatened and bargained
with his protégé's life had he been so minded, but he had never
done so. Nor, looking back now, could the boy feel that he had
ever experienced imprisonment, or felt himself to be in any danger
at Richard's hands. What he remembered was riding and hunting
in the king's company, and being praised and made much of, and
dubbed a knight. And above all, one perilous interview, after the
news had reached Ireland that his father had landed at Ravenspur
in arms, in defiance of the king's order of perpetual banishment.
In dread and confusion the boy had begged his way to Richard's
side, to plead his own innocence and helplessness in whatever enterprise his father was undertaking against the Crown. And even then
Richard had embraced him gently, and reassured him that he knew
him guiltless and would hold him immune against all reproach,
eternally his cherished cousin. Was he to forget so soon the voice
that had cajoled and coaxed him, and the kind arm flung about his
shoulders in the hour of his bewilderment and fear?

He forced his drooping eyelids wide, and the light glistened on the
oil that gilded his father's temples. It was no common oil, this, but
the miraculous phial of oil which was said to have been presented by
the Blessed Virgin to St. Thomas a'Becket, and afterwards secreted
in the Tower, where Richard had rediscovered it too late for his
own anointing. Had God, perhaps, covered it with his divine hand
to preserve it for this day, in token of his approval of the Lancastrian
accession? The boy clung to the hope with a desperation which was
its own betrayal. And yet what choice was there left? What could his
father do but step into the vacant place? And what could England do
but hale him in, and be grateful? Someone had to carry the burden.
Justice without vindictiveness—that was the significance of the load
he had carried for more than three hours this day. Richard's justice
had often been vindictive enough, but so had the justice used against
him when his star was low in the sky.

The gold and the glitter danced before his eyes. He looked from face to face along the ranks of the king's new officers, and he saw the old Lancaster household raised to a higher power with its master. John Scarle, chancellor of England, John Norbury, treasurer—who would have thought to see mere squires, not even clerks, raised to such eminence? The king knew where to place his trust. Sir Thomas Erpyngham, chamberlain of the royal household, Sir Thomas Rempston, steward—all old names associated long since with the house of Lancaster, and placing there all their loyalty, lifelong. And able men, too. Why should not the qualities that held up the duchy of Lancaster hold up the kingdom just as securely?

On one side of the throne, bearing Lancaster sword, the sword the king had worn at Ravenspur, stood the earl of Northumberland, constable of England, tall and leathery and lean, with a hawk's face and a short black beard, very splendid in his dress; on the other Ralph Neville, earl of Westmorland and marshal of England, younger, shorter, a burly figure and a chill, watchful face. They were kinsmen, and rivals. Between them they ruled the north, and each of them had always a hand spread protectively over his own share, in case the other took one step too many and infringed his border.

He turned his head a little to shake the dazzle out of his eyes, and looked into another face. The likeness to Northumberland was faint, but it was there, in the bold, arched nose, the jutting cheekbones, the line in which the crisp dark hair curved on the broad brow. But this was a wider face, with more generous features; and beardless, shaven clean from high brown temples to broad brown jaw. The dark eyes, large and very wide-set, gazed intently and candidly at the king, memorising every detail of the mystical descent of royalty, with more of detached curiosity than of envy or adulation. He stood easily, relaxed and at peace, his long mouth critically curved, watching the archbishops do their part, as he had already done his. And what filled the boy with a sudden ease and confidence, he looked upon his work as a man looks who has no doubts at all.

He was by no means the most elaborately splendid of the lords assembled close about the throne, rather sober and plain in his attire under his ceremonial scarlet and miniver; yet he wore his brown and gold with an elegance that came all from his indifference to it, and set him apart from his fellows. There would always be something to set him apart. He was not the tallest, yet any who scanned the line of heads must halt, if only momentarily, at his. He was not the handsomest, and yet the eyes that once lit on him must turn back to look at him again, and more attentively.

The boy thought, with a small shock of realisation: He looks years younger than my father, and he is nearly two years older! For he knew him well; there were none who frequented Richard's court who did not know him, and few, surely, in England north of the Humber. One of the first to ride to the support of King Henry, haring hotly down out of Northumberland to offer his sword, with his father the earl, and his uncle the earl of Worcester, drawn along irresistibly on his heels, and the blue lion of the Percies flying at his back over a formidable array of cavalry and archers. The Lord Henry Percy, knight of the Garter, warden of the east march towards Scotland, sometime governor of Bordeaux, the man the Scots raiders had named Hotspur, by reason of the ardour and impetuosity with which he hunted them back over their border as often as they ventured south. The name was in common use now, even the Londoners knew it and called him by it, so well did it fit him. And here he stood aloof and thoughtful in repose, watching the consummation of his own labours, and not angling for a leading role in the play, nor eyeing those who had managed to secure some ceremonial morsel for themselves. He had no need to call himself to the king's notice; the king could not choose but notice him.

The boy knew by this time what his own future was to be. Tomorrow parliament would reconvene, a constitutional parliament this time, called and attended by a crowned and anointed king, and one day later the king's firstborn son was to be installed as prince of

Wales, duke of Cornwall, earl of Chester, and heir to the throne. It was not merely a king they were creating, but a dynasty. The nominal command in his principality would be his from then on, but he knew his father's situation too well to suppose that as yet it would be anything but nominal. There would be a governor placed at his back to guide him and preside over his council until he came to years of discretion; and the only thing he did not know as yet, because as yet it was not even decided, was whose was to be the hand on his shoulder and the voice in his ear.

He watched Hotspur, and his heart fixed upon him and coveted him. He was mistrustful of the obsequious, the thrusting, the ambitious, he did not want to be courted and protected and flattered, hedged about with ceremony. The king owed much to the Percies. Hotspur was his friend and contemporary, knighted on the same day by old King Edward, with Richard to make the third in the illustrious company. It might well be possible to turn the king's mind towards so close and congenial an ally as the guardian of his heir. Only he must refrain from any open asking, for what he begged for would surely be suspect, and probably denied him. It was for him to conduct himself in such a way that it should end by his having Hotspur imposed upon him, and dutifully but without open gladness accepting his father's fiat. He did not even understand or question how he knew so much; it came to him as inevitable knowledge that princes, especially heirs apparent, must get their way of kings only by roundabout means, and by seeming not to get it.

To have learned that was half his battle already won. The rest, he knew, was not past his powers.

❧

At the great banquet that followed the coronation the constable and the marshal of England rode into the hall on horseback, and the king's champion, Sir Thomas Dymock, paced in after them in full harness, according to custom, and offered to do battle with anyone who challenged the king's right and title.

The king raised his voice and his head, gazing down the full length of the room. "I thank you, Sir Thomas," he said, "but if the need ever arise, you shall find I can and will defend my crown in my own person."

In the clamour and gaiety of the feasting there was one brief instant of silence, soon bridged and soon forgotten, in which every man present suffered the momentary, and of course absurd, delusion that the words had been addressed directly to him, and with intent.

On the 21st of October Lord Henry Percy's appointment as warden of the east march towards Scotland was renewed, with the grants of the castles of Berwick and Roxburgh; and some days later he was appointed justiciar of North Wales and Chester, sheriff of Northumberland and Flintshire, constable of the castles of Chester, Flint, Conway and Carnarvon, with the grant for life of the Isle of Anglesey and castle of Beaumaris, and the castle and lordship of Bamburgh. The Welsh appointment made him also guardian and head-of-council to the prince of Wales.

As for the prince of Wales himself, already securely installed in his special seat in parliament, and invested with the rod and ring of his principality, he sat with an impassive face to hear the name of his governor, and showed no emotion but that of a dutiful son acquiescing in the declared wish of his lord and father.

There was one more notable incident to record, before this parliament ended, though few recognised it at the time as worthy of note. Among the various petitioners to the assembly came a tall, black-bearded gentleman of considerable address and presence, bringing a plea for judgment of a dispute with Reginald, Lord Grey of Ruthyn, over land which the appellant claimed as part of his inheritance, but which he alleged Grey was forcibly occupying in defiance of his right. The plaintiff was himself skilled in pleading, being a scholar and a graduate of the Inns of Court, an education only the well-to-do could afford; but he had the misfortune to be

Welsh. He might hold direct from the crown lands in Wales which his forefathers had ruled as native princes, and he might be married to the daughter of a judge of the King's Bench, and be a man of substance in his own country, but in the balance against a notable supporter of the king and a pillar of English power in Denbigh and Flint he was too light to be taken seriously. The assembly declined to receive his petition.

He applied for an audience of the king. The king frowned over the request, hesitated, weighed the value to him of Reginald de Grey, and shook his head.

"The man was formerly in your Grace's service," said John Norbury fairly. "There is some small merit in his case, on the face of it."

"Grey assures me there is none. I have spoken with him. He has already had trouble with this turbulent neighbour. No, I cannot let the matter be opened. Lord Grey's lands are vital to us on that border. I will not see him."

The prince and Hotspur were entering the king's antechamber as the petitioner left it. They saw the normally expectant but muted assembly within suddenly cleft and turned aside on either hand, like soil before the ploughshare, or the Red Sea riven to give passage to the host of Israel, before the striding withdrawal of a tall personage in dark, rich clothing, who gripped with both hands a tight roll of parchments, much as the marshal of the lists grips a truncheon before the onset. They saw the glitter of fixed black eyes in a gauntly handsome face, and even the short, pointed black beard could not conceal the bitter set of the long mouth, clamped tight with rage and offence. He swept by them, the wind of his passage fluttering their hair, and the skirts of his gown swirled through the doorway like a breaking wave, and vanished. And all in controlled and formidable silence.

"Who was that?" Hotspur demanded with raised brows. "The fellow who went out in a fury?"

"Some Welsh kern with a grievance against Lord Grey. There's a plot of ground in dispute between them, somewhere in Glyndyfrdwy. The king would not see him."

"Welsh?" the prince echoed, and jerked his chin over his shoulder to stare after the vanished appellant.

"It seems we shall have interesting neighbours in Chester," Hotspur remarked, and his smile was still a little astonished, and more than a little thoughtful. "Take good note of the face, Hal, for if he keeps his present mind we may well be seeing more of it. How is he called, this Welsh kern with a grievance?"

"Oh, he's more than that, I grant you. He's a gentleman of coat-armour, and married to Sir David Hanmer's daughter, his master in the Inns," said Sir Thomas Rempston the steward. "They call him Owen of Glendower."

2

JANUARY TO MARCH 1400

B efore the new year and the new century were two weeks old, the king was shown all too clearly that the Virgin's miraculous oil and his own direct descent from Henry the Third had not yet convinced the entire world of his title to the throne. By a matter of hours he escaped falling into the hands of an alliance of earls and churchmen bent on the restoration of Richard. With London's help he raised an army to defend his throne and his life; he was at his active best when he was forced, as he himself had prophesied, to be his own champion and stand to arms for his own title. By the fourteenth of January the conspiracy was shattered and the danger over. All the chief conspirators were dead: the earls of Kent and Salisbury, Lord Lumley, Sir Thomas Blount, Sir Bernard Brocas, Sir Thomas Shelley—the list was long, and only the clerics escaped it. It was grievous that there were so many of them. The king revered the church, and felt the sting of its apparent singular want of reverence for him; but he kept his hands, as yet, from killing its priests.

It was the first reaction against the usurpation, and he knew it could not be the last. It had happened round about Christmas time, the season barely ending, and all the northern earls who were his main military strength were away keeping the feast in their own estates. The conspirators had counted on that. But they had been absurdly inefficient and disorganised, and their only achievement had been to show that Richard's influence and cause, like Richard

himself, were very much alive, that tenure of his throne by another
was threatened every moment while he, and they, continued alive.
Parliament had agreed in October that he should be kept in close
ward, and none of his former associates allowed access to him. He
had been removed quietly by night from the Tower to Leeds castle,
in Kent, and thence to the king's own castle of Pontefract, remote
from the centre of emotion and seat of government. Yet still he was
ever-present, and the silence was full of his voice.

Full also of rumours concerning him, each one as dangerous as his
very presence. He had escaped, it was whispered, and taken refuge
in Scotland, where King Robert had sheltered him and was planning
to help him recover his own. And indeed the Scottish border was
causing the king great anxiety. How better to assert the effective-
ness of his tenure than by mounting a punitive expedition against
Scotland? And how better to discourage the belligerence of France?
Let his own subjects see the power of his hand, and let the kings of
Europe take his measure, and debate carefully before they denied
his claim.

He did not wish to call a second parliament so soon, or so soon
to be asking them for money which they had already shown they
were reluctant to grant. But money he needed if he was to raise and
equip an army. For such a purpose the lords spiritual and temporal
might consent to make private loans, and there need be no publicity
and no unseemly haggling. So it was a great council that he called
at Westminster on February the 9th; the two archbishops, eleven
bishops, five earls and fourteen other lords, besides the usual officials
and clerks. The prince of Wales was away at his post in Chester, and
Hotspur was with him; what passed at this council passed without
their participation.

Whatever other business was transacted that day in Westminster,
the strangest items, in their wording if not in their content, related
to the safekeeping of the king and the kingdom, after the recent
alarm. For the council laid down the principle that if Richard were

still alive ("as they supposed") he should be securely guarded for the safety of the realm. And in the next breath they recommended that "if he were no longer alive" his body should be shown publicly to as many people as possible, to quash the rumours of his escape to Scotland.

Council had spoken with the tongues of prophecy or of fore-knowledge. For in Pontefract castle Richard already lay dead.

The bent of the prince's mind was intuitively aristocratic. He acknowledged the eminence of his position, and his heart embraced with fervour the role assigned him, and with it all its possibilities of glory and all its heavy responsibilities. The first few weeks of close association with another creature of the same make had confirmed him in all the courses his nature dictated, and encouraged him to prodigies of flattering imitation. His ambition and passion for excellence would not let him remit one scruple of the obligations he felt incumbent upon him. Innocent arrogance drove him to be unflagging in service, unsparing in consideration, always accessible, passionately just. It was not enough for him to be assured by his accountant that his bills were paid, or by his quartermaster that his castles were adequately provisioned; he wanted to be shown the books, and taught to understand and check them for himself, to go over the list of stores and ponder whether something of importance had not been omitted. He was not satisfied with reports on armaments, or assurances that his garrisons were well-housed and content with with their conditions; he would visit both the armouries and the guardrooms, and see and enquire for himself. More, through judicious study of his model he learned to do as much without affronting the lieutenants on whose efficiency he was passing judgment, so long as they had done their work properly, and were not afraid to have it inspected. He learned to compliment, but did so sparingly; to criticise, and that he did boldly, but without malice or offence; and sometimes to condemn, which he did with absolute candour and indignation, sure of his own mind. But that was rare, for he had a warm and eager heart, willing to love and approve, and childishly hopeful of inflaming others with its own incandescent enthusiasm.

And then they sent him word that Richard was dead. Suddenly, the circumstances unexplained, or barely explained, the fact gross, obstructive, cutting off the sun. And here was this prince, a public person, exposed at the age of twelve, and compelled to maintain, in shadow as in sunlight, his impassive and impartial face towards the world that relied on him. And so he did. He had not, after all, been completely unprepared; innocence was some way behind him.

The only craven thing he did—and he never quite forgave himself for it—was to suffer from a fancied fever that exempted him from riding south with Hotspur to the funeral rites of the dead king. But while he waited for his mentor to return he did not hide himself, or spare any effort of his, or let the measure of the day escape him. He had learned very much in a few months, and most of it from one man.

And when he heard the hoof-beats clash into the courtyard of his lodging in Chester, on a frost-filmed afternoon of early March, and recognised from the window of his chamber the arms and livery of Percy, he dismissed his tutor at once, and with the proud courtesy he had learned from his idol, ran down into the court to welcome him in person, holding his stirrup like a well-trained page. Princes alone may condescend to be pages for their guests; the lesser nobility have no such grace, and no such compulsion. The penalty and privilege of preeminence is that no detail is too trivial, no desert too low, to be taken into account and held in respect.

Hotspur had kicked his feet free of the stirrups, in his usual vehement fashion, to vault down unaided, but he slid his toes gently back in a token pressure into the iron, just touching the attentive fingers, and descended decorously. The hem of his cloak fell free, and encircled the prince's braced shoulder. A face as grave as the encroaching frost stared up at him, unblinking.

"You're welcome back, my lord," said the boy with ceremony, for the grooms and pages hovered, ready to take the horse from his hand, and the Percy retinue was pacing in on its lord's heels. "Lay your hand on my shoulder, and come in."

He was aware of being studied with sharp attention, though unobtrusively. "I trust I see your Grace in better health," said Hotspur.

"I am quite well, I thank you, my lord. Had you good travelling?"

"The road was well enough. The errand was not so happy. You've had quiet days here?"

"No trouble. I'm very well provided, you have seen to that. Shall we go in? I should be glad to hear your news, when you are rested after your ride."

The groom recognised the moment to take the bridle from the prince's hand, and lead the horse away. The stir and flurry of knights and squires dismounting filled the courtyard. Hotspur stooped and touched his lips lightly to the boy's fingers, and walked with him into the house. His spurred boots rang on the stone stairway.

"I had rather give it now. I need no rest, and you, as I conceive, will rest the better when we have talked." They were out of the general eye now, and in private they observed much respect but no ceremony. "God knows, Hal," he said, as he closed the door of the prince's study and drew the heavy curtain over it, "I have good reason to understand the measure of your sadness. The king asked most kindly and solicitously after you."

He dropped the cloak from about him, and stretched out his booted legs under the short, furred riding-coat, with a long sigh. Sometimes, when the matter was too heavy, or charged with feeling, speech came haltingly from him, even with a slight impediment that blocked utterance until he drove at it as at a quick-set hedge, and sheared his way through with words as impetuous as swords. But the boy already mattered to him so much that restraint was vital. Almost as vital as truth, which between these two was a matter of life and death.

He looked up at length, and fixed his eyes on the hazel eyes that gazed back no less earnestly at him, out of the long oval of that solemn face. "I never thought that it could end so, but so it ends! He is out of his pains, Hal. Whether all was done well or much done ill, only God knows, but what is done is done, and we have work still to do. I know nothing that can assoil us but doing it better than aforetime."

"He was good to me," said the prince, slowly and carefully. "There may be many have the right to say he was not good to them, but I cannot say so. Even when the event made me his enemy, he did not so use me, and when he might have made profit of me, he did not so abuse me, either."

"I grew up very close to him," said Hotspur gently, "and there was a time when I knew him well. I tell you, this Richard was as good and feeling a creature as walks in England, could he have been no more than a man. That he was born to the crown was a disaster for him and for England, and they have both suffered for it."

The fixed and guarded face quivered, like a sudden wind over still waters. "Did you see him?"

"I saw him. They brought the coffin from Pontefract by daily stages, and let him be seen wherever they halted for the night. Then he lay in Paul's for two days before the funeral service. They uncovered him for all to see. It is needful," he said gently, marking the sudden brief convulsion of the set lips, and the flutter of the large eyelids resentfully blinking back tears. "Rumour would have him already escaped and in Scotland, and Scotland is sore enough irritation without the ghost of Richard. Believe me, you would not have been shocked at what was shown us. He was not even greatly changed. Except that never until then had I seen him at peace. He was a man greatly tossed by every wind, as you yourself well know."

And the boy did know it, perhaps better than any, for the very reason that those contrary winds had never blown cold or rough upon him. He gazed earnestly at his companion, trying to penetrate where he was accustomed to entering freely; for Hotspur had never yet told him anything but truth, even when the truth was short and stinging, provoked by some negligence or levity or mistaken stubbornness on the pupil's part. They spoke out to each other, in private, and bore no grudges. No, of all people on earth, Hotspur would not lie to him.

And yet he could not give utterance to what lay heavy and certain in his mind. He needed the answers bitterly, but the questions were too terrible to be posed. He could not do it without exposing himself, and that was more than he could bear. This position he held was a fortress which, once surrendered, he would never be able to recover.

"There was no mark nor blemish on him," said Hotspur, aware of a crying need, but not yet clear how to supply it. "Only the mark of the choice he himself made. He was emaciated—so lean, so light, I could have lifted him in my arms like a child."

The prince asked, in his clear, girlish voice, and never turning away his eyes: "What have they done with him?"

"Given him every possible funeral honour. There was a great service at Paul's—the king himself was a pallbearer."

Yes, thought the boy, coldly and critically within his own closed mind, he could well afford to take some part in the charade; it would be a relief to his feelings, and more decorous than dancing on Richard's grave.

"And where have they laid him? Not in the abbey with his queen?"

"At King's Langley. The Black Friars there took his coffin in charge, and the bishop of Lichfield buried him."

Not deep enough, thought the prince. He will be out of his grave and over the border before ever my father raises these loans to fit out his force for Scotland. No matter how he hurries, Richard will still be ahead of him. And he thought of his own strange situation, prince here of a principality he desired with all his heart, heir to a kingdom he knew he could rule, bound to a people for whom he felt as his own close kin: and with what title, what morsel of right? And from the moment his fingers had closed upon the prize, he knew he could not for his life leave go.

The tide of his own outrage and grief and frustration rose in him and swept his guard away, like a straw bale poised against a flood. In a harsh cry of pain he demanded: *"And you have no doubts at all?"*

He was appalled by the sound of his own voice as soon as it was out, and jerked his head aside to stare blindly out at the grey sky above the gatehouse roof, aware of the magnitude of his self-betrayal, and shaken into as deep a desperation as that royal despair of Richard's in which he did not believe. He waited with held breath for the inevitable parrying denial; and what he heard was Hotspur's voice, roused and turbulent, saying:

"Doubts? Ay, have I, and many and grievous, too! Do you think there's one of us that is not looking back now in torment of mind, questioning at every move what we did well, and what was ill-done? Death makes a man turn his head and re-examine his conscience. Do you think any man of us all ever dreamed of driving him to his end this way, or any other way? Yet we have done it—taken away from him everything that held him back from a despair like a mortal sickness. He was fallen so low, Hal, that he turned his face to the wall and refused food, and there was not one creature there with the wit to sound an alarm before it was too late. When they brought the physicians to him, and persuaded him to take food, he was too weak even to stomach it. He starved himself to death for want of a hope of some future fit to be lived. And that was our work, whether we ever intended it or no. I tell you, Hal, I am not proud!"

The prince had turned to stare again at his friend and counsellor, his face pale and blank and bright, only his eyes shining greenly. The wide-set eyes that stared hotly back at him were clear and shadow-less, open like deep shafts into the mind and heart behind them. Hotspur had understood him astray, but answered him to the point. Dazed, the boy thought: He means it! He believes it! When did he ever tell me anything less than truth? And he drew back very gently and gingerly within his miraculously restored defences, to examine the gift he had been offered.

"But neither dare I be ashamed," said Hotspur in a softer voice, breaking suddenly into the warm smile that belonged particularly to the boy. "God knows I may have enough on my conscience, Hal, and only he knows what penance may be exacted for it in the judgment. But had I this to do again, I could not do it differently. Richard could not rule, and there was neither justice nor order left in this realm. We have done what had to be done, and put in his place a strong and able and good man who can and will rule. And on the fruits of what we have done we will be judged, not upon one most grievous and unlooked-for death along the way. Do I know when my own end may come?"

There was nothing in his voice, nothing in his eyes, to dim the dazzling fact of his sincerity. Against his judgment and almost against his will the boy felt his heart lift and lighten. He drew back in awe from such lofty innocence, examined it feverishly by the light of the spark of hope it had kindled in him, and could not bring himself to utter one word that would cast a shadow upon it. For his own sake, as well as for Hotspur's, he had to nurse it and guard it and warm himself at it until, by God's grace, he might even come to believe it justified. There was something in him that longed to probe more deeply, to say: "You know, don't you, what our enemies will say?" And even then, perhaps, since indeed he could not choose but know what many must be saying already, Hotspur would curl his disdainful lip, and shrug off what the malicious and disaffected always say when kings die suddenly and strangely, leaving the field clear for other kings.

But he did not tempt God by speaking; and it was a second and marvellous gift to him that Hotspur should answer what had not even been asked.

"I got my knighthood on the same day as your father," he said. "We've known each other many years. I've ridden with him, and jousted with him, and campaigned with him. I need not ask any man what I should think of Henry of Lancaster, I know him of my own knowledge. Whatever we have destroyed in the doing, we have put a good king on the throne of England in place of a sorry one, and I do not go back on that for my own life or another's. I may grieve for Richard, but I cannot wish the thing undone. And for you, Hal, though there may be grief, there can be no blame. You had no part in his fall. You were ever a good cousin to him, and he loved you."

No, he had no doubts at all. He knew his Henry, and that was enough for him. The possibility of murder he must have seen from the moment the news reached him, since he was no man's fool; but for him, simply, it was not a possibility.

And how if he was right, after all? The prince thought, silently and ardently behind his still face: If I could believe as he believes! Why can I not, when I believe so wholly in him? How if he is right to have faith, and I am wrong to have none? But the doubt within him, that was so close to certainty, would not be moved.

If it had been any other man, he thought, thus praising the father before the son's face, I should believe he was courting my favour by saying what he reasons will win my ear. But I have never known this man court any. And it seemed to him rather that Hotspur's intent was to make certain that the son valued the father as he should, that the favour he was wooing was for King Henry, not for himself. The thought disconcerted him, for how had he ever left room for suspicion? He searched his memory hurriedly, but could recall no failure in filial reverence on his part, nothing done or left undone that could bring his devotion into doubt. But this was not a man who reasoned and observed like other men. He sensed by touch and by affection, illogically and too often accurately; and there could have been some secret coldness that had chilled him, and made demands upon his warmth to set it right, lest father and son alike should freeze. I must be more careful, thought the prince, even with him, even against the grain. To break through the uneasiness that had fallen upon him in this long silence, he rose and went to liven up the dull-burning logs in the broad fireplace, and throw on more wood. The flickering light and the sparks made a fiery painting of his face, as good as a mask.

"If there is guilt," he said carefully, to the fire, not to his friend, "I cannot be absolved. I set my name to the declaration making him perpetual prisoner, and cutting him off from all his old servants and companions."

"And so did I," said Hotspur.

"Yes—we stand together. Whatever fears and scruples I might have," he said, "I could not wish for better than that. If you are at fault, then with all my heart I will own myself at fault in the best of company, and take the half your penance upon me." The light, girlish voice—when would it break, and behave itself seemly in accordance with his dignity?—sounded solemn and strange in this avowal. "And the task allotted to me," he said, "be assured I shall fulfil. Having your help, I may so promise."

He turned and smiled, his cheeks still flushed from the heat of the fire. "You can stay with me here a while longer? I don't yet know my father's plans for this Scottish enterprise, and I know you must look to the eastern march."

"Oh, Scotland can spare me to Wales a while yet, I hope. The money comes in but slowly, there'll be no move this side May, and my father has all well in hand along the border. But by the summer the king must stir, or the year is lost. He means to bring King Robert to acknowledge him as overlord and do homage for Scotland, as the kings of Scots have done before, as late as King Edward's time. They're toying too openly with this French alliance, we have no choice but to cudgel them out of it if they persist. If Robert were more of a king, and had not given over his power so abjectly to his brother Albany, we should not have so turbulent a border, or such frequent raids. But now Robert's heir is lieutenant for his father, the boy that was made duke of Rothesay not so long ago, and no one yet knows his mettle, or what we may expect from him. If he can hold off Albany until we get there," added Hotspur with a wry smile. "That's still to prove!"

"Will there be fighting?" He did not know whether to hope for it or not. His father greatly needed a sharp demonstration of his ability to hold what he had gained, but a diplomatic victory might be as serviceable as a military one, and less expensive. There was France to be taken into consideration. The French king had been Richard's father-in-law, and could not be expected to take kindly to his deposition and death. The complexity of all these considerations of state confounded him.

"I doubt it," said Hotspur, "but there may well be some skirmishing before there's any sensible talk. If Robert has his way, I think he'll hold off and speak us fair, and compromise if he can, but Rothesay is young, and burns to make his name. Whether he's a good general no doubt we shall learn. He's no great hand at managing his peers, that's certain. One of the most dangerous he's as good as driven into our camp already." He caught the prince's questioning look, and laughed. "The Duke was betrothed to Dunbar's daughter, the earl of the Scottish March, but now Douglas has outbid March, and got the duke for his own girl, and Dunbar's daughter is rejected and insulted. Her father's renounced his allegiance in a fury, and written to King Henry for refuge and service, and I think he'll get his safe-conduct, at least, to come to England and parley. I've fought against March on the border before now, I know his quality. Who knows, I may find myself fighting by his side yet!"

He had eased his heart; he could talk of other things, and look forward, which came always more congenially to him than looking back. The boy envied him. They had so much in common, and yet this curious purity and simplicity of mind was clean out of the prince's scope. In whom did he repose so absolute a faith?

Yes, in one man, perhaps! Supposing someone should whisper of murder against Hotspur, supposing all the circumstances should conspire to lend colour to the calumny, what would his reaction be then? Now at last, putting this case to himself, he could comprehend Hotspur's unshaken certainty. He would not even need to hesitate or question, he would know it for a lie, and one almost too trivial and derisory even to be resented.

Hotspur rose and gathered up his cloak, stretching stiffly, "I must go and wash off the stains of the road, Hal. There are letters—I'll have Audley bring them to you at once. And the archbishop has sent you some new music for your chapel. I'll bring that with me to supper."

"The archbishop is very kind," said the boy.

"On my life, I'm glad to be back. When we're clear of the frosts, with your leave, I'll send for my wife and the children to be here with me a while, until your father hales me north again."

He had thrust back the curtain, and had the heavy door-latch in his hand, when he turned and looked back, and for a moment, while he studied the prince's face with a sombre and considering eye, he seemed to deliberate whether to speak or not. The boy sustained the testing regard, and waited in some wonder, and even a little trepidation.

The words came almost violently, as always after a momentary struggle with the knot that sometimes tied his tongue: "You love your father, do you not, Hal?"

Too quickly and too emphatically the boy said: "Yes!" How else could that be answered, though his heart might lurch within him at the shock of being thus probed, and his carefully-mustered defences tremble and threaten to fall? There was no other possible answer.

"Of course! Forgive me! And are proud of him—I know! So continue always, Hal, for well he deserves it, and as I know, like any man he needs it."

The curtain swung, and the door closed after him. The boy turned back towards the fire, released from the tension that held him rigid by the sound of the latch falling into place. He was still quivering as he beheld in the dim light his own tall figure and startled, wary face, reflected in the silver mirror that hung between tapestries on the wall. There was something there already of his father, the set of the long head on the shoulders, the gait, the way the hair grew on the forehead: a slender, half-grown shadow of the king. The moment was like a foretaste of their next meeting. Clearly he saw the portcullis of reticence and watchfulness close down over his face, braced for that confrontation. And he did not even know whether his "Yes" to Hotspur had been truth or a lie.

It would never again be easy; and he would have to face his father again and again, lifelong, never acknowledging by word or sign the sickness of his spirit, never admitting even to himself what he believed. Nor could he ever again deliver to the king the confidence and trust due between father and son; there must always be a reserve between them, since there could not be truth, and must not be lies.

He was glad that he had not besmirched with a fingermark of communicated doubt Hotspur's single-minded purity, for it was his own best hope. While that endured, he could still be proved wrong, however little he hoped for a miracle. And with what joy he would acknowledge his own sin and do penance for it how ardently!

But the face he saw in the mirror remained mute, closed, and wary, like a castle under siege, with not a soul to be seen about its walls, though it was full of armed and resolute defenders.

APRIL 1402 TO JULY 1403

I

⸛

The girl had chosen to take her seat in the one spot from which the opening of the inner door would afford her brief glimpses into the prince's audience-chamber. She sat erect in her black, sombre and motionless on the bench against the tapestried wall.

Thomas Prestbury, abbot of Shrewsbury, had given over his entire lodging to the prince's party, since there were ladies among them, and the castle, tightly-garrisoned and well-supplied as a vital base against the rebellious Welsh, had little comfort to offer the Lady Percy and her women. For his own part, the prince would cheerfully have bedded down in the cramped military quarters he normally used on his periodical visits, but he was punctilious in providing every amenity for his guests, and the greater space and grace of the abbot's apartments made approach to his own person easier, and brought more petitioners in search of his favour, which at once satisfied his thirsty sense of duty, and wore him out into childish sleepiness by nightfall. He was fourteen years old, intelligent, forceful, capable of listening attentively to his ministers and then overruling them and going his own way, capable, even, or so they said, of arguing a case strenuously and sensibly against the king himself in Westminster, though he seldom won his way there; but he was still a boy, unpractised, with little experience yet of living.

The girl in black was nineteen, five years older than the boy to whom she was bringing her petition. She had watched others

come and go, and seen the hall empty round her, until only she
and her opponent remained; and she had felt no impatience, only
a growing resolution. And all this while, from behind her mourning veil, she had fixed her eyes on the inner door, and watched
for revelations from within. The narrow chink presented to her
vision showed her the spot where the prince sat. She found him
surprisingly ordinary, a solemn-faced boy in plain, clerkly brown
clothes, long-legged and angular like everybody's young brother,
with a fierce, cleft chin and huge, attentive hazel eyes. But at least
his concentration never flagged. She was encouraged, because it
seemed she could rely absolutely on that devoted attention, but
discouraged, too, because he looked and was so young, and what
could he know of marriage and widowhood, and the things that
happen to women? He might will well to her, and yet be too green
to do her anything but harm.

She never moved or relaxed her watchfulness; but in her very stillness there was something of violence, as though a touch might cause
her to spring into startling and daunting life. When the man who
waited with her crept to her shoulder and whispered in her ear, as he
did several times between his nervous pacings about the room, she
made him no answer, and never seemed even to be aware of him,
though her braced tension made it plain that nothing that passed in
this apartment escaped her instant notice.

"You'd do well to think better of it, and come home. Do you
think I won't make it worth your while?"

She gave him no sign. He ranged about the room uneasily and
leaned to her ear again: "Waste of time! He won't receive you!"
But he knew and she knew that the prince denied access to no one
who ventured to appeal to him. Those who had no case had no such
courage, either.

"Is it likely he'll listen to you, against me and my house?"

The answer to that she did not yet know, but she had her own
answer already sworn, and she would not go back on it.

"Come, be reasonable! Listen to me, girl—I'll make your fortune! I mean you nothing but good, why should we quarrel? Give over this fool plea, and be wise for yourself and your sire!"

The outer door was thrown open with haste and ceremony, to admit a cloaked and booted gentleman who swept through the ante-room on a gust of chill April air, shedding a knot of servants and gallants at the threshold, and hurling all doors open before him with an alacrity that spoke to her of royalty. She turned her head towards the servant who had just hurried to let him in to the audience-chamber, and put out an imperious hand to arrest his attention.

"Who was that? He that just went in?"

She had seen little but the outline of him, and the walk, which was individual enough to be remembered, once seen; rapid and vehement, with a long stride that barely lit upon the earth before leaving it again as vigorously. And a passing glimpse of a profile clear as bronze, and at the moment of passing as aloof and serene.

The page was disdainful. "Do you not know the Lord Henry Percy, the prince's governor? He's just ridden in from London, and his lady's here to meet him. He's newly made the king's lieutenant here in North Wales, now we're as good as at war."

"Are we as good as at war?" she asked, and there was no way of knowing whether she laughed or was alarmed behind the widow's veil.

"With this Glendower rampaging round Wales as free as a bird, and threatening Ruthyn every time Lord Grey turns his back? And urging on Ireland and Scotland to his help? Can you doubt it?"

Her face was quite still behind the shrouding veil, giving away nothing. She had said all she had to say. So that sudden presence was the great Hotspur, the most celebrated, the most gallant, perhaps the last, knight-errant of the age. A strange man—or perhaps a plain man lost in a world where most other men had crown strange—collecting superlatives to himself as Saint Sebastian collected arrows in the wall-paintings. Something had blown through the room

with him, a gust of exhilarating air trapped in the folds of his garments, leaving a breath of his own vigour behind.

"You can still withdraw," whispered the wheedling voice at her
shoulder. "Come, be wise in time! You shan't regret it."

The door of the audience-chamber had opened. She saw the prince's
chamberlain lean out and speak to his waiting page. She felt the burden
of their eyes upon her, and rose from her bench silently, waiting.

"Mistress Hussey—His Grace will receive you now. Master
Hussey, he begs you also be in attendance."

She walked into the prince's presence, her anxious enemy treading hard on her heels. And she thought as she crossed the threshold:
He is still there. You have more audience, Julian, than a mere royal
child, whatever his goodwill. You can address yourself to a man, and
at least hope for a quick ear and an open heart!

∽∾

"There is still a lady without," the chamberlain had reminded them
respectfully, "who has a petition to your Grace. And a gentleman
who desires to speak in answer to it."

They broke off their colloquy at once, postponing all that they
had to ask and to answer.

"I'm sorry!" said Hotspur. "We have time, and indeed I did mark
this lady waiting in your anteroom. Yes, surely have her in. If she
has far to go, the evening will soon be setting in."

"You'll stay with me? I should appreciate it. I have no notion what
her case may be." He was quite without knowledge of women, but
granite in the acceptance of his responsibility. "Admit the lady,"
he said, and sat down again in his chair of state; though it was but
a rather uncomfortable chair, not raised by a brace of steps like the
abbot's own judgment seat.

She came in with a light, wary step, made a deep obeisance just
within the doorway, and then advanced to the prince's chair and
sank at his feet, touching her lips to his proffered hand. The boy
took her cold fingers in his, and raised her.

"Madam, you have a petition to us. I pray you speak out, and we shall listen. You, sir, are a party to this lady's plea?"

"I desire to speak in answer to it, your Grace," said the man, stooping obsequiously to the extended hand. He was a handsome person in his florid, full-fed way, ruddy and brown-haired and aware of his consequence. The woman was a mystery, tall and slender in her black, straight and steely as a boy, and thus far silent. Silent women are always formidable, and always mysterious.

"Madam, I see by your habit that you are in mourning, and for that I am sorry. How may I help you? And what is your name?"

The girl raised her hands to put back the veil from her face. Her youth blazed at them suddenly like a torch kindled, a thin, bright, deeply-moulded face all pearl-tinted skin over abrupt, burnished bone, with a wide, firm, full-lipped mouth, and dark eyes. On either side her head gleamed coiled braids of dark-gold hair, almost pale copper in the subdued light of the room. The intensity of that face turned her mourning and her stillness into the mere dark casing of a lantern.

"Your Grace is kind." Her voice was guarded, mellow and low, a well-schooled boy's voice. "My name is Julian Hussey. I was born Julian Parry, only daughter to Rhodri Parry, a merchant of this town, dealing in wool and woollen piece goods, and married by him a year and a half ago to Master Nicholas Hussey, who held lands here north of the town. My husband died two months ago, and we had no issue. By my husband's will, and the custom of his house, all his manor and lands go to his nephew and heir, and I am without purpose in the household longer. For me there is no function left but to return to my father's house, and care for his old age." She lifted eyes like gem-stones, ruby-bright in the light of the torches, black, surely, in full daylight. They looked at the prince, and passing by him, fastened with intent upon Hotspur's watching face, as yet impassive. "Your Grace, my father is but a merchant, and to marry me into this noble family he gave me a noble dowry, eight hundred marks. Now he desires, as is but right, that my dowry should be returned with me. But my husband's heir, my nephew by marriage, will not repay what is due. And if he receive not his right, my father will not receive his daughter. I ask justice of your Grace, for unless your Grace do me right, I am without redress."

She spoke to the prince, she even looked at the prince, but what she said was addressed to the man who sat withdrawn at the prince's elbow.

"Your Grace," said Hussey, bent reverently double, and eyeing his widowed kinswoman from the corner of one eye, "if your Grace will but hear me…"

"You may speak to the matter. You are the heir?"

"Yes, your Grace. I am Edward Hussey."

"And what this lady says, is true? You have no quarrel with it?" The prince leaned back in his chair, and waited, and wondered.

"None, your Grace, so far as it goes. All is as my most valued kinswoman has told you, but your Grace will comprehend that money matters are none so simple. My lord, my inheritance is indeed enough, but my immediate resources in money are limited. I would with goodwill repay Master Parry his daughter's dowry, but at this moment it is out of my power. I have not the sum to hand, and cannot raise it even by loan. Yet I have made provision," he said fatly. "There need be no dissension. Until I can repay the dowry, I have set aside apartments in my household, where my kinswoman may keep her own establishment however she may dispose. Her keep shall be a charge upon my estate, and for company she shall be assured of the society of my own wife, her close kin and most attentive servant and friend. I cannot offer more, nor with better will."

"It would appear," said the prince mildly, "a fair offer. What say you, madam?"

"Your Grace must consider," said the girl, lowering her eyes, "that I am still young. My father may well wish for me a second marriage, and to that end I must be at offer soon, and with a proper dowry. It is well I should marry again from my father's house. And that would, indeed, be my wish."

"Nor would I stand in my kinswoman's way, my lord," said Hussey eagerly. "So soon as may be, Master Parry may make such disposal as he thinks fit, and I will never say the loath word. It is my grief that I am unable to repay at this time the money that is due. Within a year there should be no such restriction upon me. And Master Parry himself is willing to agree to the offer I make."

It seemed that with every exchange the man was growing more confident, and the girl, for all she maintained her fiery calm, a little more pressed and on the defensive.

"Your Grace," she said quickly, "even a year may deprive me of my best prospects. And what should I do in another woman's household, who have been used to managing my own? Your Grace knows that two women in one hall is not good sense."

"Yet, your Grace, with all the goodwill in the world, I cannot repay this year, or not until after the harvest. There is not so much ready cash in my treasury. And it is but right that until I can make restitution, my kinswoman's expenses should fall upon me. I don't seek to escape my duty."

He was, perhaps, a thought too complacent on the subject. The girl flashed one brief look in Hotspur's direction, and for an instant the glitter of her eyes seemed to him hunted and wild. He leaned forward to the arm of the prince's chair.

"Yet—with your Grace's permission?—if this eight hundred marks was paid over no more than a year and a half ago, surely it cannot all have been used or turned into goods so soon," he said. "Unless your estimable uncle had expensive amusements, Master Hussey, you must surely have come in for this very money along with the rest."

The girl was quick to catch at the hint, drawing breath gratefully. But so was the man; he must have come prepared even for this, and there was surely something unnatural in his readiness.

"My lord, you say truth. My uncle was already old, and not given to rash spending, indeed he carried his carefulness too far, and was something of a miser. And what he has done with such ready money as he kept about his house neither I nor his clerk can tell as yet."

"He did not trust his clerk?" Hotspur asked negligently; and it was at the girl's wry face that he looked.

"He trusted no one," she said with sudden muted violence, and paled at the bitter sound of her own voice. A year and a half ago, Hotspur thought, this fierce faun was surely no more than seventeen years old, and married off, like many another, to an old miser three or four times her age, for the sake of a noble name and a set of paltry quarterings, and the hope of a grandson set up in the landed estate. And here she is, so short a time after, widowed and childless, with nothing gained and much lost.

"The better reason for feeling certain that his eight hundred marks are still unspent, and still safely bestowed somewhere about his household. It will be needful to find them, Master Hussey. You may very well find it possible yet to send them home again in the very minted pieces in which they left home with the lady."

"So I hope, too, my lord, for then our whole dispute is solved. But if my fair kinswoman will but be patient and abide in my house until we have brought all into order, and made proper search for this money…"

Even a few weeks would do for him, thought Hotspur, and caught the girl's eyes fixed upon him in silent desperation and appeal; though indeed it was so imperious as to be more of a demand. But for God's love, he thought, half-intrigued and half-exasperated, if she has anything to charge against him why does she not speak? Why has she not spoken long ago in the right quarter? For it seems she has a father!

He leaned to the prince's ear, and said in a rapid whisper: "There's more in this! Call an adjournment until tomorrow—and have the merchant summoned to attend."

The prince, at a loss with the complexities of women, was quick enough to pick up an offered lead, and not infrequently bettered the prompting, as he did now.

"It seems to me, Mistress Hussey, that we should hear you further on this matter, and that we have need of more certain information than is available here. I will hear the case again tomorrow, at three in the afternoon, and I desire that Master Parry shall also appear then to speak for himself. It is not enough for one party or the other to tell us what his mind is, that he must do in person. And further, Master Hussey, it would be helpful if you would bring with you your manor clerk, to speak to the value of your own holdings and this inheritance. We cannot make a judgment without knowing what your resources are."

That tasted bitter, thought Hotspur, watching Hussey swallow it down perforce, for on the face of it it was reasonable, and minor lordlings from the fringes of Wales do not argue with the prince of Wales. And sweet! For the girl's eyes, which he was beginning to read as he read his own children's, had flared briefly in vindictive joy, and again veiled themselves. There goes a woman who would dance on her enemy's grave, he thought, curious and thoughtful. And lie down in her friend's, too, if need be! He understood instinctively the nature that deals in extremes.

They had both made their reverences, and were withdrawing, markedly separated by three feet or more, and shrinking fastidiously from approaching more closely in the doorway, when Hotspur called the lady back.

"Madam, I misdoubt that you should be abroad after dusk alone, either here or in the town. With his Grace's goodwill, I would offer you a night's lodging here in the safety of the abbey hospice, and tomorrow you shall have escort to bring your father to the audience. My lady and her women are lodged in the guesthouse, you need have no fears in joining their company. If you accept, his Grace's page will conduct you, and commend you to my wife."

She had risen from her deep curtsey, and stood for a long moment gazing steadily into his face. This was the moment when she elected him, with her eyes and her heart wide open, knowing what she did. She never turned back from it after; nor was it her habit, any more than his, to repent of what she did.

"My lord," she said, "I know of no greater honour you could offer me, nor any that I would more joyfully embrace. With all my heart I will go to your lady."

Elizabeth Mortimer, Lady Percy, was thirty-one years old, and had everything woman could wish for, royal blood in her veins, wit and spirit and beauty, a husband the envy of all his peers, a little son the budding image of him, and a baby daughter on whom he doted. She had also a gallant and generous heart wide-open to affection. She received the unknown and unexpected widow like a welcome cousin, asking no questions and extorting no confidences, but offering on her own part enough warmth to make the early April evening glow. She talked of her children, far away in the north at Alnwick castle with their household, and of the late Spring when she would take her husband home to them for a brief visit. He was newly come today from Eltham, the king's favourite manor, where he had been a witness at his Majesty's proxy marriage to the widowed Duchess Joan of Brittany. The king had been many years a widower. She spoke with courteous compassion of the widowed, and for her guest's sake did not dwell on their sorrows. And well might one so gloriously married feel pity for all those less happy than herself.

They were still sitting together when Hotspur came from the prince's apartments. Julian rose as he came in, and bowed herself unnoticed from the room; but from beneath her lowered lids she saw them meet, and the private radiance that lit their faces was still a dazzle in her eyes as she closed the door upon them. She saw him cross impetuously to his wife, lift her bodily by the waist, and kiss her heartily; and she knew that before the latch clashed into place they were in each other's arms. Proof, she thought, astonished, that men and women do love. For she had seen little enough evidence of it in her life so far.

She watched them in hall, from her place among Elizabeth's ladies, and they were two bright lanterns burning with sparks of laughter and joy and prodigal kindness, for pure pleasure of being together after an absence. They lit the whole of the high table, startling the prince's grave face into gaiety. Julian watched them, and every moment of watching only confirmed his election, though it set him another league away from her.

Nevertheless, he had felt her need and advanced to fill it. She did not suppose there would ever be another such moment to hope for, yet few could ever have had so much. It was unlooked-for grace that after supper he should send his page to ask Mistress Hussey to be kind enough to come and speak with him in the small chamber the prince was using as a study. And a prodigy that he should receive her there alone.

⁂

"Now that we are private," he said, looking her in the eyes, "you may speak out openly what for some reason you did not wish to speak out before the prince. Why are you so urgent to get away from your husband's house and back to your father's? Oh, the wish I well understand. You're young and handsome, and your family clearly wealthy enough, you have a life before you. But if that were all, would it be so insupportable to stay a few more weeks in Hussey's household? And you yourself made it clear to me that you would not stomach so much as one more day, if we could but be induced to open a way of escape for you. If we had not provided you this delay, and this opportunity, what would you have done?"

His voice was quiet, matter-of-fact and kind, and his eyes smiled at her with interest and curiosity, she thought, beyond the mere charm he must use by native grace upon all who came near him and were weaker than he. She debated for a moment whether to answer, and then how to answer.

"My lord, I have good reason to know that it was you who said a word for me in his Grace's ear, and gave me this day for thought, and even offered me arguments I was not wise enough to find for myself. If you had not, and the prince had consigned me again to that man's house, I should hardly have known what to do, or where to turn. Though I should have discovered a tolerable way," she said, with force and finality. "Needs must, and I have had some practice."

"And why was it so urgent to you to go? And to him that you should not go?"

"He wants me to remain under his roof," she said deliberately, "because I am young and handsome—it was you, my lord, who called me so—and his wife is neither. Widowed and childless and penniless, a woman is at the mercy of her husband's kin—or so he reasoned. He offered me a fat life as his whore, and I laughed in his face. Since then, twice already he has attempted me by force. In his house I should never be safe."

"Then why have you not spoken out and accused him?" demanded Hotspur warmly. "If he has done you such injury this fellow must be held to account."

She smiled, a small smile as bitter as rue that just curled the corners of her lips. "He has done me no injury—yet. It is I who have left my mark upon him. Your lordship may see the print of my affection scored across the back of his left hand and wrist, if you care to make him hand you his manor roll tomorrow. But give him his due, he does not give up for a scratch or two, and not even a dagger could hold him off for ever."

"No!" said Hotspur, flushed with anger. "This cannot be allowed to pass without redress! You should have spoken out boldly before the prince. Why should you hesitate? Do you think he would not see right done to you?"

"With all my heart, my lord, I believe he would, but it would be a costly redress to me and mine." She leaned forward, flushing in her turn. "I do not want right done. All I want is silence, and to go back to my father's house."

"And how much silence will there be when your father hears how you have been used?"

"He will not hear," she said vehemently. "Never from me, and never from you, my lord, if you regard my good. What I have told you here I have told you in confidence, whether I exacted any promise from you or no, and you cannot violate my trust."

"God forbid!" said Hotspur, baffled and frowning. "But why should you be willing to let so gross an injury pass? For I think it is not out of any maiden meekness in you," he said, with a sudden blazing smile that turned the stricture into a compliment.

"Because he is English, and noble, though he may be only the small cousinly fry of his house. He is distant kin to Arundel himself. And I am the daughter of a Welshman, a settler in this town for many years, but still Welsh. Your lordship of all people knows what that means now. We Welsh are all suspect since the Lord Owen raised his banner in mid-Wales two years ago. We cannot own property, or hold office, we must give hostages for our good behaviour—we are prisoners and outcasts in our own town. My father was to have been bailiff, now that and all other honours are out of his reach. He had a great and flourishing trade with the Welsh weavers, bringing their wool and piece goods into England here, and transporting them to London. Now all trade with Wales is forbidden. My father is a proud man. If he knew of the insult offered me he would want revenge—and against the Husseys he cannot possibly speed. I want my father living, not dead. What use is revenge to me if it means the destruction of what life we have left? No, my lord, I beg you keep this thing secret. I need only one thing from you and his Grace, to return to my home and take part at least of my dowry with me. And if you can give me that relief, I will be grateful."

He thought it over, to judge by his frowning face with something of a struggle, and gave way reluctantly. "Well, you shall have it as you wish, though it goes against the grain with me to see this fellow go free. But you must give me leave to confide in the prince, and I make the same promise for him. Tomorrow's audience must be managed plausibly, he will need to know what he is about."

She hesitated. "And can you so promise for him, my lord?"

"Never fear for that. His Grace is wise beyond his years. I pledge his secrecy as freely as my own."

He sat silent for a long moment, considering her soberly from beneath knitted brows. She felt that the interview was over, and yet his stillness held her still, and the solemnity of his regard filled her with a curious sense of freedom and enlargement, as though she enjoyed the very fashion of intimacy with him that he might have shared with a man and his peer, even with the prince himself. Those who were his companions in arms must have known such moments. He was at peace with her while he reasoned and thought before speaking; and the lengthening silence had neither weight nor tension, but lay between them gently like the comfortable warmth of a fire. She had never before known how to be still and wait; there had never been anything as worth the waiting for as this was.

"Lady," said Hotspur, "there is yet something you may do for me, if you will."

"I will," she said, without haste or hesitation.

"Gently, you do not know yet what it is. You said well, no one knows better than I what it means to be Welsh now in these border towns such as Shrewsbury, with trade forbidden, and restrictions bearing down hard on every man with Welsh blood. I know that for two years now Welsh labourers and students and journeymen have been stealing away out of England, to make their way back to Wales and enlist under the banner of their self-styled prince. I know the manner of this same Lord Owen's disaffection, and I tell you honestly, though I must and will fight with him wherever I may, yet I think his cause not all empty and not dishonourable, and there have been faults committed against him foolishly and grievously, which a man may well resent. It is gross waste that a man with such qualities should be turned into a traitor, when I think he never willed to be any such monster, but wanted only his native right. And if I could bring him to reconciliation with the king, without more bloodshed and without revenge, I would count it a good deed both for England and Wales. You see, I speak with you as with my own conscience. I have already attempted something in this vein, but there are those who deal distantly with such realities, and the prince and I, both, suffer from them hardly less than Owen does. Nevertheless, it is our purpose to keep a channel open by which we may still talk with Glendower."

"I have already heard," said Julian, "how in the council of last November you spoke for a parley with the Lord Owen, and told the king's ministers that he would be willing to talk peace. And how there were some there who thought no shame to recommend that you should invite him to a meeting, so that he could be taken unawares and murdered there. And I have heard," she said, "how you answered."

The eyes that dwelt upon her had opened wide in surprise, perhaps even in amusement; but the mind behind them was held and deeply exercised. How came she to know so much?

"And how did I answer?"

"You said it was hardly in accord with your rank and honour to make use of the oath of fealty to lure a man treacherously to his death. And the prince," she said, watching him narrowly, "approved you. And so the matter lay."

His eyes were very bright now, though the constancy of their regard never wavered. Looking down into them, she could see clean into his soul. If ever this man needed to deceive, she thought, dismayed, he might as well bare his neck for the axe, for he could not save himself. He has no mask to cover his intent. He is like a naked light. And his lady is no different. Does that come from living and loving together? Or from choosing after his own kind?

He said drily: "You are very well-informed concerning the work-ings of the king's council."

The Welsh are all wizards," she said. "And the Lord Owen is the greatest wizard of all. Have you not heard as much?"

"Lady, I study to learn. There are more secrets than those be-longing to the English, and well I know it. Your father, as I hear, was the main channel through which the Welsh woollens reached England. Parliament in its wisdom or folly has banned all such trade, true enough. But parliament is far away, and the border of Wales is very near, and is there a soul in these parts who does not know that smuggling goes on day by day, and that life here would be impos-sible if it did not? Almost half of Shrewsbury has Welsh blood, or at the least friends in Wales. How can such a border be blockaded? It cannot, nor it is not. The Severn, even in spate, is not impassable. Now supposing, lady, supposing, I say, that there are traders who have kept their contacts across the water. Then such men can be of use both to England and to Wales. Peace is in the interests of both. You believe me? You trust me?"

"I believe you," she said. "I trust you." She did not say: "I love you."

"Good! You have spoken openly with me, and I speak openly with you. No penalties! I am neither a bailiff nor a tax-collector. What you say to me has been said only to me. *Is there a reliable man who goes back and forth freely into Wales?*"

"Yes," she said, "there is such a man."

She had said it, and she was committed, and had committed others along with herself. The thought did not daunt her, but she had great need of a moment of silence, to take breath and consider how much she dared tell. He had dealt with her honestly, not as with a mere woman, one who must necessarily be only on the fringes of her menfolk's concerns. He had asked her only for what he needed, though there must be many blunter questions he could have put to her had he been so minded. She trusted him, for her own part, without reserve or doubt; but she was trusting him for those who crossed the river and took the risks. Moreover, he himself had loyalties of his own to preserve, and it was well for him that he should not know too much.

"Yes," she said, picking her way delicately for his sake, "the cloth still finds its way in, though not so freely and not so profitably. Yes, the money still finds its way out to pay for the cloth."

"And letters can find their way both in and out," he said, "by the same route?"

"Yes," she said, "they can." Can and do, she thought, ever since that September of two years ago, before I was given in marriage, when Owen fired Ruthyn, and his men plundered Oswestry and Welshpool, and the king came storming through here and across the border with all his army, but never found any enemy to fight. The Welsh had all vanished into the hills, as they always vanish, and Henry marched his army back through Shrewsbury empty-handed. The despatches that mapped every move he planned went into Wales ahead of him by this same route. And that was only the beginning.

"Will you bring me in touch with this messenger?"

She hesitated, pondering means. "You must meet him?"

"I think it may be even more important that he should meet me. Will he take your word for my good faith?"

"Do you take my word for his?" she said.

He smiled. "Come, then, let's be plain. I have warrant from the king to deal—to keep open, if I can, a means of communication with Glendower, any honest way of continuing the debate that may yet stop this fighting, and let tradesmen and students and friars move freely about their business again. I want pacification. I want an open border, as you do. I want Owen back lawfully on his own lands and in good odour again with his king. What I do in approaching him thus I do with the king's goodwill. But well you know, it seems, that one such attempt has been ruined and rejected by the council, and it may take us a weary while to find a fair agreement and a council sobered enough and sensible enough to abide by it. Yet I think the trying well worth while. If I move as privately as possible, it is to hold off the fools and rogues until the thing has a chance of success. And if I handle all with my own hands, and keep the prince clear of it—though he knows my mind, and it is his mind, too—I do so to preserve him from harassment by those who will hear of nothing less than Owen's head on London Bridge. The letters your man will carry will be in this hand! He has a right to come face to face with me, and judge for himself whether he can honourably deliver them, and never fear that he is helping to lure a brave man to his death."

"My man knows your reply to the council," she said, "as well as I do. But your lordship says right, it is better there should be as few hands in the chain as may be. No one between you and Prince Owen but one man."

"Will you bring me to meet this man?" he asked.

"He cannot well come here. Or to the castle."

He nodded assent, and did not ask for a reason.

"I would rather come to him. There must be no suggestion of the prince being involved. If your father will receive me in his house, I should be glad. I would not have him think I have taken advantage of his daughter, and shun facing him. Nor that I will to borrow his messenger without his knowledge. I need not ask if he can be secret."

"He can be the most secret man alive."

"Will you be my go-between to him?"

"Yes," she said, "I'll be answerable for my father."

There was nothing he could have asked of her that she would not have done for him. She had never been afraid to look straightly at whatever fortune sent her, to map its every feature, and acknowledge it for what it was. She had examined with analytical precision her empty and disgusting marriage with an impotent old man, and her candid delight at the death that had put an end to it. She had even considered the possibility that the old fool's frantic efforts to

match a young wife had been the cause of his death, and the idea
had not caused her to turn her eyes away and evade the issue. She
had rejoiced at her childlessness, and even found the heart to laugh
at the lamentable end of her father's fond dynastic ambitions. If
there was one thing not ugly and absurd about that marriage, it
was a small but irreversible change in her own situation. She was
no longer an unmarried daughter, but a widow, and widowhood
represented status, and liberation not merely from spinster hood, but
also from any expectation of fulfilment in marriage. Through that
illusion she had walked with blessed speed, and out beyond it into
a world of other possibilities. Eventually the experience might have
to be repeated, in her own defence, but she could not hope to find
much more in it than she had found in this first venture. There were
other relationships. Whatever she could look for in the future must
be looked for outside marriage. What was here being offered to her
she took with both hands, roused and grateful. She had not yet even
recognised what it was, but she knew it for better worth than she
had ever yet been given.

"You will go home with him tomorrow—"

"If he gets his money," she said with a rueful smile.

"He'll get his money, or part of it, at least. How soon can you
bring me to meet the man you speak of? If he goes and comes, it
may be days yet? Or weeks? I cannot afford weeks."

"He is here in Shrewsbury," she said. "It can be tomorrow. Give me
but one day, and by night he shall be waiting for you at our house."

"I will come there after dark. Tell me how to find the place."

"It is a house in a court behind St. Chad's church. You may come
there by the alley from the town wall, and leave the church on
your right. There is a sign over the gateway, the Fleece. Or if you
will, I will come to the abbey gate, and bring you there by the least
frequented way."

"I would not so burden you. No, I will come, and alone. You
and your house shall take no risk by me. Oh, I know," he said,

"the pains of being Welsh, and too close neighbour to the English, when the standards are out." He took her hand, not to kiss, but as he might have taken a man's hand who had met him fair and done him honour. "I am ashamed that I have kept you from your rest, after so troublous a day. Go now and sleep, and have no fear for tomorrow. I will take care that you shall not be persecuted further."

She crossed the chill, moonlit parclose of the abbey of St. Peter and St. Paul, the faint smoke of frost from her breath going before her. The great church was mute and dark, for compline was long over, since the routine of the house clung as yet to its winter timetable, and the monks were in their beds until midnight should rouse them for matins. She walked alone in the silence, hearing her own muted footfalls like echoes of past or future, she could not distinguish one from the other. Faithful to his orders, she had no fears for the morrow. There was no man but one who could trouble her rest ever again, and whatever disorder or ordeal he cast into her path she knew she would go gladly, and gather like flowers.

She entered the warmth of the hospice as Lady Percy was leaving the hall to go to her own apartment, attended by a single demure damosel. Elizabeth saw her, and stretched out a generous hand:

"Mistress Hussey, I missed you! Margaret has orders for your comfort. Sleep well, and be sure they will see right done to you. Good-night!"

Julian looked after her, the high, exultant step, the reared head under its coronal of brown hair, the lofty joy in every movement. And she thought: What must it be like to go to one's marital bed with delight, instead of disgust? And to such a man, instead of an old fool with the shakes, and sweating like a pig in an ague?

And how strange, she thought, that I have come from him, and you are but now going to him, and yet I do not envy even you, the most enviable of women! For God's sake, what is it I have got from him, that it sets me so high?

2

She suffered one paroxysm of doubt, the first and the last, and a matter of shame to her as often as she remembered it after, when the hour of noon came and passed, and no one sent for her to go into the town and fetch her father to the audience; and when she ventured to enquire, she was told that one of his Grace's clerks had already gone to summon Master Parry, and she need not concern herself in the matter. That struck her hard; but the shock passed as quickly. It seemed the prince would not have a witness influenced, even by his own daughter. She had relied on having time and opportunity to confide in him, and set his mind at rest about the unexpected summons. She knew him, and could imagine his state now, half surly defiance, half anxious and defensive fear. He was not a brave man, and often said so, brandishing his supposed nervousness like a banner. If they did not let her see him until they both appeared before the prince, what wild errors might he not commit in his insecurity?

Yet she could not, once that first convulsion was past, feel any unease. Hotspur had promised her a fair deliverance, vouching for the prince no less than for himself, and in his promise she believed as in the mass. So she waited for the summons to the prince's presence, and went with a demure step and a high heart when she was called at last.

Her father was in the anteroom, waiting for her with a dour face and uneasy eyes, but so closely attended by page and chamberlain that barely a word beyond her submissive greeting and his mumbled acknowledgement, phrased as a blessing but uttered like a malediction, was able to pass between them. Then they were ushered together into the presence-chamber.

She looked round for Hotspur, but he was not there. She was not to be trapped into suspicion again; if he knew his power so well that his presence was unnecessary, that was enough for her. The prince was seated, not in his chair of state, but between two of his clerks at a trestle table, with a quantity of papers and parchments spread before them; and his treasurer stood at his shoulder, ready to advise if requested, but looking on so impartially that it seemed to her he had already done his share. Before the table Edward Hussey stood hunched in defensive composure, very plainly dressed—had he set out to demonstrate the modesty of his means?—and with his countenance fixed in an expression of resigned and dutiful benevolence. It was somewhat of a disappointment to her vengeful mind to consider that he might have taken yesterday's omen to heart, and prudently drawn in his horns, resigning his pretensions on her rather than venture even token opposition to the fiat of the prince and his governor. It was, she supposed, a possibility. The girl was well enough—all the better for hating and fighting him!—but not worth that risk. There were plenty more to be had cheaper!

"Mistress Hussey," said the prince as she entered, "we beg your forgiveness for keeping you waiting a little beyond the time we appointed. Master Parry, pray pardon also a summons at such short notice, but the case we have to judge concerns you nearly, and I make no doubt that your daughter's wellbeing is your first anxiety. We have pleased to reserve this hearing until we had had an opportunity of acquainting ourselves with all the circumstances." He lowered his eyes for an instant to the parchments that littered the table. The hovering clerk at Hussey's back was watching them narrowly every moment, as though one of them might elude him when he came to gather them up again. "The matter at issue, as you no doubt know, is the return to your household of your daughter, now widowed and without children, and the repayment of her dowry. Madam, it is your personal wish that you should so return, is it not?"

Julian inclined her head and veiled her eyes.

"To the end that you may make a second and happier marriage from your father's house—is that so?"

This time she raised her face, blazing with candour, and said: "Yes!" boldly. She was not one of those who cannot lie with wide-open eyes and angelic faces when needful.

"Such an intent we find wholly commendable," said the child gravely, monumentally sure of his shaky ground, "and we confide that your father must feel with you, as is but natural."

He is acting, she thought, touched and elated, he is prompting my father; he has learned his lesson well. But then she looked into his eyes, which dwelt upon her in huge solemnity, and knew that he was burningly sincere. If he delivered her, with her endowment secured, as she had been promised he should, he did so of his own will, because he was convinced of her need and the justice of her complaint. And he had been left to conduct this hearing on his own, secure that he would make the decision both Hotspur and she needed. Never had he surrendered, or been asked to surrender, his independence of action. Had Hotspur even confided to him all that she had urged and confessed, yesterday evening? But yes, surely he had. He had given the boy all the evidence, dumped it in his lap without ceremony, and left him to examine all, and act as the prince he was.

That argued a very profound knowledge of the royal mind on Hotspur's part, and an even deeper confidence in its infinite will to justice. On what grounds, she reflected now, enlightened, had he vouched for the boy? He had never said: "The prince will do as I tell him," but simply: "The prince is wise beyond his years."

Why, after all, should that cause her any surprise? The boy had been in his tutelage now for two and a half years, closer far to him than to his own Lancaster kin.

"Very well! We have now examined into Master Hussey's means, and we are satisfied," said the prince, very gravely and courteously, "that even though no exact inventory has yet been made of all the property passing to you, Master Hussey, by your uncle's will, yet you have certainly acquired assets which must be disposable, and of such a nature as to be very readily disposable. You are already possessed of a substantial household, and have here been visited with a second. We are taking into account that both manors must be properly manned and maintained. But there is still a handsome balance of advantage to you. And it is our judgment that you can and should pay at once a portion of Mistress Hussey's dowry, so that her maintenance may be assured, and she may return to her father's house from this court, as is her wish. We cannot feel that such an arrangement is in any way unjust to you. Even if we were to order the repayment of the whole sum at once, the amount would be less than if you were paying tax of a lawful fifteenth of your movable goods. Which could well happen," said the Prince—was it possible that he was capable of a strain of malicious humour?—"whenever parliament meets. But we are not demanding the whole. One half of the dowry, four hundred marks, you will pay to our treasurer here by this day week, and we ourselves will see it conveyed to Master Parry. The remaining four hundred you will pay through the bailiff of our town of Shrewsbury within six months from today. We have given our judgment," said the prince formally, and sat back in his chair with an authority and finality that no one cared to challenge.

There was nothing for Hussey to do but bow before the wind with as good a grace as he might, profess his resolve to do all that was required of him—at whatever penal cost to himself, his martyred countenance implied—reverently kiss the prince's hand, and withdraw to his plain, melancholy wife and his two fat manors up-river.

Julian made her reverence in her turn. Over the extended hand she looked up into the prince's eyes, and saw there the same candid regard she had seen in his model; yet the shafts that pierced into this boy's inmost being were somewhere shuttered close, standing off all communion. There was no obliquity, no deceit; neither was there any revelation. The boy had learned what the man would never learn.

She watched dispassionately, concealing a faintly malevolent smile, as her father's inflexible knee forced itself to bend before the wrong prince of Wales. The return of his four hundred marks was a strong inducement, nevertheless it went against the grain with him to do homage to an Englishman.

"Master Parry," said the prince, innocent of his offences as of the benefits that spoke loudest for him, "we will make it our business to see this money duly paid to you. Madam, I pray you may enjoy a more fortunate marriage hereafter."

They were blessed and dismissed. They went out into the precinct of the abbey church, and the showers had passed, and April wore its radiant face. Distant across the river the towers of the castle rose against the sky, straddling the only land approach into Shrewsbury. Pale, rushing clouds danced across a blue almost as pale.

"And what the plague," demanded Rhodri Parry irritably, grasping her arm as they crossed towards the guesthouse doorway, "did you want with starting such a frantic legal bother, without a word of warning to me, without a hint of your purpose? Could you not have sat tight in the fellow's house for a few weeks longer?"

"Not a day longer! I could not stand another hour of the man himself or his bleating sheep of a wife," she said tartly. "And moreover, could I know how long the prince would stay here? It might have been no more than two or three days. I had to strike now or never. And you had best be grateful to me, for if you had left it to the little men of law he could buy better and shiftier than you, and you would never have got your money at all."

The old man—she was the child of a second marriage, and he had been well past forty before she was born—snorted his disbelief, but she knew he was doing little more than vent the nervousness of the past hours, now that the suspense was over. "He could not have denied me. It was due. Or else he could have fed and kept you for the rest of your life!"

"Then there would have been bloodshed, for I tell you I could not be in the same house with them and keep my temper. And as for letting go of what he had, he would have gone to every possible shift first. It might have cost you more to get it than the gold was worth. You should never have been so eager to pay so much for so poor a privilege."

"Poor? Do you know the value of that manor of his? It is a noble name and a noble family."

"Very like, and I make no doubt there are even some noble members somewhere within the clan, but my husband was none, nor is this nephew of his. I suppose if he had been wifeless you would have had me married off to him as soon as I was out of mourning!"

There had never been a time when they had not wrangled, and yet after his fashion he was fond of her.

"You might have done worse. But let it go—the man is married, and there's an end of it. And I'm glad enough to have you back, since you could not give me the grandson I hoped for—"

"I could," she said fiercely. "Will you have me prove it? On what stock shall we graft? You should have bought me a man, and not a threadbare purse."

"In God's name, girl," he protested, shaken, "what devil has got into you, to talk to your father so? You were not wont to be so loud and bold."

"I was not wont to be a married woman, and now a widowed woman. The degree loosens the tongue." And she meant to use it to the full, though perhaps not in this wasteful way. In one unwelcome marriage you learn much about the means of evading a second, and still retaining the consequence gained by the first. It had been her only gain; she did not mean to let it be whittled away. "Wait but a few moments here for me," she said more gently, "for I must make my farewell to the Lady Percy, who has been more than kind to me."

Elizabeth gave her a warm, vivid smile, and her hand, and good wishes to go home with her. Her faith in the prince's justice—perhaps larger than that, in God's—had never admitted any question of the outcome, assured that a plaintiff her husband favoured must be in the right. Julian went out from her strangely uneasy for creatures who walked through the world so openly and confidently. It is too simple a matter to damage those rare few who are too brave, too scornful, and too trusting to put on armour.

"Lady Percy!" said her father, musing, as they walked side by side towards the gatehouse. "That's Harry Percy's wife? He they call Hotspur? He was not there with the prince at the audience?"

"No," she said, "he was not there."

"A pity! Since you needs must drag me here, I should have liked to see this Hotspur men talk so much about."

She said nothing to that. It might be needless caution, yet she kept silence by instinct in all public places upon all that touched Hotspur's affairs, and more because they were his than because they affected the state, and such gravities as peace and war. All the way home she held her tongue, answering only in monosyllables to her father's habitual complaints and strictures, which never were meant to be taken too deeply to heart.

It was not so long a walk, though it led her back in twenty minutes through a year and a half of her life, and was quick with memories both sharp and sweet. The sun had come out fully over the abbey mills and the narrow bridge of Meole brook, and in the foregate there was bustle enough. This English gate into Shrewsbury was guarded less stringently than the Welsh bridge on the further side, and therefore used more freely, and the drawbridge was lowered from earliest dawn. The river was high and sparkling, piling light debris of branches and leaves against the piers of its four stone arches; and beyond, the walls of the town rose, and the tunnel of the open gate. Down the steep slope from the walls to the shore the narrow terraces of the abbot's vineyard ranged like a staircase, the vines like charred black stumps as yet barely showing the first shadowy tint of green. Reflected light shimmered upwards from the rapid water, and rippled along the stone of the ramparts. A fair city, something dishevelled after uneasy times, and hampered and straitened now by the loss of the thriving Welsh trade which was half its life, but still capable of living on its own fat for some while yet, and still hard to take and invaluable to hold.

"You'll not find it easy to get the keys from old Joanna," Rhodri remarked with malice, as they passed in through the archway and continued along the town walls. "She's had her own way too long now."

She cared less than nothing for the privileges of the housewife; the old woman could have kept the keys for ever, and Julian would have been indifferent. Yet her homecoming and remaining at home would have to be justified, and there was no other immediate way except by assuming the direction of the household. "Leave me to fend for myself," she said. "What's my due I shall have, and today."

She had not tried, as yet, to see beyond today; she sensed that what she saw when she did lift her eyes might well be a void, and as bleak as winter ice. Another marriage—probably as chill and loveless as the last—or a comparable prison in her father's house. Some women found at any rate a sanctuary behind the veil, but a convent was more likely to be a hell of rebellion and constraint to her. And yet, she thought, as they picked their way gingerly along under the stooping eaves of the alley that led to the rear of St. Chad's church, to avoid the running kennel thawed and filled by the morning showers, the finger of God had intervened in her life only yesterday, and might again lean down to point out for her an acceptable and fruitful way.

What she wanted was not a sanctuary, but a battlefield. But nobody less than God was ever likely to offer her one.

The house of the Fleece was timbered and dark and beetle-browed on the side next the street, with jutting upper storeys and shuttered

windows. There was an arched cartway into the yard, and a narrow
wicket let them in through the thick oak portal to the cobbled court,
ringed round with stables and storehouses. Another prison, indeed,
but at least this one had a visitation promised.

Not until they were within, the door closed after them, and the
silence of the thick walls like a seal against the world, did she tell him
what manner of guest she had invited to his dwelling, and how soon
he was to have his wish.

It was past nine o'clock when he came, late enough to have emptied
the streets. The house of the Fleece was fast shuttered by then, the
wicket in the yard door closed but not barred; and Julian was waiting
in the doorway of the undercroft, her ears pricked for every footfall
that passed along the alley. She knew him when he came; though he
trod quietly his step was unmistakably light and long and confident,
and he was one of the few who came that way by night alone, yet
not furtively. She was at the wicket before him, and because the yard
was dark, put out a hand to guide him within. The implications of
the contact she honestly had not considered; she would have done
as much for any who came by night. He accepted the service as
naturally, closing long, hard fingers on hers to read the hints they
gave him. Her veins ran fire, flashing back like a powder-train to the
heart, and there bursting in a brilliance and violence such as she had
never experienced or dreamed of. She contained it and gave no sign,
for she was enlarged, as the night is by the moon. She even detached
herself composedly when he was within, to have both hands free
to drop the heavy wooden bar into place and fasten the door, and
then took him by the hand again to bring him safely to the door
of the undercroft, across the uneven stones. Only when they were
within the house, in the timber-scented darkness of the staircase, did
she halt to kindle a light. The tinder caught and glowed, the candle
billowed, a small orb of yellow light between their two faces, and
they were looking intently into each other's eyes across the flame.

"You keep close and careful house here," he said, with a small, grim smile.

"The Welsh in Shrewsbury do not invite notice, especially by night, my lord. And my father is a timid man. These precautions are not all for you."

She had answered him, as he had spoken, in an undertone. He cast a glance about him, noting the half-empty spaces of the undercroft, and the faint gleam of light from above-stairs. "Are there servants in the house?" he asked in the same low voice.

"One old woman—deaf, and in bed and asleep in the garret long since."

"Your father has no journeymen living with him?"

"Two, but they sleep across the courtyard, above the storerooms. You may be private enough, my lord. The house is sealed."

She held the candle steady until it burned tall and pale, and the light swelled and smoothed the mellow wood of the walls, calling gaunt shadows out of empty air. Then she lit him up the stairs, and went before him into the panelled solar, where Rhodri rose from a tall chair by the fire to receive him.

"Father, here is Lord Henry Percy." She was quiet, muted, moving before her sire with downcast eyes and dutiful voice, and withdrawing into the shadows as soon as her errand was done, as though she had no part in what was still to do, unless to wait on their requirements. For a moment Hotspur almost believed in her extinction, her relegation to the servant's role which was the lot of daughters in their parents' households; and even for a moment it grieved him to believe in it. But the face into which he had gazed across the candle-flame had been neither tamed, nor troubled by any foreboding. She did what she chose to do, and was as for the time being she chose to be.

"Master Parry," he said, "I must thank you for granting me this interview, so strangely requested. No doubt your daughter will have told you why I am here."

"You are welcome to my house, my lord," said Rhodri. "For your kindness to my girl I am in your debt, as she is. Yes, she has told me."

Hotspur had felt some curiosity about this father of hers, for she was not a woman whose antecedents could easily be guessed at. What he saw was a man of about sixty years, older than he had expected, but still hale, and of a powerful frame. He stood no taller than his daughter, probably she exceeded him by an inch or two, but he had the shoulders of a bull, and a great head of brindled brown hair laced with grey, like his short, square beard. He leaned and peered a little, but not from any weakness of the eyes, rather out of a fixed suspicion that caused him to study with narrow attention all who came near him, and especially strangers. His gown was rich and sombre; he knew cloths, and had the means to buy the best. He valued ceremony, too, perhaps as a barrier, negotiable when desired, but inestimable as a means of maintaining distance during a parley. On the heavy oak table beside him there were good silver goblets set out, and a flagon of wine.

"Be seated, my lord! Put off your cloak and draw near the fire. You'll drink a cup of wine with me?"

Hotspur put up a hand to the furred collar of his cloak, and let it slide from his shoulders; and like a silent and attentive valet the girl came gliding out of the shadows and took it from him. He was plain and sombre, dark brown from head to foot, to pass in the night unnoted though undisguised. As soon as he was seated at the table she poured and handed wine, and he marked the breadth and strength of the shapely hand that offered the cup, and realised suddenly, noting the blue cloth sleeve of her gown, that she had already shed her mourning.

"Master Parry, I have so much confidence in the good offices of your daughter that I have brought with me the letter of which I spoke to her. Is he here that should deliver it?"

"He is here," said a soft, deliberate voice from the darker side of the room, remote from the fire. The narrow inner door had been invisible in the uniformity of the panelling, and its latch had made no sound as it was lifted; but suddenly there was a man framed in the doorway, a lean, wiry, lightly-built creature, stepping out of the wall with a conjuror's aplomb and a deer-hound's lanky grace. Hotspur had swung round in his chair to face the voice, which had an aloof, noncommittal sweetness of tone, promising nothing. It did not disturb him that he had been under observation; he was not accustomed to deprecate what he was, or to undervalue it. He looked up with interest, candidly returning the inspection, at Rhodri Parry's agent.

The young man—perhaps not quite so young after all, he might have been as much as thirty—came forward into the room, closing the door behind him. He wore the usual faded, dun-coloured every-day clothes of the peasant and labourer, coarse woollen chausses and short homespun tunic, with a capuchin pushed back from his head and dangling at his back; but the belt that circled his hips was of finely-tooled leather, and had straps to attach both sword and dagger, though he wore neither; and his boots were knee-high, and also of soft leather, no doubt hand-worked somewhere in Wales, from native deerskin. His face was long and gaunt, tanned by outdoor living in all weathers to a deep olive tone, but his eyes, deeply-set beneath black brows that flared upwards like wings, were unexpect-edly blue and cool and far-looking. He wore a short, close-trimmed beard that scarcely veiled the shape of a wide, mobile, quirky mouth like a jester's; and though his thick crop of short, curling hair was black, there were twin streaks of mingled rust-red in the beard's blackness, sharpening and tapering his long chin to a fiery point. The corners of his mouth bit inward deeply; it was sometimes difficult to know whether he smiled, or had a wry taste on his tongue.

He stood unmoving to be examined, in no way disconcerted by the length of the scrutiny, and feeling no need to break the silence, until Hotspur said at length, with slow consideration:

"Somewhere I have known you before."

"It may well be, my lord. At any rate, your lordship will know me again."

"I think so. You might be all too easily remembered. Yet I cannot call to mind where I have seen you."

"As good a gift as being easily forgotten," said Rhodri Parry drily. "Your lordship desired to meet the man who can carry messages freely into Wales, and out again. Here he is, and for his ability I can vouch."

"I pray you—with your leave, Master Parry!—sit down with us. It is fair you should have time to consider well. You are vouched for," said Hotspur, with the large simplicity that was warp to the weft of his equally vast pride, "but no one has vouched for me."

The young man sat down readily at the table, leaning his home-spun elbows at ease; and Julian, without being bidden, came forward noiselessly and filled a cup for him. Rhodri watched them with his hooded, wary eyes, and said nothing.

"He has avowed only that I can. Not that I will," said the young man coolly.

"That he can hardly promise. Only you can do that. May I know your name?"

"My name is Iago Vaughan. I am a Welshman from under the Berwyns, and distant kin to the Tudors of Anglesey." Hotspur smiled, for the sons of Tudor ap Goronwy were first cousins to Owen Glendower, prominent in his counsels, and in his war-bands, too. "Does your lordship require to know more of me?"

"Not even that, if you had not pleased to tell me. But I like a face to have a name. And it is a fair exchange, for mine you know before I name it." He turned suddenly to Julian, standing silent and attentive in the shadows, and said to her, with a hand outstretched: "Hand me my cloak!" But he did it with a warming smile and a ready assumption of her allegiance and willingness, more as if he had asked a small current courtesy of his wife than given an order to a servant. And when she brought it to him, he did not take it from her, but only felt in the deep pocket stitched into its lining, and drew out a parchment rolled and sealed, which he reached across the table and laid before Iago Vaughan.

"You can read?"

"In four languages, my lord. I was brought up in the cloister, and have Latin and French as well as English and Welsh."

"Faith, I wish I could say as much, for I never mastered Latin, and have no Welsh. But I write a tolerable hand in English. I trust the superscription is clear? I have not named the place where he is to be found, since I do not know it, and a week hence it may be very far from where he bides today. Yet I make no doubt he can be found." By one of the Tudors, he thought, a finger could be laid on him any day of the year, I'll swear. But he asked nothing; it was not his habit to woo men from their clan allegiance, or try to make dishonest use of a man he wished to employ honestly. He leaned back in his chair, leaving the letter in Iago's hands. "Will you take Owen my message and bring me back his answer? Will you undertake as much again, if this bears fruit?"

He looked at the old man, peering darkly under his down-drawn brows; and there was one who would have questioned and writhed and wondered, pondering long before he would have given any answer, and then, most likely, regretting the answer he had given, whatever it chanced to be. But he looked at Iago Vaughan, and was suddenly aware that his motives would not be questioned nor his matter suspected. The thin, clever, spatulate fingers—they could have been an apothecary's or a musician's—held the roll of parchment delicately; the light blue eyes studied Hotspur's face without disguise and without wavering.

They saw a man curiously like and curiously unlike himself; like, in that he was no man's man but his own, and what he pledged, he would perform; unlike in his innocence, pride, and primitive simplicity. A man without a glimmer of serpentine wisdom about him, for all the sword-sharpness of his mind, a man who thought with his blood and his bowels, for good or evil. A dangerous man, and a man who lived eternally in danger. He wrote English vehemently, scoring deep into the vellum:

> *"To the most excellent lord, Owen ap Griffith, lord of Glyndyfrdwy and Cynllaith."*

From one haughty and courteous prince to another.

Only a few months ago, after this Lord Henry Percy had withdrawn to his other urgent command on the Scottish borders, Owen had run wild over most of North Wales, and made himself master of the counties of Carnarvon and Merioneth; and while the woollier heads in King Henry's council had seethed and talked bloody war, Hotspur had come swooping back to hold the balance so sturdily that he had been allowed, on the king's warrant, to approach the Welsh prince, and attempt to bring him back to his allegiance, on promise of honourable terms. There were still Welsh grooms and servants and even lawyers about Westminster, to listen and observe and send word. And there was no man in the kingdom who knew better than Owen what Hotspur's disdainful answer had been to the council's shameful proposal of murder in place of magnanimity. This new approach, it seemed, was not to be made so publicly, not to be exposed to the expedient treason of little devious minds far removed from the battlefields on which honest men met, and contended, and killed one another without malice. Yet the girl had said that what he did, he did with the king's warrant, and the prince's approval. They had learned, apparently, not to let the pack near the scent too soon.

"I will do your errand, my lord," he said, "and I'll bring you word again from the Lord Owen. And for the future, so long as there is hope that this may speed, I will be your go-between."

"God speed both it and you!" said Hotspur, and sat back with a short, sharp sigh of satisfaction. "When do you set out?"

"Tonight. But for your lordship's visit I should have been gone before this."

"And how soon can you be again in Shrewsbury? No, never tell me more of your goings and comings than is my due, I need only to know, as nearly as you may judge, how long I must bide here to wait for the answer."

"Within a week, unless the Lord Owen move too often and too fast for me, I shall be here again. How may I come in touch with you?"

"Why, that's no great problem while we remain at the abbot's lodging, since half of Shrewsbury and a good part of the shire goes in and out freely at the abbey, and you may ask an audience when-ever you will, and always find yourself one of three or four, various enough to keep any man in countenance. But it's well," he said seriously, "that you should have a token about you that will get you in to me or the prince at need, and stand you in good stead if ever you should fall foul unawares of any of his officers or mine. I need your discretion, yes, but I will not have you brought into need-less suspicion or danger upon this account. Here, wear this!" He plucked a heavy silver ring from the middle finger of his left hand, tugging it over the knuckle impetuously, and held it out across the table in his palm. The single stone with which it was set, opaque in browns and golds, passed from hand to hand like a glowing eye. "It is known to be mine, and I will give my chamberlain orders that it shall admit the bearer at any time. If ever you have word when I am not by, it will bring you to the prince in my place. I'll see to that." He smiled, seeing his pledge lie in the other man's palm, as yet only half-accepted. "Put it on, and wear it. It's yours, whether we speed or no, and some day you may need it."

"I take it, then," said Iago Vaughan slowly, "since there may be a time when there'll be little leisure for persuasion. Are you not afraid, my lord, that I shall use it upon my own occasions?—which may not always be yours? A princely warrant to pass where I will could be a godsend to such a man as I am."

"Unless I have lost my judgment," said Hotspur bluntly, "you would not be beholden. Though so it serve our purpose, I would not quarrel with a little license."

Iago slid the ring on to his finger, and admired the deep sheen of the polished stone. "If I have not lost my cunning, as you have not lost your judgment, it will never be used but to come to you with that which belongs to you. What is it, this stone?"

"The Scots call them simply pebbles. I got it while I was prisoner there, after Otterburn." He smiled a little ruefully, remembering his captivity and his costly ransom, fourteen years past now, before he married. "And take this also, for you will have charges to meet on your journey."

He had not asked, nor would he ever ask, what provision was normally made for these frequent and illicit journeys, the relays of horses, the hire, perhaps, of boats, transport for the cloth. That was Rhodri's business, and if it was illegal, it was also inevitable and understandable. He laid upon the table a drawstring purse of soft leather, that chinked faintly as it shifted and settled. He saw Iago's lean and secret face stiffen, the blue eyes shrink to points of steel, and the linked hands draw back from touching.

"Ah, never look so, man! I have not bought nor bribed you. I am asking a service of you, and I will pay the expenses, as is but right. You need not feel your hands tied—if you can bring that prince of yours and his armies victorious into Shrewsbury over my body in fair fight, go do it, and I'll never cavil. You are as free a man as I am, we do but agree over the hire of a courier. So you give me that service, there are no debts between us, and no obligations."

Iago looked up at him over the wine with a face suddenly bright, astonished and disarmed, and burst into a muted crow of laughter. "By God, my lord, I think you are a man after my own heart! And I pledge you my word, and I take my fee. I shall use it only on your business, and if your business is done and myself discharged before your gold is spent, you will take back the balance, or I will break your teeth with it. And if I play you false, you may break mine. Within the week I will bring you back your answer."

He reached for his cup, and there was Julian with the flagon lifted, ready to refill both his and Hotspur's, so silently and impassively that they might almost have dreamed her into the fringes of their conference, but for the fourth cup which had appeared beside theirs, and which she was also filling to the brim. Her hand—that firm, forceful, boy's hand of hers—lifted the goblet as they lifted theirs. She drank with them as they pledged each other. Her face was tranquil and still, but her eyes flashed like arrows from one face to the other, observing and remembering, before her large, creamy eyelids veiled their light.

Iago could not recall that he had ever truly noticed her until that moment. She had a tension about her like a strung bow, and every bit as lethal, and she had a piercing beauty—why had he never marked it, he who had known her nearly three years?—that made his heart contract as he looked at her. He could afford to study her, for she was not looking at him with any but surface attention. She recorded everything that passed in the room, but she cared for only one person. Nor was that one altogether unaware of her, or unappreciative. But on what curious terms, only God knew. He had never before seen man and woman regard, consider, and touch each other as man with man. No, even that fell short of truth; there are degrees that cannot be accurately plotted. They made their own terms of reference; she, perhaps, with knowledge and calculation; the man, after his kind, by impulse and the blind brilliance of his own nature.

He was on his feet, roused and content, and looking round for his cloak; and she was there with it, lifting it to his shoulders. His eyes encountered hers, and smiled in pleasure and gratitude; hers smiled, too, but mutely, making no marked acknowledgement. Rhodri Parry thrust himself stiffly out of his chair.

"I shall look to hear from you," said Hotspur, fastening the clasp of his cloak, "in a week, if all goes well. God speed you, and bring me a hopeful answer—both for England and Wales!"

"So I pray, too, my lord."

"Master Parry, I owe you my thanks. Should I ever be able to serve you, I pray you let me know."

"We are still in your lordship's debt," said Rhodri formally.

Hotspur had withdrawn a step or two towards the door when he turned again to look at Iago. "Carry my respectful greetings and compliments to your kinsmen, Gwilym and Rhys ap Tudor and their brothers, and say I still owe them a shrewd knock for their taking of Conway on Good Friday of last year. It cost me a deal in time and labour and money to get my castle back from them, and if we had not had such a pious garrison—all but the lame and bedridden in church!—they would never have prised their way into the place. I look for an adjustment some day."

"I make no doubt they will accommodate your lordship," said Iago. "Yet if I speed too well you may have no remedy."

"I'll bear that as the yoke of God. Mistress Hussey—Master Parry—Master Vaughan—I bid you good-night."

"I'll light you down to the gate," said Julian, the candle ready in her hand.

The door of the solar closed behind them; their feet felt a way silently down the staircase. At the house door she left the candle burning upon a shelf within, and took him by the hand to lead him across the stones of the court to the wicket gate; but he halted her suddenly, drawing her back within the shelter of the doorway. In the soft, still light she felt his eyes earnestly and faithfully searching her face.

"Madam, are you content?"

She knew he did not mean with their night's work. Evenly she said, in the same undertone he had used: "All is very well with me, my lord."

"I would I could be sure of it. I have in some sort made myself a party to your situation, and it will go hard with my conscience if you find yourself no better blessed than in your old condition. If ever you should be in need of a place of refuge, you have a resort in my wife's household. You need only come to her."

She offered her thanks with composure. In her heart she thought: Kind as she has been to me, and much as I respect her, your wife, my lord, is the last lady living to whom I am likely to apply. Nor is it a place of refuge I want, among the women of a countess's retinue. I do not know as yet what it is, but I know it is not that.

"Well, bear it in mind. In case of need, it will always be open. God be with you!"

"And go with you, my lord," she said.

His hand withdrew from hers, and he was gone, stepping silently through the narrow wicket into the darkness of the street. But the warmth of his touch remained with her, in spite of the chill of the night, as she dropped bolt and bar into place, and fastened the house door.

She let herself into the comfort and glow of the solar to hear her father's querulous voice complaining, in terms in which surely he himself did not believe: "My mind misdoubts me we have done wrong to have any part in this. How if he is sending you with a bait to bring Owen to his death under cover of a parley, as the king's council urged? Our lord would not be the first to come to bargain and stay to bleed."

"You trouble needless," said Iago, undisturbed. "You know as well as any what answer he made to their urging and how fast they dropped it, at least in his hearing. Do you think they would send such a lure through such a palpably honest man?"

His eyes, fragments of pale, clear sky, and yet so impenetrable, were on the doorway, waiting, she thought, for her. They did not leave her as she closed the door and drew the curtain over it, and came forward into the room. He saw his own words sink deep into her mind like water into a secret thirst; but her face was motionless and indifferent.

"Fool," said Rhodri impatiently, "would they be likely to send it by one palpably dishonest? There's hardly a man in England but this one to whose lure Owen would stoop now. And perhaps his father! And why? They're well-disposed enough, all the Percy tribe, because their own holdings are in the north, and they have nothing to lose here on the Welsh border, it would be a different tale if they were in the king's own shoes, for he's a marcher lord himself by reason of his Bohun marriage, and when Wales is in question he thinks like a marcher lord, and there's an end of it. No, if they want to flush him out of hiding, there's hardly a man they could use but Hotspur."

"I would stake what I have," said Iago, still watching the girl, "that this Hotspur is not an easy man to use. And in November at the council he let see how much trust he was ever again likely to put in the little law-givers at Westminster. Never be deceived by his simplicity and honesty. In defence of that same honesty I think he could be shrewd enough, and ruthless enough, too. And as for deliberately lending himself—why, he would cheerfully hew off Owen's head in fair fight in the field, and never lose a night's sleep for it, though he'd grieve for the loss of a grand fighter. But as for putting poison in his wine, or setting a pitfall under his feet at a hunt—no, he'd hew off the head of any man who tried to put him up to it. What they call policy nowadays he'd still call by its old and uglier names. And he has a sense for it, as the cleanly know by instinct how to avoid filth."

The girl had lifted her head and turned her face towards him, though he could not flatter himself that she was looking at him; rather at the image he drew before her, that spare portrait of the departed visitant, sketched in so few lines on the firelit air. He saw her breath quicken ever so slightly, and her chin lift, and the light glittered in her half-hooded eyes, red as the embers. It caused him to look back in some compunction, in case he had lied to discover what he wanted to know; but he could find no lies. Hotspur was as he had painted him. He seldom had to meet a man twice to be certain of his ground with him. Women were another matter. How was it that it had taken him so long to see Parry's daughter thus clearly?

"In any case," he said, rising and stretching lazily before the fire, "you lose your pains if you trouble on Owen's account, unless you think him easily gullible. A letter in a man's own hand is evidence to be read, along the lines and between the lines, and Owen can read as well as any, and better than most. You think he will move unless he's sure of his ground? And now I'm off to pick up my cloak and pack, ready to shift before dawn." He had put away the letter, somewhere inside his ample tunic. He moved towards the inner door by which he had entered, no long time ago.

Before he reached it he was aware that Julian's eyes had shortened their focus, and were fixed with sharp intelligence upon his face. She said nothing, but she met his gaze fully and did not veil her own. Rhodri was still muttering, unwilling to give up his customary pessimism, but he might as well not have been in the room with them, he counted for so little at this moment. As little as she did to him, Iago thought, for now that he was to have half his money back, that he had staked on her ennoblement and his grandchild's inheritance, he scarcely noticed her. She filled her place, she fetched and carried for him, but any tame girl would have done as well. He had no need of this mewed, motionless falcon, waiting now only for the moment and the means to shake off her jesses. In the world into which she intended to soar there was little room for Rhodri Parry. But there might, he thought, if he knew how to wait, be room some day for Iago Vaughan.

3

In the foothills of the Clocaenog forest, snugly folded within the pleats of thickly-wooded ground, the camp was invisible from all sides at any distance, covered on one flank by an upland bog, and guarded on the other by a line of outposts. Long before an enemy could get near enough to distinguish any glint of arms, the whole company could fold their belongings and slip away into the mountains at their back. They needed little and carried little. They were expert at vanishing silently and reappearing suddenly in some unexpected place; and in case of need the Lord Owen's main strong-hold of Glyndyfrdwy was no great distance away, mound and manor guarded by a curve of the Dee, down there to the south in the close confine of the valley.

The weather that mid-April had turned fair and mild; the trees were coming into delicate leaf, and ladysmocks fluttering over the marsh meadows. It was pleasant to live in the open, and easy to provision both men and ponies; and the courtier and man of law who had lived a high life in the London Inns and colleges, and been in the king's own service, was nonetheless a hardy Welshman, well able to campaign in the hills winter or summer, and never complain of a hard bed or a scanty meal. He was the master of most of North Wales and part of the central lands, but a swathe of bracken and heather covered by a skin rug and his own cloak was bed enough for him, and he ate what his men ate, and wanted no more. He had the roads to Ruthyn and Denbigh under his eye from this eyrie, and Mold was not too far for a raid if the weather and the omens were good; but since his active autumn of last year he had contented himself with holding and consolidating, and swooped down in the occasional raid along the border only to keep his hand in for greater things if the season should indicate the necessity.

He sat on a couch of deerskin, under the awning of his tent, a long, sinewy man in the prime of his powers, forty-eight years old, black of eye and black of hair, but for the first frostings of grey at temple and lip. He was changed since his days at Lancaster's court; with all his polish and scholarship, which neither time nor place could tarnish, he had nevertheless shed all the cramping tensions of city life, and moved like a young stag, long-stepping in motion and magnificently abandoned in repose. His armour was piled not three yards away, arrayed ready to be donned at short notice. Everything he bore in hand was but half-achieved and for ever in the balance; yet if at this moment there was a prince in Wales, his name was Owen, and Owen knew it.

Outside, on the grass stippled with the bright embroidery of light and shadow under the trees, Iago Vaughan sat clasping his little travelling harp. Of the prince's bards he was the least, the stray; but his touch on the strings was no less sure than that of Owen's court poet.

"And he said he had known you somewhere before?"

"He said so."

"I doubt it may have been somewhere in a circle of exiles, plucking that familiar of yours." For in England every bard was an incendiary, with however much deceptive mildness he chose his songs; he was the voice calling the Welshman home, and for what purpose except to join the golden dragon in arms? There had been disaffection among the Welsh in the universities for more than eighteen months now, and many a wandering musician had been thrown into prison for stirring up sedition with his tribal songs, and more than one had been put to death. Welsh labourers, however indentured, however bound, had somehow found a means to slip away, and England well knew where, and for what purpose.

Iago shrugged and smiled, muting his vibrating strings with a flattened palm. "It's true he was in Oxford while I was there, and the schools were no very safe place to be singing about great Llewelyn in his seven-foot grave, or making verses after the manner of Cynddelw. God knows we were not always as discreet as we might have been. But more likely it was some time in London. He has his own town house in Bishopsgate Street. Does it matter?" he said, lazily watching the dew distil into vapour as the sun drank it. "Even if he remembers, it's a year and more ago now, and he'll remember to forget."

"You at least have confidence in him," Owen said, thoughtfully frowning down at Hotspur's vehement hand.

"Yes. Confidence in his will to end this war, even upon terms not ungenerous. By comparison with that, what is it to him if one bard goes free? I'm of more use to him, if I carry his letters faithfully, than all the statutes and limitations and restrictions they've clapped on the Welsh trade. He knows them for folly, and has no patience with the little, grudging, timorous minds that made them."

"Will you hear what he writes to me? Listen, then, you've seen and spoken with the man, and have some insight into his mind."

The prince unrolled the scroll, and read aloud:

> "'To the most noble and puissant Owen, lord of Glyndyfrdwy and Cynllaith, Greeting and Respect!
>
> "'By this it will have come to your lordship's ears what little success my attempt to put forward your terms for negotiation achieved in the council. There are those among the ministers and members who have little knowledge of Welsh affairs, and are not well-disposed to proffer any concessions. But I beg you to believe that there are also men of a wiser and more experienced sort, who by no means decline all consideration of negotiating terms.

For my part, I promise you I will continue at all times to have
this possibility in mind, and to take every opportunity of bringing
it to the minds of those who can best move in the matter. The
same guarantee I can offer for all my house, whose will to you is
as mine. And I am in haste to get this word to you, that you may
know your affair is not in abeyance, and that the undeclared truce
which has held good, but for some small brushes, since the council
met in November may continue unbroken. This circumstance of
restraint on your part is the most favourable argument they can
have, who are your well-wishers here. Every day that passes
without further raiding speaks for you, the more confirming those
who give their voice for reconciliation, and by little persuading
those who were against. But if you again burn and provoke,
for every enemy you slay you raise up in England a score of
enemies, and do but increase the odds against your cause. Which,
as I esteem it, is a cause not all unjust, and not to be distorted
by ill-judged action.

"'I charge you, therefore, for the present abjure all fighting but
that is forced upon you, when no man can blame if you do valiantly in your own defence. But forswear all attacks upon cities
and towns, upon travellers going their way without ill-thought
towards you, all provocation of all kind against the borders, and
avoid, so far as ye may, any meeting with any English soldiery.
You well may do so, as I know, where every valley and hill and
track is known to you. And in return, I promise you that if I
get from you the reply for which I hope, I will be about your
business presently.

"'But further, my lord, one stipulation I make, for your own
protection: do not upon any consideration come to any meeting,
or respond to any advance, however seeming honest, that does not
come to you by my hand, and by this same messenger. For notwithstanding I trust to bring you off happily, with the goodwill
of our lord the king and all who best speak for this land, yet I do

*know there are some who may have other thoughts concerning
you. Therefore bide your time and refrain from all action, until
I send you word that you may come with my warranty to the
council table. Which warranty, when I have given it, I will make
good with my life.*

*"'I trust to have word from you by this messenger, and delay
only to know that you wish me to proceed. Thereto I pray all
good both to you and to Wales, again reconciled soon, I trust, to
the king's Grace.*

*"'Given by my hand at Shrewsbury, the seventh day of April,
this year of our Lord fourteen hundred and two.*

"'Henry Percy, Knight.'"

"By God, he goes a degree beyond even what I had thought," said
Iago, roused and vindicated, "to warn you not to put your trust in
princes and councillors. Surely he knows you're well warned already,
but for his honour he cannot keep from underscoring it three times."

"It was he laid my terms before them, and put the idea into their
heads," said Owen with a wry smile. "He may well feel the need
to scare me off. But I grant you there are not many would have
gone to the trouble. You'll need a fresh horse, Iago. Go and see
to it. Einion will find you whatever you need. And ask Philip, and
Griffith Fychan, to come to me here. I have a letter to write."

"You'll remember, my lord," said Iago, rising with alacrity from
the grass, "that he is but an earl in the making and has no Latin."

"It shall be in English," the prince promised him drily.

"And favourable?"

"God granting, everything shall be as he wishes. I will keep my
hands from the English—any and all but one," he said grimly.

Iago slung his harp over his shoulder, where it carried snugly
under his cloak on horseback, and hunched one shoulder slightly
under the cape of his capuchin when he went afoot in England. He
had made no more than half a dozen strides towards the heart of

the encampment when Owen called him back suddenly, in a sharp, changed voice; and when he looked back in surprise:

"What was that you said of him?—of Hotspur? '"He is but an earl...'"

"An earl in the making, I said, but it was a foolish saying. In what does he fall short of an earl now? Why, my lord, what is it?"

Owen's black eyes, deep-set and far-seeing, stared blindly inward, narrowed after some vision they had almost captured, and yet let slip. His face was honed bright, like carved ivory.

"Nothing! I cannot be sure now. The fire kindled, Iago, when you spoke. Now it's gone." Colour came back into his weathered cheeks; the volcano of prophecy that was known to burn in him had cooled and crusted over. There would be no further prodigy. "I have it in me, Iago, that this Hotspur, whatever he be, will never be an earl. Strange! Less and more I see him, but never that. Never Northumberland!"

❧

Iago ambled down out of the forest in mid-afternoon, on a Welsh mountain pony with a barrel like a butt of wine, a cross-grained temper, and a turn of speed no one would have credited from her build. He wanted no more showy mount; for all his notably individual looks, he could jog like a pedlar and fade anonymously into any background when he chose. He had Owen's letter in the breast of his tunic, and his harp tucked away behind his shoulder, and three days of his promised week left for getting back into Shrewsbury. He could have moved directly south into the valley of the Dee, but instead he chose to head eastwards towards the vale of Clwyd, to take a cautious look at the borders of Lord Grey's domain before he turned south to cross the mountains to Valle Crucis. The truce, after all, did not depend all on one man's goodwill.

The sun was high and bright as he dropped gently out of the hills towards the vale, faintly misted with vapour, and saw in the far distance before him the mole-hill of Ruthyn, hunched and veiled

in the smoke of its house-fires, a delicate blue flower in the sparkling folded green, with the giant hogback of Moel Famau towering
beyond. And he saw, too, narrowing eyes that were used to singling
out detail at great distance, the betraying glitter of sunlight upon
arms, below him in the copses of the valley. A crackle and sparkle
of steel, spitting light and vanishing into shadow, but to reappear by
spasmodic flashes thereafter, moving up towards him. They were
no threat to him; they were far away, and he was in tree-shade, and
had nothing bright about him to catch the light. He was invisible;
and at need he could better their speed. He loitered, untroubled but
curious, for they were no small company, and by the line of their
march they had come from Ruthyn. Reginald de Grey reckoned
every Welshman a thief and an outlaw, and had his borders patrolled
as though against the entire army of France, in great measure creating the animosity and disorder he saw everywhere; and this company
might be no more than a routine patrol meant to impress and in-
timidate on his usual terms. Yet they moved with more than usual
purpose towards the hills; and it was always a possibility, however
remote, that some vagabond poacher or time-expired soldier living
wild had hit upon Owen's outposts without being detected, and
thought it worth his while to carry a tale to Ruthyn.

He did not take it too seriously, but nonetheless he wheeled his
pony and made off at speed, back towards the fringes of Clocaenog,
where he had passed the last of the prince's watch. The man looked
down at him from his perch in a beech-tree above the track,
and laughed.

"You think we're asleep, up here? A runner went to the prince
half an hour since—by now he knows better than you. Get on
your way, and watch how you cross them, for it's Grey's livery
they're wearing."

It was true enough, he had good need to take thought for his own
safe passage, for his course must somewhere cross that of the armed
company. To avoid their notice, and give them time to get clear

of the folded valley before he ventured it, he turned on a contour course towards Ruthyn, and kept in the fringes of the forest, watching the glint of steel come and go on the track lower down the slope, drawing steadily nearer to him, but some half-mile below. And having found a vantage-point where he had a clear view of the meadows and was himself sheltered, he halted his pony and stood to watch, narrowing his eyes to single out coat-armour, and number the forces in the English party.

There were archers with them, but not a great company, and some three-score men-at-arms, all mounted; and a knot of bright devices he could not quite read at that distance, though their colours did almost as well. Four knights at least, all Grey's men; and a rugged, thickset figure in half-armour, whose seat in the saddle was familiar, even if the black horse under him had not been so signally ornamented with his blazon. Reginald de Grey himself was on the move, with a strong and well-mounted party in arms.

They passed, and left the valley free for him to cross. He waited until they were lost to sight beyond a fold of ground and a belt of trees, and then made good speed down to the little river, splashed through it where the banks were level and firm, and climbed the slope on the other side. Clocaenog village he left at a distance on his left hand, and wound his way up into the hills again. But his mind was not easy. It was an ill omen that Grey should appear on this day of all days, so close to where Owen lay hidden, newly resolved to take Hotspur's advice, bide his time for peace-making, and forbear aggravating the English further. Any and all but one! And that one had to appear, like a spirit raised by necromancy, suddenly almost within grasp of his hand. And for what purpose, with such a force, unless he had some word of power to lure him out of his castle?

The old quarrel, sprung from a tract of land in dispute, had been fomented by many acts of hostility since. When King Henry had summoned his muster for Scotland, the year after his coronation, Grey had been charged with delivering the summons to his Welsh neighbour, and had withheld it until too late, so that the lord of Glyndyfrdwy was exposed to the charge of being a traitor. Out of this personal feud had burned up, like the sudden flaring into splendour of a bush fire, the old, old quarrel that belonged not solely to Owen, but to Wales. After so long of acquiescence, the Welsh felt themselves Welsh again, a nation with a prince and a prophet of their own. And yet the personal bitterness still rankled in the heart of the fire, and as it had kindled it, so might it sour it and put it out.

His uneasiness grew, and yet he could not tell why, for the prince was warned, and could very well deal with this matter. Avoidance would be easy, the camp could dissolve into the hills like mist within half an hour. More likely, if the force from Ruthyn seemed to be passing without ill intent, they would merely sit still and let the enemy go. Yet Iago suddenly wheeled his pony again, and made for the highest point of the ridge, where he could look back over the valley, and see as far as the scattered outer copses and the rim of the forest.

Far below him the river was a silver thread, curling and twining through meadows freshly green in sunlight; and beyond it the folded hillocks rose plumed with clumps of trees, heaving and falling in a series of green bowls all along the flank of the dimpled ridge that soared to the dark green of woodland above. He saw, as though some wall painting had come to life before his eyes, the glitter of steel and the minute clusters of rainbow colours just moving over the crest of one rise, to descend into the next bowl; and riding towards them, negligently like men out hawking, he saw a smaller group, no more than half a dozen mounted men, who had been until this moment hidden from them by the lie of the land.

There was an instant when both parties halted at gaze, no more than a quarter of a mile apart; and though they were so far from him across the valley, he felt the shock of confrontation and recognition quiver through his own body as they measured each other. Then the handful of riders wheeled their mounts in wild haste, and rode back by the way they had come, and after them in headlong pursuit streamed Reginald de Grey and his knights and men-at-arms. The quarry must needs have ridden steeply uphill if they were to gain the cover of the trees, and he saw that they were not even attempting it, but climbing only very obliquely towards shelter, preferring to gain distance on the level. And as the half-dozen lengthened into a line, he watched them like a file of horsemen on a hanging tapestry, each separate, and the last flagging. He saw the tall grey horse stumble, or seem to stumble, and recover but lamely. The pursuers saw it, too, and lingeringly across the valley, long after they had launched it, he heard their shout of triumph. The Lord Owen was taken at a disadvantage, surprised in the open, hunted like a hart, and his horse fallen lame.

The men of Ruthyn had abandoned all caution, spurring their horses furiously, lengthening out in their turn into a long frieze parallel with the edge of the forest, every man mad to be the first to lay hand on the arch-enemy. Iago felt in his blood the coming of the climax, the moment when Owen had drawn them, with his body for bait, exactly where he would have them, with all eyes on him, and never an archer ready to string bow, or a lookout to shout an alarm. There had never been a more insolent ambush. He did not know whether to laugh or to weep.

Suddenly the grey horse was lame no more, but picked up his heels and leaped ahead with stretched neck and lunging shoulders, the prince lying forward over his neck and thrusting with him, as though he and his beast were one flesh. The gap between him and his pursuers widened; and at the same moment, though they were invisible and their volley could not be followed by eve or ear, the Welsh archers deployed all along the rim of the forest loosed their shafts together.

It was like corn falling before the scythe. They had every man his mark, and they loosed at leisure; not at the horses—good horses never came amiss, and certainly never were wasted—but at the men.

The mounts, suddenly lightened and without hand on the rein, wheeled and circled curiously in the heaving bushes and trampled grass, more at a loss than frightened. Without a sound the men of Ruthyn, more than half of those leading the pursuit, fell with the impetus of the arrows that pierced them, heeling out of their saddles like a breaking wave, downhill from the forest. Some were dragged by a foot still caught in the stirrup, round in a circle in the turf. Some shook themselves clear, and even rose again, but many lay threshing, and some lay still. And before those following could rein in and look for cover, or dismount and string their bows, or drive headlong into the trees from which their death was launched, the second volley followed the first. At that range, Welsh arrows could shear through plate-armour and fine mail shirts within, and these were riding half-armed.

Owen and his half-dozen were in the trees by then. They took breath for a few moments before they emerged, after the third volley, to finish what they had begun, the Welsh swordsmen boiling out of the bushes joyously on their heels. Iago watched that fight to its end, and saw the survivors haled away into the forest and silence. A few, those who had been last in the line, turned their horses in time and rode for Ruthyn to carry the news, and were not hindered in their going. All the wilds of the Cambrian mountains were at Owen's back, there were plenty of places where Reginald de Grey could safely be hidden, long before any party ventured out of Ruthyn to collect and bury the dead.

Iago dug his heels into his fat pony's ribs, and took the shortest way down into the Dee valley, riding hard for Shrewsbury. And still he did not know whether he should be laughing or weeping.

He came into Hotspur's presence in the abbot's lodging at Shrewsbury abbey, still stained and dusty from the road, a thin brown packman with some plea about a permit to carry his goods to Chester. His extraordinary eyes he veiled with lowered lids and humility, and only

the satirical curve of his long lips, accentuated by those twin russet
flames that forked upwards through his short black beard, caused
the chamberlain who admitted him to look at him a second time.
Both chamberlain and clerk accepted it without question when they
were dismissed from attendance. There were no other petitioners
waiting, and they had routine work to do. This fellow's matter was
simple enough.

"You've made good speed," said Hotspur when they were alone.
"Better even than you promised me. You have a letter for me?"

"My lord, I have." But he held it in his hands still, not yet proffer-
ing it; and his eyes were unveiled now, two slivers of clear sky, but
a winter sky. "My lord, I entreat you to believe that what you find
in this letter was honestly written and honestly meant. I pledge my
own honour for it. But there has that happened since that may well
have changed all."

Hotspur sat very still, watching his visitor's face. "What has happened? There has been no news here."

"Not yet. But there will be. I have come straight from the event,
and as your lordship sees, I have wasted no time in applying to you."

"I am content," said Hotspur quietly, "that you have fulfilled all
terms, and done everything you undertook to do. What more has
happened cannot be of your doing. But I need to know."

"Read the letter," said Iago.

Hotspur broke the seal in silence, and unrolled the parchment.
Owen had written to him in his own hand, a fine and scholarly hand.
He read it through, while Iago watched his always eloquent face.

> "To the most noble and excellent Sir Henry Percy, Knight,
> Greeting and Love!
>
> "For your lordship's letter, duly come to hand, I send you my
> thanks and my grateful sense of your lordship's kindness and good
> feeling towards me. I have, as I ever had, the fullest confidence
> in your honour, and am willing in all things to deal with you as

man with man. But I confess that I have not the same trust in some your peers. Nor does the issue of life and death rest only with your estate, as we have well seen in the fate of those earls lately in dispute with the king's Grace who fell into the hands of certain lawless gatherings of commoners, and were shortly done to death. I will well, therefore, that you should, as you have said, deal for me as you may, and when you summon me to conference with your own warranty, I will not hesitate to come. But for no other will I come in confidence, unless it be for Prince Henry, whose mind I conceive as noble, and his word as his bond.

"And to the end that you may deal for me without hindrance, to bring about this peace, I undertake that I will not henceforth, at least until I do withdraw this word, have any ado of my own willing with any English company in arms, but will forbear them as you counsel. And for the rest, if any do challenge me, and I cannot but defend myself, you shall hold me justified and excused. Though whether any other of your part will, neither you nor I can well determine before the event.

"I greet your lordship well, in the hope of a good deliverance for us all, and look to hear from you again, God willing.

"Given under my hand, this eleventh day of April, the year of our Lord fourteen hundred and two.

"Owain Glyn Dwr, lord of Glyndyfrdwy and Cynllaith."

He looked up from the scroll, thoughtful and faintly frowning: "You know what the Lord Owen writes to me?"

"I know what he gave me to understand he would write. And I know it was written in good faith."

"That I never doubted. So what has befallen to make this of none account? And how came you to know of it, if it befell, as it seems, after you had left the Lord Owen?"

"I myself witnessed it, my lord, though from a distance." He told it, exactly as he had seen it, not concealing that there were curious and doubtful points in it which even witnessing could not make plain. "Sure I am that until this party was sighted, the Lord Owen had no thought in his mind of any such happening, and no plans to provoke it. But when the word reached him, and especially when it was seen that Lord Grey himself was with the party, thereafter I cannot be sure. I tell what I saw. The English came over a crest, face to face with the Lord Owen in open field. And they spurred forward to pursue and take him, no doubt believing it a happy chance for them, and the Lord Owen caused his horse to appear to drop lame, and so encouraged and led them until they were spread all along the field in open order, within close range of the bowmen in the woods. When he had them so placed, he spurred ahead and drew clear, and the archers cut them down like corn. Only a few of the rearmost broke away and escaped back towards Ruthyn. But whether they came out knowing of the Welsh camp, and with some plan of attack, which the Lord Owen by his own stratagem forestalled, or whether they were on other business and would have passed by but for this lure, I tell you honestly, I do not know. And even if they meant him no threat, how could the Lord Owen be sure of it? And with all his force to guard, how dared he assume it?"

"You argue well," agreed Hotspur, watching him keenly, and with a sudden remote spark in his eyes that looked like involuntary laughter. "And whatever the way of it, had I been in the Lord Owen's place, with my chief enemy thus presented naked into my hand, I doubt if I could have resisted the temptation. Certain it is, if he had more than three-score armed men with him, he was not on his way to church! Well, tell on to the end. The archers cut them down—a few broke back for home unscathed. Some, no doubt, made their way back later with their hurts. Were there prisoners taken?"

"My lord, there were. I saw two or three of the knights haled away into the woods. And after them," he said with deliberation, "Lord Grey himself. If he was hurt at all, it was but a minor hurt— he walked where he was led." He caught the wide, levelled eyes watching him with the first faint shadow of doubt and disquiet, almost distaste, and laughed shortly. "Oh, never wonder about me, my lord! You are the first of the king's officers to know that Lord Grey of Ruthyn is carried off prisoner into Wales, and if this moment you turned out the muster of every shire between here and Denbigh, and loosed them into Clocaenog forest, do you think you would find hide or hair of a Welshman there? I would not have told you place or time if I did not know that every man of them is far into the mountains and out of your reach long before this. And I tell you now in order that you may reckon well what chance is left of keeping any hope of peace alive, after this skirmish. For I do believe you honest in desiring it, and so it deals fairly with the Lord Owen, I desire it, too, and will still be your instrument in pursuing it. But I tell you plainly, I count the chances as low enough."

The shadow broke like a cloud, and was blown away in a gust of rueful laughter. "And so do I, Iago, so do I! What can follow now but renewed war, and hotter than before? Can I argue and persuade for moderation, when every baron along the march will see himself in Grey's shoes? I am sorry, Iago, that it is so soon over."

"For this time," said Iago, and slid the ring from his finger. There is also money which is yours."

"No. Keep it—keep both. I hope there will yet be occasion to make use of them again in the same cause, even if we must wait now for a better opportunity. Or a verdict in the field," he said, abruptly flashing fire, "for if you have occasion to speak with the Lord Owen again, you may tell him I will not spare to do my uttermost against him."

"That he knows," said Iago, "and would expect of you."

"Yet I would rather a resolution less wasteful. So, Iago, keep the ring. And if you ever have word for me that may bear fruit, come and ask entry to me wherever I am. And should I need you, can I find you or get in touch with you at Rhodri Parry's house?"

"They may not always know where to find me. But they will

always know the times when I shall be here in Shrewsbury, and I will see to it that whenever possible they shall have word of my moves between." He thought of Julian in her drab housewife's gown, with her still, tense body and her hungry eyes, and he said, hardly knowing why, or whether it was mischief in him or mercy: "If you need me, apply to the girl. She keeps at home now, and she can be as secret as any man."

But into that flight, though he looked at him thoughtfully and searchingly, Hotspur would not follow him. And so they parted.

When the prince heard the story, over a conference table uttered with notes, despatches and letters, he first opened eyes and mouth wide with shock and disbelief, and cried: "Never say so!" and then as suddenly laughed aloud, crowing: "A judgment!" looking, for once, a year or so less than his age and capable of mischief; and then he looked very grave indeed, and sat staring moodily at his table-full of papers, and said, dismayed: "The king will be out of himself with anger. He values Grey."

"Too well!" said Hotspur grimly. There was no third present, and they spoke openly as they always spoke together. "I don't say the man could not be of the highest value, if he did not ruin everything he touches with his implacable spleen. He fights well, he mans and maintains his castles well—God knows not all in the marches do so!—and he has a good grasp of tactics in the field. And yet he is the man who first made this needless quarrel, and now inflames it even when Glendower is disposed to be reasonable. He would never in life agree willingly—or let the king agree—to any settlement but a total victory over the Welsh, and the hanging of all their leaders into the bargain."

"To be fair," the prince pointed out generously, "in this case it seems to have been Owen who took the offensive." And briefly, before resuming his burden of responsibility with a resigned sigh, he laughed again. "It must have been a rare sight! I wish I'd been there to see."

"Faith, and so do I, but we're like to pay dear for it. And what do you think Grey was doing, skirting the forest with such a force? No, he had his information, no question—only it seems it was none too accurate. And the upshot is, there will be war on hotter terms than ever, and no more listening to counsels of peace. And we had best get our fences in order, you and I."

"We must get back to Chester," the prince said, "and call a council at once. We can better keep care of Denbigh and Mold and Flint from there, and I must see to it that Ruthyn is properly garrisoned, now that Grey's gone. Where do you suppose they have taken him?"

Hotspur laughed shortly. "Where no one but a Welshman is likely to be able to track them. The king had his fill of trying to find the Welsh in their own mountains, a year and more ago. The most we can do is expect Owen everywhere, and be strong enough to match him wherever he strikes. For strike again he will, now the die's cast. There's no going back from Grey's capture—not until time has dulled the sting, at least, and made it possible to mention peace without being called a traitor by some city haberdasher in the commons. I've already written the news to my uncle of Worcester in Cardigan. Who knows, the next foray may be into the south. And, Hal, from Chester I must go north to the march as fast as I may, for Walton sends me word there are new raids threatening, and it's his belief and mine there are French knights serving there with Douglas."

"France has declared its intent to maintain the truce," the prince objected.

"To send a force with King Charles' official blessing is one thing," Hotspur agreed with a hollow smile, "to finance small parties of adventurers and let them slip away privately to Scotland is another. It's cheaper than out-and-out war, and they can be disowned if things grow too difficult. But trust me, they're there. And both France and Scotland are receiving Glendower's letters, and finding them tempting too. We may yet find ourselves fighting a war on three fronts, and all one war."

"I know it is a possibility my father has much in mind," the boy admitted soberly.

They did not speak of what lay behind France's bitter enmity, though it was always present in their minds, a spot too sore to touch on lightly. Charles of France might shrink from fomenting a direct war, but he would be glad to use every oblique weapon against the upstart king who had deposed his son-in-law, and sent his little widowed daughter back in clumsy state, but without her dowry, which had been fed of necessity into King Henry's treasury to keep it solvent during his first year of kingship.

"Dunbar is there in the north," said the prince, offering what even he felt to be dubious reassurance.

"The more reason I should be there, too," said Hotspur tartly, "for a man who can turn his coat once can turn it again as readily. I'll take my wife home to Bamburgh, Hal, and go north to Berwick myself for part of the summer. If you need me, I'll be in Chester within three days. But to say truth, I trust this border to you with a far lighter heart than I trust the east march to Dunbar."

He hungered for the north, too, the prince knew that. It was his country, and campaigning across those noble moors under the Cheviot was his true life, as natural to him as to the hawks hovering on languid, sinewy, expert wings above the heather. He did his work here well and thoroughly, but he hankered, every so often, for the rough grey seas and painted, cloud-dappled hills of Northumberland, and his children, and the soil that knew his step and warmed under the sole of his foot, like a caress.

"I'm faced with this business of the Danish marriages," the boy said without enthusiasm. "I shall have to go to London, perhaps in May, to appoint proctors. I suppose I must at least be civil to the Danish envoys, and offer them some entertainment. I shall not linger."

Hotspur forgot his preoccupations for a moment, and looked more closely and with quickening affection at his friend. To be thinking of marriage, at this age, to a girl he had never seen, who might be ugly, stupid and inert, where he was handsome, intelligent and almost excessively alive! He felt a wave of almost incredulous pity for princes. "Are you happy about this proposed match, Hal?"

The boy shrugged, raising his brows with a mild affectation of surprise that it could be thought to be important; but the stillness of his face and the steadiness of his eyes on Hotspur went some way towards betraying him. The three northern countries had recently agreed by treaty to unite under one king, the fifteen-year-old Eric, and Eric had sent envoys to propose a marriage for him with King Henry's second daughter, Philippa, and as an opportunist gesture by the way, a second match between Eric's sister Catherine and the prince of Wales. The boy had lived through the negotiations, rather less sordid than most of their kind, for his sister Blanche's marriage, and had got the tune of these affairs very well off by heart now. It was no shock to him that he should be marketed in his turn. And yet the Danish princess was no great catch for the heir to the English throne. He knew that, too. By this time there was very little he did not know about being a prince; and long before he came to it he would know more than most men born to it about being a king.

"Why, it's nothing yet but the beginning of talks. They'll play with it for two or three years yet, and in the end very probably nothing will come of it. After all, Philippa is not yet eight years old. I was but an afterthought, and I doubt if they're bidding high enough for me."

His voice was cool, even a little cruel, in its effort to be adult and civilised. For when it came to the point, he would probably do what was expected of him, whatever that might be. Marriages were an acknowledged part of the to-and-fro of barter and bargaining that royal children were born to. (But there was always the sudden stab at his heart when he reasoned thus, because he had not been born to it!) And that thought brought him sharply into collision with the one marriage that stuck most obstinately in his throat.

He had not mentioned it in all this week that Hotspur had spent with him at the abbey, had asked no questions but the most current politenesses about his stay and his journey, and had shown no interest at all in the ceremony from which he had come. But now suddenly he came out with it violently, almost in the manner of Hotspur himself over-riding some constraint that tied his tongue:

"Harry, what does my father hope for from this marriage of his?" And as Hotspur turned to face him, in mild but sympathetic surprise: "He cannot suppose that allying himself to the duchess of Brittany will either placate or frighten the French. It will not even give him any power in Brittany, for if she comes here she loses whatever sway she has there. He neither gains an ally nor sweetens an enemy, and say she brings but a token household with her, yet it will cost him dear to keep them. And you know how willing the commons will be to grant an aid for a foreign queen! They starve him of funds even for paying his soldiers. No one knows it better than you—we've both pledged our own valuables before now to keep our archers from deserting. What does he want," said the boy, pale and passionate in resentment, "with a new expense? What does he want with a queen? He's lived content enough these eight years since my mother died."

He had put a finger too accurately on the true cause of his indignation, and flinched away from it hurriedly.

"And if it is not some political advantage he is after, what else is there? Why, he can have seen the duchess no more than once, and that at least four or five years ago, when she was a wife." Wife to an elderly duke, he could have added, and his third wife at that; it did occur to him fleetingly that she, perhaps, had something to gain, a brief recapture of life and youth before it was too late. "So what is it he hopes to get out of it?"

True enough he's seen her but once," Hotspur said gently, "and by the same token he must have liked well what he saw, for he's been in correspondence with her ever since he was crowned. And but that he had many things to occupy his mind, and she no less, I think something would have come of it before now." It was hard to urge forbearance and sympathy with the father on the son, all the more in face of that bitter resentment that was all for poor Mary Bohun, mother of six young children and dead at twenty-four. More than likely his younger brothers and sisters would welcome a new mother, but he was too nearly a man to take kindly to any woman set with so little warning in his own mother's place, especially when this new incumbent stood to gain a crown as well as a ring. The earl of Derby had never offered Mary a crown.

"You must not think," gently said the man who had married for love in his late twenties, "that the king has always reasons of cold policy for what he does. What does he hope for? A little happiness, perhaps, Hal, nothing stranger than that. A little happiness, while there's still time."

4

It was a grim summer that year. There were torrential rains, rivers burst their banks and flooded standing crops, churches were struck by lightning in heavy thunderstorms. After the first fair flush of spring, nothing went right. Like the weather, the fortunes of the time were soured. Nothing but bad news came in from every frontier.

The king withdrew in great weariness and exasperation of mind from his son's manor of Kennington, where he had presided over an anxious council on Wales, and took refuge in mid-June in his castle of Berkhamsted, with only his intimate household about him. Strange how wide a gulf he found between these old retainers of Lancaster and the full council of the realm, let alone the unpredictable vagaries of parliament. Nothing could shake the steadiness of such men as Hugh Waterton or John Norbury, who had been in his service from the time when he had been merely Henry of Bolingbroke, earl of Derby, and even that title borrowed by courtesy from his father. On these, on the Leventhorpes and Rempstons and Erpynghams, he could lean when he would, and they would not let him fall. But the council of England turned in his hand, Parliament crossed him, always with the greatest respect but implacably, criticised his use of the council to levy an aid for the marriage of his elder daughter without consulting them, doubted if there was a precedent recent enough to justify the aid, and periodically and obstinately restated to him the principle that the king should live "of his own," without demanding that parliament should raise money by taxes for his expenses. Had not John of Gaunt been reckoned the richest man in the kingdom? And so might his son have been and remained, with only a duchy to administer, but a kingdom was a different thing. How different, he had never dreamed until he made the assay.

They had declared at his accession, they had repeated often since, that they desired him to reign upon the selfsame terms as his predecessors; and yet they made him aware, whenever it was needful to ask for a grant of money, that in fact he stood upon ground subtly changed, and must ask as a favour what had been Richard's unquestioned right. But there were never any open words expressing the inflection, never anything to which he could raise objection. Only the feeling of mute resistance, the chill sense of acquiescence so grudging as to give pain. It was, perhaps, partly his own fault. In that first parliament of his, immediately after his coronation, he had refrained from asking for money, had even prided himself on his princely forbearance, and believed it had won him friends and trust. Fool, he should have known that that was his one chance to strike, and make known his mettle, and assert his right once for all. It would have been time to win them with clemency later, when they knew his power and will to dominate, and could be stunned into love by the unexpected mercy. Now it was too late. They had his measure.

But was this indeed his measure? He knew he was no such man! What had gone awry, that he should have been led to this pass, and even now he felt himself following, perforce, the twists of his fortune, headlong as a fall, when he should have been steering his own course and bearing them strongly with him?

He had been king for two and a half years, and he was aged by ten. When he peered into his mirror he saw himself already a little stooped in the shoulders, a little heavy in the body, the full cheeks beginning to hang, their old ruddy colour grown muddy and pale, strands of grey in the short, forked beard and at the high temples, and above all, that permanent, aching double pleat between the long, thin brows, scored a little deeper every day. He was thirty-six years old, and his youth was gone, and even his prime was passing.

He came from hearing vespers in his chapel, and shut himself early into his private chamber. The wind tugged at the banner-pole that carried his standard, outside at the turret, and made a dolorous creaking sound that accompanied his steps along the chilly corridor, and whined faintly in his ears even after he had closed the door and shut out the sound of the rain.

Such a night for a ten-year-old child to be out on the North Sea, as by now she must be, if contrary winds had not driven the ship back into port. Blanche, born an ordinary little noblewoman, and now a princess, and bound for Cologne to meet her bridegroom there, Louis, son of Rupert, king of the Romans, duke of Bavaria and Count Palatine. She was small and fair like her name, shy like her mother, and his favourite child, dearer even than Thomas, for daughters are more fragile and vulnerable than sons, and she was his first daughter. And though she had been excited and proud about all the frantic arrangements for her state departure, when it came to the point she had been frightened, and sad at going, though she would not complain. He prayed that the boy might be fine and gentle and kind, and take good care of her. At least she had her uncle Somerset to watch over her on the journey, and the countess of Salisbury to be a mother to her until she was handed over at Cologne to Louis.

Even this, in its way a successful transaction, had done no better than limp lamely to its achievement. He flushed with anger when he remembered how the legal aid he had levied to furnish her to her wedding had brought in only miserable trickles of money on the date appointed, and how he had been forced to send out letters to all and sundry requesting loans to help to pay for her clothes and dowry, and even to borrow abjectly from the City of London and some of its richest citizens, with all the members of his council pledging themselves for repayment, so low was his own credit fallen. Even so, only a negligible part of Blanche's forty-thousand-noble dower left England with her. Even her departure had been delayed for weeks for want of the funds necessary to fit out her ship and escort.

And had there been any real need to send the child away to her bridal so soon? True, Rupert had proposed the match, and sent envoys a full year previously to treat for Blanche's hand, and the alliance was not one to be despised. But had he not fallen in with it too readily and too rapidly simply because it was a testimony to his secure tenure, a declaration before the world that he was a king indeed, and his progeny fit mates for the royalty of Europe? Was he clutching too eagerly at every such evidence? To flourish before whom? Charles and his quarrelsome relatives in France? King Robert and his dangerous regent Albany in Scotland? Or Henry of Lancaster, here solitary and discouraged in Berkhamsted? Did he need Rupert's reassurance to prove to him that he was indeed king of England? And was he to be as abjectly grateful for proffers even from young Eric in the north lands? For only a month ago he had seen his eldest son and his younger daughter appoint proctors to treat in the matter of their proposed Danish marriages. And the little one, Philippa, barely eight years old!

He was not committed, of course. The discussions would move languidly enough, the parties being so young, and there was time to extricate either of them, or both, at whatever stage he found it desirable. Yet the first step had been taken, and an inexpressible sadness closed in upon him, as if he had stripped himself wantonly of the children who were his own flesh. He saw himself, ten years on, a querulous old man complaining in self-pity: What company have my children ever been to me?—and forgetting that he had sent them so lightly away from him, Blanche across the sea to Heidelberg, to a husband she had never seen; Philippa, possibly, to remote Denmark; Thomas, only this Spring, to be titular governor and keep his court in Ireland, and try to make good the wrack and ruin of castles and garrisons there. A good boy, Thomas, keen and ambitious and full of filial zeal. He understood Thomas.

And his heir, Henry, only a year older, could he claim to understand him, too? So different in every way, even in looks, so grave and contained, so full of contrary ideas, and, sometimes, so blunt in uttering them, yet himself so perilously elusive. Deep as a well, and for all his strength and prowess—for he could hold his own with any boy of his age, afoot or on horseback, when he chose—looking and bearing himself like a clerk, and sometimes even like a clerk in orders. Not one easy to fathom, or comfortable to frequent. Though it hardly arose, for the boy was engrossed in his Welsh affairs, and came south as little as he could. He had put in an appearance, perforce, at the ceremony at the Tower, to appoint his proctors, but returned to Chester as soon as he decently could, and had not left it again to come to the council at his own manor of Kennington, sending only one of his esquires with a report on the situation—admittedly an admirably full and expert report—to lay before the assembly. He made no bones about stating his own views or criticising theirs. He was too free with his strictures, and too impatient with restraint. Because he was on the spot, and had established a surprising, and surely almost heretical, chain of friendships there on the border, he thought he knew better than these older and cooler heads in London.

There were letters from the boy here in his closet, no more than a week old, cold-blooded enough in their analysis of the military situation since Grey's loss, and ruthless enough in their acceptance of the necessity to deal in extremes in the last resort, but still arguing the advantage of restraint, even daring to suggest that Lord Grey's capture made no substantial alteration in the case for negotiation, since he was the original party to the complaint which had never actually come to a judgment under law. There was something of the lawyer about Hal himself. Perhaps that was what he respected in Glendower.

No denying the boy was dutiful and punctilious in all things, however opinionated he might be. But unsparing in his pressing of points he thought vital, and eternally urging the need for money. It was the same burden Northumberland was always singing in the north, and Hotspur from whichever front of his double responsibility was occupying his immediate attention. Always the money that had not arrived, always the arrears of pay causing disaffection, and even if they had been sent substantial tallies on regional treasuries or port taxation officers, still the endless complaint that the money simply was not there to meet the bills. What was the use of tallies that might, perhaps, be valid in theory, and even capable of being turned into cash in six months' time, or a year, but were so much paper now, and no use to disgruntled archers and men-at-arms whose need was for coin that could be spent at once? As if he did not know all this for himself, and was not endlessly wrestling, valiantly and incredulously, with the problem of his own chronic poverty! He had had three treasurers of England already, good men every one, and two treasurers of his own household, and none of them had made ends meet yet. It was an unfathomable mystery how a once-wealthy magnate could become so poor merely by the act of assuming the crown.

But penury, though exasperating enough, was not the whole of his distress. If only it had been! He looked back upon the month of May, and stood aghast at what he recalled, so far were these extremes from the whole habit of his mind. When had he taken any delight in killing? In defence of the faith, in defence of his crown, he had no choice but to stand rigidly upon the law, but every cutting off of the least citizen was a maiming of his own nation and his own body, and he found no remedy against the grief and horror into which his own procedures cast him. Where did they come from, those sudden rumours that ran about the country like little trails of fire spread underground in a dry summer? As fast as the council ordered the arrest of one carrier, the story ran to the opposite end of the land

and broke out afresh. Ever since the proxy marriage it had been so.
The king was about to sail for Brittany to marry the duchess, and
in his absence from the realm Richard would come again with a
great host, Richard who was not dead, but alive and in safe hiding
in Scotland, and had never truly relinquished his own. In the middle
of May they had imprisoned Sir Roger Clarendon, who was, so the
common people said, natural son to the great Edward, the Black
Prince, and half-brother to Richard the king. But the story could
not be shut up with him, and before another week had passed
they had been forced to commit to the Tower six more persons,
four friars minor, Stephen Lene, parson, and the prior of the friars
preachers of Winchelsea. The prior of the Austin canons of Launde,
in Leicestershire, followed these into captivity, and shortly all of
them had been put to death for treason. But no matter how many
friars died, the story would not die. And only two years ago the
common people had risen in anger, and themselves done to death
the rebel earls and knights who had dared to take arms for Richard!
They should have waited two years more, Henry thought bitterly,
until the people had come to hate me even more than they hated
Richard. How was such malignant hatred brought to birth, when he
had meant nothing but good, and tried with all his soul to work no
evil against them? Is to be a king the same thing as to be the object
of universal hate?

The council had done its best, formulating a writ to all sheriffs
to issue proclamations forbidding the spreading of lying rumours
that Richard was alive, and committing to prison all culprits on
whom they could lay hands. But the secret wandering singers from
Wales and the itinerant preaching friars still went their ways, and the
prodigy still washed like a wave before them, whispering treason.
There is no way of stopping the seeping of water, by every valley
and hollow it still finds its way.

Strange, he thought, aggrieved, that the friars should be so implacably his enemies, and stranger that by becoming his enemies they

should regain a little of the credit they had lost among common men. As though he had not tried always to be God's knight, and do the church clean service. He had been a crusader in the north, he had made devout pilgrimage to Jerusalem, a soothsayer had promised him he should die there when his hour came upon him. What clearer mark of grace could a man have? But still they slandered him and conspired against him, not only the Welsh Minorites of Llanfaes, whose house he had burned last year, but the Franciscans everywhere, in Norfolk, in Leicester, in Kent. First he had forborne them, and then he had punished, but still there was no amend.

But this was self-pity, to which he had never been addicted, and he must shake it off at all costs. Everything would be magically changed when Joan came to England. She had her difficulties, too, or she would have been with him by this; but she was as much the prisoner of circumstances as he, and could not well take ship until she had established a firm and safe regime for her young son. But she would come, and surely bring sunlight and a blessing with her, to his great hope and help. He clung to the thought as to a talisman, or a reliquary of supernatural power.

He had seen her only once, and that briefly, no more than a few days, when she had come to Richard's court on a state visit with her ancient husband; but he had never forgotten her, and after the duke's death, which by some dispensation of providence had taken place shortly after Henry's coronation, he had taken advantage of every courier to France to send her devout greetings. And she had replied warmly and kindly, and at last sent him her picture. Though he needed no picture to see her very clearly, a tall, fair, calm lady with a high forehead and blonde hair, her features regular, smooth and serene, not beautiful, but possessed of such a quality of gentleness and repose. Everything his heart needed, even dreamless sleep, she would be able to give him.

The rain had stopped; even the wind seemed to have eased, and the banner-pole no longer creaked so eerily above the roof of his chamber, as though the calming thought of her had its benign influence even on the elements. The king sighed and stirred in his chair, and reached out a hand to ring the small silver bell on his table for his chamberlain.

Strange, even when he looked at his eldest son, whom he knew to resemble her, he could not remember Mary's face.

Owen Glendower, lord of Glyndyfrdwy and Cynllaith, and master of most of North Wales, came south that June into central Wales, his raiding parties materialising like shapes of flashing, thundery sunlight out of the rains and mists of the hills, and eating at the borders of the Mortimer lordships in Radnorshire. When least expected, they struck, plundered, and withdrew. Reach for them, and they were mist between your fingers. Every castle mustered its defences and stood by to repel the normal sharp and brief attack; for only when they were insolently sure of their supremacy did the Welsh assay a siege. Their strength was in their mobility, and in the contemptuous austerity with which they could discard their meagre establishments and take to the hills with their real possessions, their liberty, their horses and cattle, their tribal loyalty and their weapons. Much had changed in Wales in the two hundred years since Llewelyn ap Iorwerth the Great; but this was not changed.

The earldom of March was in the king's ward; for Roger Mortimer, earl of March, had died in action in Ireland, leaving a six-year-old son to inherit. But Roger's younger brother Edmund, twenty-six years old, high-spirited and impetuous, was at large about his border lordships, and very much inclined to resent the incursions of his Welsh neighbours. He mustered from his family's many garrisons a substantial army, and went out to patrol his borders and look for his enemy.

He found him, or was found by him, on the 22nd of June, in the valley of the river Lugg, near Pilleth, where the steep slopes of Bryn Glas hurtled down to the track on one hand, and the flats and meadows of the river hemmed it on the other. In the wet, wild June the grass was tall and lush, and the heather on the hills stood high and bristling like wire. Beyond the river, which was wide and hasty in spate, Llan-fawr soared into cloud. And out of the bracken and the thin, fine rain the Welsh boiled like foam out of a hound's jaws, to confront the English in the narrows under the hill.

Edmund Mortimer kept his head, deployed his archers in what cover there was, massed his knights and men-at-arms on firm ground clear of the marsh meadows, and stood to receive the attack, braced to hold back his horsed companies until the bowmen had had the chance to loose from cover three or four volleys, and reduce the odds. He withheld the signal until the range was close enough to be deadly, and the stocky Welsh ponies were stretching their frenzied necks and rigid nostrils for the impact, and then flung up his arm, and waited for the tremendous thrumming in the air, that maddening, intoxicating sound like a thousand wild geese all taking flight at once.

It did not come. The volley of arrows was thin and broken, its unevenness jangling in his nerves even before his senses recorded it. He turned, incredulous, to stare, and saw half his array of bowmen, the Welsh-born half, standing mute and grim with bows on shoulders, some slowly raising them, some fitting the shafts; and he knew, by their faces and their movements, where those shafts were bound. He uttered a great cry of anger and shame, without words, and then the words came following, so hotly that they burned in his throat:

"Traitors—traitors! You've eaten my salt and taken my pay…!"

But they were Welsh! He should have foreseen it. Mercenary soldiers are mercenary only skin-deep, they still have blood, and the blood can out-argue the indentures and the oaths of fealty sworn for pay. In his heart, even as the first shaft sliced into the flesh of his left arm, he did not really blame them. But now there was only one thing left for him to do, and that he did, before the shock of Glendower's assault sheared deep into his ranks, hardly slowed by the few casualties caused by the English archers. He wheeled his horse, and roared his own knights round upon their bowmen; and the loyal among the marksmen set up an answering howl, and fell out as best they could, leaping sidelong into the bushes and up the heathery slope, to stand clear of the slaughter and find a vantage-point again from which they could play their part. Edmund rode with slashing spurs and flailing sword into the ranks of the mutinous archers, his knights hard after him. Before that killing was over, the vanguard of the Welsh charge struck them in side and rear, and swept the whole mêlée two hundred yards down-river in a tangle of steel and blood and shrieking horses, inextricably mingled.

A few of the rearmost fled down the river valley towards Whitton, and made good their escape, but most stood their ground as soon as the hurtling, heaving mass lost impetus and came to a seething stay. The loyal archers climbed into the wet furze-tangles of the hillside, and did what they could to pick off the outliers among the attackers, and those in the rear, where they were less inextricably tangled with the English. But Owen's bowmen were swarming along the higher shoulders of Bryn Glas and shooting down upon them, and upon the struggling men-at-arms; and they had the advantage of better positions and better sighting, and skill and marksmanship at least equal. Most of the loyal archers died where they fought, picked off at leisure from above. A few, when the field was plainly already lost, crept away into cover as best they could, and lay hidden in the valley of the brook beyond Graig Hill until nightfall, to make their way home in the dark.

In the meadows by the Lugg, driven by its own weight ever closer to the edge of the water, and trapped by its own trampling ever deeper into the quaking marshy turf, the mass of struggling, hampered men and horses wallowed like a bogged ox. In the heart of the press one or two died of suffocation, and many were ridden down and crushed to death under the horses' feet. There were horsemen snared in the vortex who died unable to free an arm to defend themselves. One or two, their horses killed under them, were held for a time unable to fall, and others slithered into the river, its shore by now churned into slime, and drowned there in their harness.

This lasted but a little while, for those on the fringes, both forward and aft, drew off as soon as they had room and control, and sought firmer ground and more elbow-room. The swords which had been clubbed or shortened into daggers for want of space to use them, now came into more orthodox play; and the Welsh archers above on the hills were able to select their targets again without killing their own comrades, and worked with supercilious skill as long as there was light to slay by, and an Englishman still alive.

Edmund Mortimer, with blood running down inside the plates of his armour, heaved his mount out of the mire and up to firm ground, and wheeled to take his first brief survey of the field, and locate the main body of the Welsh cavalry, for only in hand-to-hand combat with them was there any respite from the steady and murderous attentions of the bowmen above. They would not dare risk a shot at anyone within a sword's reach of their prince and his guard. He found the raking black horse that stood a head above the tough mountain ponies—Owen was a long-legged man, and liked a tall mount—and the knot of unmistakable knighthood around it. He saw the flaunting, rosy feather in the prince's helmet, and the golden dragon outlined on the white surcoat. Edmund rose in his stirrups, and bellowed against the uproar all round him:

"Mortimer! *À moi*! Mortimer!" And those who could dragged themselves clear to re-form and charge with him.

They presented a target thus for only a matter of seconds, though three of them fell in that time; then they were hand-to-hand and at blows with the prince's bodyguard and this was battle as it had formerly been understood between knights, and the hovering archers were crippled and out of the fight. And yet this field was like every other since the archers had become the terrible force they were; their part was done first, but nonetheless at the end it was seen to be the determining part. There were so few left active to sustain the burden afterwards.

The lord of Glyndyfrdwy had been as well-tutored in arms as in law, and as apt a pupil; he had, moreover, all the experience that Edmund lacked. It was all one to him whether he directed a battle or a raid from his headquarters and left the action to others, or himself went to work with lance or sword in the centre of the din; they were merely complementary skills in the same comprehensive expertise. He unhorsed Edmund, knowing very well whom he held at his lance's point, with economy and address, and without damaging the horse, for of fine horses there can never be too many. When the boy rose at him on foot, none too steadily but with grim gallantry, and dripping blood from the finger-ends of his mail gauntlet, Owen vaulted promptly out of the saddle to match him, and waved off his companions, who would have borne the young man down by sheer weight. No one wanted to kill him, no one wanted to spoil him; he was too precious for that, and already too securely theirs, for hardly a whole man was left to back him. Owen drew on him, and let him attack as he would, approving the pointless but touching valour with which he came on. He had lost much blood, his helm was notably dinted, and the head inside it already dazed and misty as the dusk coming down on the hills. He wavered and lurched as he came. Owen measured his distance, and as he swung, struck the sword with well-judged force out of his failing hand, and clubbed him senseless with the flat of his blade. The boy dropped at his feet, in a single, total fall without a movement after, like a stone.

"This one," said Owen generously, looking down at him, "may not be over-valued at the price. I'd as lief have him on my side as against me."

He looked round him, upon the desolation of the field between Bryn Glas and the river, littered and faintly heaving still with bodies and cast arms, and groaning with the last convulsions of struggle and pain. The dusk was coming down fast. Horses threshed feebly, pounding the earth in a frenzy to get to their feet, and falling back again. The men lay more quietly; some, not a doubt of it, still alive, some even lying mort until it should be safe to rise and go. Let them go who could. The Welsh wanted none but valuable prisoners, and had no interest in killing the others, since they would surely leave this place more nimbly and rapidly than the English survivors, and be as inaccessible as the stars by the time another force looked for them.

"My lord, there are three knights live and yielded. Shall we bring them, too?"

"Can they ride?" For the company would move fast this night, lie but briefly, and double again; and even the prisoners must stand the pace.

"Yes. And the horses are blown but sound."

They had remounts not two hours away; that was no problem.

"Yes, bring them. If they give their parole, take it. But keep archers at their back." Even a knight was worth a fair ransom; and better worth if he decided, upon consideration, to enlist upon the other side. He looked down at Edmund Mortimer, motionless at his feet, his mailed hands relaxed and empty in the turf. "Bind him on his own horse—it will go better under him than another. We'll have the harness off him at Llanbadarn, and see to his hurts. I would not lose him for every noble we'll get for him. But have him out of here we must, and quickly."

They hoisted him into his saddle and bound him there, lying forward upon the beast's neck with his arms lashed about it to hold him secure, and a folded cloak under his breast and cheek They took what there was to take, all the mounts that were fit to travel, all the arms that lay masterless about the field, and vanished in the dusk up-river into the mountains with their prisoners and their triumph. The night came down over Bryn Glas, and the remnant of the Mortimer forces crept out of hiding, salvaged what they could, and made lamely for home with their wounds and their disgrace.

The squire who carried the news to the king at Berkhamsted reached him on the evening of June 24th. The young man had ridden hard, and was stained and tired, and not a little frightened at the magnitude of the disaster he reported. When he had finished, the king was motionless and silent for so long that the messenger held his breath, in dread of the repercussions that commonly attend the bearer of bad news. But when at last Henry spoke it was mildly and quietly enough, though his eyes, deep-set and haggard under their drawn brows, looked curiously opaque, like grey glass with no light behind it of lantern or sky, and his hands, slightly gnarled like the hands of an older man, gripped hard at the arms of his chair.

"Carried away prisoner, you say. And alive? You are sure he was alive?" A strange question; who would burden his raiding party with a dead man? "Was he wounded?"

"Your Grace, I saw him felled. It was not a killing blow, it was meant to stun. But I think he was already wounded."

"Gravely?"

"No, your Grace, for when he mustered what force he had left and drove at the Welsh knights, he could both ride and fight, and so did, and well. And they were careful of him, knowing his worth."

The king thought long, or perhaps sat silent long without thought, hardly yet fully grasping what had befallen. Then he asked slowly: "What other losses have we suffered in this battle?"

"My liege lord, three knights killed, and as many captured, and of others killed, some three score archers, men-at-arms, and squires. The Welsh losses were but light, but for the archers of Welsh blood in our forces, who are all dead or deserted with the enemy."

"You have been at some personal pains," said the king in the same quiet voice, "to bring us an eye-witness's account, and for that we thank you. How came you off so fortunately?"

"Your Grace, I and two others were some way behind, bringing up the spare horses, and came on the scene only in time to see Sir Edmund at grips, and the battle all but done. When they saw us they pursued us, but not far, for it was growing dusk. And when they gave over I ventured back to see from the hillside, where there was some cover. So we rode for Whitton, and were able, as soon as the Welsh were gone, to bring off some of our wounded safely."

"You could do no more. Very well, you may leave us. Take your rest and refreshment here, and when you leave tomorrow I will send letters by you to Wigmore."

And when the messenger had made his reverence and limped out from the presence, Henry turned his head a little, and looked at his closest confidants, but obliquely, out of the corner of a sunken eye, and dismissed them, too.

"Leave me. I must have time to think. This cannot go on un-checked. I'll call you when I need you."

The door closed on them. He was alone; he could let his face fall, and his eyes open and cast their shutters. There was no one to see in him either dismay or glee, or the furious fusion of both that raged in him. He lay back in his chair limply, and felt himself begin to tremble. He could not have borne a mirror in the room with him now, for fear of what he might see; in his heart he knew that it would be unrecognisable, as he failed to recognise the turmoil of his own feelings as having anything to do with the self he had always known.

Bad news, so bad the boy had almost been afraid to utter it! If only he had known enough, he might have come privately and hoped for a reward!

Grey in April—that was one thing. But now Mortimer in June! Of all men, Mortimer! Great-grandson to King Edward the third, and by a branch senior to Lancaster, even though his descent came through a woman. For Edmund's mother was Henry's cousin Philippa, the daughter of Lionel, duke of Clarence who had been born before John of Gaunt. And no matter how the experts argued about the legitimacy of descent through the female line, nevertheless the people recognised no bar, and the council had accepted it as just and right when Richard, in view of his childlessness, had been urged to name his heir presumptive, and had named Philippa's elder son, Roger, earl of March. Well, Roger was no rival now. He was dead in Ireland, four years ago, in Richard's service; but he had left behind other Mortimers, far too many Mortimers, to inherit his claim: Edmund and Roger, his sons, Anne, his daughter. And if all these should flicker out like candles, still his young, lusty brother Edmund, strong as a stag, and ripe for marriage, capable of getting more sons, more Mortimers to carry on the line and the claim to eternity. And if this second branch failed, there was yet another Mortimer, Edmund's sister Elizabeth; and like Philippa, even if she was but a woman, she had given birth to a son, the youngest Henry Percy, Hotspur's heir.

He sat staring before him, seeing nothing but a long line of Mortimers, inexhaustible and prolific to the end of time. True, Roger's children were all in the king's wardship, the boys far too young to cause trouble, and in reliable hands even if they should try, or others should try on their behalf. Yet they lived—and all men knew they lived. And this elder Edmund, their uncle, he was no child to be held in fosterage, but a young man of power and property and ambition. Why could not Wales have taken care of him as efficiently as Ireland had of Roger? "Captured" was well enough in its way, at least it disabled and immobilised him. But it might so easily have been "killed"!

The king seemed to himself to turn suddenly, and gaze back into his own mind, and it was like peering into a cavern where dangerous creatures lurked, such as he had never suspected could habit within him. He willed to turn his eyes away, but he could not. Once having looked, he could never again be unaware. And yet it was false, he had no ill intent, he had done no wrong to Edmund or to any of them. Was it any fault of his if the Welsh rebels had made prisoner a Mortimer, at this moment the most formidable of the Mortimers? Had carried him off into the mountains, in this

harsh summer of storms and floods? And wounded, if only lightly!
Perhaps not so lightly! Perhaps gravely. And such a forced journey
after—Who knew where death was lying in wait for him? No, he
had done nothing to harm Edmund, nor would he in the future.
Only let be, he thought, hardly knowing he thought it, *and there may
be no need*!

And yet this matter of the battle at Pilleth could not be left un-
answered, for the sake of his tenure. The blow to English arms
was bitter, and he felt it as an insult to his own person. The threat
from Wales grew steadily, and could not be suffered any longer. It
was time for him to take action. He had left things to others too
long, and his sovereignty was in danger of being slighted. In this
matter, too, he hardly recognised himself. When had he ever had
to be pricked into action before? He was at his best when reacting
promptly and powerfully to every threat, how had he let himself
be hemmed in thus by forms and processes and the operations of
incompetent deputies? It was easy now to decide what to do, both
for outward appearances and for the comfort of his own spirit. He
must and would take the field himself against Glendower, and make
an end of him.

*(Yet if he did so, was not Edmund Mortimer let loose again from his
prison?)*

He rang his silver bell, and it was John Norbury himself who came
in to answer it.

"My lord?"

"John, I must write to my council. Send Nicholas Bubwith in
to me. And bring Thomas, too, and do you stay with us. I need
your advice."

And when they were come, and settled into conference with him:
"I desire your views upon the decision I have taken in this matter
of the Welsh war. It is in my mind that this last outrage cannot be
allowed to pass, nor can I longer leave the handling of the affair
to Prince Henry or his advisers. I purpose, therefore, to wage war

myself in Wales, and I intend to set out from Lichfield on—let me see, this is the twenty-fourth of June—on the seventh day of July. Draft a letter to my council, Nicholas, notifying them that I have already had the news of the action at Pilleth, and asking them to send out orders for the knights and squires of all the midland counties to meet me at Lichfield, fully prepared, mounted, and arrayed for war, by the seventh day of July. You may say also that I think it well that the musters of the northern counties should prepare themselves for possible action against the Scots at the same date, and those along the south coast should be ready to resist any assault by sea from my enemies in Europe. For we already have knowledge," said the king, "that our enemy in Wales has sent letters praying aid to all these potential foes of our state, and a joint assault is more than a possibility. So write, Nicholas," he said, leaning back relaxed and smiling in his chair, "and I will sign it. And you, my friends, show me your will, and say if I do well."

His eye had regained its clarity, and his head its proud poise, as in the days when Norbury had accompanied him in his Prussian crusade with the Teutonic knights, long ago. With one voice they told him that he did well.

At very much the same hour Edmund Mortimer came out of the deep sleep that follows fever, and opened his eyes reluctantly, remembering instantly and ruefully a day and a night of indignity and discomfort before he had lost all sense of place, time, and direction, and finally of his own identity. He had no idea where he was, except that it must be somewhere in the wilds of Wales, well hidden from any possibility of rescue; and he took his first unwilling look about him in the conviction that captivity could mean nothing better than solitude, close confinement, and squalor.

He opened his eyes upon discreet candle-light, upon a small room hung with tapestries and green fir-boughs that smelled of spice and resin and open air; and upon a girl's face bent solicitously over him.

She could not have been more than eighteen years old, golden as a kingcup and white as windflowers. He had never seen hair of such a full, glowing gold, or a fairer brow underneath it. The great thick braid of spun metal hung over her shoulder, and brushed his cheek as she leaned over him. Her eyes, which were blue-black, were very large, grave, and kind. As soon as she saw that he was awake she slipped a hand expertly under his head, and held a cup to his lips, and he drank thirstily, like a child, all the more willingly because it was plain that his docility pleased her.

He must, of course, be dreaming her. During the fever brought on by wounds, forced marches, wet and cold he had dreamed many odd and discomforting things, but never anything like this.

He tried whether he had a voice in the dream, and it seemed that he had, though a curiously meagre one, for she leaned still closer to hear what he wanted, inclining her earnest head to bring a small, close-set ear almost within touch of his lips.

"Madam, I see that—after all—I have not been too much a sinner. For you can be nothing—but an angel."

She heard and understood him. She drew back a little, and let him see her face whole again, and in focus. The briefest of smiles took flight from her lips to her eyes, and away, leaving her portentously grave again; and with careful, frowning concentration she said in English, her bright, light, child's voice forming the words as gingerly as a novice using an untried weapon:

"Oh, no—I am only Catherine."

5

King Henry's moves that summer afforded a curious study to an observant man. His decision was taken, and the orders sent out for the triple muster, yet even after news from the northern border confirmed only too clearly that Scotland intended to take a full part in the harrying of his realm, he was slow to move. He was still at Berkhamsted at the end of June, but at least then he had the relief of writing to his council with somewhat more reassuring news from Northumberland. The earl had successfully held minor raids near Carlisle, apparently launched to sound out the defences of the western march, and at Berwick the garrison, with the help of George Dunbar, that angry refugee from over the border, poacher turned forester, had decisively defeated a party of four hundred Scots. But this was no more than the beginning; for by now they knew very well that there were French knights fighting with the Scottish companies, and in fair numbers, too, and the south of England had been warned to look to its defences in case of a direct assault from across the channel.

In July the king finally moved north, took up his residence in the abbey of Lilleshall, and made it his headquarters while he reviewed the defences of the Welsh border. He remained there long enough to draw many camp-followers of various kinds, including several of the merchants of Shrewsbury, who had an interest in the supply of gear and provisions, and smiths and other craftsmen who could pick up lucrative jobs among the armouries. It was easy to move among this great, churning concourse, and hear all there was to be heard, and no great trick, for an intelligent man, to winnow the less likely rumours out of the crop, and be left with the grain.

The king, so they said, had made four new commands on the Welsh front, though it was only four months since he had made the previous appointments of the two Percies as lieutenants of north and south Wales. He hardly knew his own mind, they said candidly among their own intimates. His executives went in and out of office like dogs at a fair, and so did his treasurers. True, Lord Henry Percy had his hands full on the eastern march of Scotland, and could hardly be in two places at once, but the earl of Worcester was still in Wales, and acting as the prince's governor and head of council, too. The only magnate who kept his place unchallenged for long was the prince himself.

And now that he had his muster here, what would the king do? Strike directly into Wales? Surprisingly, he turned not westwards, but eastwards, to Lichfield again, and on to Burton-on-Trent, where he issued orders for the victualling of all the border towns by the 27th of August, ready for an advance into Wales.

Thus far Iago Vaughan, like many another displaced labourer tramping the roads in search of casual work in these disturbed times, had followed the unwieldy cavalcade and kept his ears and eyes open. But if the victuallers were to have their stores ready only by the end of August, and the king was intending, as it seemed, to continue his journey eastwards across the centre of England, equidistant from the possible battle-grounds of the Welsh and Scottish borders and the threatened south coast, and ready to move in whichever direction should first require his presence, then there was no longer anything to be gained by loitering here, and he had better be making his way over to Owen with what information he had, and whatever intelligent inferences could be drawn from that information.

"We need not expect him, then," said Owen, "until the beginning of September. And these estimates you bring me of his numbers—since they can but be estimates—have you shot low or high? He'll have more, or less?"

They were sitting together over a rough table in a room in a farmhouse outside Abergavenny. Owen distrusted castles unless he had had the ordering of them and the garrisoning for a year or more; there was infinitely more safety in the hills, because the hills were his castle and not another man's, and could not be betrayed or easily taken by storm. The English feared for their lives to be shut out of a keep; but the Welsh were more wary of being shut in.

"My lord, as I think, less. If I am in doubt, I overshoot. And as you see, the numbers with which I credit him are more than enough. But more important is how he will use them. And—my lord—there is here something more than strange."

"I am listening," said Owen.

"I have studied this Bolingbroke carefully and long. I know his record, before he became king and after. So do you, better than I, and you must check me if I stray. For my life I cannot understand, what is it makes this man now so lame, so hesitant, so crippled, who was wont to be hale and prompt enough. He moves about his business, life or death, like one with a broken back. He can, but he will not, or he will, but he cannot. He knows what he wants, and he means to go forward and grasp it, but ever he turns aside, or his feet lag. I have seen the son, and he is no such being. So far as he's let, he knows his mind very well, he determines and he does. What has happened to this Henry, since he landed at Ravenspur and struck out so baldly for a crown?"

"He has won it," said Owen, his mouth curling in a dark, private smile.

"Should that unman him?"

"He was ever a man of terrible rectitude," said Owen dispassionately, half-closing his eyes to peer back into a past he hardly ever dwelt on now. "Narrow as a lance, but sure of his own probity, and very well able to act if his rights were infringed. What has he to be sure of now in that quarter? As certain as he thinks "my rights" and puts out his hand to strike in defence of them, he knows they're none of his. How came the son of a younger son to have any "rights" in the throne?"

"Make no mistake, my lord," said Iago vehemently, "he'll stoop to any shift now to keep his hold of it."

"So he will, I know it. So he must. But his arm will be lead to lift, and his feet chained when he seeks to stride. Like a man in a dream, that must for his life run like a deer, and can only crawl like a broken worm. When most he wants and needs to strike home, he'll find himself shuffling and stumbling and hesitating, waiting to see what his enemy will do. You cannot be a man of such icy probity as he was, and not be crippled when your credit's gone."

"Don't underrate him, however. Even a broken worm can kill, if it happens to be an adder. And he is not yet so low that he cannot bring down many a better man. For with all his rectitude," said Iago, coldly considering, "I think him but very small in goodness, and very drear. He is a winter man, and his frost drives away even those who most willed to warm him."

"He was not always so," said the greatest of those he had yet alienated and turned into enemies. "It is a part of his malady. And now there is no cure. He must live with his disabilities as we must live with his abilities. We shall see who calculates most accurately. The twenty-seventh of August! And you say he plans a three-fold advance, from Chester, Shrewsbury and Hereford?"

"That was the talk of his camp. I think it could well be true. Certainly they are victualling all three towns."

"Then the prince will move in from Chester. It is his headquarters." He who was the effective prince of Wales spoke easily of "the prince," and never grudged him his courtesy title. "Henry will take Shrewsbury for himself, the central base. And Hereford—that will be either Worcester or Stafford." He had already noted all Henry's new appointments. The young earl of Stafford was coming early into prominence, for he was one of the new knights Henry had made on the eve of his coronation. "Well...well," he said, narrowing his far-sighted eyes upon the beloved map in his mind, "they shall be somewhat too far north by then to find any trace of me. And while they feint at shadows, I will be busy with the substance. For it's time they saw more of me in the south, Iago, where I shall not be expected. I have a fancy to show myself as far as Newport and Cardiff, while they lose themselves in the mountains of Maelienydd and Brecon."

"And I, my lord, what shall I do?"

"Go back to Shrewsbury. It is his main base, and where the news will be. I'll send letters by you to Rhys and Gwilym, and they'll have a man waiting across Severn at Guilsfield, ready to pass on any word you send him. Go and be a hanger-on at Henry's storehouses, and pick up what grain you can. As for me, I shall move south by Usk and Caerleon. And I warrant I shall be ready for the twenty-seventh of August before Henry will. It will be a testing month," he said, smiling a little to himself, "more ways than one."

Iago rose to take his leave, but the prince called him back for a moment. "Will Percy come south to Wales, think you, or stay on the Scottish march?"

"He'll stay in the north, my lord. He must. There's not a mile of that border safe if he turns his back now, and they know it."

"You think he knows yet that I have Mortimer? But he must, surely. He'll be pinning his faith on Henry and his autumn parliament to raise the money for the young man's ransom, no doubt. Should you, by some far chance, rub shoulders with him again, Iago, let him know his brother is well healed of his wounds, and in good fettle. He had a zealous nurse," said Owen, and laughed at some thought of his own.

"And will you let them go for ransom? Mortimer and Grey both?"

"What use is Grey to me now? I cannot fight him while he's my prisoner, I cannot kill him until he's free to face me again in arms. And his price—his price can be of enormous use. Ten thousand marks it shall cost them, if they want him back. And as for Mortimer, they shall pay dearer still for him. But whether in money or kind," he said, a suppressed smile tugging the corners of his mouth inward in very private amusement, "may well be another matter. I doubt if it rests altogether with me or with Edmund."

The entire vast enterprise lurched into uneasy motion at last, in the first days of September, in the strange, ominous hush of the end of that disastrous summer, while France sat mute and made no sign, and the Scots, for all their gadfly raids, seemed to hold off from testing the defences of the north. It was King Henry's one great gesture against Glendower, and nothing had been spared of loans, and exhortations, and massing of stores, to ensure its success. It was his misfortune to envisage every such encounter as a matter of life and death, though by now he should have been used to anticlimax, and to the survival and tenacity of both parties to fight another day. He wanted an ultimate solution, and life does not deal in such simplifications.

The prince, who took his force into Wales from Chester in good tight order, and at every mile ensured his lines behind him, was on his guard against his own instinctive enthusiasm as well as against Welsh armies, and knew enough about them by this time to feel no surprise that he should probe ever more deeply and carefully into North Wales, and never touch hands with anything more than a darting patrol, gone almost as soon as sighted. He threw out no sounding parties too weak to guarantee their own safety, and he lost none of them. Past Ruthyn and Clocaenog and into the Cambrian mountains and the Berwyns, hampered by vile weather, and impeded by swollen streams and misty hills, he moved methodically on the lines laid down for him, and made no contact with any substantial enemy. He made no attempt to touch Owen's ancestral hold of Carrog, because he had no orders to do so. His advance had been laid down for him in definite terms, and he held to it, but taking his own precautions along the way. In any case, he knew who would be in Carrog—the women and children and those unfit for warfare—and he knew how quickly they would remove before him if he went near them. There would be men enough left with them to ensure their safe withdrawal, not enough to make it worth his while disabling them. What he wanted was the main force, mobile and sudden and a prize fit for his steel. Some day there might be a time for setting light to both Carrog and Sycarth, and driving their households homeless into the hills; but not now, that was to fritter away all these preparations upon a minor consideration.

He went his way across North Wales, probing as he moved, but he never saw hide nor hair of Owen.

The force from Hereford had the choice of two ways in, the more northerly by Hay and Brecon, the more southerly by Abergavenny, and by ill-luck chose the first. At Talgarth they got wind of skirmishes in the south, and set off southward over Mynedd Troed for Tretower; but because of the time they had lost they were always too far behind their quarry even to realise the magnitude of the chance that persistently slipped through their fingers. By the time they reached Abergavenny, Owen was at Cardiff, and while they were pressing hard from Usk to Caerleon, Owen was withdrawing in excellent order into the wilds of Brecknock. They never got so near to him again. They had suffered less than the other armies from the evil weather up to then, but in the days that followed Wales and September did their worst, and it was difficult to keep open their lengthening supply lines.

King Henry himself, with the third army, struck due west from Shrewsbury for Welshpool, strongly garrisoned and lavishly provisioned as an advanced base. From there they moved on into the Cambrian mountains; and for three days they toiled through the worst storms of the year. Every brook coming down from the heights was swollen into a torrent, every valley river gulped these tributaries into its heart, and burst out over the narrow meadows into languid shallows, while in the centre it rushed ahead with treacherous force. Some of their stores were swept away, some of their mounts and pack-horses were bogged, or foundered and damaged themselves in the stones of the river beds. In the upper levels of the hills the occasional pools had grown to three times their normal size, and turned every bowl of rushy upland into marsh, where the army laboured perilously for every half-mile of painful progress.

On the seventh of September the clouds broke for the first time, the wind subsided, and the sun came out. That evening they pitched their camp on a shoulder of dry ground above a valley, thankful for the respite. The king slept half-armed in his tent, the remainder of his plate-armour massed just within the entrance, and his lance with its pennant fixed upright in the turf outside. Strung out along the shelf between hill and vale, with outposts covering every approach, the army settled down for the night.

In the third hour of darkness the climactic storm seemed to materialise overhead out of a sky barely dappled with clouds. Those who were waking said afterwards that it did not move towards them across the sky from any direction, but burst suddenly, directly above them, in a great whirlwind and a peal of thunder. Then every star vanished, and the sky was instantly one piled mass of black cloud, out of which lightnings flashed and rain streamed in a circling torrent, swirled by the terrible wind. One sentry almost drowned on his feet, for the wind had pinned him against a rock, and he could not free himself or even turn his face into shelter, while it dashed into his mouth and nostrils unceasing volleys of rain so heavy that he could not get his breath; and if two of his companions who had their backs turned upon the blast had not been cast against him, and so afforded his face shelter enough to breathe, he must have died spread-eagled there. Some in the low-lying places, who were heavily asleep, did drown as they lay, the water gathering so rapidly in every hollow.

The king awoke out of his sleep to a frightful sound, like a great crash of thunder and the hissing flight of a thousand arrows. He sprang up with a cry, and in the same moment the tent collapsed upon him, pinning him to the ground under its heavy folds, and the hammering rain held it there, flattened crushingly over his breast, moulding itself to every feature of his face, so that he was nearly suffocated. And yet the place was drenched, as with water, so with a fearful smell of burning. He had laid by his sword, but he had a dagger still upon him, and managed to draw it and slash through the folds that smothered him; and Norbury and Erpyngham and half a dozen others of his own people came plunging and splashing through the storm to help him out of these ominous grave-clothes.

Then they all saw that the royal lance, which had stood upright at the door of the tent, had been flung down so violently that its point had pierced the breast-plate of his piled armour; and the shaft of the lance was twisted and discoloured, all the armour dinted, and the royal pennant charred as if it had been burned. They began to shake, for this was too close to hell-fire and witchcraft. No one then had time to utter what he dreaded; but afterwards, though those about the king held their peace doggedly, and spoke only of phenomenally bad weather against which no man could guard, in the ranks men were saying to one another that this was no natural storm, that there had never been known so strange and violent a tempest, that it was sent out of malice against them, either by Owen himself, or by those stiff-necked Franciscans of Llanfaes whose house the king had burned, and who were allies of Owen and the devil to the last man.

But this was afterwards. There was no talking that night in the darkness, men had enough to do to stay alive, and salvage something out of the ruin. For after the rain came hail, to batter and crush what the water had left undamaged, and after the hail, snow, sudden freezing squalls that piled white drifts in every cranny and across every open space. And towards morning, when the snow turned again to rain, the whole hillside under which they were camped had become furrowed and scoured by a hundred brooks scurrying and leaping downwards into the river valley, till the level of the flood crept up towards their outposts, and its tributaries carried down into it everything movable that came in their way, including some of the hobbled horses, and the wreckage of tents, and drowned men.

When the light came they mustered what was left to them, and knew without many words spoken, even when the storm subsided at last into mere mist and drizzle, that they could not advance further. Half their provisions were lost or ruined, many of the horses dead or hurt, and a number of men drowned. They had little hope of bringing up fresh provisions in these conditions, and if they lengthened their lines by a few more miles they would have no hope at all. The army turned back in drenched and miserable retreat towards Welshpool, without having so much as sighted a Welsh force of any kind. And the soldiers muttered to one another as they limped and splashed back towards England that the black friars had not only sent the terror, but withdrawn it from them as soon as they turned back, and the devil their master could call it up again in an instant if they so much as looked over their shoulders.

In Welshpool they halted to rest, and make good what losses they could, to dry out their arms and reflight their arrows; and there was a brief council of war. But the issue was never in doubt. Some said the king was gravely shaken by his narrow escape from death, and the implied threat that still hung over him. Some said merely that the money was not available to fit out such an expedition a second time, even if the spirit had been willing; and that was certainly true. But all agreed, even before the order was given, that when they moved from Welshpool it would be back to Shrewsbury. And all agreed most bitterly, though no one uttered it, that they would be going back derided and disgraced.

No one knew it better than the king; and no one felt it more corrosively.

It so happened that on this same 7th of September the inner circle of the royal council was meeting in a small room in Westminster to hear the report of the treasurer, the king's old and loyal servant Henry Bowet, now bishop of Bath and Wells. Among those present was Master John Prophet, dean of Hereford, who among his pluralities numbered also the deanery of St. Chad's at Shrewsbury, the king's privy clerk, and soon to be his secretary.

The treasurer's lament was not new to any ear; it was the unceasing accompaniment of every expensive undertaking. But this time it had a note of desperation which rendered it almost novel even to those who had heard it so often.

"I have employed every way I know," said Bowet wearily, "to procure money for his Grace's needs. I have offered bonds under my own seal, as well as the royal seal, but without result. They will not lend any further sums unless they hold jewels as security, and more; unless they may have letters patent to give them the right to sell if they do not get repayment by the date appointed. We have no authority to issue such letters, yet the matter is urgent, all the more as his Grace is absent in such a vital cause. He cannot be reached at this moment, and the question cannot be shelved. The money must be raised, and at once. I ask the council to advise."

They debated unhappily, reluctant to commit themselves to an opinion, until John Prophet suggested sadly that in the circumstances it might be well to consult the archbishop of Canterbury, and in some relief they agreed on this course, and carried their problem that same afternoon to Lambeth; where Thomas Arundel, on the force of whose word and influence they could rely, advised them, in consideration of the desperate need, to issue the required letters patent, and he would be responsible for defending their action to the king, should it need any defence.

Accordingly the lenders got their security, and leave to turn it into good cash if no other cash redeemed it in time. There was a proviso that should the value of the jewels exceed the amount of the debt, the excess must be paid over to the king's treasury. But no one wasted much attention on that. It was a practical certainty that he would be trying to raise more loans long before these were ever repaid. But at least they could hold off within the value of what they now held, and were empowered to dispose of to advantage.

So low was King Henry's credit fallen with those who lent money to him. But lower still, infinitely low at this moment, with himself.

The news of the retreat came into Shrewsbury only a day ahead of the returning vanguard, and filled the town with rumours and counter-rumours. Some said there would be no more than a brief lull to refurbish and reprovision, and then another attempt; others maintained that the troops would be paid off—if they were so lucky as to be paid!—and disbanded from Shrewsbury, for it was too late in the year now to favour an invasion. And many whispered of witchcraft; and some, in very low voices and in trusted company, said that the judgment of God was sometimes miscalled the malice of the devil, by those who must pass off their devil as God. There was even some whispering, in secret and in Welsh, of birthrights; for the lord of Glyndyfrdwy was the lawful living heir of the princes of Powys Fadog, and his mother, Helen, was great-grand-daughter to Llewelyn ap Griffith, the last revered and lamented prince of North Wales; and Henry of Lancaster was the son of a younger son, and the stars and the elements could not be deceived.

But those who could speak English spoke no Welsh aloud in Shrewsbury in those days, for feeling was running all the higher because the two races bred and mingled so closely here, and it was well to be known as a loyal king's man, and indulge other sympathies only in low voices round the hearth, or better still, in silence within the heart.

But Welsh and English alike took care to put their valuables and their armour, if they had any, safely under lock and key, for if the returning troops were to be billeted in the town, even for a few nights, there would certainly be some looting, and no sane burgess was so loyal a king's man as to be complacent about losing goods and gear without a struggle to preserve them.

And some, and among them Rhodri Parry, had more dangerous and precious things to hide from the retreating soldiery. A town filled with disgruntled men-at-arms, more than ready to pick an easy quarrel to pay for the hard one they had lost, was no place for a fugitive Franciscan friar escaped from the Leicester convent, and suspect of treason along with several others of his house, some already executed. He had lain in one of the lofts above the storehouses for several days, weak and sick after zig-zagging cross-country ahead of the hunt, moving by night in this foul summer, and lying up in woods and trees by day. Iago had brought him, and Iago should have been here within two more days to take him away, somewhat recovered now and strong enough to continue his flight into Wales. But the disfavour of heaven had driven the royal army back too soon, and there was no Iago here to relieve the house of its dangerous guest. And within a day there might well be ten men-at-arms bivouacked in the house and the store-rooms.

"He must go," fretted Rhodri, tramping the length of his solar like a caged wolf, "or he's a dead man, and his blood will be on our heads. By tomorrow night it may be too late. And how are we to get him past the gates, with the town in this ferment? The guard will be on its mettle, with the king not a day away, and the sheriff alerted to expect him. I would not give a solitary noble for his chances by the Welsh gate. Where is Iago, for the love of God, when we need him most?"

"About our business and the Lord Owen's," said Julian, with a vicious snap that belonged rather to a wife than a daughter, "and worse pressed than we are, very likely. Hush your noise and see to your journeymen, and I'll do the rest."

"You?" he said with unflattering disbelief, and laughed.

"What else am I for in this place? You are the one that might be missed about the house and the business. Nobody asks me to be answerable for anything here. Keep the boys to the cloth warehouse after noon, and I'll see to it that Joanna has things to do above-stairs. She would not hear the crack of doom, and I'll ensure she shall be satisfied where I'm gone. Walter will find him safe lying at the holding until Iago can ferry him over and see him on his way. And you need know nothing, not even what we bargain among us. Who knows nothing can tell nothing, nor be convicted of anything, either." She had not quite the disdain of him that she put into what she said; and perhaps he knew it as well as she did. They had been father and daughter, and sworn enemies, for a long time now; they understood each other too well for comfort. "Give me your bless-ing, sir," she said, the devout child, "and be about it, and never look over your shoulder."

He cursed her, and blessed her, and fumed away on her errand as far as the door; and turned there to say with genuine fury: "Am I mad, that I turn you loose to take your chance among wolves? Say you put a foot wrong, are you not game to be coursed and spoiled, like other women, that I listen to you like a craven creature as I am?"

"You need not fret," she said equably, with the darkling smile that disquieted him more than her enmity. "I was spoiled long ago by that maudlin old wreck you bought for me, what more can happen to me now? Yes, there is somewhat in me still virgin, but not my body, and not at any man's beck and call like my body. Never have any fear for my virginity—it is not in danger."

❦

He was a poor, meagre creature, this Brother John Caldwell, thin as a rail from long starving in the woods, and by no means fully recovered as yet. His tonsure had grown out raggedly, and grown out white as ash, and the six-weeks-old beard he had acquired from living wild was streaked with grey. They had thought it well to keep that, trimmed into a square shape that concealed his lean jaw and fallen cheeks as much as possible. In Rhodri's cast-off clothes and worn shoes he looked like a penurious wandering scrivener of sixty; in truth he was barely forty, and had been a tall, strong man of his hands once, and would be as good again after a month of eating regularly, and nursing his frayed body and broken and blistered feet.

They would not normally have dreamed of attempting to get him into or out of the house except under cover of darkness; but now there was no certainty that they would have even one night of grace. Julian left him lurking in the shelter of the cart-house while she kept watch from the wicket for the most favourable moment, and beckoned him through quickly when the alley was empty. They were in luck, for the sky was still murky and a thin drizzle falling, excuse enough for him to cover his head and shadow his face within his capuchin, and for her to pull forward the hood of her old cloak, and hide within it.

Once away into the open street they could breathe more freely. He leaned heavily upon her arm, with a shambling lameness which was only half assumed, for he had gone barefoot for three weeks before he reached the refuge from which Iago had conveyed him west to Shrewsbury. They moved slowly through the crowds in the streets, glad of the obscuring numbers and the bustle and the noise, and the quivering, suppressed excitement, a thick veil behind which they walked, unnoticed and anonymous, towards the High Cross, and the long, gentle descent to the castle gate.

She knew better than to take a wanted man near the Welsh gate; but the castle gate was the one land approach to the town, the east-ward and inviolable gate, overshadowed by the bulk of the castle and the strength of its garrison. Where men feel most secure they keep least suspicious watch. It would mean a longer walk for them round the northward coil of the river, but that was a small matter once they were out of the town.

The great corner tower of the curtain wall loomed above the street on the right hand; and here the crowd was thicker, and the babel of voices louder and more excited. It seemed that somewhere ahead of them, towards the gate, all motion had ceased, and the press of people heaved and shifted, but made no progress. Julian took her companion by the hand, and wormed her way round elbows and between shoulders as far down the street as she could, drawing Brother John after her; but before she was close enough to the gatehouse to see what was happening there she was brought to a halt, and could move no farther. Others thus jammed beside her were shouting questions to those before them, and craning to peer over their heads. And up from the barbican of the castle, heaving the crowd aside by force on either hand as a plough turns the soil, came the clatter of hooves and a flurry of plumes, and resolved themselves presently into a posse of horsemen, breaking open a clear passage before them with staves, and thrusting the watching crowds back to the walls.

She watched the leaders ride slowly by, edging their horses mincingly along the fringes of the road, and shouting orders to give warning ahead:

"Stand back, there! Clear the way! Make way for the king's heralds!"

Crushed tightly together, the mass held its ground stolidly, and watched curiously for what would happen next. The town bailiffs passed slowly—she knew them well, Robert Thornes and John Scryveyn, both gentlemen of coat-armour. Their under-officers fell out one by one and took station along the way to preserve the channel they had opened.

"What is it?" Julian asked in the ear of the man in front of her. "What's happening? I'm late with getting back home as it is. Will they keep us here long?"

"So am I late, my girl, and many another here, but there's no help. They've closed the gate. There'll nobody get out of the town by this road until the king's officers have passed."

"They say the king's left Welshpool with a small escort ahead of the army," volunteered a boy a yard or so in front of them, turning an excited face.

"Is he coming here, to the castle?"

"Nobody knows. Some say he is, but last time he went to the abbey."

"No, he'll go on to Lilleshall. You'll see, they'll quarter the soldiers on us, but the king's officers will be pushing on for London as fast as they can."

Julian looked about her, and took heart. There were any number of laden country folk in this concourse, and within the hour there would be still more crowding down upon them from the town, after the market. If they had closed the gates to guard against any untoward incident until the king's men had passed, they would be the less inclined to make any checks of those passing through afterwards. It would be a case of opening the gates thankfully, and letting them pour out and disperse over the neighbouring villages as they would. The wait would be well worth it for such a blind release; and in this motley crowd, drawn from a dozen hamlets outside in addition to the town, her companion was nameless and faceless as a hunted man could wish to be. She pressed his gaunt hand with vital, confident fingers, and looked anywhere but at him. He must bear his soul in patience; he was safe enough.

Over the crest at the High Cross, erupting suddenly out of the declivity beyond, and certainly from the Welsh gate, the hard drumming of hooves burst upon their ears, coming at a gallop. Every head turned towards the sound, and every tongue stilled. A small party of riders—she counted eight of them—swept at speed along the channel cleared for them, the royal pennant at their head, two squires and four lightly-laden sumpter-horses following hard on their heels. Two riders turned in at the approach to the castle, the rest of the cavalcade swept onward through the gate, flung open to give them passage, and vanished in a flurry of spume and fine mud along the foregate.

The echoes subsided after them, but the under-bailiffs kept their place, patrolling nervously along the edge of the crowd, and all but trampling toes, though the horses sidled delicately away from contact, and shook their ornamented heads in distress at being held so close. Evidently there was some further party expected, and there would be no move until it had passed.

They had a long wait for this one, almost an hour. Julian looked sidelong at her charge, for he was weak as yet, and in this press, even if he swooned, he would not be able to fall. But he stood like a rock, his burning eyes fixed. She ceased to wonder that he had survived his long ordeal of flight and hiding and hunger; he was durable beyond most men.

There were more horses coming now, less hurriedly than the advance party, but still approaching at a brisk speed from the Cross. Craning and peering, they caught glimpses of a minor forest of lances and standards, though the number of riders was probably no more than a score; and rumour on rumour flew down the street before them, and name on name.

"I see Arundel's livery—and Stafford's..."

Silver swallows and a red chevron, and the purple lion of the Lacies; and another standard, lions and lilies quartered.

"The king..." someone said, in a vast, wondering sigh.

The horsemen passed. The marks of their campaign were upon them all, in the dulling of their armour and the soiling of their harness, in their stooped crests, and most of all in their fixed and frosty faces, the chagrin of paladins repulsed withe it a blow, out-ridden, out-manoeuvred, outdone in every way, and no remedy in gallantry. Shrewsbury had never until then sensed the bitterness of this recoil, or its galling comedy. The crowd fell absolutely silent, beholding the humiliation of the crown.

"The king..."

King Henry rode with eyes fixed before him, and brows drawn taut above them, as if his head ached. He had put off his armour, and rode in black and gold, with high gauntlets of purple leather, and a fine, extravagant capuchin in the same purple draped and twisted into a flaunting hat that drooped a long liripipe about his shoulders. It made a brave picture, for he was a fine figure in the saddle, tall and erect and well-made, and looked younger and more athletic than when he went on his own two feet. But his head, Julian thought, staring up into his face with intent and passionate attention, was a death's-head, drawn and pale about hollow eyes. He let his gaze rest upon the awed and silent faces that fringed his passage, but without seeing them. There was even a moment when he looked directly into Julian's eyes, and she opened them wide to take him in, but there was nothing alive in him to enter. He brushed with the same dead regard the face of the man his agents were still seeking in the matter of the Leicester treason, and Brother John gazed back at him earnestly and impartially, and was moved to distant pity. But no spark passed between them. The party clattered by, the gate opened to give them passage. They diminished steadily, shadowed under the archway, smoothed by the soft grey light beyond, riding onward towards some unknown destination.

No, he was not going to linger here. He had sent his outriders on ahead to make ready for him at Haughmond, or Lilleshall, some retired place where he could swallow this wormwood in solitude, out of the eyes of men. Julian felt no pity, only a detached curiosity and wonder; for he was not quite as she had imagined him, neither so malevolent nor so formidable. She was chiefly aware that his passing had served them well; for the under-bailiffs had relaxed their vigilance, and were moving slowly downhill towards the gate, and suffering the crowd, those who willed, to move in that direction with them. Who was going to check on these hundreds, all bent on getting home with their purchases, or the profits of their sales? They let them surge out at the gate and shake themselves loose of restraint to take their several ways. It was simplicity itself.

"Then that was the king. I never saw him before," Julian said wonderingly as they took the path that wound along the riverside, and the high walls of the castle fell behind them. "But it is not a bad face—only bleak and suspicious, not evil." She looked at her companion; they made their way at ease now, no longer in haste or fear, with a two-mile walk before them. "And did you really conspire to depose him?"

"We never willed to do him wrong," said the Franciscan of Leicester, treading gratefully in the thick turf with his crippled feet. "King he is not and cannot be, for King Richard was well alive when this man took the crown, and an abdication under duress is no valid abdication and cannot confer a valid right. And if King Richard is now dead, then it was by Lancaster's order he died, and whatever title Lancaster might otherwise have possessed to inherit from him is forfeit. No manner of election can entitle him to a siege which is not vacant. And no murderer can enjoy legitimate rights to the fruits of murder. Duke of Lancaster he is, with every right, and we never denied him that title, and never would. But king he is not. Neither crowning nor anointing can change the nature of truth."

"Excellent law," said Julian, sourly smiling. "You should have said as much to him as he passed."

"No need," said Brother John Caldwell tranquilly. "God has already shown him by the lightnings what I do think he already knew in his heart. For this is too just a man not to recognise his own offence."

She was thinking then of another man, and did not answer him. For it had dawned upon her suddenly why she had been able to take such pure pleasure in the Lord Owen's triumph, unspotted by any tincture of regret or sympathy for these humbled princes driven so ignominiously out of Wales at his hands. It would not have been so light a thing to her if Hotspur had been among those dour-faced lordlings clattering through the streets of Shrewsbury with their shame. But that was folly! If he had been there, he would have come out of it with his lustre still upon him, and his crest as high as ever. No matter how, no matter what the lightnings that assailed him. She could not associate him with any loss of dignity, or credit, or grace, not because he felt these too nearly and jealously, but because he wore and used them with as little thought as the breath he drew, and they were as natural a part of him, and like breath, when they left him they would leave him dead.

But not even the contagion of disgrace had touched him through his king's disastrous venture; for he was in the north, far away from this debacle. And in whatever enterprise he was engaged there, in that far-off region she had never seen, and never would see, where his heart was, she knew in her own heart that it could not be less than glorious.

6

They had held back at Milfield on the Till, biding their time, until their scouts came in with exact information of the movement of the Scots army. For this time it was an army, no less, ten thousand strong, though its actions were still those of simple border reivers. It was fourteen days since the force had crossed the Tweed, eluded the levies that rode to intercept it, and roved south towards Newcastle, pillaging and burning what was left of the standing crops. And Northumberland had chosen, rather than pursue them with a force then quite inadequate, to gather his and his sons' levies and wait for the marauders to return. His spies had plotted their course all the way, sending back word by a chain of messengers, until now they knew numbers and names, and were well aware that what they awaited was a national army, glittering with noble pedigrees, not all of them Scottish. The earl of Douglas was their general, and he had no less than four other earls as his lieutenants, Moray, Angus, Orkney and Murdoch Stewart, earl of Fife, the regent Albany's eldest son. But among his knights there were at least thirty who were French.

It went against the grain with Hotspur to let such an illustrious company move south unchallenged into England, merely because they had not been intercepted in time to confront them on reasonably equal terms. But George Dunbar, whose renegade's knowledge of his countrymen and their terrain King Henry had seen fit to use where it could be most effective, on the Scottish march from which he derived his title, had counselled the waiting game, and Northumberland had come down upon his side.

"Hold your hand," Dunbar had said, "bring up all your force, and make sikker. Most of your harvest's in the barns, your folk will be into the towns and the peel towers at a word, cattle and all, what's to lose? And everything to gain!"

And there was much in that, for the policy of these raiding parties was always to loot, never to attempt the towns or the castles if there was strong possibility of resistance. They were happiest on the move, never constant in siege. Where there was a stout tower, they would prefer to pass it by and take what came easily; and most of those Northumbrian herds and farmers would survive. Most, but not all. And Hotspur was restive with his new ally's counsel, wise though it might be, as he was in the company of the new ally himself, however often proved the wilier tactician.

He was at his elbow now, a long-stirruped, loose-riding knight in modish plate-armour, peering keenly out of his helmet with half a face, the chin erased in steel. The high cheekbones showed, powdered with red freckles, while the redder hair was hidden. His eyes were blue, beneath sandy brows, and very keen and bright, missing nothing favourable or unfavourable to himself, and the mind behind them recorded all, and forgave nothing. He was much the same height as Hotspur, and much the same build, though twenty years at least older, and a century more crafty, and there was always the curious suggestion about him that he was ready and waiting to fit himself into the void if ever Hotspur slipped out of being. He had, after all, cut off all his sources of wealth and honour and position in Scotland, and a man must take care of himself and his own, at whatever cost to other men. He had cast in his lot with England, and there was no going back.

But of his courage, though it was not of a kind that Hotspur admired, there could be little doubt; and of his ability and calculating detachment, none. Northumberland had more use for him; he was temperamentally closer to this coldly thinking man than to his own son. Father and son were fond, but different. It never troubled them, and never divided them. Where family affection was concerned, they were both marvellously simple creatures. Blood was blood, and sacred.

They had moved their army south from Milfield yesterday, as soon as they were sure by what route the Scots were returning towards their own country, and chosen their position on the northern bank of the Glen water, a mile and more from its confluence with the Till. From here they could control both river valleys, and deny Douglas his passage home by either. Their front was protected by the Glen, and the foothills in which they deployed their forces, low though they lay, were well-grown with bushes and clumps of trees almost to the waterside, and afforded a clear field of vision before them. They had placed small groups of bowmen wherever this rich cover offered, keeping their main companies higher along the hills to shoot over them. Between the archers were set the formations of pikemen and swordsmen. The cavalry were drawn up in three companies, on the wings and in the centre. And on a high point forward of the central company Hotspur and Dunbar sat their horses, and studied the sweep of country before them.

The Glen came down from their right turgid and fast, shut in by hills on either side, round the rim of the Cheviots and the great curving flank of Yeavering Bell, and across their front to empty itself into the Till. By this valley of the Glen water Douglas had surely intended to make his way back to Kelso, for he had brought his army out of the cleft of Wooler close under the hills, bearing west, and only when they were clear of the town and close to Homildon village had they become aware of the English army drawn up facing them, closing this route, and in a position also to deny them access to the more easterly route by the Till. Their preference was understandable, for Till was in flood, spreading in lead-grey pools across the water-meadows, and flashing suddenly into silver when fitful gleams of sunshine broke through the mask of cloud overhead. Here, as in Wales and the south, it had been a black, malevolent summer.

The Scottish host was drawn up now along the flank of Homildon Hill. They could distinguish the four orderly schiltrons of solidly-grouped infantry, ready and able to bring their pikes to bear in any direction. When a shaft of sunlight crossed their ranks the steel heads of the lances glittered and defined them clearly. Between them the light-armed men-at-arms formed smaller companies with room to manoeuvre at need, and the knights and cavalry, visible in snatches of blazonry and colour against the dun-coloured slopes, were drawn back somewhat higher in three squadrons. They had an excellent position, but for the fact that there was an army between them and home, and with England at their backs, and bitterly conscious of their recent attentions, they could not afford to sit still and wait to wear out the enemy.

Hotspur looked up, and above the enemy ranks the hill soared rounded and perfect, the shape of a woman's breast, with a sunlit nipple pointing at the sky, that vast, spacious sky of Northumbria that he missed even above the grander mountains of Wales. And beyond that, the outliers of the Cheviot swelled, dappled with cloud-shadows and stained russet and purple with bracken and heather, rolling away in waves to the distant and invisible summit of the Cheviot itself.

"Take my counsel," said Dunbar at his elbow, "hold back as long as you may, and the archers'll do all for you."

"Very like!" he said, knowing it was true, and knowing that he would not hold back so long as to let it be true. There were lives to keep, yes, valuable to their lords and their wives alike, but he had learned warfare in another school, and without the shock of arms and the life staked there was no savour. Somewhere there must be an honourable compromise, just as the van chasseours and the parfytours shared the work of the chase, the first coursing the deer and the second pulling it down, equal in achievement. The archers to start and wear down the game, and the knights to capture it; for bowmen can kill, but not make prisoner. And it would be shame to him to hold back and let a fighter like Douglas be shot to death from a distance, with never an enemy at hand to exchange blows with him. A brave man deserves an opponent he can reach.

"First we've to get them within range," he said grimly. "And how if they sit it out with us?"

"They'll not do that. Now they've seen you, little choice they've got. You need not so much as move a company across the Glen to fetch them down. Wait, and they'll come to us."

And he was right, for unless they could lure the English across into the open they could not make use of their greater numbers or the advantage of the ground. And they knew that they could expect no reinforcements from Scotland, while they could have no certainty that a second force was not closing in behind them from England, since clearly their movements had been known, and their return anticipated. They would not wait it out like this for long. Nevertheless, the English had prepared for the unlikely event of a contest in patience. There was a bridge below, where the track crossed the Glen, and there were three good fording places, level and safe, for even in spate the Glen was not a deep or dangerous river, only an unruly one. The English could use these at will, and looked to do so later; the Scots could not approach them without coming into close range of archery they had learned to respect.

"Look yonder! They're moving!"

The bristling pikes were indeed on the move, the whole mass shifting down the hill, the cavalry pacing slowly with them. They would drop almost into range, and then make use of the slope to give impetus to their charge. Dunbar was grinning in high content as he wheeled his horse to trot back to his own division. "You've only to hold on, and let the archers begin and end it." He rode away complacently, sure of his countrymen, whose deaths he had been so busy arranging, and meant to buy as cheaply as possible.

The knot of squires at Hotspur's back hung close and eager, ready to carry his messages. Their eyes were fixed and intent upon the mass of heraldry and steel sliding in formation down the flank of Homildon Hill.

"Master-bowman!"

"Here, my lord!"

"When the first ranks are within range, hold your volley until I signal. They'll try a feint to bring us out before they risk all, and they'll want to bring up their pikemen as close as may be. We'll waste no arrows until they make their true attack."

"Ay, my lord!"

This they had done together many times, though never in such a pattern setting as now. Dunbar was not the only man who knew how to use archers, even if it went against the grain to leave too much to them.

"If it goes as we expect, then your task, when they are close enough, is to split me a way into the ranks of the two central battles of pikemen." Cavalry cannot break into a solid phalanx of pikes until a way has been cut for them, but once in they can do fearful slaughter. "Concentrate on the centre of their ranks, and if they try to close, keep the gap open at all costs."

"Ay, my lord. Every man knows and understands his orders." He looked at the hillside across the river, where the moving masses had halted, still just out of range even for the most expert, to redress their line. "Now they'll come." And he went to his place jauntily, without even hurrying.

They came, with a yell that crossed the fields ahead of them like a sourceless bellow out of the air. The cavalry surged suddenly ahead, streaking downhill to the meadows, the massed pikemen broke into a measured run, keeping formation, and followed them. A quiver passed along the English lines, the horses stirred and shuddered, but no more. Hotspur sat bolt upright in the saddle, his eyes narrowed on the hurtling horsemen, and never moved a hand. All the bows

braced and drew and leaned, like hawks about to stoop, fixing upon
their prey before it was in range. And now his experienced eye told
him that the foremost ranks could be reached, but still he did not
move, nor did any of the bowmen loose. Their nerve was a match
for his; they had most of them served him several years, for his men
did not leave him.

"They'll turn!" whispered one of the squires at his back confidently; and he smiled, noting the voice. And on the very word,
the Scottish wheeled in two wide circles, to form again ahead of
the pikemen. There was a strange, silent pause. The English did
not come. They would not come. There was no way left but to go
to them.

The pikemen had never lost the impetus of their tireless running,
the deceptively slow-looking running of mountain men, that
covers the ground with frightening speed and ease. When the
knights reformed in front of them they suddenly launched a wild
shout, and welded into one moving weapon, that aimed itself at
the enemy beyond the river, and this time did not halt. Even so,
Hotspur held his hand until the issue was certain, and the thunder-
ing vanguard of cavalry well within range, and plainly bent on
driving home. Then he raised his lance, and a shaft of sunlight
from beyond Homildon Hill fired its point like a captive star,
before he drove it down again. The radiance burned from it as
it fell; and the master-bowman, somewhere below him with his
men, bellowed: "Loose!"

The air quivered and thrummed and shook, the horses shuddered
to the vibration, and their manes rose erect, bristling and undulating
to the contractions of their twitching hide. The pent arrows took
the air like a flight of hawks, and in the charging ranks across the
river sudden gaps were ripped and flattened like corn before the
wind. Horsemen heeled sidelong out of the saddle, crests sank and
pennants lurched low, fouling other riders, startling other horses.
After the first volley there was always more chaos from the terrified

horses than from the loss of men. And always it gave time to fit the second shaft and loose the second volley, and redouble the boiling turmoil that was held at a distance by nothing more deadly—but there was nothing more deadly!—than cloth-yard shafts of wood and steel flighted with a handful of feathers.

A few shook themselves loose from the tangle, and pounded onward, others skirted the fallen and fell in behind them. And now the archers were shooting at will, selecting their targets where they best offered, without haste and without respite. But what was left of the line of knights after every fall always came on, implacably brave; and Hotspur's heart started and complained grievously whenever the foremost fell, still short of the river bank. Dunbar had said no more than the truth, the archers could do it all. But so much gallantry to be squandered with so little hope!

Nevertheless, he held his heart in check until the schiltrons of the pikemen were in close range, and being harrowed like arable fields by the steady volleys of arrows. There was place enough there for a knight, after the archers had done their work. He had stood it until his heart bade fair to burst with longing, and if they could not cross the river, then he must go to them. He launched a great shout of: "Espérance Percy!" behind him, waved a hand at the squire who carried his guidon, settled his lance, and plunged headlong down into the river at the ford they had marked out for the centre, and out again in a flurry of muddy spray on the levels beyond, with the whole company of his knights and squires and mounted men-at-arms hurtling after him.

On the right, his father was not many yards behind him in that charge. On the left, Dunbar held his hand and re-deployed his archers to pick off any strays who might still offer a safe target. He would risk his life coldly where there was need, but here he saw no need. Why exert himself to win a battle the bowmen had already won? When he crossed the Glen it would be in his own good time, and with an eye to what prizes were left alive for the taking, and for them he would fight as doughtily as any man if he must. But he would not be fool enough to fret if he need not fight.

What remained of the Scottish chivalry had re-formed in haste to face the English charge. Hotspur's lance, steadily lowered as he came, selected its target, the foremost knight on the tallest horse, and struck the uplifted shield so strongly that the shock flattened its bearer back upon his horse's crupper; but he kept his seat gamely, rolling under the lance as it flashed by, to recover dizzily and swing a vehement though ineffective stroke with his sword, before the lurch and sway of the press carried him away. Hotspur wheeled to keep touch with him, pleased by the ready retort, but his impetus had swept them apart, and from that moment it was hand-to-hand work with whoever was cast up at him, horsed or afoot, until he could find room enough to choose his man and use a lance again. The warm, wild joy came over him that never failed him when he met hand-to-hand on an even footing with his peers—his peers whatever rank God had given them—in courage and spirit and tenacity, without a grain of malice or hatred. He heaved his snorting, raging mount out of the press of dismounted men, swung him round in a trampling circle to clear ground about him, and drew off to realign his vision and find a just opponent. The field was chaotic now, the archers had done their part, and could do no more from this on but let fly at the occasional fugitive. For some on the fringes were already in flight.

Therefore this was a battle now as he understood a battle, however mangled beforehand by being half-decided at a distance. And his heart sang as he settled his lance in rest again, and drove at the first and readiest knight who caught his eye. This time his lance struck accurately in the throat of his adversary's helmet, too fast and too high to be warded off, and hurled the rider to the ground and his mount off-balance, dragged by the tightly-gripped rein, to roll upon his master. The lance shivered, the shaft splintering halfway down to the guard, and Hotspur hurled it from him, and reached a long arm to snatch at the bridle as he was swept past, and drag the terrified horse to its feet again. The man kicked and struggled wildly, and rose on his knees. He had fallen in soft, lush ground, still water-logged after the flood had somewhat subsided, and he came to his feet whole and angry. But the tide of flesh and steel tore them apart, and Hotspur saw no more of him. If he had known his man, and cared for what he knew, he could have battered Albany's son and heir into surrender, instead of hauling his horse off from crushing or smothering him in the mud. But he did not know him, and would not have cared too greatly if he had. He was looking for the Douglas.

He was glad for them, they fought so ferociously, as if they had never heard of defeat, they who were already defeated. He turned his horse time and again, and went ploughing through the thickest of the struggle with bared sword, exchanging strokes with any who cared to stand and debate with him. Time did not exist for him now, as long as any challenged him. He did not even know that most of the Scottish host had already cast off everything that weighed it down, and taken to flight, acknowledging the truth of this meeting. They were pursued, some into the Till, where many drowned and some swam to safety—if it was indeed safety, so far into England—on the further side, some as far north as the Tweed and the border, thirteen miles away. But the Tweed also was in flood, and many perished there.

But Hotspur was more concerned with those who stood and traded blows as long as they could stand, and some even longer, on their knees and still defiant. These he understood and worshipped, and went about to salvage if they would be salvaged, for they were far too good to waste. He had barely a scratch upon him, he was hardly blown by comparison with these, and he stood off while they breathed, and at the last lighted down from his tired horse, to meet with the most valiant on equal terms. But the terms were not equal, for his assailant bled from the head, under his conical helm and gorget of chain mail, and from some wounds under his plate-armour, also, for there were red seams in his body-harness, and he leaned to his right side, favouring it as he fought.

Hotspur hung back from him, and let him gather himself, waited, indeed, for him to make the first assay, and put it by when it was made with the utmost care and forbearance. When it was pressed again, doggedly but almost blindly, he struck the questing sword expertly out of the hand that held it, with only the measured force required, and reached a hand eagerly to his adversary as he crumpled to his knees.

"Be ruled, man, yield yourself to me, you've done enough! I promise you all possible honour, it is but your due. I am Henry Percy." He had uncovered his face; the field was fallen into a curious quietness about them, as though they were alone.

The mailed hand in his kept hold firmly enough to draw him down to his knees as its owner sank back into the turf. "Is it you, Hotspur?" said a thick, bubbling whisper out of the broken helmet. And again, just distinguishably: "I surrender myself to you. None but you…" The steel fingers loosed their hold, and slid down to lie lax in the grass.

"Do off his helmet, quickly," said Hotspur, tearing off his gauntlets and himself stooping to fumble at the mail gorget, "he's breathing blood!"

They got the harness off him, and turned him to bleed into the grass rather than into his own throat. It was a young face, surely not past the early thirties, comely, dark, passionate in line and feature, with reddish black hair and thick, straight brows. From the eyelid down, one cheek was a mask of blood; the eye stared opaquely from under a half-closed lid. Dunbar came picking his way between the debris and the fallen, and looked down calmly upon the son and successor of his old enemy.

"You've taken a fair prize there," he said dispassionately, "if he lives. Yon's Archibald Douglas."

"Bring a horse," said Hotspur, rearing up fiercely and looking about him for the nearest serviceable squire, "and get him on to it. We must have him away into shelter in Wooler. If he dies on us, so gallant a man, I'll never forgive myself."

Seven Scottish nobles were killed in that battle under Homildon
Hill, five earls made prisoner, Douglas, Fife, Moray, Angus and
Orkney, and twenty-three other noblemen captured, as well as three
of the French knights. In all, eighty barons and knights of rank, and
a host of men-at-arms and archers, besides those killed in action,
or drowned in Till or Tweed in their flight. And this battle took
place on the same day that King Henry in retreat from Wales rode
through Shrewsbury, the 14th day of September.

The squire who was sent south to carry the good news to King
Henry overtook him at Daventry on the 20th of September. The
young man, whose name was Merbury, was eager and inexperi-
enced, and took it for granted, as an honest man well might, that
his story of complete and shattering victory, of the capture of so
many of the active nobility of Scotland, and of a bright lustre added
to the name of Percy and of England could not fail to be pleasing
to his sovereign. He told it well, with a wealth of detail, for he
had been there, and was proud; and at every word of praise for his
Northumbrian lords he rubbed salt into sore and festering wounds.

So apt, so malevolently timed, one more great benefit conferred
on the one side, one more debt incurred on the other! Who could
choose but look on this picture, and on that, and acknowledge
and be shocked by the inevitable comparison? And I must sit here
and smile, thought the king, to hear him praised for his valour and
impetuosity, and worse, worst of all, for his success, and say some
good and gracious words in return, with my mouth full of wormwood. And is he to carry away his laurels thus unchallenged and
undespoiled, while I am famished?

But he found good and gracious words to say, and the
Northumbrian squire in his simplicity was well satisfied, and did the
rest of his office joyously.

"And the Lord Henry Percy and his lady in especial greet your

Grace, and pray you be of good cheer in this happy news, for that the price set upon these Scots prisoners, such as belong to the Lord Henry, shall be at your Grace's disposal in the matter of the redeeming of their beloved kinsman, Sir Edmund Mortimer, out of his captivity in Wales. For they would not that burden should be borne all by the crown. And they wish your Grace joy, and comfort in the favour God has shown to your arms, and the Lord Henry trusts to see you in health and spirits at the assembly of your parliament at the month's end."

He was thanked and rewarded for his embassage, and dismissed in great content. And King Henry, alone in his chamber, held his head between his hands for fear it should burst with anger and chagrin, and something else which he did not or would not recognise for pure hatred.

"—joy and comfort in the favour God has shown to your arms!" Was there ever such insolent irony? As though some evil genius had inspired the man to find the most mortifying words possible in which to signify his loyalty and goodwill. True, he could hardly have heard, when he despatched his messenger, of the shaming tragicomedy in Wales. And yet how could a man so beset fail to hold it against him? Too happy Harry, the darling of fortune always, and always so sure of the love other men bore him. The fruit of his prowess to be sold to ransom Mortimer, and a graceful by-gesture made to his king in the process! And no doubts, never any doubts at all, that men thought as he would have them think, and would always be as he had always known them.

How was it possible for any man who fell within the circle of his radiance to forgive Hotspur for being Hotspur? In and out of season he must give off these sparks of personal brightness, to dazzle as he had dazzled James of Lusignan, King of Cyprus, with his "singular courtesy and noblesse" when he was governor of Bordeaux. Even the loss of Conway castle in his absence, a ridiculous incident enough, and costly, he could turn to appreciative laughter, and never grudge that the laughter, at second-hand if not directly, was against himself. So over-blessed a nature must bring a man either to a throne or a grave before ever he lived to be old. But I am no such creature, the king thought, burning in his own fury and grief, I cannot be thus constantly outdone and bear no grudge. And he shall not, he shall not, walk onward like this over my discomfiture, secure that his foot cannot slip. He shall feel the ground give under him, if only once, he shall fall, and men shall see him fall, and know him for a man like other men. And then if I please to reach him a hand and pick him up again, he shall know and acknowledge to whom he owes it, and walk more humbly thereafter.

And I will love him the better, his heart said, turning rebelliously in his breast. At St. Inglevert—do you remember, Lancaster?—he was the match of any he met in arms, if not the master, and so were you, and together you two held any two that France could set up against you, and Jean de Boucicaut himself acknowledged it.

But those were the days of innocence, long ago vanished and past recovery.

I will give him sharp orders, he thought, and bring him up on a short rein; and I will see him come to terms, and kiss the hand that curbs him. And then, then, I will restore him what I denied him, and graciously accept the proffer of it again as a tribute to me, so that for ever afterwards he shall know who is master between us two friends. He shall give, and I will deign to accept. And I will give, and he shall be mortally glad to accept.

But he was careful not to think, because some corner of his mind knew that that way lay a kind of death, of Hal in Chester, quite certainly notified, or soon to be notified, by Hotspur or another, of the long day's work done at Homildon Hill six days ago. The one thing he could not have borne, the one thing he could not completely shut out from the fevered fringes of his mind, was the thought of the boy's chill assessment of his father's achievement and his friend's. Hal had sent a messenger only yesterday with a dutiful report on his fruitless sally into North Wales, and his orderly return. Nothing could have been more controlled or correct, as if he did not know that his father had been driven out of the principality like a half-drowned rat, or a hound caught in a thunderstorm, and running for shelter with its tail between its legs. And now to think of him listening to the rhapsody of such another youngster as this Merbury, besotted as they all were on their paragon, Hotspur! From the contemplation of this inescapable judgment he turned his face resolutely away. There should yet be adjustment between them, and the boy should be made to witness it, whether he would or no.

When all the hot bitterness in him had cooled and congealed into a hard and reasoned purpose, and he had command of his face and his voice, he sent for his secretary, and dictated a letter to his council at Westminster.

In Bamburgh castle, where they had carried him from Wooler as soon as he was fit to be moved, the earl of Douglas took his ease in a very light and illustrious captivity. They had found no less than five flesh wounds on his body when they stripped him of his armour, but all clean and none dangerous, once the draining of his blood was staunched. But there was one loss that could never again be supplied to him: he had lost the sight of his damaged eye. All he could discern on that side was a shade of difference between dark and light; but with the one eye remaining he missed very little of what went on about him, and within the week he was out of his bed and trying his skill at aim and balance about the rooms and staircases. Since the light hurt his blinded eye, and indeed the cut which had damaged it was not yet healed, he went with it bandaged and darkened with a black shade. Hotspur's wardrobe furnished him with clothes, and Hotspur's stable, when he was strong enough, and already restive with inaction, supplied him with a mount. His parole was given and taken, and there was no need for him to lack exercise. They rode together, hawked together, played chess

together, and to work off the convalescent's stiffness as his wounds
healed, essayed a little mild sword-play together. The prisoner was
popular with those who attended on him, adored and followed
round faithfully by the children, and well-liked by Elizabeth, to
whom he was heartily gallant.

"Your lady," he said warmly, "has been to me the kindest of
hostesses and gentlest of nurses. Were I her honoured guest, she
could not have used me more generously."

They were walking their horses among the sand-dunes south of
the castle, and on their left hand the sea ran high and grey, and the
gulls were uneasy, aware of coming wind.

"Why, so you are. And she's trying to buy a little justice from
fate," said Hotspur, with an overshadowed smile. "As she uses you,
she trusts, so may Glendower use her brother Edmund, who is also
a prisoner."

"She uses me according to her own sweet nature, and could do
no other for her life. But I've seen," he said, grown serious, "that
she frets over him."

"So do we all. It's three months now, and no news, not a word of
ransom yet. Though when parliament meets—it's no more than six
days now, we shall be leaving tomorrow—I hope the matter may be
quickly resolved. She has lost one brother already," he said sombrely,
"of the two that she doted on, when Roger was killed in Ireland, four
years ago. Now she fears for the one remaining like a hen for her only
chick. It's been so ever since I've known her—she was the eldest, and
felt herself a mother to the pair of them. And Edmund was always the
more venturesome, and the one that frightened her most. He's five
years her junior. And, faith, since we married I've been pressed into
service as one more brother to him, a father, too, since his own father
died when the boy was barely thirteen. I'm very near as fond of him as
Elizabeth herself. I wouldn't for the world he should miscarry."

"He'll do well enough with the Welsh," said Douglas stoutly,
"why should he not? This Owen's an able prince, no more like than

any other prince of Christendom to do harm to a prisoner, or let harm come to him."

"That I believe, but Owen is mortal, and hunted hard. How if he be killed, then who follows on? And in such a state of war as we have now in Wales, mischances can happen all too easily. Their way is to pick up everything movable and retreat into the mountains when pressed, and in such rapid removals and sudden onslaughts a man can come by his death by pure accident. And in sickness, say—and wounded, as he was—how if a prisoner hampered their movements too much? They might be forced to discard him—and a stray company working at large would not scruple to cut his throat, though Owen would. He is not in a court captivity, he must live wild like the rest, and founder if he cannot keep their pace. I shall not be easy until we get him back."

"For a Mortimer," said Douglas, "they won't haggle over the price."

Hotspur laughed aloud, startling his horse into a side-long dance. "Not haggle? If you knew how many complaining letters I must write before I get the means to pay my men their dues! God knows how the treasury comes to be so desperate poor. But there isn't an officer of the crown who hasn't had to put his hand deep in his own coffers to make good what should be crown expenses. Else none of us could keep an army together."

Douglas was laughing, too, though a little ruefully. "Faith, I begin to see how I may be serviceable to your lady. If coin's so short, it might be simpler to offer me to Owen just as I am, in exchange for Mortimer. If the price of an earl is what he asks, send him an earl. But I doubt he'll hold out for the money. I'd best be sending out letters to see how my credit stands at home."

"The thought," admitted Hotspur, grinning, "had entered my mind. But I'm not in such a hurry to be rid of you just yet. So we'll sound out parliament first, and hold you in reserve, my lord, for a last resort."

They rode back together very companionably; their rides were short

as yet, for Douglas was still weak, and tired soon. Hotspur watched
the marred profile beside him curiously as they paced side by side,
for he was greatly drawn to his prisoner, and could not reconcile the
many stories concerning him with this man he had begun to know.
He had come into his earldom only two years ago, very shortly after
the scandal which had sent Dunbar storming over the border into
England in dudgeon, and asking for a safe-conduct to King Henry's
court; for the old earl had died very soon after the coup on which he
had staked so much, leaving this new Archibald Douglas to step into
his shoes. Only two years established, barely thirty-three years old,
and already he had a reputation as formidable as his father's. Perhaps
the most powerful man in Scotland now, excepting only Albany, the
regent. King Robert himself hardly counted, poor soul. Fifty-three
years old when he came to the throne, and crippled by the kick of a
horse in his youth, what could he do against all these turbulent and
forceful lords, his brother Albany, his son Rothesay, and these Black
Douglases who bore almost the prestige of a royal dynasty?

And now this dark story that had leaked out of Scotland earlier
this year of the death of the duke of Rothesay—the husband of
Douglas's own sister, and the brother of his wife, doubly close kin
to him! Certain it was that the young man had died at Falkland
palace in Fife. Of a bloody flux, the official proclamation had said.
But unofficially the word ran that he had died of plain starvation. It
was Albany's castle, and it was Albany who had shut up his nephew
there, and must carry the burden of his death. Scotland had proved
too small to hold two such power-hungry men. But there were
those who said that Douglas had known of it and connived at it.

Watching him ride thus, strongly recovering from wounds that
might have killed a lesser man, and whistling softly and content-
edly into the sea wind, it was impossible to think evil of him. And
after all, Rothesay, so they said, had led Margaret a dog's life after
all her father's pains to secure him for her, and been by any standard a poor bargain for any girl, having worn out so many before

her—including, the bolder gossips whispered, Dunbar's unhappy daughter, affianced and bedded but never wed. Who could say if Margaret was not better off a young widow, able yet to make a humbler and happier match? And yet murder was murder. Hotspur could not conceive of such doings in the dark; but neither could he connect his prisoner with them. The man's heart, even in captivity, was light as a bird. Even with an eye covered, he was debonair to look upon. Even in bodily weakness and misfortune, he charmed all who came near him. And of all fighters Hotspur could remember holding at the end of his own sword, this was the bonniest. And he could not choose but love him.

～∽

Elizabeth rode with her husband as far as Alnwick, to spend one more night with him there; and Douglas added himself to the escort which was to bring her home again to Bamburgh afterwards. The distance was not more than fifteen miles, and he was beginning to feel his strength returning, and to look round for employment, feeling himself for the first time a little cramped in his enforced inactivity.

They came down through the woods to the bridge over the Aln late in the afternoon, when the light was beginning to change from clear pale gold to grey, after a sudden bright day of recovered summer; and at the head of the rise beyond, the castle cast the shadow of its towers and curtain wall across the river, standing guard over the town. Of late years, since the death of his second wife, the earl had begun to feel happiest and most at home at Warkworth, nine miles or so down-coast at the head of the Coquet estuary, but Alnwick was full of childhood memories and family warmth for Hotspur, and he never rode across the Aln bridge without being moved to spur into a canter up the winding hill to the barbican, the last stage of the way home. Elizabeth set spurs to her mare and kept pace with him, and Douglas and the squires of the escort fell back a little, and let them pass through the gates alone. Hotspur was happy that day, for no great reason except the late benediction of sunlight and blue sky, and the unhurried and companionable ride. In the shadow of the barbican he waited, and reached out an impulsive hand to her, and hand-in-hand they entered the castle precinct.

Grooms ran to take the bridles, and a squire to cup Elizabeth's foot in his hand and lift her down; but Hotspur was before him, plucking her boisterously out of the saddle between his palms and setting her softly on her feet. The escort came trotting in after them just as the earl emerged from the doorway of his great hall, long and lean in a dark gown of brocade and fur, with George Dunbar at his heels. The earl of the March of Scotland, like his host, was bound for the parliament at Westminster, and it was reasonable enough that they should travel together on the morrow; yet Hotspur's brow clouded faintly at the sight of him here.

"Sir, your son and servant!" He leaned to his father's embrace and kiss, and held him off afterwards at arm's length to look at him more closely. The gaunt, hawkish face was glad of him, and yet not wholly glad; there was a slightly grim set about the mouth, and the brows were drawn a little too straight and low over the bright black eyes. "Someone is in your displeasure! Not I, I hope?"

"I never knew you care overmuch for that," said Northumberland drily, and turned to take Elizabeth's hands, and kiss her warmly. "My lord of Douglas, I'm glad to see you so well recovered. There are letters," he said abruptly, turning back to his son. "For you, and for me. The king's messenger was here yesterday, and hearing you would be riding this way so soon, he left them here with me."

His voice was perfectly flat and inexpressive, and that in itself said more than his words. There was something here that was not in accordance with his will, and certainly not to be communicated here in the courtyard. "Come, we'd better go in." He led the way, with patent purpose, into the retired room he used for his own private business. But he did not scruple to draw in Dunbar and Douglas to join them, and called for a page to bring wine before he closed the door.

There were two sealed scrolls lying upon his table beside the window. He took them up, one in either hand, rather as if he held a pair of daggers, though his face was mute and controlled but for the glitter of intent eyes. "These, for you. This, from the king's council. And this, from the king."

Hotspur took them without a glance, his eyes steady upon his father's face. "You know what is in them, I think." And yes, someone was certainly in his displeasure. The council, or the king?

"I have received the same. So has March. Here are no favours, and no favourites. You had better read."

He hesitated a moment, still trying rather to read his father's face; then he shrugged, and broke the seals. It did not, after all, take a great indiscretion to fire his father's ready resentment, or a great gesture to cool it again. And what could be amiss with Henry, when they had just presented him with the most valuable victory of his reign?

He unrolled the council's communication first, and they watched him read it through with brows sharply contracting into impatience, then into half-incredulous anger. He looked up with the warning golden flare in his eyes, and the sting of dark colour in his cheeks.

"But this is insolent folly! No such order has ever been issued before. How dare they so presume without authority?"

Northumberland uttered a short bellow of laughter. "Without authority? They had authority enough to set them scurrying to do as they were bid. Read the king's letter!"

"What is it?" Elizabeth asked, looking in wonder and anxiety from one face to the other. "What order have they issued that can disturb you, Harry?"

But he had turned to the second missive, and spread it brusquely between his hands, frowning over it fiercely; and when he looked up again the slumbering fire blazed.

"What the plague has got into the man? He cannot do this! He has no right, and he knows it. I sent to him, I made generous offers, far beyond any duty I owe him, and he strikes me in the face now with *this*!"

"He has done it," said Northumberland grimly. "And he would say that he has a right. It was common practice formerly that the crown should enjoy the right to dispose of important prisoners, though always with respect to the captor's honour, and his right to fair compensation."

"No such claim has been enforced now for years. Though God knows," he said, flaming, "there are other outmoded rights he has not scrupled to revive for his own profit, now I call them to mind. How long has it been since any sovereign levied an aid to marry his daughter? Sixty years? Seventy? King Edward never asked any for his girl."

"From all I heard of it," said Northumberland sceptically, "that did him little enough good."

"Neither shall this, I swear it. And "fair compensation"! From what funds? He has none! No, that's but a form of words—it means he takes from us what might in part supply what he owes us, and in return he'll give us another bad tally, life-long, never to be re-deemed. And after I'd made known to him what I intended! It's from Edmund he's stealing, not from me!"

It was a strong word, and they stiffened at hearing it. Elizabeth, quivering as much with exasperation as with anxiety, struck her hands together in entreaty.

"Harry, for God's sake, will you tell me what this means, for I'm lost here. What has he done? What has Edmund to do with it?"

"I misdoubt I'm the bone between two hounds," said Douglas at her shoulder, and laughed, but for once wryly.

"Why, the king writes me here that it was he directed the council to send out this order—that none of our Scottish prisoners are to be ransomed or freed without the authority of council. But in his own letter—in his own hand, mark you—he goes farther, for he orders that all the noble prisoners shall be delivered up to him in the term of this parliament. And he promises—promises!—that there shall be fair compensation made to the captors! He does not say from what fool's gold! He does not say when! Simply, he will take to himself all those prizes we won honestly while he was trailing his draggled plumes out of Wales."

"He writes thus crudely? To *you*?" She meant: To you who made him, and set him where he is!

"He says there are urgent reasons. But he does not say what they are, or give me one word to justify himself."

"The ransom price of an earl or two," said Douglas ruefully, "is urgent reason enough, if your Henry is as beggarly as you make him."

"But what did you mean, Harry, what did you mean—about Edmund?"

He looked at her, and his roused and formidable face softened. "Why, I did not mean to keep anything from you, but I thought it too soon and too cruel to raise your hopes and have you bedded on thorns. I sent him word by the courier that so far as any ransom monies accrued to me, they should be at his disposal to defray Edmund's ransom. And here he seeks to take this means out of our hands."

"He cannot have received your message when he sent out such an order! He cannot have known!"

"He did know. Merbury reached him on the twentieth. The order is dated two days later."

He saw that there were tears in her eyes, and misread them, for it would have seemed to him then unthinkable that these edicts he held in his hands could have been conceived for the very purpose of denying freedom to a kinsman and a loyal subject. It was she, not he, who read more deeply into the letter she had not even seen. He saw nothing but a clutching at one means of gain, and even that chilled his heart. But she saw a dynastic quarrel deeper than blood itself, and she would have done anything, uttered any lie, to keep him from the same vision.

"No, trust me," he said warmly, "he has not understood. When I

meet him we shall resolve everything. I will not believe that he has
thought clearly what he does. He'll listen—I know him! But I will
not resign any part of my rights," he said, stiffening. And he turned
and stared, with eyes like levelled lances, at his father and Dunbar.
"And you, my lords? Do you stand with me?"

Dunbar shook his sandy head weightily, and looked sidelong with
his blue, bright eyes, scrubbing with dubious fingers in his beard. "For
me it's none so easy. I'm a Scot among the English, in no case to stand
too high upon principle. "Fair compensation," his Grace says, and for
my part I'm bound to trust in his word. I had lands in Scotland, and if
we win them, I'll be in the king's debt if he'll but make me free of my
own. I rede you do as I do, and bow to this decree."

Hotspur looked long at his father, and Northumberland took his
time about responding. He was not in need, he felt in no necessity
to quarrel with his king, though he did feel some annoyance at the
want of civility and humility in this utterance from a made king
to an earl who had made him. He felt no fear, and therefore no
compulsion to appear fearless. The matter, on the whole, was too
small for a breach. And Mortimer was no close kin of his, though he
respected his son's affections, and knew their strength.

"Harry, there's matter for thought here. I'm the king's man, and
have shown myself so many times over, and I incline to go with
the king's order as far as I honourably may. Tomorrow we head
for London, and there'll be time to talk of this. For my part, I shall
reserve my rights, and trust to have speech with him. I'll make up
my mind then whether I surrender my prisoners or no."

Hotspur looked from his father's face to Dunbar's, and thought,
some way beneath the level of his own personal anger and intransi-
gence: He is taking note of all. He sees himself as the king's jackal. But
he wastes his efforts. Henry is no such dupe, for all this present greedy
folly he knows who his true friends are. He looked at Elizabeth,
pale-faced but calm, willing to go with him unquestioningly wherever he saw fit to go, and at Douglas, whose wild, ebullient spirits

were curbed now by his new and voluntary regard for his captor. He turned the uncompromising stare of his brown eyes on them both, and embraced them with his heart and love.

"Well, do as you think best. That's every man's right and duty. But for me, I pledge you now I will not surrender one grain of my rights. What I took, I took, and by God, I'll keep it, too. Take her home tomorrow, Archie, and never look back to watch what I do, for you know it before. I would not give him one knight who had confided himself to me and none other, much less you. Only over my dead body," said Hotspur hardily, eye to eye with the friend he had made under Homildon Hill, "will King Henry ever claim you as his prisoner."

7

King Henry's third parliament went the way of all parliaments, beset with a host of private petitions, local grievances, problems of finance, complaints of discrimination, and the fretful and continuing menaces of Wales and Ireland. But early in October, with unusual cordiality, the estates took occasion to present a loyal address of thanks to the sovereign and his family for their tireless labours in the service of the realm. To Henry, for his great exertions against the Scots and the Welsh, to the prince of Wales for his direction of the struggle in the principality, to Prince Thomas for his industry in Ireland. And through his Grace they desired also to express their thanks to the earl of Northumberland and his forces for the notable victory of Homildon Hill.

Finally, whether spontaneously or how prompted it was difficult to say, they respectfully entreated the king to sanction the raising, through Lords Willoughby and Roos, of a loan of ten thousand marks to ransom Lord Grey of Ruthyn out of his captivity in Wales; a request which was graciously granted.

No other prisoner was mentioned.

On Friday, the 20th of October, in the White Hall at Westminster, parliament met in a special and ceremonious assembly, with prince, lords, and commoners all in their due stations, and King Henry on his throne of state at the upper end of the hall. Only the constable of England, the earl of Northumberland, was absent from his place, and that was for a purpose. The king was already advised of the ceremony to come, and had graciously assented in it; privately he had known for some days that certain of the prisoners of Homildon— such as were in fit case to travel, naturally—had been brought south to London. He had even been faintly surprised, and deeply gratified, at the earl's compliance and complaisance. This solemn presentation would set the seal on his authority and prestige, publicly redeeming that disaster of Wales which he still could not get out of his dreams.

Northumberland, always an imposing figure in any picture, was monumentally impressive now as he made his entrance at the far door, very splendid in cloth of gold.

"Your Grace, give me leave here to present before you these knights and noblemen of Scotland and of France, taken in battle at Homildon Hill, and here delivered to your Grace's charge."

They came in singly at the earl's back, and he named them as they came.

"Murdoch Stewart, earl of Fife."

Albany's son was tall and reddish fair, a handsome young man, fretted now with his captivity, and limping still from his fall at Homildon. He came in proudly enough, but he was unlucky in bearing a famous, even a notorious, name, and he glared and flushed to the hair under the bombardment of inquisitive stares. Tradesmen of the City craned and stood on tiptoe to gape at him, the son of a royal duke and nephew of a king, directed now to kneel on Northumberland's right before another king.

"The Lord Montgomery."

He stepped to the left with a closed and stony face, and kneeled, looking at no one.

Close to the throne, the prince shifted unhappily in his seat, and looked away; and it was not quite chance that he looked to where Hotspur sat, erect and cold in distaste, his broad brown forehead lofty and blank as a castle wall, and the corners of his lips curled.

"Sir William Graham—Sir Adam Forster…"

There were three Frenchmen after, Sir Jean de Heley, Sir Piers Hazars, and Jean Dormy. They joined their fellow-prisoners, kneeling just within the doorway until the king inclined his head and beckoned them to advance.

The entire company came forward, kneeled again in the centre of the hall, and a third time immediately before the steps of the throne. Hotspur watched them sink to their knees, one or two painfully, being so recently wounded, within touch of Henry's hand, and smiled for the first time during this spectacle, thinking involuntarily: Douglas would have stood his ground rather, and spat in Henry's face! And again, devoutly: I'm glad I did not subject him to this. He would rather I'd run my sword through him on the grass at Homildon!

The prince was beset with equally ungovernable thoughts, for what had flashed irresistibly into his mind was: Richard would have swooped down from his throne and lifted them by the hands, and himself seated them with all honour, like a squire attending his lord. He knew when to humiliate, and when to humble himself for his better exaltation. But you cannot learn it. You have it or you have not.

Yet he knew in the same moment that he did his father an injustice, for whatever Henry might lack, it was not a sense of the courtesy of kings, or the wit to know how best to burnish his own image in such a planned and rehearsed scene. No, there was something deeply wrong here, something that had distracted his mind and caused him to miss his moment. It was as if he had been waiting for something more, some following name, a climax which had failed to come, and could not yet believe that he was to be forced to make do with this. With these! There should have been at least one more, the greatest, the most eagerly anticipated. And there were others present, too, who had sensed the lack almost as soon as he, and were leaning head to head now in half-gleeful, half-appalled wonder, and whispering another name. For where was the earl of Douglas?

The king looked up once towards where Hotspur sat, stared briefly at the high and stony front that encountered and repelled him, and made shift with what he had. His grievance burned in him, for he had been robbed not only of the crown of his triumph, but even of the spontaneity with which he might partly have atoned for what was lost. He rose valiantly, and took Murdoch Stewart by the hand, but there was not a soul present who did not sense that it was done with no more than the half of his attention. He raised his enforced guests graciously, and dismissed them into Northumberland's care until they should all meet at the royal table in the evening. And all was done well enough, and with impressive majesty, if only it had been done in time, and with his whole heart. But his heart was not whole, it was corroded with bitterness and anger. He had essayed a public demonstration of his power and his magnanimity, and it had been turned into a public humiliation, not of his prisoners, but of himself. A king who gave orders, and was flouted coldly, openly, to his face! He knew, none better, that all that muted buzz of excitement as the lords and commons dispersed from the White Hall was a threnody on the names of Douglas and Hotspur. They knew whose prisoner the great earl was, they knew who had denied him.

The king kept his face heroically until he had withdrawn into his own apartments in the palace. He felt hazy of vision, and dizzy, though perhaps that was only the pressure of anger within his brain. Of late he had been troubled with an irritable, swollen eruption that marred his face in moments of stress, and he felt it rising now to complete the anomaly, and mark him, not the insolent vassal, with the insignia of shame. Afterwards in calm it always subsided, leaving as yet no mark behind; but always it came when most he needed to be free of it, and magisterial, and royal.

"My lord of Worcester, remain here with me. Heron," he said, to the steward of his household, "ask my lord of Northumberland to join us. And send to the Lord Henry Percy to bid him attend us here at once."

William Heron, Lord Say, was an old adherent of Lancaster, and knew his master well, though he had been his steward only a few months. He was accustomed to doing such errands as this without too much haste, for not even kings can lose by being given time to think again; and often enough he had been called back from the doorway by a change of heart. This time, too, he had barely reached the door when the king called after him. "William…"

"My lord?" Say turned without eagerness or surprise, either of which would have been taken ill. But all the king said, and with dark intent, was: "Send also, William, for our son, the prince of Wales!"

The first person Hotspur saw, when he entered the room, was the prince, very slender and aware on a stool by the king's right knee, his large, intelligent eyes, at once so candid and so consciously guarded, wearing here one more film of withdrawal, though his delicate nostrils dilated and quivered like those of a high-bred horse scenting thunder. Veiled though they were, the eyes clung to Hotspur's eyes, and it was with deliberate purpose that Hotspur kept his gaze neutral and turned his head away. The boy should not have been here, it was unfair to try to use him or influence him thus. But whoever assayed it would find that there was a highly individual mind to be reckoned with behind the eyes. As for Hotspur, he willed to be alone with the king, and from this moment, father and uncle and prince notwithstanding, those two were alone. Northumberland on the king's right, Worcester on his left, stood ware and watchful to prompt him or throw him lifelines as they might, but he ceased to take them into consideration from the moment his eyes met Henry's eyes.

"Your Grace was pleased to send for me. I am here."

The king looked ill, blotchy of cheek and feverish of eye, braced back tautly in his great chair with hands spread on the lions' heads that formed the arms. Hotspur was momentarily shaken by a recollection of the great, agile body sweeping through the lists at St. Inglevert on a tall, raw-boned destrier as grey as cloud. He tensed his own easy, never-questioned muscles wonderingly, and recaptured briefly the knowledge that one part of him, at least, was nothing but joy. And he nearly two years the elder! And a part of his chilly anger at least warmed, if it did not depart from him.

"My lord, you have somewhat to answer for to me."

"I shall answer whatever your Grace is pleased to charge me with." His voice was equable, clear of all impediment; he was not yet roused, and his will was to be placated upon reasonable terms.

"My lord, you, like your father here and certain others, received not my orders merely, but my council's, concerning the disposal of your prisoners taken at Homildon. Yet you have not delivered up to us your chief prisoner, the earl of Douglas. We expected he should have been brought to us today with Fife and the others. Why was he not?"

He had changed to the royal "we" and "us." The temperature fell with the mutation. It was a mistake; they had been so close that its inappropriateness here in private jarred sadly.

Northumberland said, brusquely but readily, the honest father speaking up for the obstinate son: "My liege, the earl of Douglas suffered five wounds at Homildon, and lost the sight of an eye. Can a man put that load from him in so short a time? It would be barbarous to ask him to ride so far so soon."

The king looked wordlessly at Hotspur; and Hotspur smiled, though disdainfully. "My liege, the earl of Douglas is indeed in no great case to try his strength too far as yet, but by stages he could have made this journey very well. He rode with me and hawked with me before ever I left Bamburgh. It is not his health prevents, but my honour."

"Your honour? Are you not sworn my liege man? Do you not owe me fealty?" The king was leaning forward, gripping the arms of his chair with hands like talons, and his face was blotched from brow to chin with rafts of angry red. "I ordered you to surrender your prizes to me. You have not done so. Not Douglas only, but some number of knights you also hold. You say the earl can assay this journey without danger to him. Very well, I take your word for it. Since he can, he shall, and forthwith. You will send orders this day by a fast courier that he shall set out under escort and be delivered here to me within seven days from the time your messenger reaches Bamburgh. This you will do this very hour, before you quit my court, and you will submit your order to me to be despatched."

"No, your Grace," said Hotspur, burning very quietly before him, with a smoky, smouldering glow, "I will not. I will not write such an order, I will not give you what is mine, I will not subject so noble a creature to such a Roman parade as we have seen this day, not for my life. He would liefer be dead, and that I know and understand, for so would I. My lord, in no other matter do I dispute your overlordship, and in none, God knows, do I resist your sovereignty. Have I not been its prop, as early as Doncaster, as late as Homildon? Am I like to change now, unless you change me? But Douglas is mine for that I took him and he gave himself to me. Such a confiding cannot be passed from hand to hand, like slaves in some Roman market, for gain. He was but slain, and I uncovered to him and offered him honourable peace, and he surrendered himself to me—to me, my lord, not to you. "To you, and none other!" he said to me. How can you claim what was so given, and so received? This is a bargain between my lord of Douglas and me. I can sell him his own freedom, and at a high figure, if I please, or I can give it with my goodwill, if that suits my humour, but hand him over without his leave to a third, king or no king, this I cannot do. He is not merchandise."

"You are on rotten ground, my lord," warned the king, quivering. "It is old and established custom that the sovereign enjoys the right to take over all noble prisoners, though he must hold the captor immune from costs and compensated for the captive's value. Do you deny this right?"

"I do not deny it, though for long time past it has not been exerted. But I deny that it can be exercised where the terms of surrender do not admit it. There are two partners in our agreement, my lord. Write also to the earl of Douglas, ask him if he agree to your claim, and if he answers ay, then I will not say no. But the exact opposite he said, with witnesses enough, when he surrendered himself to me."

And as yet he had not lowered his eyes, bright gold flames in their onyx-brown irises, nor, which was more formidable still, raised his voice by so much as a tone. A clear voice, and carrying; it seemed to find echoes in every corner of the room to underline the words it uttered, but still it remained low and reasonable. He could not deny to himself that he was being stubborn, but he could not believe that he was unjustified, nor that he would not be understood.

"Custom does not delve into such niceties," said the king viciously. "If you have foolishly entered into undertakings you cannot make good, you must be answerable for that, not I. I have my right as overlord, and I assert it, and will maintain it. I guarantee you the compensation due. But the earl I will have."

For the first time Hotspur's subversive tongue knotted, and silenced him. His face was convulsed for a moment with the struggle, then he forced his words past the barrier in an abrupt explosion of anger.

"Your guarantee, your Grace, can hardly stand without some security offered, even if I would deal, and I will not deal. My house already holds some four thousand pounds' worth of unredeemable tallies issued by you this year. Reckon up for yourself the amount owing to my father and me for our management of the Scottish march, and see for yourself how an enterprise so successful may yet come near to beggaring the wardens. We have paid out thousands from our own revenues to make good the pay of the army that won Homildon. True, we may recover it hereafter, but soldiers cannot wait, and our coffers are not inexhaustible. Put it no higher than this level, and even so you owe me any claim you may have to the earl of Douglas, over and over you owe it, before ever he came into my hands. Yet I would not argue on this level, and I will not. Even if you had his price," he said hardily, "and you have not, the earl is not for sale."

The reproach was too true, and therefore too bitter, to be endured. Henry knew himself bankrupt of money and credit, and the sting of being told so openly and roundly was too sharp an offence. No one knew better than he did that he had nothing to give to Northumberland for these prisoners so prudently and dutifully handed over today, except perhaps their lands in Scotland, and even that he was loath to do because it would involve his honour in assisting in their capture, else he was again merely defrauding one already his creditor. Was not Dunbar, too, hovering, demanding recompense for his services? And what was there to bestow, except his title to his own lands, title he already possessed, and no more real after the king's gift than before? To help him to the real enjoyment of his own was another matter. There were Scots of the earl of Douglas's mettle in the way.

He felt the whole encounter slipping out of his hands, even the command of his own tongue threatening to leave him. And all this while the boy sat here at his side with a back straight as a lance, and a face so withdrawn that there was nothing to read in it, neither approval nor disapproval, neither loyalty and indignation nor distaste and resistance. Once only he had lifted one hand some inches, as though to lay it on his father's arm, but then had lowered it again and refrained from touching. And on whose behalf he had gone even so far there was no knowing.

"Do not try me too far," said the king, in a voice thick and choked with gall. "What you in your arrogance decline to sell, as you call it, may yet be taken from you, yes, along with much else, if you put yourself in opposition to the crown's due rights."

"So it may, your Grace, by any that has the hardihood to come and take it. Yet it behoves the crown to remember that others, too, have rights, a right to the prizes of their own prowess, a right to the sanctity of their word, a right to be considered equally with others in equal case, and not taken contrary. For I give you to know, my liege, that we are concerned here with more prisoners than one, and more prisoners than mine." And now he had raised his voice for the first time, it rang out loud and indignant, and colour had flamed into his cheeks, burned brown by wind and sun. "Why have you said no word and made no move to bring home my brother Edmund Mortimer from his captivity in Wales? For Lord Grey, the chief cause of this dissension in the first place, and who fomented it as long as he was free to act, no price is too high! You give your gracious consent to the raising of a loan of ten thousand marks for him, but not one word is uttered concerning Edmund, your kinsman, your Grace, as well as mine, who was taken in battle in your cause as surely as was Grey, and more effectively, too, for as I have heard, he left some fair number of Welsh dead on the field by Pilleth, which is more than ever Grey did at Clocaenog. I waited and was certain that you must speak for him, if no other did, but never a word. He might be dead, for all the mention I hear of him from you! Now if you care as much as you have said for justice and right, then do Edmund justice. Give me your royal sanction to raise a comparable loan for him as you have agreed for Grey, and I will speak for your wish to the earl of Douglas, and if he so free me as to come willingly to your court, I will not gainsay. But if he hold me to my troth, I cannot give him to you."

He had come thus far with the impetus of one of his own moorland burns in spate, and though hot and vehement now in voice and eye, yet with less affronting haughtiness then before, for he had forgotten himself and his own grievance in Edmund's, and his eloquence, though still intransigent, had turned to a kind of passionate and imperious pleading which might even have been expected to assuage, in some degree, the king's outrage, and bring him gratefully a step towards reconciliation. It would not have cost him much, on the face of it. And Northumberland, who had all but bitten his own tongue at least a dozen times in these exchanges, holding back remonstrances which he knew would only have driven his son to worse extremes, drew back with a secret sigh of relief to let things go their own way from here, secure that the worst was over. But Worcester, on the other side of the throne, stood in silent watchfulness still, too wise to intervene, but by no means yet reassured. And he watched most narrowly of all, not Hotspur, but the prince of Wales, tensed on his stool like a young leopard in ambush, only his hazel eyes moving in quick perception from one antagonist to the other. Northumberland might be relaxing in the belief that the climax was past; but this last proposition had meant to the prince something different, something charged and perilous. Not an end, but a beginning, and incalculable in its possibilities.

The king shifted forward in his chair, staring balefully, with little hope of staring down the bright, demanding eyes that challenged him. He tried for utterance once, and his voice foundered in his throat for pure desperation and bitterness; and when it came at the second attempt, it came a tone too high, fevered and hysterical, and he could do nothing to subdue it, or silence it once it was launched.

"You do ill—you do ill, Sir Henry Percy, to speak of Mortimer in the same breath with Grey. Lord Grey has been always my most faithful servant in North Wales, and if I had had a dozen such, or one such, perhaps, in command to aid my son, we might have fared very differently in this contention. Mortimer was not on my occasions, but minding his own boundaries, when he fell into Glendower's hands, and little enough have I ever had to thank him for in those regions, and nothing—you hear me? Nothing!—do I owe him. Let him shift for himself, for I will not lift a finger for him." The note of frenzy crept in again, shrilling in his own ears with frightening malevolence. Half on his feet, he shouted his refusal into Hotspur's stunned and incredulous face. "I will not, and you shall not! No, you may not with my sanction make any move to raise a loan for his ransom. I will not countenance such a measure. And I will make known to all lenders that this is my will. You hear me, my lord? Are you answered?"

Their faces were scarcely a yard apart, each peering with strained attention into the other's eyes, trying to penetrate darkness where once all had been crystal. And it was too late now for anyone to reach out a hand to stop the avalanche, for everything was in motion, everything was toppling, and nothing could now arrest the fall. For one long, blinding moment Hotspur saw Henry's private countenance naked and plain, and after that it was too late to forget anything or explain anything. He saw him more clearly than Henry had ever yet seen himself, even in nightmares, and knew more evil of him than Henry would ever know of his own suspect heart.

This was no mere matter of money, after all, or even of preferring Grey, wisely or unwisely. The man was glad that Edmund should be prisoner, and meant to leave him in hold until he rotted. More, he would have been better pleased still, though he himself hardly realised it and would never admit it, if Mortimer had been killed at Pilleth instead of taken. It would simplify everything for him if Mortimer were dead. All the Mortimers! For somewhere in his tormented mind brooded the fear that every one of them threatened his security and his peace. If King Edward's granddaughter Philippa could transmit her claim to her sons, so could Elizabeth transmit hers, if all other Mortimers failed, to young Harry. And if fear and enmity could reach as far as Edmund, it could reach as far as Elizabeth and her son, as far as the last of all the Mortimers, for its corruption was without limit.

His heart cried out in him that this was not what Henry had been, that it was utterly against his nature. But that was no answer and no reassurance, for as surely as he stared into this face now, it was what Henry had become. The corrosive suspicions of the usurper had eaten out the heart that had once been his.

Strangely, in the turmoil of this revelation and shock and grief, Hotspur felt a convulsion of guilt, too. For had not he done more, perhaps, than any other man to put this sometime friend of his on the throne, and drive him to his damnation? And, worse, if the mind behind that face could dwell thus hopefully on the possible death of Mortimer, then what of Richard? Richard, who *was* dead! So aptly, so opportunely dead! That death shone forth to him now in another and sinister light, matter for far more than regret. And the little boy Edmund, earl of March, the next legal heir to Richard's throne, what of him? Safe kept and safe watched in Henry's fostering! Safe? At any moment, if it became necessary, a hand could be laid on him. A few more friars burned or hanged, a few more rumours of conspiracy, and how much longer would the child live? The child? The children! Even the baby, Anne!

Still frozen in fascination, he saw in the king's eyes an awareness of change as keen, if not as clear, as his own awareness. Henry knew that something had happened, that something unidentifiable was lost to him; and he was the more desperately sad because he did not know what it was, but only felt its loss. Something they had possessed between them, trust, respect, the confidence that was better than understanding, had suddenly flowed away like water between his fingers, and would never again be recovered.

"I am answered," said Hotspur grimly.

"Is that all you have to say to me?" He reached after some word that would either turn the fury aside or cause it to burst in ultimate ruin, it hardly mattered which if only it would end this scene, and lift, for the moment, the burden of his sick despair from him. "I have heard no word of submission and obedience, none of your duty, none of all the favour I have shown you. My lord, I think you are no better than a traitor! Did you not swear an oath of fealty?"

"Ay, so I did!" cried Hotspur, in a sudden white blaze of rage. "You do well to remind us both. So I did, my lord, long since. *And so did you! Traitor to whom?*"

The king uttered a wordless bellow, and lunged out of his chair; and suddenly the boy made a small sound that was like a distant echo of his father's cry, and started up to catch at his father's arm. For the king had a dagger naked in his hand, and the sheath swung empty at his hip. The blade flashed, a blue glimmer. Hotspur stood his ground motionless, his lips curled in arrogant contempt, and spread his empty hands tauntingly, daring the stroke to fall.

The king's hand sank. Silently, stealthily, almost tenderly, the prince slipped the dagger out of his unresisting fingers.

"Not here," said Hotspur abruptly, "but in the field!"

He turned, without another look, without haste, without regard to anyone present but the man to whom he had spoken, and walked out of the room.

The king looked round him dazedly, at the three faces that scrupled to look too closely into his, at his open and empty hand, at the curtain still swinging in the doorway. And suddenly he cried out in a sharp voice of realisation and distress: "Harry!"

But the door had closed between them, and Hotspur did not hear.

8

They came after him to his town house in Bishopsgate Street, his father and his uncle together, urgent to repair what could be repaired. They found him standing alone beside a fire of logs, staring into the blue blaze in search of some clarity that might light his own understanding. His face was still and dark, and though he stirred himself to offer them fruit and wine, it was with no more than a corner of his mind that he seemed aware of them.

"Nothing's lost yet," urged Northumberland, pacing the room hungrily, and glittering in its dim corners in his cloth of gold. "I tell you, after you flung out he called after you, if you had but had sense enough to linger within call. And the prince will work on him, be sure of it. Neither of them wants this rift, nor will the king press it to extremes. He owes us too much, and besides, he does value you, he is no such fool as to lose you lightly. If he had not a temper as curst as your own it would never have come to this. But all you need do is show some patience and caution, and for God's sake a little humility if he offer you the chance to approach him."

"He shall not have Douglas," said Hotspur, who did not so much as recognise the name of humility, though he did very often show it to creatures weaker and less fortunate than himself; but he spoke almost absentmindedly, still watching the flames with a darkling face.

"Fool, do you think he'll ask for him again? He has had a lesson, if you have not. He brought the boy there to see you humbled, you know that, don't you? He will not tempt God again! Not that way! And I don't say you did ill to out-face him, though you risked more than you know. But you had better not tempt God too often, either. Draw in your horns now, and show some will to be reconciled with him, and you may keep your Douglas, and your office, and get his favour again, too, if you do your part. But if you cannot walk gently for a month or so, and speak him fair, you may ruin us all."

"Not least, Edmund Mortimer," said Worcester in his wry, measured voice.

Hotspur turned his head, and looked at him for the first time as if he saw him. They were very close, although they were opposites and anomalies, the uncle thoughtful, subtle, a man of many parts and ahead of his time, the nephew a dazzling ember after the fires of the past had burned out. Worcester was as tall as his brother, and made in a broader mould, a grand, well-formed man a shade fairer than the rest of his tribe, and more than a little quieter, with a short brown beard, and shrewd, illusionless eyes. He had been many things in his day, notably grand admiral of England, steward of King Richard's household, and lieutenant of South Wales. And whatever else might dismay him, he was beyond surprise.

"Yes. I have been thinking," said Hotspur, "how best to care for Edmund."

"That we foresaw. For clearly Henry will do nothing, and after what's passed today we could hardly ask him for anything. But we're not without resources. We can and will dip into our own treasuries for Elizabeth's brother. That is not the present problem. *You* are that." Hotspur looked back at him from over a doubled fist with impenetrable reserve, and said no word. "Harry, you must make your peace with him. Or at least—for I think he will make the first move—let him make his peace with you."

"Peace!" burst out Hotspur, rearing his head from his hand and turning on them in a convulsion of passion. "You've understood nothing! Peace…reconciliation! This is a man I do not even *know*!

One that has been my close acquaintance and my friend from child-hood, and suddenly I look into his eyes and see a different being—a stranger and a murderer! In will, if not in deed. And I think—I think even in deed! You want me to go back to such a man, swear my fealty to him afresh, give him earnests of my goodwill? How can you ask it of me? Never again can I feel towards him as I used to feel. You're mad if you can contemplate it. How can I ever be sure that Roger's two little boys, and Anne, and Edmund himself, won't go the way Richard went? I saw it in his face that he begins to see them all as threats to him—that he'd be glad to have them dead. And the children out of our reach, already in his care, attended by his creatures!"

Over his tensed shoulder the two elders looked at each other, and recognised each his own thought in the other's face: It has happened, he is awake. Now it will be like holding unbroken horses. Others can note and reason, calculate and bide their time. Not this one! The only other name he knows for dissimulation is dishonour.

"He will not touch the children," said Worcester with considered emphasis. "There is no need, since they are in his care, as you say. And whatever fears and doubts he may have, he is not the man to take kindly to murder, or use it unless he feels himself forced."

"He *was* not such a man. He is now. Not kindly, no, that's true, it will be utterly against his nature, but he is already twisted into conflict against his nature, the battle is lost and won. He cannot go back to the Henry I knew. And yet," he burt out helplessly, drumming his fists down hard against the arm of his chair, "I saw Richard's body! There was not a mark of violence on him. Not one!"

"There are precedents," said Northumberland, with half-contemptuous bluntness. "They showed Edward's body, too, in my father's time, after Berkeley. Much can be done with a body, once it ceases to make any resistance."

"But everything appeared as they claimed—he was whole, but emaciated—they swore he'd refused food in his despair..."

Northumberland uttered a brief, hard bark of laughter at such innocence, and swung away impatiently to pace the room again.

"And did you ever know Richard persist in either elation or
despair for more than three days?" asked Worcester, ruefully viewing
his nephew's shocked unhappiness. "More often he scaled the one
and plumbed the other in the same day. If he had resolved on death
in the morning, he would have recovered hope of rescue and restoration before night. Only those very resolute in despair carry it
to the death. It was another resolution, not his own, withheld food
from Richard."

"Like Rothesay, this very spring at Falkland," said Northumberland.
"Albany was resolute, and Rothesay is dead. It's an old way enough
of getting rid of the inconvenient."

Hotspur looked slowly from his father's face to his uncle's, and
back again. "You have known this all along!"

"We knew and we know no more than you," said his father
brusquely.

"But you believed it! While I shrugged off all the whispers.
There are always whispers. No such death can ever happen without
someone saying: Murder! You went into it with your eyes open."

"And so did you!" snapped Northumberland.

He opened his lips to protest fiercely that it was not true, and was
brought up short against the inescapable image of his own guilt.
What evidence had they had, that he had not had? Of course he had
heard all the rumours that passed in secret about the city and the
countryside, but he had taken them for granted as inevitable in any
such situation, a part of the common-place of crisis and upheaval.
Because he had known Henry, or thought he knew him, as he knew
his own heart. All men were fallible, that he knew, all men could,
when pressed, do terrible things; yet he had believed himself capable
of judging what Henry would and would not do, and never for a
moment had he entertained it as a possibility that, however pressed,
he would put Richard to death. Was it arrogance to make such

passionate judgments, to be so sure of one's friends as to come near
to blindness? All his life he had taken men as he found them, and
staked fearlessly on his estimates of them, and all his life remaining
he must do the same, he could live no other way. Yet in his wrong
judgments he was guilty.

But his guilt went back still further. It had begun in very natural
and not ungenerous resentment of Richard's high-handed dealings,
and hot sympathy with Henry in his unjust banishment, and even
more in the expropriation of his estates, flagrant, bare-faced robbery.
No doubt where the right lay in such a case. And who had been
the hottest of the Percies then to ride to meet the returning duke
at Doncaster, and support his claims to his own? These two had
followed more prudently, weighing the consequences, perhaps even
foreseeing much of what was to follow, but he had plunged into the
adventure in heat, as he did everything, never looking beyond the
immediate issue.

"It is true," he said, stricken. "I have been to blame. It is no excuse
for me that I could not or would not see. I went in to it with my
eyes open."

"And when you were in," Northumberland pressed mercilessly,
"do you think your responsibility stopped there? Whose fire was
it set light to this Henry of yours, slow-burning stuff as he is, and
drove him on headlong through his own rights to grasp at more,
and more, until he had little choice but to grasp at the crown itself,
where he had no rights? Do you think you can start a mountain
sliding, and then halt it when you will?"

"It is truth," he said again, but more calmly now, with a grave,
uncharacteristic quietness, for he had already accepted his own role
and Henry's. There was a logic in events, once they were set in
motion, that had left neither of them much choice. He recalled the
oath with which they had begun, at Doncaster, asserting only their
just and limited demands. Had Henry been a hypocrite then, tongue
in cheek? No, surely not. He had meant what he swore as fervently

as had Hotspur, and they had both broke their troth. For the tide into which they had waded so singlemindedly had swept them and their oath away. He remembered the succession of parliamentary orders and contrivances to which he, like the others, had assented, every one of them whittling away a fragment of the justice of their cause, almost unnoticed, almost in innocence. But not quite! The order decreeing Richard's perpetual imprisonment—Yes, Hal had signed that, too, Hal who had loved Richard, but as a boy of twelve, dazzled, disorientated, anxious to be loyal to his father. For Hotspur there could be no such excuse. And yet at the moment there had seemed to be no alternative. And at every succeeding moment of pressure, none. And so they were come in the end to this, to today.

Only the death…In the death he had never believed. Richard's despairing withdrawal had come almost as a deliverance from an intolerable situation. Now it was the rock on which he had come to wreck. For the tide no longer carried him.

"Very well," he said slowly, and his voice was harsh and distant, arguing, from somewhere deep within his own conscience, with the God who judged him, and wanting to evade nothing, to excuse nothing, which belonged to him by right. "I have been to blame. I did what I did, and I did wrongly. But I can go no farther along this road, now that I have seen where it leads. For my misjudgments I must answer, and I will answer, whenever account is demanded. But there are others. And now I want Edmund out of danger, and the two little boys and their sister, and by God, my own Harry, too, for through his mother he's nearer the crown, even he, than this Bolingbroke king we've set up between us. I would not trust him now with any one of them. And they, at least, have done no wrong."

His elders exchanged glances, and as one man drew nearer to him, but with careful gentleness. Worcester took him by the shoulders, and turned him to face him.

"Harry, it's for their sakes that you must practise caution and pliancy and patience, all that comes hard to you. Do you not see the peril in which you place them if you make one wrong move now? For Edmund we can deal ourselves. But for him, for us, for Elizabeth and your son, and Roger's children, everything depends on you. Unless you cover them with your compliance and moderation, they may fall into the very pit you've imagined for them. You must master yourself if you're to deliver them. You must come back to court, to parliament, to your proper place, and keep your countenance and your patience. Until," he said, very softly, "the favourable hour comes. We cannot make it overnight because you have seen visions."

"The favourable hour," Hotspur repeated to himself, and the inward stare of his eyes turned outwards shrewdly enough for a moment, to consider their watchful, appraising faces. "Favourable for what enterprise? The removal of the children out of his hand?" But he knew better than that. There was that in the very tone of their approaches now that went beyond the condition of Roger's orphaned brood.

"Not, perhaps, of the children," said Worcester softly.

"Do you think," said Northumberland, low-voiced, "that we are any happier than you with the state of our affairs? Or England's affairs? Or the monster we've created?"

They drew in on him with careful gentleness, one from either side, not hurrying him, not even pressing upon him too fiercely what they had never even said to each other until now, scarcely even thought in any formulated terms. They were speaking to each other and to themselves as surely as to him; for if he had suddenly achieved this prodigy of recognition, then the time was come to speak, and if he had reached the point of absolute severance with the past—and for him nothing less was now possible—then it was high time to think of the future. For he was a natural force that could not be contained for long.

"What we did we did for the best," said his father, "but the worst has come out of it. And a situation that cannot be borne can always be changed."

"It would not displease us," said Worcester, "to unking this king we made. And we have a close and recent precedent, have we not? Kings *can* be unmade. If Richard, with his God-given right, then why not this Bolingbroke, so lightly rooted, with so little right? He has shown us the way himself, and what has been done once can more easily be done the second time."

"But not yet. There's no virtue in plunging blindly into such an enterprise. You must come back to parliament and to court, meet him halfway if he offers it, patch up this untimely quarrel…"

He let them talk, persuasively, fervently, discovering for the first time the depth and bitterness of their resentment and disillusionment. He himself said little; his mind was on something else, something to him more immediate, while he listened and noted, missing nothing.

By the time they left him he had grown so thoughtful, and so apparently docile, that they were encouraged to believe he had resigned himself to the necessity of dissembling, and would consent to a meeting with the king, if one were offered. They withdrew with their eyes still on him to the last, distrustful of this uncharacteristic quietness, but assured that he had given up all thought of precipitate action.

When they were gone, he turned to what was more urgent in his eyes. There was no longer any help for Edmund in the king, no deliverance to be hoped for from him, nor any security in his vicinity even if deliverance were possible. What mattered most at this moment was that Mortimer should know how the land lay, and take thought for his own future. He was a man, what right had any other man, even one that loved him, to do his thinking for him?

On his knees beside his father's chair, the prince clung to the cold, rigid hands that hardly acknowledged his touch, and argued, pleaded, reminded, cajoled, until his eyes filled with tears of pure exhaustion from so much outpouring of love where he could not be sure he felt any. Once Norbury had ventured to open the door and look into the room, and it had been the prince, not the king, who had turned fiercely and waved him away, scrambling up from his knees to secure the latch after him, before he returned to his place.

"Father, don't press him, wait, let him rest. You took him too fiercely on a point of honour—you know him, if he gave his word he will die before he breaks it, even for you, though for you he would do more than for any other man." Was that even true? He could not be sure. He knew only that three times at least Hotspur had sensed some want of filial love in the son, and spoken out for the father as no other man would have done, "Is not that the best of reasons for valuing him? Do you think such a man would ever break his troth to *you*! What use to you is a vassal who takes back his faith upon orders? Don't follow this quarrel, let it lie, let it sleep until it can be mended, or you will have lost the best man you have, the best you will ever have. As you know!…As you know better than any!"

He did not know this wisdom for folly, being sure in his own mind that he mattered too little to his father, in any personal sense, to allow of any jealousy; but his fervour and praise were at once bitter and sweet.

"Was he not one of the first to ride to join you? Did he wait then to see which way the wind of success would blow? You know he did not. He came on the instant, and he and his forces were your mainstay. And how has he failed you since? Sir, you were too hurtful pricking him so sharply on the very occasion of his greatest gift to you. Was Homildon a small thing? Had he not a right to be proud? And it is no falsehood that he needs money for his men, and ready money *now*, and surely he welcomed and was glad of this means to furnish it. If you must have his submission, you could have asked for it in private, man to man, and not so matched one provocation with another."

Try as he would, he was dismayed to find his tone veering towards blame upon the one part and excuse upon the other, and he was wise enough to know that for folly. He laid his cheek against his father's knee, for no better reason than to hide his face a moment and draw breath, but the gesture reached a heart at which, just then, he had not even been aiming. One of the king's hands drew itself out of the boy's clasp and was laid, almost gingerly, upon his head. A moment it lay stiffly still, and then warmed and curved, inexpertly caressing the bright brown cap of hair. And suddenly Hal's tears gushed over the one hand he still held.

"The man loves you!" he sobbed, blurting out what he had always known as truth. It was not his fault that he uttered it too late for truth. "If you knew, if you knew, how he has always spoken of you to me! And not of design! He does nothing of design. He says what is on his heart. You have not a truer lover in this land than Hotspur."

The king's hand, which had lain in his as inert as marble, stirred into tentative life, opened and shifted, and closed about one of the slender hands that cradled it.

"I drew on him," said the king's voice, helplessly grieving. And the prisoned hand tightened and quivered, and the boy clasped it gratefully, his long lashes brushing the backs of the strong fingers with the soft, rapid friction of a butterfly's wings.

"He won't hold it against you."

"But he defied me! He denied me!"

"You pressed him too hard—and too rashly…"

"How could this happen? I cannot understand! I never wanted this, I never meant this…"

"Nor did he," said the prince, trembling under the hand that stroked him in so moving and timorous a manner, as though nothing but Hotspur's thunderbolt could have brought about this scene of clumsy and terrifying tenderness. "He never wanted it, either. Oh, why, why did you force it on him?"

There again came the partisan note that he most wanted to avoid, and he wept over it like a distressed child even as he plotted his way round it like a general, and a hardened one, too. "If he had not been so dearly your friend, he would not have felt your orders as such a slight. You have hurt him as he has hurt you, and needless."

"It was not my intention," said the king heavily.

"He knows that, now he's had time to cool. Nor was it his intent to affront you, sir, I swear it. You have driven each other, and that was wasteful."

He was not yet old enough and practised enough to measure the personal griefs and problems of the father who had engendered him; it would have taken a greater effrontery than he possessed, to make the leap into understanding. He experienced, but could not yet comprehend, the loneliness of the spirit that cannot express its feelings or show its affections openly; and he was moved to a compassion he did not know how to employ. He fumbled as best he could for a rational means of using it for good.

"Let me go to him! Let me bring him to you! He'll come for me."

The king heard that, and his caressing hand halted and stiffened on his son's brown hair.

"He knows the value you and I set on each other," said the boy. "He would not come for an official messenger." He was learning fast, with every breath, but the process was painful. He looked up, his face now under firm control. "Make your peace with him! You know you desire it. And so does he. Only your enemies and his rejoice to see you estranged, do not give them that comfort."

The hand lingered, inexpressibly timid and fond and irresolute. The boy held his breath.

"Bring him," said the king, with dread and constraint. "Ask him to come to me, of his kindness."

❧

The prince, again a prince to view, armed against any resistance, did the errand himself. He was in some embarrassment, unwilling to leave his father to other care in his absence, but even more unwilling to trust the mission to another. In the event, he closed the door very gently on the king, leaving him solitary, and himself chose a mount from the stables, saddled him, and rode to Bishopsgate Street. For tonight's mood, thus softened and vulnerable, would not endure long, and he could not afford to lose the tide while it lasted.

Even so, he was late. At Sir Henry Percy's house the steward informed him that his lord had taken horse and ridden forth half an hour earlier.

"To what destination? Did he say?"

"No, your Grace. He left us no word, except that he said he might be away for four or five days."

"And he took no escort with him?" asked the prince, in consternation.

"No, your Grace, not even a groom. His lordship rode alone."

To the steward it was not so strange. Hotspur rode as he pleased, and often alone. But Hal went back reluctantly and anxiously to the palace of Westminster, his hands empty, his heart uneasy, and his mouth barren of reassurance.

The king was in his bedchamber, dressing carefully to face his prisoner-guests in hall. There was no one with him except his valet, and they were about the business of making royalty appear even more royal as though nothing more urgent awaited attention. The king turned upon his son a changed face, composed and aloof, marked his momentary hesitation, and smiled grimly.

"I thought you were too hopeful. So he will not come!"

"No, sir, it's no such case. I could not deliver your summons to him. He has left his house and ridden away, they were not told where. Perhaps for four or five days, they said. Half an hour earlier, and I should not have missed him. He could not know," said the prince, watching his father's flinty face with wonder and misgiving, "that you would call him back to you so soon."

"He has left London? He is abandoning us and parliament like this?"

"No, that's impossible, his household has no orders but to expect him back in these few days. When, if you will let me speak with him again, he will surely come to you."

"He may not get so magnanimous a welcome by then," said the

king, turning under his valet's hands to settle the folds of his gown. "It seems to me that you have been over-hopeful, and I over-persuaded. If he had cared greatly for my regard, would he have taken himself off so lightly and promptly? What business can he have that takes him out of town so suddenly, unless it be matter as seditious as his own speeches? If he is loyal, his business is here, in my council and at my court while parliament sits."

"Sir, you are unjust. He is gone away alone, and I think it is not hard to see his need. He wants time for thought, after such a sore contention, as hurtful to him as to you. I pledge my word he will come back to his place, and fill it as he always did, nobly and dutifully."

The king smiled, but it was a sour, cold smile. He cast a critical eye on his son's muddy boots and plain riding-clothes. "Well, you have done what you could, Hal. Now you had better be making yourself presentable, had you not? We at least have places to fill, and cannot ride away and leave our duty."

"Yes, sir," said the prince, chilled. "I shall not fail you. But I beg you not to judge him in his absence."

He went out slowly, puzzled and anxious, for it seemed that this mere mischance of Hotspur's sudden departure might have undone everything he had achieved towards a reconciliation. Something, at least, had greatly changed his father from the sad, tired man he had left not an hour ago, grieving over the rift with his friend. Yet now he looked more closely, the change had been there from the moment he opened the door and entered the king's room. There before him, and waiting for him. The wind had swung into a harsher quarter before ever he came back with his news. The spurt of cold suspicion of Hotspur's motives and errand had done no more than reinforce a mood already determined. He has come to himself, the boy thought uneasily, or been brought to himself. He has remembered his grievance and repented of his repentance.

In the passage-way he met John Norbury, ready to attend his master, and on impulse halted him with a hand on his arm.

"John, who went in to his Grace, after I left him?"

Norbury pondered no more than a moment. "Only one that I recall, my lord. The earl of the March of Scotland."

9

It was past ten on a fine, moonless night when knuckles rapped sharply at the shutters of the lowest window on Rhodri Parry's house. The summons might easily have gone unheard if Julian had not been making her rounds before sleeping, as she did with more than usual care on these evenings when she was left in the house alone. She was just passing through the undercroft to secure the bolt and latch on the yard door when the knocking came, and she halted with held breath and reared head to listen. She was safe enough within, short of fire and sword the house was a fortress, and there was no need for her to open; but she knew that she would open. Perhaps in hope that God was opening another door to her; perhaps out of a sense of her own destiny which would not let her refuse any challenge.

She crossed the yard to the wicket-gate in the cart entrance; and as she put her hands to the wooden bolt she heard the length and lightness of the step without, quiet but not stealthy, and knew it. She had never doubted that some day he would come again.

She drew open the wicket gladly, and reached a hand to guide him as she had done once before; and as his fingers closed strongly on hers she heard him draw breath for the shadow of a laugh, in pure pleasure at the ease of their confederacy. But neither of them spoke until they were safe inside the undercroft, and the door closed after them against the world.

"My lord, you're dearly welcome! I'm charged with a message to you ever since Iago was here in September, if I'd had any way of reaching you."

"From Edmund?" he said eagerly.

"No, but concerning him. It may do as well. The Lord Owen sends you word he's well healed of his wounds, and in good heart. I did make shift, at least," she said, "to pass on the news to your lady, by a clothier who trades as far north as Newcastle, in a little piece of embroidery. But he'd be some weeks on the way, I doubt if she has it yet. I knew no other safe way."

"God bless you for the word and the thought!" he said warmly. "You ease my heart of the worst load before I so much as ask." They stood face to face, close and kind, in the dimness at the foot of the staircase, only a thin chink of light coming down to them from the solar, the yellow of a candle and the last gleams of a fire burning low. "Julian, I need Iago now on just such an errand. Is he here?"

He did not even know that he had used her name for the first time, as simply as he used Iago's, for she was one in the brotherhood of those he respected and trusted. "I have letters for Owen and for Edmund, and the matter's urgent. Iago said you should always know of his whereabouts if I needed him."

"He is not here," she said, "nor my father, either. I'm alone in the house, but for the old woman. But come up to the fire, why do we shiver here in the dark?"

"No, God forbid, if you're alone I must not trouble you—" he began.

"You don't trouble me. It would only trouble me if you went away troubled. And you said it is urgent."

"Not so urgent that I need bring you into question or distress. I must wait until Iago comes." He was disappointed and uneasy, stirring restlessly in the dark beside her, beating his gloved fists together softly and tormentedly as he debated within his own mind what to do. "How soon do you expect him?"

She was silent for so long that he put out a hand and touched her shoulder, and marvelled at the braced tension he felt beneath his fingers. "I do distress you! There are things I must not meddle with, I know it. And I'm ashamed, when you've already done so much for me and mine. Tell me when I may come and visit your father, and I'll leave you in peace. Or if I've already trespassed beyond what's allowed me, tell me so, and I'll find some other way. You shall not suffer by my means."

"No!" she said quickly and fiercely, gripping the wrist of the hand that held her, and would as abruptly have quitted her. "No, don't go! You would not be leaving me in peace. You mistook me, I was thinking how best to deal. This is vital? No, tell me no more than if it matters dearly to you, and that's enough."

"It does, dearly. But if Iago is not here—"

"He is here," she said. "No, not here in the house. But unless he's moved ahead of his time, for some good reason, then he's within three miles of us at this moment. And before morning he sets out again into Wales."

"He's so close?" he said eagerly. "And I can still reach him? Tell me how to find him!"

"No! I could tell you, but you could not pass that way alone, and though you, I daresay, could command a way through the gates even by night, as we could not, yet by that road you might be too late. And even if you were not...My lord, desperate men don't take kindly to strangers galloping suddenly upon them in the night. I would not like them to end in prison, nor you in the Severn. But I can take you to him."

After a moment of abrupt stillness and silence he said gently: "I understand you. And I do not think I should let you either go with me into danger, or endanger yourself with your own people for my sake."

"If I come with you, there will be no danger. And as for any man blaming me for admitting you to too much secret knowledge, Iago's word will stand by me against all others, and Iago's word is what counts. You will make no use of whatever you learn by my means, that I know." She smiled suddenly, and though he could not see the smile, he heard it in her voice as she said: "That was like you, to call them my own people, and allow them rights like other men."

"I give you my word," he said, "nothing I may see or hear shall be used against any man, whatever his allegiance."

"That must be enough for them. And as for me, I did not even need that. I'm putting the safety of other people in your hands, but I have great trust in your hands. Let's be plain! My lord, my father and I are Welsh. We have been made to know all too well that we're Welsh, here in this town, where once we wanted only to live and work as peaceful citizens. Very well, Welsh we are, and now we claim the right to fight for our own country as you English do for yours, having been brutally shown that England is no country of ours. I tell you," she said more gently, "because I would not have any concealment between us. You must know what you are doing, as well as I."

For answer he said only: "Where are we bound?"

"Out of Shrewsbury, first. You came on foot? There's no horse to be hidden? I can't get a horse out the way we are going."

"I came from London alone," he said. "The horse is at the abbey stables, but not left in my name."

"Good! We shall have two miles or more to walk, but there should be time. Wait for me!"

She went away from him in a rustle of skirts and a gust of cool air, up the staircase and into the solar. In a few minutes she came back to the stairhead, drawing the door securely closed after her, and descended to his side, swathed in a dark cloak. They went out silently together across the yard, and through the vicket door into the deserted alley.

Instead of turning towards the town walls, where there was always the chance of encountering a stray patrol at night, if the watch had a zealous officer, she chose the narrow ways through the town itself.

There were still a few people out and about, enough at least to prevent them from being too conspicuous, until they had left the centre and the market-place, and turned towards the walls and the river again, by the street called Romaldesham.

"How do we pass the gate?" he asked in a whisper in her ear.

"We don't go near the gate. There are other ways."

They were walking now along the inner side of the town wall, and the street was black and deserted around them. Julian hugged the wall, and drew him suddenly into the embrasure of a narrow doorway sunk deeply into it, and rapped with her knuckles at a small grilled panel set into the wood at eye-level. There was no light within, but in a moment there was the faintest of movements close to the grille, and the soft sound of breathing.

"Brother Richard!" Julian whispered, and waited to be sure she had the right man before she went further. "It's I, Julian Parry. I need to pass, with an urgent messenger for Iago."

There was a moment's pause, and then the door gave inwards and let them through. They were in the vaulted tunnel of the gateway, and before them, to one side of the entrance, a faint gleam of light came from the open doorway of a small stone lodge. The porter was closing the door and making it fast behind them. A tall, thin, black figure, a moving shadow among shadows; by his long habit and rope girdle Hotspur knew him for a friar.

"Richard, ferry us over and bring the boat back. We may be the whole night away, and we can come in at the gate by daylight. You may pass," she said to Hotspur, "right round the coil of the river on the far side, and come to the abbey without entering the town. I'll show you."

"Nothing's gone amiss?" the friar asked in an anxious undertone.

"No, all's well. But there are letters for the Lord Owen. We must reach Iago before he leaves."

They emerged from the thickness of the wall into a broad enclave that seemed to slope away outside the wall of the town, and here the starlight had some effect. Hotspur's eyes, growing used to the night, found about him the outlines of large buildings, one surely a church; and open spaces between, where the friar led them silently down slopes of grass to avoid even a footfall. There were trees, too, on one side, perhaps an orchard. Yet the whole seemed to be enclosed by another wall, like a bastion built on to the original town walls to make this broad and pleasant ground safe. Two small towers jutted against the sky. They had passed the main barrier only to be shut in by a secondary one.

He went where he was led, trustingly, and asked no questions, here where voices might betray not only them but their guide. They reached the lower wall, and here again, it seemed, there was a small postern gate. The friar unlocked it with one of the keys at his girdle, and they emerged above the grassy bank of the Severn, a ribbon of faintly-gleaming silver open to the starlight. There was a worn path through the shoulder of meadow down to a shallow cove where two boats were beached, and one rode softly nodding in the water, moored to a small jetty. If this enclave within the wall was indeed one of the friaries, then the brothers would have their own fishing rights in this stretch of the river. Even at night a boat might not be too sharply suspect, if it was noticed; and since the main, manned wall of Shrewsbury lay some way behind them, and obscured by the church and the friary buildings, boats upon the water here in the hours of darkness might never be noticed at all. It was one way out of a city.

"There's a quiet old horse at graze in the field over yonder," said Brother Richard in a hoarse whisper, as he untied the mooring rope and stepped in after them, "if you can manage him without saddle or harness. But only the one. He's ours and short of work this autumn. He could well carry two a short way."

Hotspur was fitting oars into rowlocks, silently and gladly, strangely enlarged into a brief renewal of boyhood in this nocturnal adventure, so gentle and so dreamlike. He felt and heard Julian quiver beside him with equally irresponsible laughter.

"Two miles, Richard, and a way I know well enough, dark or light! We'll let your old horse rest and grow fat. Though a knight without a horse," she said, with a flash of her eyes towards her companion, that was almost palpable though not visible, "is a poor, lost creature."

"In the dark," said Hotspur, "and on a way I don't know, I'll trust my two feet rather than his four."

"As you will," said the porter, and sat down beside Hotspur placidly, taking one of the oars from him. "Pull yonder, for that white stake, there's a good, hard gravel there, and we needn't drive her aground. The current goes crosswise here by the shore, and then strongly in the centre. Along the bank opposite you may idle as you please, there's no current at all."

He knew his river. He set them ashore dry-shod, with a leap of a yard or so to be negotiated, over which Hotspur hoisted Julian in his hands, like a child, for all her height.

"God speed!" said the porter, and poled the boat about, standing, and took both oars to strike out again for the friary landing-stage. They watched him dwindle into mid-stream, and then turned to climb the high bank above them. Hotspur had his bearings now; he knew the angle of the wall they left behind them, outlined in black against the sky, on the far side of the silvery Severn. The Welsh bridge was only one curve of the stream away from them.

"Your way out of Shrewsbury is through the domain of the Austin friars."

"Since Brother Richard became their porter," she said, "yes. The friary knows nothing of it, and we have used it only three short weeks. We must change often, as each becomes dangerous."

"And if this way out becomes dangerous first to Brother Richard?"

"Not through you," she said serenely, and smiled. "But yes, it well may. Then, if we know in time, we take him away, that way or another, into Wales. His name," she said in explanation, "is Richard ap Llwyd. He is a good man."

"I do believe it. I think," said Hotspur, "that you have found in this cause something for which you were seeking."

She said nothing to that; it was a perilous remark to answer, with her heart rising in her like a lark, and like a lark singing. From the moment that she shed from her the shadow of the town she was strangely happy, as if no yesterday existed, and no morrow.

"They call that enclosure the New Work," she said. "Like a wen grown on the wall of the town. It was a burial-ground once, when there was an interdict upon England, and no one might have funeral rites. And yet I think they have fair enough lying, under the orchard there. When they let the friars build there they had to make them a way through the wall for access."

"You know the way we must go?"

"Do you think," she said, "I have never done this before?" But never, she thought, with you, and perhaps never shall again. "Give me your hand. The ground's uneven here, but I know it."

He gave her his hand, trusting like a child; and so they set off at a good, brisk pace, across the neck of land to the next coil of the winding Severn, skirting the Frankish suburb outside the walls, and heading north-west for Shelton and beyond.

"My husband's manor," she said, pointing across the river, "lies over there. Do you remember?"

"I remember. I trust your father got his money back?"

"The first half was paid. And the remainder surely will be, or the sheriff will need to know why. Strange," she said, "how change begins. How a life can turn suddenly and move away on another course."

"Yes," he said, "strange indeed." And he was thinking of Henry's eyes, stripped clear of all secrecy for one instant, hungrily desiring the death of the Mortimers. He was thinking of his own life, so open and thoughtless and clear, turning away upon a new course from the revelation of murder.

"And there," she said, "beyond his manor, the old Leybourne lands begin. There are no Leybournes now, they're all dead, the land fell into the hands of Sir Roger de Trumpeton, but he never comes near it. He has leased it out, like so many others, and sold parts of it. You cannot work land here now by feudal labour. My father bought a holding there, with fields running down to the river, but for a Welshman it's impossible now to buy land, and unwise even to keep what he bought before. An old journeyman of his owns the place today, Walter Hanner. A simpleton, but an English simpleton. It was a way of keeping it. A farm by the river here is worth a great deal. Far enough from the town, close enough to a clear run westward."

"You store the woollens there, until they can be moved south?"

"And other things," she said, "until they can be moved west."

"Men?" He could ask it simply enough now, between two friends who had no secrets.

"Men and arms—bows, arrows, swords, pikes, lances…Even money. You cannot fight without money."

"That I've found out for myself," he said ruefully. "Though I had thought it hardly applied to Owen. He seems to keep men in the field with nothing but the splendour of his countenance and the promise of plunder."

She smiled. "That may once have been true of our people, but you've changed us to your own pattern. Look, ahead there where the trees begin. Did you see a gleam of light across the water?"

They had followed the long, soft winding of the river upstream, north-west from the town, first at a distance, glimpsing the metallic sheen of the surface only occasionally, but now they drew close to the banks again; and ahead of them copses of scattered trees closed in above the shores, an ideal screen.

"Yes, there!" It came and went in one instant, tall and upright like a thin lance of light kindled and put out in one breath. "A door opened and closed!"

"Walter's toft. It lies on the edge of the trees. The barn beyond, in the field, is bigger than the house. And such a riverside toft needs no excuse for having its own boat. There's the elver run in the spring. And good fishing—even salmon in season."

"It was well chosen," he said appreciatively. For men on the run from north or midlands there was no major water to cross to reach this refuge, and north-west to Glyndyfrdwy, or due west for Montgomery and beyond, there would not be wanting, from this point on, way-stations where a Welshman might lie overnight in safety. He found his mind assessing the need and the means, as though he had been Welsh himself.

"We're in time," said Julian, satisfied. "Watch, and when next the door opens, you'll see that a shadow slips through the light. A man. I've counted four. There are still two to come. One boatload must be already on its way."

They were in the trees now, and almost opposite the distant cottage. "Hush!" she said, stiffening into stillness and holding him still by the hand, which had grown to her hand like body to soul. Somewhere close, they heard a horse blow placidly through distended nostrils, and the shifting of hooves on solid soil, muted and soft, felt rather than heard. But there was another sound also, the faint ripple of water in regular rhythm, sliding along muffled oars.

She drew him on again, glad and content. There were horses hobbled among the trees, he counted six, but thought there were more. And suddenly out of the shadows before them a man started, and stood in their path, plucking a long dagger half out of its sheath. The darkness hid the weapon, but the ready gesture they both knew. Julian stretched an imperious arm across Hotspur's body and drew him close behind her, holding him there between her hands.

Nothing stranger had ever happened to him. It caused the breath to halt in him for a moment, though not with fear, and not with shame. He felt the laughter of astonishment and joy and admiration rising in him like a tide, and would have picked her up bodily and lifted her aside out of harm's way, but that she was his captain here, and he had no such right. She knew what she was doing; it was for him to obey her.

"Brother John!" she said softly. "You know me. I am Julian Parry. Where is Iago? We have letters for him."

There was little of the Franciscan left about Brother John Caldwell, after a month of rest and convalescence and labour here on Walter Hanmer's farm. His grey hair was cropped, his beard shaven, he moved firmly upon those once crippled feet, and wore the homespun tunic and chausses of the peasant cultivator as if he had grown up and grown old in them. She was lucky to have encountered here on watch a man who remembered her with gratitude as his hostess and guide; a stranger might have struck first and asked afterwards.

"Is it you, mistress? Who's that with you?"

"A friend—Iago knows him well. He has letters for the Lord Owen. Where is Iago?"

"Down there by the water. Go down to him." And he came a part of the way after them, to be sure of the import of that meeting. Well as he knew her, he watched narrowly; women, even men, could be duped into treason.

Between the trees the water gleamed, shaken by the motion of the boat as it came quietly in to shore. Three men in it, and a fourth to take the boat back for the remaining three. It seemed a light load, until they saw the bundled, straw-wrapped pikes being lifted ashore, and leather rolls the length of a cloth-yard arrow. They slid down the last grass-slope into the gravel, and the men who had jumped ashore saw them and clapped hands to daggers, looming about them suddenly and ominously, in black silence.

"I am Julian Parry," said Julian, spreading her empty hands to view, and putting back the hood of her cloak, but never moving from within touch of Hotspur, and never ceasing to interpose her body between him and the hesitant steel. He was ready at the first move to swing her into cover at his back, but he would not have had her know it for anything in the world. "Do you think," she said scornfully, "that Brother John would have let us pass if he had had any doubts. We want Iago Vaughan. We have letters for him."

He came round a curve of the bank from where the pack-ponies stamped and grazed, dropping with the lightness and aplomb of a deer to the waterside. "I heard my name. Who wants me?"

Then he saw her, and even in the dimness, familiar now and no trouble to him, and quickened by the lambent light from the water, he knew the man she had brought with her. For an instant he stood stock-still, taking into swift reckoning every consideration for which he was accountable; and every man present froze with him. And Julian smiled, though no one saw the smile clearly, and only Hotspur knew, from the touch of her hand and the ease of her body close to him, how sure she was of the outcome. Because Iago knew him so well, and trusted him so unquestioningly? Or because she had power over Iago, whether she knew it consciously or not, and defied him to meddle with anything she did?

"Very well met, my lord!" said Iago, breaking out of the ice that had cased him, and starting all his men alive in the act. He looked about him sharply, and they bent to work with the bundled arms. The boat had already touched at the far shore, and was on its silent way back again, laden low with five men aboard. "What brings you out here looking for me?" he said, and held out his hand like a prince upon his own ground.

"You recommended me to Julian," said Hotspur, "and now she must recommend me to you. I came tonight asking her for a means of getting urgent letters to the Lord Owen, and at my entreaty and under my bond she has brought me here. Tomorrow would have been too late, you would have been somewhere in Wales. And we had no means of knowing how long it would be before we could hope to see you here again."

"She did well," said Iago. "I'll take your letters gladly."

The boat touched again, a faint, hissing ripple running before it into the gravel. Four more shadowy shapes came up laden from the shore to hem them in, and the fourth was Rhodri Parry, girded for action in a short woollen tunic, and booted to the knee, with a dagger at his belt, half a world away from the wealthy merchant in his long, furred gown, with his barred and locked treasury and his carved chair by the solar fire. He stood and looked upon them steadily and long, calculating; but he said nothing above an undertone, for sounds carry in a still night, and by his own estimate he was a timid man.

The scroll that Hotspur took from the lining of his cloak was thick and closely sealed.

"It is superscribed to the Lord Owen. But there is a second letter enclosed, for Sir Edmund Mortimer. The covering one is to ask the Lord Owen's courtesy in delivering it to his prisoner."

"He shall have it. And say he does so deliver it, and Sir Edmund desires and is allowed to reply—where shall I find you?"

"So he reads and heeds what I've written," said Hotspur, "the reply is not urgent. Leave the answer for me with Mistress Parry or her father here, and I will enquire for it when I ride north from this parliament."

Rhodri heard and did not demur. The letter vanished into the breast of Iago's cotte. "I will do so," he said.

It was done; the act contemplated had become an act committed, the first rustle of an avalanche, though as yet hardly a grain of the ground on which he stood was in motion. Nor was there any course recommended to Edmund in the letter, and yet he felt that he had loosed an arrow that could not be called back, even if he would.

"It is plain," he had written, the bald facts having been recounted, "that the king will neither move to ransom you himself, nor listen to any proposal to that end from another, nor, if he can prevent, will he even allow your friends and kin to ransom you themselves at their own expense. I am forced to the knowledge that he is set against you, and against all your house, and since you have always done him honourable service, it can only be for a reason which is not far to seek. No other family in this realm stands legally between him and the crown, as yours does. So far as I can see, this sick disposition in him cannot mend, but must worsen. I can only advise you, therefore, not to place any trust in his goodwill, or ever allow yourself to be kept too close to him or too much hemmed in by his power or his officers, when you shall be at liberty again, but to stay within the safe borders of your own estates, where you are at the advantage, and to have loyal persons always close to you. In this pass, dear Edmund, it is for you to take thought where your best interests lie, and to do everything to ensure them. On the affections of your kin, and most of my Elizabeth and myself, you know you can rely. And should there be any further happening of which you ought to know, I will get word to you by the same hand. For Roger's children, I would I might withdraw them out of his hold, but the means to that end is not yet in sight."

And so with family news and the greetings that pass between brothers, to the end. It would have been treason to Edmund not to write as much.

"There are horses across the water," said Rhodri, gruffly offering what hospitality he could here. "If you care to cross, you can ride back to Shrewsbury, but it means waiting until the gate opens in the morning."

"I thank you, but no, I'd liefer not meddle in your moves more than I have already, and I can be at the abbey before light, without, I'm told, entering the town."

"I am coming with you," said Julian, "to show you the way."

"No need, I shall find it, and I've tired you out enough. You can return in safety with your father."

"No, for I must be ready to pass through the gate as soon as the bridge is lowered at dawn. The fewer who know I've been out of the house, the better."

She had her way. They walked back together.

"And he has been doing this now for a year and more?" he asked wonderingly, as they walked through grass now heavy with dew.

The Welshmen by the waterside had ceased their loading of the horses and stood silent to gaze after them until they vanished, their eyes suspicious though their tongues made no complaint. After they were gone perhaps there had been complaints, too, questions, doubts, even blame. But she had no doubts; she answered all such queries without hesitation, letting him into intricacies he need not have shared. And suddenly he trembled for her and for himself, as though everything they did and said together was driving them softly but certainly into some action they would not, in the end, be able to avoid.

"Yes, before ever I knew you. But I was not in all his secrets then, and I did not know what risks he was taking. He always used to claim that he was a timorous man," she said, and laughed.

"Faith, with a few thousand such timorous men I could win a kingdom, and so may Owen yet."

He was an officer of the king, and he was in possession of knowledge of the king's enemies, and fully intended to withhold that knowledge, to make no use of it, not even to disrupt the traffic itself without penalty to those involved. A private promise counted for more than his oath of allegiance, and a private affection than his duty to the crown. The paradox baffled him. And yet he was a man not accustomed to question the promptings of his blood, or to lose any sleep over things done and never to be undone.

They walked at ease, for they had time enough, all the rest of the night to employ before he could well go in at the abbey gate and retrieve his horse, and she pass in by the English gate of the town and slip unnoticed, if possible, back into her own home. It was late October, but mild and still, several warm days past, and a few yet to follow before the season turned unkind again. And they were lightened in heart at having done what they had set out to do, and at peace now in the night, their eyes gifted with sight, and their ears sensitive even to the rare nocturnal stirrings of bird and beast.

"Julian—it's a rare name. She's one of your patron saints in Shrewsbury, I think?"

"They give it to their daughters sometimes in St. Julian's parish," she said. "She was a virgin martyr. The Romans killed her. She was eighteen years old—I've already outlived her."

"You? You have a whole life before you yet."

"Certain it is," she said, "that until this year I have nothing resembling a life behind me."

"Then there's all still to come, and you are blessed."

"It is truth," said Julian, exultant, "so I am!" For walking thus beside him in the night, speaking with him, being silent with him and still companionable and close, touching him for guidance where the way was complex, once lifted between his hands across a brook that came down to the river: conscious of all this, and having achieved with him some prodigy not yet fully understood, which neither of them could have done alone, and which bound them lifelong in this rare union for which no name or comparison existed, she would not have changed places with any creature on earth.

The way back was longer, since they had to skirt round half the town, keeping to the high ground on the western side of the river. But the miles passed merrily, pensively, tranquilly, without any thought of haste or ending, the dawn being so far away. It was as though they had set out together on a walk that would continue thus confidently and single-heartedly to the farthest reach of their vision, to his life's end or hers.

10

As suddenly as Sir Henry Percy had left his house in Bishopsgate Street, he was back again; and almost before he was missed in parliament or in the king's council, he was there once more in his place.

His reappearance was so calmly managed and so clearly to be taken for granted that those who had rumoured storms behind his back felt themselves on very insecure ground, and moderated their predictions of a rift with the crown. True, the king did not, so far, admit him to intimate speech or include him in his personal invitations, nor had Hotspur himself sought any audience of the king. But they met, watched by every eye, in the sessions of parliament and the meetings of council, they exchanged decorous and unremarkable words upon those topics on which Hotspur might be expected to have special knowledge, they brushed sleeves at court and treated each other with restraint and reserve, but with every proper consideration.

"You took too great a risk," said Worcester in private, but without any note of blame. "The boy had brought him to send for you and patch up the dissension, and you were gone. It was the wrong moment to vanish out of his reach, and there are those who have made use of it."

"I doubt not," said Hotspur, unmoved. "I have come back, have I not, and behaved myself very seemly, and so I'll continue to do. But don't ask more of me."

"Or of him?" said Worcester, and smiled. "He has not let the prince work on him again. And as well, or he'd have had the thankless task of working on you, also. No, I don't ask more of you, Harry. God knows I could not stomach it myself to suggest that you should come to heel and make offers to him of what you first denied. But that he'll never ask of you again, for fear of a further shame. No, all we need of you is that you shall carry yourself thus quiet and serviceable and without reproach, and leave it to others to plant the idea in him that you will yet come round out of your anger and offence to be his loyal and loving vassal as before."

"And am I not?" said Hotspur, with lifted brow and curling lips.

"That, you best know, Harry," said Worcester softly, and so left him.

The prince came, also, and that was difficult, painful and endearing, for the boy all but apologised for failing in a mission in which he could not possibly have succeeded; and if there was anything in the world that could have brought Hotspur to a reconciliation, it would have been the prospect of assuaging Hal's distress and rewarding his heroic efforts. But he was spared that, for it seemed the king would have none of it now. He wanted no open break, he wanted no break at all, short of desperation, but neither would he bend his own neck again and admit his own vulnerability so far as to make the first approach. It suited him better that the clash should be smoothed over by day-to-day contacts and a measure of restraint on both sides, until all interest in it died.

"As it will," said the prince eagerly. "You see he means to pretend, even to himself, that nothing has happened. In a while he will even believe it. He thinks of nothing now but the duchess's coming to England to join him. You know he hopes to bring her over from Brittany for Christmas, if he can, or very soon afterwards."

Always he spoke of her as "the duchess," never "the queen." And indeed, she was not yet crowned, nor could she be until she reached England, but by proxy she was already his father's wife.

"I know. My uncle of Worcester is going with your uncle of Somerset to fetch her, as soon as parliament rises."

"My two uncles," Hal corrected with a thin smile. "The bishop of Lincoln goes with them." He was on good terms with his Beaufort kin, the fruit of John of Gaunt's long liaison with his daughters' governess, whom he had scandalised England by taking as his third wife after his royal consort's death. Sometimes Hotspur had felt that the boy had more use for these belatedly legitimised Beaufort bastards than for his own brothers, though he was indulgently kind to the younger boys, almost as to children of a different generation. But when the Beauforts were sent as escorts to his new step-mother, even they came within the range of his sore animosity.

"Don't judge the poor lady too soon," Hotspur said good-humouredly, "she can hardly be blamed for looking to her own defences, and arguably she must be truly fain, or she would not have risked so large a step. You may yet find her as kind and true a friend as a second mother can be."

"I am past the need," said the boy with a forbidding face, and laughed at himself the next moment. "Oh, Harry, my little brothers are looking forward! They've ordered a pair of gold tablets for her as a gift. And I must do my part, too, it would not be seemly to hold back. And indeed, if she gives him, as you said once, a little happiness, she'll have done more than I can do, perhaps for us all. For he is *not* happy!" said Hal, grieved and impatient and censorious all at once. "What is it he wants?"

A quiet mind, thought Hotspur; but he did not say it. "A crown is no light weight," he said, and meant it as sacredly as if he had uttered his first thought.

"No—I've already made note of that. It will touch me, in the end, will it not?" His voice was wary and measuring, but quite unafraid.

The boy felt cheered before he left, though he had come rather to cheer Hotspur. In the doorway he hesitated, which for him was rare enough, and meant a balance of judgment equally rare.

"Harry…do you remember we spoke once, in passing, of the earl of the March of Scotland?"

"Dunbar?" said Hotspur, surprised. "Why, what of him?"

"I think—I fear—he is not your friend. If you suspect he may use the king for his own ends, having forsworn his own king in Scotland for a grudge, so do I suspect he may make use of your house, which is the chief power in the north, to cultivate his own interest with the king. I have no sound reason…" (He was lying, of course; his cheek—that smooth right cheek turned upon his friend—always reddened to scarlet when he lied.) "It is only a feeling. But never trust him too far."

"Why, the man is anxious for himself and his own, as we all are, Hal, and no doubt my eclipse would leave room for his star to rise. But we all direct our own fate by what we do. If I fall, it will be by my own hand, not Dunbar's."

"And by your own folly, you would say?" The boy smiled, for he thought of Hotspur as a repository of pure natural wisdom, not his own kind, but a kind he would most gladly have had for his own.

"Folly, wickedness, virtue, ambition—who knows what it will be called? But above all," said Hotspur, holding the torch high on the staircase as they went down together, "and past doubt, mine own."

On Sunday, November the 26th, after the rise of parliament, the king feasted all the members of his lords and commons, the earl of Northumberland conveying his gracious invitation to both houses. Sir Henry Percy was gloriously present among his peers, moving inviolable among those who had speculated pleasurably upon his disgrace not long ago. And the king, after the wine had flowed freely for a while, was notably civil to him, and showed him some favours that caused a further drawing in of horns. The Douglas episode was past, clearly, and the withholding of that turbulent foe accepted in order to avoid a more disastrous conflict. Percy was worth a modicum of restraint, even if it meant swallowing a rebuff not normally endurable to kings. Those who were courtiers born came to the conclusion that it was a good investment to court the Percies, for clearly their sway was strong.

Hotspur, who could not love courtiers, found the occasion irksome, and practised restraint in his turn only at his father's reminder and entreaty. There were Roger's hostage children to be remembered.

But even that night of festivities ended at last, and they were all free to disperse. The good commoners to their boroughs and shires, their wives and children and Christmas cheer, the lords to their own estates, to keep the feast in their own regional style, the earl of Worcester, with his fellow-envoys the bishop of Lincoln and the earl of Somerset, to take ship from Southampton, bound for Brittany to bring the new queen home, and the king to settle down at Windsor for Christmas. Hotspur separated himself, upon the excuse of business in Shrewsbury and Chester, from his father's processional north in state, and rode with a small escort westwards to the abbey of St. Peter and St. Paul, to hold open audience one day for any who came, and by night, and alone, to walk up into the town and make his way to the house of the Fleece near St. Chad's church.

He was prepared, this time, to be face to face with her as soon as the wicket opened before him, and have her hand reach out to guide him. It would have seemed to him a jarring discord to be admitted by any other at this door.

"How did you know? Who told you to expect me? *What* told you? Do you stand always just within this doorway, waiting for certain people to come? Iago...myself...who else?"

"They said in the town that you were at the abbey," she said, "and that you would go north tomorrow. There was no possibility but tonight. Surely I knew you would come. The letter is here for you, more than a week ago."

"Is your father within?" He would not enter unless he knew. His conscience was not easy about this young and beautiful widow, with a whole life before her, untroubled, God willing, by intrusive lords and inconsiderate politics. He touched her hand quickly to his lips, a motion of contrition rather than anything more personal, but the contact flamed through him painfully. He was back with her again by the Severn, Julian the virgin martyr, not the muted widow, the soldier of Wales who had put an English general behind her and held him there between her peremptory palms from Welsh steel.

She drew down their linked hands strongly, and swooping with that dark-gold head of hers, returned the kiss upon his hard male fingers. There was nothing he could do to reprove her or restrain; she was her own law. But he was so shaken and moved that he reached up to touch her cheek with his free hand, in a motion of distracted and bewildered tenderness.

"Julian, Julian...where are we going, you and I both?"

"Where we must," she said, "both you and I. But where that is I do not know or care. I am going. I shall find out where."

"And I? How am I to know if I'm going right?"

"I believe in your rightness of judgment as in the Host. Come in, my lord, and read your letter."

He went with her, the candle lighting them up the stairs and into the solar, where Rhodri Parry rose in ceremony to receive him. That was good, it set him back firmly into the framework of state and rank, loaded him again with the obligations of his office. Drinking wine gravely with this Welsh magnate was only an apparent paradox, not a real one.

They brought him the letter. "By your leave!" he said, and broke the seal and read.

"Most dear brother Harry,"

Edmund had written:

"For your warning I send you my heartfelt thanks, and give you to know, by this writing, that what you have told me concerning the king's mood and intent does but confirm an inclination which

has been budding within me now some weeks, and wanted only the impulse of your news to prompt me to act upon it.

"To make all clear, I have been received and entertained here with a courtesy and care not always to be found by prisoners of war, and I owe my present rude health and spirits to the usage I have encountered, being now completely restored, and healed of my wounds. Having given my parole, I ride and exercise as any free man, and enjoy the privileges of a guest. But I have more than this, and your word of the king's mind towards me has caused me to consider, indeed, where my best interests lie. If I decide with my heart, you will be the last to blame me.

"I have been blessed here by the ministrations of a most lovely and accomplished lady, not only my kind nurse while I was sick, but my dear companion now that I am well. She is young and tender, and I have not ventured to make to her any earnests of my love, but she in her goodness has afforded me signs enough that she returns the feeling I have for her, and as I believe, her family would not be adverse to my advances. Conceive, then, with what convictions of the guidance of God I have received your letter. You urge me to give thought where my best interests lie, when I am in torment to turn in this one direction; and truly it does seem to me that you have pointed me the way my own heart desires to go. For if I have nothing to hope from England, who live and rule always in some peril on its borders, may I not in all earnest look rather to Wales, in contact with which land, no less, my estates lie, and from which land I can as well receive support?

"In short, Harry, I am resolved now to approach—as up to now I have not done—the Lord Owen, my captor, and ask him not simply for terms of peace, as I well might have done in whatever case, failing the king's interest, but also for the hand of his youngest daughter Catherine in marriage. For I love her as never I thought to love any lady, and will have none other but her, whether she will take me or no, as long as I live. And so be my *messenger to my sweet sister, and assure her of my love second only to that I bear this gentle jewel, my Catherine, whom she, too, will love if ever I may bring the two together. Hers was the first face I saw when I opened my eyes in this place, and she has been to me ever as friend, sister, protector, and lover, so my sister cannot but love her in return. And you must do as Elizabeth does, for I well know that you enjoy even such a love as I now feel, and cannot therefore grudge me the fruits. And as for the Lord Owen, I do believe he is already ware, and will not deny what I ask. And the more surely to disarm him, what his daughter asks!*

"Harry, if I do ill by your measure, believe that I do right by mine, for I can no other. And carry my love and service to my own Elizabeth, until I can bring to her—if God so grant ever— my dearest Catherine, to be my best advocate. Until which time I take my leave, with the promise to send you word of whatever further decision I may take. And in the meantime, I beg you care for your own wellbeing, and guard yourself from every enemy, for surely they are legion, and come in many guises.

"With my most humble duty to my true brother and my loving sister, in all affection,

"Edmund Mortimer."

He looked up from reading, and found Julian's eyes upon him, black and grave. "All is well?" she said.

He pondered that without haste, and said at length, with deliberation and decision: "All is well. All is very well!" And it seemed to him that all occasions, all omens, all prophetic utterances, everything that had befallen him since first he had set eyes on this girl, combined to drive him in one direction and toward one action, and that would be the climactic action of his life, for better or worse. The tide which had carried both him and Henry far beyond any goal they had ever set themselves had ebbed now, and left him isolated in the race of a contrary tide no less irresistible. But this time he saw, however dimly and imperfectly, where it was carrying him; and this time he was faced with the final judgment, and must of his own will go with it, or of his own might tear himself out of its power and strike out strongly against it. Old impatience with London policies, old sympathy with a gallant enemy and a genuine grievance, the almost accidental involvement with this patriot household, the well-intentioned approaches which had wound him deeper and deeper into their secrets, the strong loyalty to his blood-kin ill-used and imperilled, indignation over his own shabby usage, everything flowed into one powerful stream threatening to sweep him away. But he was still on his feet, and he could still choose.

If Edmund had not just taken such a giant's stride towards making the decision for him! For between king and kin, between the oath of fealty and the bond of the blood, dearly though he valued both, the choice for Hotspur was no choice at all.

"I think," he said, his eyes holding hers, "there will be some further letter for me, all in good time. And I think it cannot be long. Ask Iago, of his kindness, to make use of my purse and my ring this time without stint, and bring or send me my kinsman's letter at Bamburgh, by whatever means and whatever safe hand he may. His messenger shall not lose by his journey so far north. And if he come himself, the more welcome," he said. "There will be letters for him to take back into Wales."

⁓⁓

The envoys to Brittany embarked from Southampton on a stormy sea, and beat southward as best they could, only to be driven back by contrary winds, and forced ever westwards until they were obliged to put back into harbour in Plymouth, far off their course. There was no possibility of putting to sea again but in a refitted ship, and in better conditions. At Windsor the king received their letter reporting their disasters and asking for fresh orders and more liberal funds, and it seemed that even the winter was evilly leagued against him, to keep his bride from him, and with her that lost content he had hoped to regain from her hands as a wedding gift. His own gift to her, a jewelled gold collar of wonderful workmanship, was ready and waiting for her coming, but the severing sea would not let her come.

This was his case, some ten days into December, when word came to him, a thunderbolt out of a grey but tranquil sky, that Sir Edmund Mortimer, prisoner in Wales, for want of any prospect of ransom by his peers, had made terms of peace with Owen Glendower, man to man, and taken to wife the Welsh prince's daughter, Catherine.

Here was he, King Henry, aching alone, separated from his queen by a wintry sea; and somewhere in the western mountains the Welsh rebel's daughter had opened her bed to a joyful bridegroom, and worse, one who brought with him half the territory of the upper Wye, and much of Maelienydd, a great tract gouged out of the centre of the march, lost to England. Lost, if "terms of peace" meant what he dreaded it must mean, a simple transference of allegiance in this marriage. Though that did not necessarily follow, for supposing even Glendower had doubts of the ending, and might be glad to see a daughter of his set up on English soil and consort to an English nobleman? Young men do love, and Mortimer was young, and the girl, they said, very young, and there might yet be no more in this than a love-match, and the compounding out of good will for a ransom paid gradually from revenue, and the security of one, at least, of Owen's household. For he had other daughters to provide for. Even older men, the king thought, aware of the ache of longing within him, for some private peace that no one but Joan could supply, do love. It is not a legend.

But he could not subdue the dread that once again a Mortimer was to be the rock on which the sovereign came to wreck. With all that good border country lost to England and added to Wales—if the Mortimer castellans held to their lord rather than their king, and when had they chosen otherwise?—what was there to keep Owen from encroaching far into the marches, eating away the territory of Shropshire and Herefordshire? No, this was to be too gloomy a prophet! To hold the Mortimer lands was not necessarily to be able to use them for assault purposes, rather they would be always beleaguered. Hal was there, sharp as a lance and steady as a Cheshire bowman between Chester and Shrewsbury, with quick sense and merciless judgment.

No, it was too soon to judge and condemn. What Mortimer's bargain meant would come out soon enough, no need to rush ahead too fast into despair. Before Christmas the issue might show plain to be read. And before Christmas, or very soon after, these contrary winds must cease, that kept the escort still fuming helplessly ashore, and Joan would be able to make the crossing. And after that he would never again be so desolately alone.

He turned his mind wholly to perfecting his feverish preparations for her reception. She loved music, as he did—they had corresponded, he knew her tastes as he knew his own. His musicians attended him everywhere he went, but of late his interest had flagged sadly. And his flute—he had not practised now for many months, he must get his hand in again during the festivities, ready to play for her. The choir of the household chapel, too, had been somewhat neglected in the press of affairs, he must give his mind to choosing some new music for them in her honour.

Once, he remembered strangely, his heart turning in him with a sharp pain, Mary had sung to his flute, a middle voice, full and sweet and true, a half-fledged nightingale…

Mortimer married to the Welsh girl, his peace made…And what of my peace, the king thought, counting the days in Windsor.

It was on the 15th day of December that a solitary horseman, warmly cloaked and shrouded in a furred capuchin, rode up the coastal track from Embleton, and climbed the great ramps of the hill towards Bamburgh castle, looking eastwards over the undulating dunes and the bleak and troublous sea. He was well mounted, having changed horses no farther away than Warkworth, upon the mandate of a ring known to carry the authority of Sir Henry Percy. The same ring let him in without question at the Constable tower, and up the steep rise to the bailey gate.

They brought him at once across the inner ward and through the great hall to the small cabinet where Hotspur was conferring with his steward. At sight of the ring in the page's hand he started up from his chair and pushed the rolls away from him, and the steward, interpreting his look, rose and shook his papers into order, and left the room. Elizabeth, who was stitching at a dress for her little daughter by the fireside, gathered up her work and would have followed his example, but Hotspur laid a hand on her arm.

"No, stay with us. This is Edmund's messenger, who has a better right than you to welcome him?"

The stranger came in on the heels of his guide, and the chill of the outside air, close to frost, entered in the folds of his garments. He had tossed back the cloak from his shoulders and the capuchin from his head, a faun's narrow, fleshless head, with eyes like two slivers of wintry blue sky, and a short, clipped dark beard through which two curving russet streaks flared like flames. He was plainly dressed under his winter cloak, like a peasant or a small yeoman, but on this journey he wore both sword and dagger, and wore them casually and gracefully, as one well able to use them at need. He was lean and wiry and moved like a lusty hound, yet it seemed to Elizabeth that he had one shoulder a little hunched and misshapen. Then the cloak slipped back from that shoulder, and uncovered the worn and polished frame of the little harp he carried there.

"You're welcome to Bamburgh, Iago! My lady, I make known to you at last Master Iago Vaughan, who has done his own lord and our house very valuable service."

"You are he," she said, holding out her hand to him warmly, "who restored me my peace of mind concerning a dear brother. You and the lady—I remember her well. How glad I am to be able to thank you in person!"

When he kissed her fingers, barely brushing them with his lips, the chill of frost touched her there briefly; it was a bleak road up from Warkworth in the winter months, with the sea wind blowing.

"Madam, I am your servant." She was aware that the blue eyes, so clear and pale but not cold, rather of a fiery brightness, observed her attentively from under his lowered lashes. For this was the candid face and the bold and generous hand that had welcomed an unknown young widow at Shrewsbury abbey as guest and friend, without question or condescension.

Hotspur weighed the pebble ring lightly in his palm, and held it out to be slipped back upon Iago's finger. "You may need it still on the way back. Had you to use it often?"

"There was a check on your borders, my lord. I had no need of it until then, and from then on I did not scruple to show it at once, to speed my passage and pick up fresh horses." He brought out a sealed roll from the lining of his cloak. "For you, my lord, from Sir Edmund Mortimer."

"He is well?" Elizabeth asked eagerly.

"Madam, he is."

"And happy?" she said.

"And happy." He said it gently, for in a sense she was losing a great part of her right in Mortimer, not only to his young wife, but to those new brothers and sisters he had acquired in his marriage, a whole novel life opening to him and leading him away from her. But her face as she heard of Edmund's wellbeing was entirely joyous and grateful. "You must not leave us soon," she said, like a child wishful to reward someone who had given her pleasure. "Bide with us over the feast."

Hotspur sat with the unrolled letter spread between his hands on the table, and pondered for a long minute after he had read it to the end. He heard but hardly marked their exchanges. It was very well that Edmund should be happy, but even that felicity must be paid for by someone; and perhaps not Edmund himself, or his unknown

Catherine. Here there was far more at stake, and upon this chess-board Iago was as vulnerable a piece as they.

"Listen," he said abruptly, "to what Edmund writes." And he read aloud:

> "*Most dear brother,*
>
> "*I send you by this messenger word of my considered intent, as I promised; and I write it upon the same day in which I have written certain other letters, all of the same tenor, to Sir John Grendor of Herefordshire, Hywel Fychan of Rhayadr, and others my associates and castellans in those parts. These letters will be despatched two days after Iago sets out with this to you, that you may be among the first to hear what I purpose, and be prepared for whatever may follow.*
>
> "*To all my captains and garrisons I have written that as from this date I have adopted, and will adhere to, the programme of my father-in-law, the most noble prince, Owen, lord of Glyndyfrdwy and Cynllaith. That is: in the room of the usurper Henry of Lancaster, now reigning, to place upon the throne of England, which is rightfully his, my nephew Edmund Mortimer, earl of March, and to secure to Prince Owen for all time his right in Wales.*
>
> "*This is the cause to which I am pledged from this day forth, and I desire to proclaim it before all who know me, and to devote to its fulfilment all the resources I possess both in lands and men.*
>
> "*That you will approve this act of mine I do not dare assume or declare. Indeed I make it public to all the world that neither you nor any other has ever prompted me to it, that it is my decision, and mine alone. I do but set it forth to you in all humility, dear Harry, and leave to your own heart what your part shall be. And whatever it be, I will never say the loath word, nor suffer any man to speak blame. I would not upon my life speak out thus for any man but myself, but for myself I can neither do nor say any less or any other.*

*"'And so with my reverence and love, and in the happiness of
my heart, I greet you and my Elizabeth, and trust in God's time
to see you again in peace.*
"'In all respect and affection,
"'Edmund Mortimer.'"

There was a brief and absolute silence when his voice ceased.
Elizabeth had grown pale and tall and still as she listened, her lips
parted, and her eyes suddenly fixed upon a distance where many
impulses contended. She could be as quick as any man to weigh and
compare and choose, and as bold as any man to make that choice
and abide by it once it was made. She could even stand back from
the natural desires of her own heart, and see them for the perilous
things they were, able to ruin and kill; and still, if that remained
her choice, go after them with all her might. Yet now she held
marvellously still, containing her ardour and her doubt, and even
her maternal, protective ferocity, everything that prompted her to
prompt him. Where all things conspired to urge him, she would
not join the conspiracy. He saw her withdraw mysteriously behind
the veil of her womanliness, leaving him unfurnished. The focus of
her eyes changed and shortened, coming to rest in his. She smiled
at him. Where he went he must go because he willed; and what
her choice would have been she would never reveal, now or at
any other time, in success or failure, triumph or ruin. Simply, she
would go with him wherever he set out to go, and never complain
of the hardships on the way, or repent the journey though it ended
in disaster.

He smiled at her, rolling up Edmund's letter gently between his
hands. And he wondered if the news had yet reached Windsor,
or was about to break there like one more baleful echo of the
September storm.

"Yes, stay, Iago," he said mildly, "spend Christmas here with us.
Why not? What need will they have of you while the frost holds,

who is going to disturb the peace? This is not the time for battles and couriers and campaigning."

Iago shook his head, though he smiled. "I would, gladly, but I have work still in Shrewsbury. I must set out tomorrow, or the next day without fail."

"Then for two nights, at any rate, you are our guest. And at last I may hear you harp for your supper. Before you go south," said Hotspur, "with my answer to your lord, and to Edmund Mortimer."

They sat long in hall that night, and there was good music and good wine. And Iago Vaughan, having drunk as deep as any and being as well advanced into intoxication as his impervious constitution would let him go, took the little harp in his arm, and played and sang while the musicians of Bamburgh drew breath. He began in English, but soon fell into the trance of his own art, and strayed into his native Welsh, where few or none here could follow him. He fixed his eyes upon Hotspur at the high table, and thought of the girl in Shrewsbury who never ceased to see that wide brown gaze and lofty brow, and could not see the rest of the world, not even Iago Vaughan, for the dazzle of their brightness blinding her eyes.

Presently, because it was December, and the Welsh were in arms again, his tongue wandered back with him in time to another December, more than a hundred years past, to the fields on the banks of the Irfon, close by Builth, where an obscure lancer struck down the last prince of Wales in the native line, Llewelyn ap Griffith, in the half-melted snow, and never even knew the magnitude of the disaster he had wrought, the great body lying cold and unrecognised all that day.

The wine went round, the hall was hung with green boughs, and Christmas was on the doorstep; but Iago Vaughan lifted to the dark Northumbrian night his sweet, poignant, inconsolable lament, in a language no one about him understood, and felt within himself not

only the long-drawn grief of remembrance, but the ominous fire of
prophecy, as he sang of the death of princes:

"O God, that the wind and the rain should carry it,
And the sullen waves along the shore, and the oaks
  threshing and crying,
The name of the lost one, the valiant one, never to be
  recovered.
O God, that the sea might roll over this land
Rather than leave us to this waste of sorrow without end
For the bright golden eagle, the great one, the gallant one
  gone from us!"

11

✦

Joan of Navarre, duchess of Brittany and queen of England, left Nantes on the day after Christmas, and set sail from Camaret for Southampton on the 13th of January. The contrary weather that had kept her English escort still kicking its heels helplessly on the other side of the Channel permitted her to embark from the southern shore, but did not give her an easy passage, for the fierce easterly winds continued, driving her ship far west, and only after five stormy days was the vessel able to put in, not at Southampton, but Falmouth.

The king's desultory after-Christmas progress had brought him and his household to Clarendon, in Wiltshire, when he heard the news that his bride had landed safely in the west country. It was like the breaking through of the sun and the promise of spring. Everything that was evil and threatening, the march in jeopardy, his purse, as usual, empty, his parliament critical and parsimonious, his council divided, Mortimer a defector, everything that irked and depressed him was swept far away to the back of his mind, not solved but in abeyance, and grown transparent and unreal in the radiance of Joan's arrival. He chose a small party as escort, with John Norbury as always close to his elbow, and rode away like a love-sick young squire to meet his bride.

The queen and her little daughters, with their servants and steward and retinue, had a long and wearisome journey from their far western harbour; but before they reached Exeter they were met by the English escort, and brought into the city with grand ceremony. And there Henry and his party joined them, and husband and wife met at last.

He came to her as soon as he had had time to wash away the stains of his long and precipitate ride, and make himself fine for her. When the earls of Somerset and Worcester announced him to her, and he entered the room where she sat waiting to receive him, his hands shook, and his heart rose into his throat in a surge of joy and fear. He had not seen her for five years, and then only briefly. The woman he knew was the woman who wrote warm, calm, affectionate letters to him from across the sea; her mind he did know, but its mortal envelope he might scarcely recognise.

All her attendants drew away from her chair on either side, and made deep reverences to the king of England; and Joan rose, came a few steps forward with hands extended, and laid them in his hands.

They had to cross only a few yards of paved floor, but they were crossing five years of divided living, and reaching out their hands to take up a physical acquaintance which belonged to the past; and whether it would be changed out of all knowledge, enhanced in value, or disclosed as barren and savourless, these were things they had to discover in this moment. They had eyes for no one but each other as their hands met.

Henry saw a slender, fair woman in a tight-fitting blue cotte and a gold-bordered surcoat, her hair braided high at temples and crown, and confined in a net of gold filigree. She was above the middle height, but small-featured, with fine, delicate bones, and her expression, like her movements, was eager and gentle.

Joan saw a big, heavily-built man of reddish-brown colouring and commanding presence, very splendidly attired and attended, with a short, forked beard and curling moustaches. He was as she remembered him, and yet changed. She would have known him again, and yet she might well have had difficulty in being sure that she was not mistaken. The powerful features she had known had thickened and relaxed in discouragement, there were pouches under the full brown eyes, the head stooped forward a little. His face was marred by patches of a roughened, pink eruption which she could not yet know was the consequence of emotional excitement at her coming, and would be cooled and invisible when he was rested and calm. And though he was smiling with evident and touching delight, the two upright furrows between his eyebrows were now scored far too deep for even the power of joy to erase them.

Her first marriage had been to an old man, and she had been his third wife. She had affianced herself for the second time as her own heart inclined, happy to be sought in marriage by a fine, vigorous king only five years her senior, a soldier and crusader, renowned for his exploits in tournament and field. This time she would rest in her husband's strength and regard, cared for and cherished and protected lifelong. Now she saw him again, and he was already ageing, tense and overshadowed by cares. And she knew, as he bent over her hands and kissed them, that once again, if this union was to be a force and a reality, it was she who must kindle and keep alight the flame at the heart of it.

He was not yet thirty-seven, and he looked ten years older; and if he did not at this moment look harried and tired, yet the shadow of irritation and weariness had grained itself into his face like that hectic stain into his skin, and even present joy, the depth of which she could not doubt, had no power to banish it.

She was a woman of tranquillity, decision and generosity, at least towards those who depended upon her. Before he looked up at her, over her still-cherished hands, and began to address her in somewhat insular but fluent French, she had put away out of her mind the rosy image of her own hedged and indulged security in the ward of a grand paladin, and accepted in its place, with all her heart and with little regret, this troubled and fallible man who had such hungry need of her loyalty and serenity to hedge him from the world's assaults, in private at least, if she was powerless in public. And love did not diminish as it metamorphosed itself into compassion; rather it seemed to her greater and more assured than before.

"Joan, lady, most beloved spouse, you are devoutly welcome into your realm of England, and into my heart. I have longed for this day, and its coming is inexpressible joy to me. I fear you have suffered much upon the sea, and somewhat, too, here upon our land. I trust all shall go well for you hereafter. It shall be my own special care."

"My fair lord," she said, "I rejoice to be in your presence at last, and I doubt not to be in love and goodwill with your people, now mine, as I am with you. The sea was harsh, but you see I am arrived in good heart. Whatever you propose, you shall not find me weary. And whatever you shall ask of me, you shall not find me unready. It was a winter passage, but I am here." And she smiled at him, her pale, mild, constant smile, warming him to the heart. As she had intended. It was not demonstrative passion he needed from her, but something durable; and that she had learned how to give.

"Praise be to God!" he said reverently. "You and I shall give Him thanks together that we meet at last."

The escort made their reverences, and went quietly out of the room. So did her children's nurse, marshalling the little girls by the hand, and after her the squires and the damosels, the valet and the chamberlain, all the attendants of every degree, to whose untiring attendance she was accustomed. Upon their going something grave and silent and nameless came in, no trespasser upon their solitude.

"Lady, God knows how I have longed for you," the king said, and dropped her hands to cast his arms about her and draw her into his heart. Clenched into him like one already flesh of his flesh, she felt the strong pounding of that heart, and measured her own pulse to its beat. "Joan, we shall drive together, you and I, as far as Bridport, and then I'll ride on to Winchester and make all ready for our second marriage. My brother of Lincoln will marry us. Love, consider how you will have all disposed, and it shall be done as you decree. There shall be nothing wanting that can please you…nothing!"

She freed her arms, and with dedicated deliberation folded them about him, holding him close and tenderly. "My sweet lord, there is nothing wanting. So you love me, I cannot go hungry." She took his head between her hands, that heavy, discouraged head, and kissed him on the brow, and on the lips. "I am your Grace's loyal and loving wife. Be pleased to share with me all your joy and all your grief, for there is nothing of yours I cannot bear…"

It was unfortunate, and in its small way characteristic of the fate that dogged him, that when King Henry rode joyfully ahead from Bridport to prepare his bride's royal reception at Winchester, he should forget to confirm that the bishop and the earls of her escort were left with sufficient funds for the remainder of her journey. At Dorchester, Worcester and John Norbury were compelled to borrow in order to see the queen fitly conducted to her second and resplendent marriage. But Joan was happily unaware of their embarrassments; to which, indeed, they were by now so used as to be hardly embarrassed at all. So they got her with due ceremony to Winchester by the 5th of February, to be feasted loyally there. And on the 7th of the same month the bishop of Lincoln, her new half-brother, married her formally to the king of England in Winchester cathedral. Her younger stepsons met her, flushed and eager and self-important, with their wedding-gift of gold, and the prior of Winchester lent two hundred marks of his own money to make good what was wanting when the bills came in.

So then they were man and wife, no less than king and queen, and in the midst of the hectic splendour they were islanded alone; and in the night, in the blessed quiet of their bed, they lay wreathed in each other's aims, released from the daylight necessity of being royal, a man and a woman meeting in some field of half-glad, half-sorrowful tenderness and restraint. They loved, and she pitied. It was not the best of grounds for a marriage, but it sufficed. She had, after all, had to make do with less. And he, she hoped, found a measure of happiness that somehow redounded to her pleasure, as well as her credit.

Her little girls were shy and uneasy with him. He did his best to unbend, but he was too stiff and sombre for them. He was happiest when they were out of his sight, and he could forget that they existed. She was early aware that she must always have an eye to their interests, or they would be without advocate. And girls are vulnerable in this world, and need a protector, as she knew, having been born a girl. Her loyalties, though staunchly reinforced, began to be in some sort divided; she balanced her priorities and held her peace.

After the wedding Henry and Joan journeyed together in state to London. At Blackheath a deputation of the citizens came out to meet and escort them into the city. Through Cheapside they went in procession to Westminster, and there, in mid-February, the queen was crowned and feasted with much splendour, with jousting and banqueting and every mark of reverence.

One of her stepsons, Thomas, was busy in Ireland, acting, under tutelage, as his father's viceroy. She divined, from her husband's way of speaking of his children, that Thomas was his favourite, perhaps the one most like his sire, and easiest for him to understand. The younger ones were no trouble to her, they were eager and excited, and took delight in all the ceremony and splendour that surrounded her coming. The eldest, the heir, as preoccupied in Wales as Thomas in Ireland, she had yet to meet; but Wales, after all, was not so far a journey, and did not entail a sea crossing, and her cool senses told her that he could very well have been in Westminster to greet her had he been so minded. He was the one of whom she was a little afraid. A boy of fifteen, and by all accounts alert and adult some way beyond his years, can be a formidable opponent.

He came at length, early enough to make his excuses acceptable, late enough to confirm in her everything she had decided about him in advance. And he came, not to his father's palace of Westminster, but with his own very handsome retinue to his own house at Coldharbour, in the City, and from there paid his new stepmother his first visit in great state, like a native prince making an imperial gesture towards a foreign visitor. His gift was generous—and paid for, for he had learned to be a good manager of his personal funds—his approach reverential, and his conversation adult and graceful. His father was charmed and relieved, conceiving that the boy felt the need of all this ceremony to support a natural youthful shyness. Joan made no such mistake. She had marked no less that Prince Henry's face was stiff and cool—which could also have been a sign of shyness, but was not—and his eyes aloof and hostile. She knew then that she would never win him; effort would be wasted. All she could do was behave with patient gentleness towards him when they were together, will him no harm, and be ready to defend herself and hers; and, perhaps, encourage every move that might keep him permanently apart from her and from the king. He had Wales to care for, had he not? It was his own particular principality, which could not be taken from him. And the more he was married to it, in turmoil as it was, the less time he would have for undermining her position here in London. She did not conclude at once that he had any such purpose; it was entirely possible that he would welcome the means of remaining at a distance as much as she would, and make no assault upon her if she made none upon him. But she had to be prepared for his enmity, and take measures appropriately.

She was the more inclined to be wary of closer contact with him because she, a woman and a stranger, saw with peculiar clarity his attraction, his ability, and his stature. Of all these children of the royal house—though John was engaging, able, and intelligent—this Hal was the only genius, the only creature dauntingly above life-size. A little larger—she was woman enough to see and acknowledge it—than the father who begot him. Perhaps even more than a little!

So she praised him, whenever his name arose between them, even after he had taken himself off again to his headquarters in Chester.

She assuaged Henry's anxieties whenever he fretted about his heir, and told him that the boy was chafing against his leading-strings. He was obviously far ahead of his years, and this year he would be sixteen. What did he need with these lieutenants of Wales set over him? It was time to give the boy his head, and entrust the total command in Wales to his discretion, clear of restraints.

"You have great confidence in this youngster of mine," said the king, astonished and gratified, smiling at her with absolute trust in her sincerity and her judgment. "Do you truly think him ready for such a charge?"

"It may be," she said, returning his smile with indulgence, aware of her power, "that I see him clearly because I see him with new eyes, not as a parent. I do believe he can do whatever he sets out to do. And I counsel you, give him the opportunity and he will soon show if he can use it." She leaned and touched his hand, her long fingers grown expert in caressing thus discreetly. "Do you think you can breed small, fearful sons, my dear lord?"

He had every hope, then, of more sons by her, for she was hardly turned thirty, and had proved that she was not barren. He had lost the nervous habit that brought out that ugly blotching upon his face, and inclined him to look morbidly to his health and think upon his end. He responded ardently to her every touch, folding his hand upon hers with passion and desire.

"My love, you do convince me. Hal shall have his chance to show his mettle."

She convinced him of other matters, also, for she, too, had needs, for her daughters and for her own peace of mind. It was essential for his new queen to have a jointure of her own—she did not say in so many words, but mercilessly she made it plain to him that even kings are mortal—for her protection in time of misfortune or bereavement. He listened devoutly to all she had to say to him. And for payment, she loved him as women do the husbands who are utterly dependent upon them for all their joy, for what little joy there is to be had in this world, and gave him all she had to give that was available to man. He was the only love of her life in the marital way, and she valued him accordingly; but she had daughters, defenceless creatures in a male world, and she balanced her responsibilities as best she could. She had many dependants to provide for, all victims, all with rights. She did her best for all of them.

On the 8th of March, Queen Joan was granted in council an income of ten thousand marks annually, dating from the day after her marriage. The king immediately began to grant her lands to the same value, to ease the drain upon the exchequer, transferring the burden from the royal monies to the queen's own land revenues as soon as he might. Joan was assured of her income, from whichever source, and could breathe easily again.

On the same date Prince Henry of Wales was made officially lieutenant of the whole of that grand principality in his own right, as an adult prince, clear of all tutelage and entrusted with his territorial administration for all time thereafter.

In this same month of March, moved by certain impulses of shame and indebtedness towards the house of Percy, the king formally granted to the earl of Northumberland, for the use and advantage of his house at his pleasure, all the forfeit lands of the captive earl of Douglas, to wit, all the land of Scotland south of the Tweed, with the addition of the lands of Galloway, in requital of the surrender of the earl's Scottish captives from Homildon Hill, and in recognition of the services rendered by the illustrious house of Percy to the cause of Lancaster. The said territories were not, in practice, in the king's gift, being held and garrisoned, where castles existed, by the Scots. The gift was a gift to be won in arms, or not at all; but capable, upon exertion, of being turned into a reality. And the Percies were expert in turning visions into realisations.

It was the first gesture of conciliation, the first acknowledgement that he had robbed Northumberland and his son of a source of revenue they could ill afford to cede to him. It looked well, and it cost him nothing; it even promised him substantial gains, for if the Percies set to work to secure what he had merely offered as hypothetical bait, all that noble tract of land would be added to the territory of his realm. Northumberland, with his shrewd sense of values, might think it well worth his while to make good his claim, and with his hard efficiency might very well establish it; if he did, he could not but extend his liege lord's domain, and enhance his stature.

It seemed a very adroit move; and Henry was gratified when he received the first reports from Northumbria, indicating that the earl was taking him at his word, and making his dispositions to possess himself of his new lands by conquest. All would yet be well. He saw a future of hope and accord, a reunion with all his old associates, the beginning of something more than a domestic happiness.

◦◦◦

"Say what you will," said Northumberland, pacing his solar in Alnwick, and pausing at every circuit to peer hungrily at the rough map he had sketched upon the table, "there are prospects here of great enlargement, and if we throw them away, we do so at our own risk. I am no happier with this Lancaster king than you are, but he has made the first offer towards us, and that's no mean achievement. If he can be bent once, he can be bent again. It would be folly to throw away that advantage without considering it carefully."

"He has given you nothing," said Hotspur indifferently, for neither gifts nor denials had any influence on his mind. "He has merely asked you to get for him what it would cost him plenty to get for himself. You are doing his work for him yet again without pay."

"Not so! He's given me, this time, the needed leave to pay myself, and so I will, with interest, for all I spend in the getting."

"But not at his expense! At the cost of such poor souls as inhabit these lands—and for Henry's greater glory. He stands to gain and gain from you if you prevail, and you to lose and lose without loss to him if you fail."

"And am I failing? You know I hold a part of this disputed land already and but for these two fortresses of Ormiston and Cocklaws I could take all at small cost. I think it worth the spending of some few thousands of marks to close the bargain And I think you may trust me to see he does not drain away from me all the good I shall have gained by it. Well I know I led you to believe I would go with you against him—no, that I would be before you in the advance! But this does somewhat alter our interest, as you must see. The main grievance we had against him he begins to acknowledge and amend. Is that a small thing?"

"The main grievance?" said Hotspur wonderingly, and turned with some difficulty to try and see with his father's eyes. He smiled. Richard in his grave at Langley was but a minor item, and Roger Mortimer's children in close ward hardly an embarrassment.

"Am I asking that you abandon your project for ever? I say only that there is no point in being too precipitate. Caution and patience will bring a better opportunity. Since we are contending for stated ends, what folly not to gather in what fruits offer by the way, and then, and only then, pursue what still remains unsatisfied."

"You waste your breath," said Worcester gently, from where he sat in the embrasure of the window, his head leaned back against the yellowish-grey stone. "If you gave him Scotland now you would not halt him." And he turned his head a little and looked from one face to the other, still ruefully smiling. The father so bold and shrewd and adaptable, and the son so obstinate, and single-minded, and incorruptible. "He'll help you to take your two castles," he said philosophically. "What more do you want from him?"

"I want his head safe on his shoulders, and my grandchild ensured in his succession to this earldom of Northumberland," said the earl furiously. "Is that a base ambition in me? I did say, I still say, that we did ill to support this King Bolingbroke, and it would be well to set him down from that eminence in which it was we who set him up. But this is a perilous enterprise, and I am not satisfied that this is the time or the manner in which it can be done successfully. For my part, I say wait, and tread carefully. There'll be a better time."

"And Edmund will have spent his fortune and his life to no purpose, for want of us," said Hotspur violently. "My uncle has told us how the prince has carried the war into the Dee valley, and burned Sycarth—and praise it is to him, and no blame, that he does his work so well. But what sense is there in waiting until we are without allies? It would be great reproach to me if I failed now of what I have undertaken, for Edmund's sake and for Owen's."

"It would not so! You could turn back now without harming them. There's time to give them due warning, and they have the whole of Wales, that sufficed Owen well enough before, for their sanctuary. You've waited this long, why not longer?"

It was late May, and the prince had been in control of his own command for two full months, and made redoubtable inroads, in his new enthusiasm, into Owen's ancestral lands; though the inhabitants, as always in Wales, disappeared with unruffled contempt into the mountains, and left their frail homesteads to be fired without a backward glance, and for every house thus lost to them had ten yet left to retire to.

"I've waited because Edmund needed time to muster and organise his defences. And because it is now done I cannot wait longer. Nor will I," he said, with immovable resolve. "When my uncle goes back to his post with the prince in Chester—"

"In Shrewsbury," said Worcester abstractedly. "Did I not tell you? He's moved his main body and his own staff there. It makes a better base for raiding central Wales, and the boy is keen. He has your old trouble, though," he added, and laughed. "Never a courier goes to London without a letter to the king, begging, bullying, demanding money to pay his men. Those who have the means could buy half that force tomorrow for ready money."

"We are no richer in that than he is," said Hotspur with haughty distaste.

"But we are, Harry! I do not go penniless into any venture. I have already withdrawn my treasury," said Worcester, "both from London and from Chester, and have it always close about me. When the time comes, leave it to me to do the buying. Bring your own men south with you, and pick up what you may in Cheshire as you come, and I shall meet you by the way with whatever force I can draw off from the prince's army. And if I do not bring you more than the half of it—and not all bought, at that!—charge me with treason to you as well as to Henry."

"*You* don't urge me to turn back," said Hotspur, shaken and shocked by the sudden vision of Hal isolated and forsaken in Shrewsbury; and forced, upon that revelation, to look the boy in the face, and contemplate what must be done about him.

"I know," said Worcester simply, "that if God himself urged you to turn back now, you would not do it. I doubt if you could. There are thoughts in you that will not let you look back. It's gone too far, you've seen too deeply and understood too much. There's no going back, and no standing still, only a progress, and that ever more rapid. And to what end we cannot know."

"For you," said Hotspur in a low voice, "there could be a turning back. I don't ask you to see with my eyes, or judge with my mind. How could I?"

"Harry, where you go, I go. You are all the remaining sons of my brother, and you are all the son I ever had or wanted. If you think I would let you go into this venture, and stand aloof from you, you are mad. And that being so," he said practically, "we had better take good care to see that we make a success of what we're about. You began to say, Harry, that when I rode south again...?"

"I am coming with you, to see the last letters despatched to Glendower and Edmund. There must be good timing and utter surprise, or the children will be at risk. Once he knows we're in arms and close upon him, he'll have no time to threaten them. And I should like," he said, his voice carefully level and quiet, "to visit Hal again while I'm in Shrewsbury."

Worcester had brought him a letter glowing with confidence and grand intentions, pouring out to him all the prince's hopes of victory in Wales, undeterred by sympathy, ready to go to all lengths to achieve the task committed to him. A just judge! Hotspur remembered the twelve-year-old face, pale and fixed behind the blue blade of the Curtana at Henry's coronation, with huge hazel eyes dazed by glory but never wavering from the contemplation of duty. A lovely, terrible child! And a friend of such fierce loyalty that disloyalty to him, however inevitable, was a kind of death. But he did not look too long at that grief. He was about something he had to do, and for all his father's arguments, there was no choice left.

"Why go near him?" said Northumberland in exasperation. "You are urgent for sorrow. And all needless—needless! You could call a halt now, warn your allies in Wales, sit close and still, and watch events. But since you will not, I have done!"

"And you stand in with us?" Worcester asked sharply.

"Since needs must, yes. If we cannot turn this mad-head, we may well consider how best to turn all other things to account. If we are to strike," he said, and came back to the table to frown down upon his scrawled plan, "let's strike as effectively as possible. You say the prince has moved his headquarters to Shrewsbury because of the flare-up along the Dee?"

"So much the better," said Hotspur with decision, "for it's more accessible than Chester. And before we do anything else we must secure the prince, and put him out of the reckoning."

Northumberland approved. "Good! If he has but half an army left to him, you may get hold of him and immobilise his men before they can make a move, and you'll have a garrison town with two river crossings to serve Glendower and Edmund. Yes, you must begin by occupying Shrewsbury."

And a royal hostage, he thought, warming almost to the idea of rebellion, to which his subtle mind saw so many practical objections, while his discontented and disaffected heart still desired it. Who put this man on the throne? How could he ever have carried his way without us? Yes, if we do move, if we must move, let him sweat for his heir. It's good tactics.

He said so, when they were alone, to Worcester. His brother looked back at him with wide, inscrutable dark eyes, that seemed to have seen already everything there was for a man to see between birth and death, and smiled, saying never a word. This was not a matter of tactics. It went far deeper. For his soul's sake Hotspur had no choice but to remove the prince from the battlefield before the onset. Never could he bear to confront the boy with the choice between his father and his friend, and never dared he risk meeting his protégé in arms. For not even for his life, not even to preserve himself for the sake of lives doubly dear to him, would Hotspur have touched the prince.

Prince Henry, prince and lieutenant of Wales, had taken up residence this time in the castle, having no ladies to indulge, and being himself content with a narrow cell and a hard bed along with his garrison and his standing army. The bailey of Shrewsbury castle was always alive with comings and goings, with the bustle of armourers, of fletchers and master-bowmen at the butts, and young men-at-arms at exercise with lance and sword about the wards; but the prince had a squire always alert to whatever coat-armour entered at the barbican, and would have arrivals reported to him as soon as identified. The blue lion of Percy was enough to bring him leaping down the stone stairway and running in person, with the vehemence that created its own dignity, to hold Hotspur's stirrup as he eased himself out of the saddle.

"My lord, you're most heartily welcome! Your uncle of Worcester told me you would be coming. I've looked forward many weeks to seeing you. Lay your hand on my shoulder, and come in!"

The hovering groom reached forward to take the bridle. The men-at-arms and retainers moving about the ward paused and loitered to look again at the visitor, passing his name from lip to ear wherever they went. The Lord Henry Percy was above and apart from all the vagaries of the king's policy. The king's heir ran to honour him. Who did not?

"Harry, I've hoped to see you this long time. You'll make the rounds with me, and see how well I'm keeping my garrison and armoury and stores, now you're here?"

"Faith, not I!" said Hotspur, laughing. "It's you who carry the burden now, Hal, and indeed, so you have for the greater part of a year. How often have I visited the march these last months?"

"Not often enough," said the boy heartily. "I've missed you."

"By all accounts you do very well without me. I hear you've made havoc of Owen's lands along the Dee."

"It seemed to me time," said the prince seriously, "to try if we could not root out his main refuges, not merely to loot, or take what prisoners did not slip through our fingers—that we know they always do, like water—but to destroy every shelter there, and make it useless for any return. He must have places to store his dependents, his treasure, his reserves of weapons and stock, and in summer it may be no problem, but if we can raze his main holdings past repair, then the winter will be a hard enemy to him, and an ally to us. We let them alone for a long time," said the boy, with perfectly detached reasoning, "while we hoped for a mutual settlement. Now I mean to deny them to him one by one, until he has no shelter left. Once razed, it is not so hard to deploy force enough to keep the Welsh from slipping back and rebuilding."

"And the women and children?" Hotspur asked. The boy gazed back at him, sternly sure of his own duty, a rock from which regrets fell back like spray; and yet he cared greatly that his mentor should approve him.

"There were none there. They had notice enough. And they are not yet without a roof to cover them," he said drily. But he had flushed faintly. "I have been given work to do," he said, "I must do it as quickly and as cleanly as I can. It would not be merciful to prolong a resistance which cannot succeed. I do what I may to make defeat human, but first to make victory sure. Everything I know of this game," he said earnestly, watching Hotspur's face. "I learned from you."

"It seems to me you have bettered the instruction," said Hotspur mildly.

"You mean by that, that I have gone further than you would have gone," said the boy, squarely but sadly confronting his own dilemma and his own grief.

"So you have, Hal, but never think I blame you for that. You are right, and I approve you. It is a reproach to me, not to you, if you have done what I could not have done. For it was my duty as surely as it is yours."

They had reached the door of the prince's apartments, but above that level a winding stair led up to the guard-walk on the wall, and the sun of a June afternoon was bright and inviting through the arrow-slits over their heads. He flung an arm about the boy's shoulders. "Not indoors, let's go up on the wall. What do we or the Welsh want with a roof over us, a day like this?"

They stood leaning on one of the embrasures of the wall together, looking down over the coil of the Severn, the steep terraces of the abbot's vineyard, and out to the abbey and the stone bridge. Beyond, the green plain of fields and copses rolled away into summer mist, gently undulating under a blue sky. They talked of the years they had spent working together in this troubled region, before the prince came to man's estate, and the campaigns they had conducted along the marches of Wales. The boy was not too proud to discuss his proposed future moves, and ask for comment and advice; and Hotspur responded without reserve or pretence, giving whatever wisdom he could, though with some amused wonder at himself, and much respect for his listener. If Hal had asked him how best to combat the determined assault of a Northumbrian army led by a

Percy and reinforced by Cheshire archers, he would still have had to answer to the best of his ability. How else could he deal with this young creature who placed absolute trust in him, and whom he could not choose but love and trust in return?

"You'll stay a few days with me, now you're here? You come so seldom now, and I need to lean on you now and again."

"You need no man to lean on," said Hotspur with conviction. "I never knew any man stand more solidly upright upon his own two feet. No, Hal, I wish I could stay, but I must be on my way back before night. You know my father is set on reducing the two castles that stand between him and his enjoyment of those Douglas lands your father has granted him. And Dunbar is no less eager, for whatever we can recapture of his properties will be his again. I can't hold back, I must go and do my share. We have both Cocklaws and Ormiston under siege, and both have agreed to surrender if the Scots don't relieve them by the first of August. But the word we have is that they mean to raise a relieving force, and if we're to keep the ring tight round both castles we need all our forces."

"Stay overnight, at least. What difference can one night make, and you'll have the advantage of a fresh and early start."

He smiled, turning his head to look the boy long and earnestly in the eyes; but he shook his head, saying gently: "No!"

He felt no shame or constraint at doing what he had to do, and yet being here as friend with friend; but he would not, in these circumstances, sleep beneath Hal's roof or eat Hal's bread. Some day, when everything was known, they might come to clear speech even about this interlude, which he saw now was an indulgence to himself, and perhaps an injury to the boy.

"No, let me go, and think no ill if I leave you. We have both things to do that we must do. Take it that I go because I must—that what I do, I do because I cannot do otherwise. And that nothing I do can change the love and honour in which I bear you." He said it in a light voice and with an easy smile, as if by way of graceful apology for an abrupt departure; and yet the words had a weight about them, that anchored them fast in the prince's mind, and made him look again, more fixedly and deeply, into his friend's face.

He turned away suddenly, and stood looking out over the glittering bow of the river, his smooth cheek turned upon Hotspur; and after a moment he said, in a low voice:

"Harry, is it answer enough for *any* act, do you suppose, to say that we do what we must? Isn't there always a choice?" He spread his long young hands restlessly along the parapet, and stared down at his splayed fingers braced against the stone. "Can a man plead compulsion to *anything*? Even—what can never be undone? I've often meant to ask you...Do you remember once when you came to me in Chester, from seeing King Richard buried?"

There was a silence between them that lasted too long for candour. Now they were both feeling their way, and how strangely, the man lost between enlightenment and relief on one hand, and a sense of wondering compassion on the other, the boy pierced to the heart by this pregnant silence where he had expected an instant, open response. Not even the kind of silence that wrung the air when Hotspur's unruly tongue had knotted itself and caused him to struggle for speech, but a still, wary silence, astonished and dismayed. *Something has happened*, the boy thought, shaken and amazed. *Something has opened his eyes. He does not speak out now for my father's stalwart innocence. He cannot—he knows!*"

"I do remember," said Hotspur, too gently and too late.

"Often it's hard to find a right way, for there seems to be none, only one perhaps less wrong than another. But there are things that must not be done...I have been in great perplexity and torment of mind," he said, "concerning Richard."

Hotspur said: "I know only that for what we do we must be answerable. Whenever we may be called upon to pay it, there will be a price."

"Harry...I have never told this to anyone but you...I have made a vow, as soon as it's in my power, to bring King Richard out of his obscure grave, and bury him like a king in the tomb that was made for him, in the abbey, with his dear Queen Anne. Not that I dare assert," he went on quickly, "that he was without fault in what happened. Doubtless he did some wrong, and much injustice. I doubt all kings do so. But I cannot on that account forget all the good, and all the kindness that was in him, or let what was ill-done blot out what was done well."

He had said what he had to say. He turned again to face his friend, and suddenly smiled at him. "How solemn you look! Is that my doing?"

The full gold sunlight of a better summer had burned Hotspur to a deeper brown, and polished his broad forehead and the jutting bones of his cheeks and jaw. For a moment his face, normally so mobile and expressive, was quite still, caught in distant and inviolable serenity, like a hieratic bronze head on a tomb. Then it quivered and melted into glowing life again, returning the prince's smile.

"Well, God keep you of the same mind, and preserve to you always as loyal a memory. For some of us, I doubt, will stand in great need of advocates before we come to our life's end. By your judgment," he said whole-heartedly, "I will gladly abide, and whatever dues you charge me with, I will pay with a good grace."

12

King Henry was well-informed on the history of the sieges of Cocklaws, by Yetholm, and Ormiston, by Hawick, that summer. In May Northumberland had written urgently to the council for funds due to him to pay his men, and on the 26th of June he wrote again, from his manor of Healaugh in Yorkshire, this time to the king himself, reminding him of the possible lustre in prospect for English arms if the fortresses were successfully carried at the beginning of August, and the inevitable disgrace if they were allowed to be relieved for want of the money to pay the troops. Moreover, a successful attempt to raise a Scottish relieving force, and thrust back the English encroachment, would be a danger even to lands which had always been English. A successful thrust seldom stops at any border. It was a warm and even indignant letter, bluntly assessing the crown's present debt to the Percies at twenty thousand pounds, but it was confident and loyal, too openly aggrieved to be read as anything less than loyal.

The earl had shut his eyes to all uglier possibilities when he wrote it, and believed absolutely in what he set down. It was still his devout hope that fortune would avert all action, and allow him to go on as before. Not out of fear, but out of a strong middle-aged disinclination to break violently with what he knew and had grown accustomed to, and set out despairingly afresh.

He signed the letter with his own hand, styling himself, in an affectionate flourish which the king would understand, "your

Mathathias," thus aligning himself with the loyal band of the Maccabees adhering staunchly to their chosen champion. What if his son had sent and received letters to and from the alliance in Wales, arranging times and movements with them until all was polished into deadly perfection of form? Plans made could still be silently shelved, even in the last few days before the cataclysm, and no one any the wiser upon one side about this sudden access of wisdom on the other. Meanwhile, he encouraged events to intervene, to provide reconciliation and requital, to make rebellion pointless and out of date before ever its hour arrived. And if the storm could not be averted, with all his efforts, then he could go out into it with his son as he had promised, and stand or fall with him.

Henry was at Kennington with his household when the letter was delivered, about to set out on one of his normal summer progresses. He was in good health and in good heart, and some months of modest domestic happiness had eased him of the ever-tightening stress that was making him old before his time. Northumberland's bluntness and warmth moved and melted him. He had been in danger lately of feeling himself almost of Northumberland's generation, he who was a year and more younger than Northumberland's son. Now he felt himself being chided, with affection and indignation, by a second father to whom he certainly owed much. He had been something less than generous to the Percies. He felt ashamed of the hypocritical gesture with which he had made that grant of the Douglas lands, giving away, in payment for the prisoners of Homildon, what was not his to give, and leaving the earl to turn an empty formula into a reality. And here was he, far away in the north, busy doing as much, and needing at least his due in money to help him to the achievement.

He took the letter with him as he moved northwards at leisure to Higham Ferrers. From there he wrote a buoyant letter to his council announcing to them, in an access of energy that was partly Joan's gift to him, and partly the fruit of a burst of filial feeling towards Northumberland, that he had made up his mind to proceed immediately to the Scottish border in person, to give whatever aid and support he could to the earl. Thereafter, the fortresses of Cocklaws and Ormiston successfully occupied, he would return to give his attention to Wales, and with his son's aid to terminate, once for all, the long rebellion there.

Two young squires bore this optimistic letter south; and Henry went on blithely, braced and heartened by this evidence of renewed vigour in himself, to Leicester and Nottingham, where he arrived on the 12th of July. Thence his usual route north was by way of Pontefract, that castle of his which had scored its name into history as the place of Richard's death.

He never reached Pontefract. For at Nottingham his rest before supper was rudely broken into by John Norbury, the one person who dared bring him bad news.

"My lord, there are messengers here from the north. You must hear them. There's word of armed revolt. Sir Henry Percy has abandoned the siege of Cocklaws with all his army, and is on his way south. He has left the earl of the March of Scotland waiting in vain for him—they had a rendezvous there…"

The king sat up stiffly, staring, the morbid rash starting angrily on his face. "No—impossible! Rumour, nothing but rumour…it cannot be true!"

"My lord, it may be no more than rumour, but you must listen and judge, for it may be sooth! Only hear these messengers!"

There was an agent of the earl of Westmorland, haggard and dusty from the road, and a terrified merchant of York, who had heard the stories in that city, and brought them south with him. They poured out everything they had heard. The Lord Henry Percy had entered Cheshire, and there issued proclamations in which the king was spoken of crudely as Henry of Lancaster, and Richard as lawful king of the realm of England, and alive, and returning to reclaim his own. And the nobility of Cheshire, always Richard's men, had pricked up their ears, and were furbishing forth their musters to go and join the

revolt, to put back the true king upon his throne and reinstate him
in all his rights, and do justice upon the usurper.

Mere mischief and rumour, it could not be more! As if Hotspur,
whatever he was about, would ever issue such a lie! He had seen
Richard dead, had himself examined that exquisite, tranquil body,
that work of art, unmarred by any wound. Arrogant he was, and
proud he was, almost beyond the title of pride, and he might without
offence to his nature flame into rebellion, but into such petty lies he
would never stoop. It was not his territory. But the act of abandoning the border, of sweeping southwards in arms, thus without a
word out of his tongue-tied mouth—yes, that could be true, if he
hated enough... *if he knew enough*!

Counter-rumours crossed swords with the first. The rebels were
not yet in Cheshire, but had raised the Percy standard in the north.
Richard himself had crossed the Scottish border from his secret
refuge, and joined his loyal forces in arms. Composed so beauti-
fully for his lying-in-state, nailed down, lapped in lead, Richard still
would not stay in his grave. Murdered men cannot rest, nor let their
murderers rest.

He still could not believe that there was any truth in it, but since
the stories insisted that the rebels were heading south-west towards
Wales, he, too, turned west from Nottingham, spent the nights
of the 13th and 14th in Derby, and on the following day reached
Burton-on-Trent. And there the rumours of conflagration came
blowing more strongly, like smoke from the fires of discontent.
If he had not, in the warm, hopeful impulse of his heart, set off
northwards to the aid of the Percies, leaving the queen behind at
Higham Ferrers, he would not have received the news for several
days more, and would have been several days further removed from
effective intervention. His gesture of conciliation now seemed a
miracle of salvation.

For there was no more disbelieving. This was hard, black fact.
Hotspur was in Cheshire, with a strong force from Northumbria,

and recruiting from among the conservative Cheshire nobility as he came. The confederacy embraced the Welsh rebels, and Sir Edmund Mortimer with his feudal force, all these lately engaged in ferocious sorties into South Wales which were now seen to be a calculated diversion, damaging though they had been in their own right. All eyes upon South Wales, and in the north the standard of rebellion had been raised almost silently, almost invisibly. Moreover, the Percies had issued in Chester a long manifesto setting out their complaints against King Henry, and the list was long and bitter, meant to canvass support among a nobility always discontented enough. They accused him of exacting taxes and tallages he had sworn not to demand, and putting the money to other uses than the right keeping of the realm and the due protection of its borders; of having broken the oath sworn at his muster at Doncaster on his return from exile, to claim only what was his by right, to make no bid for the crown, but only to ensure that Richard should continue to rule under the guidance of a properly constituted council; of manipulating parliament by ordering the county sheriffs to return only knights favourable to the royal interest; of having, out of personal malice, refused to ransom or countenance the ransom of Sir Edmund Mortimer, and of keeping the younger Edmund Mortimer, acknowledged heir to King Richard's throne, a prisoner and deprived of his right. And clearly they said that they had done amiss in supporting Henry of Lancaster's claim to that throne, and could no longer continue in so flagrant an error. Their avowed aim now was to set Edmund, earl of March, upon the throne of England.

Only in that last abrupt declaration could Henry recognise the voice of Hotspur. The rest surely came from another and a different mind, subtle, legal and cool. Who, in any case, could imagine Hotspur sitting down at a desk to compose such a document? Yet not Northumberland, either; the language was not his. Nor, so far, had anyone brought in evidence that Northumberland himself was in arms, or meditating action. Reports said he was certainly not with the host in Cheshire, though it was natural enough to assume that he might follow on to reinforce his son's numbers with his own.

From Burton, upon the assessment of all this evidence, the king wrote in frantic haste to his council, urging all its members to join him at once, except for the treasurer, whose task it was to raise hurried loans to support an inescapable campaign; and to all the sheriffs of the midland counties, ordering them to raise their musters instantly and prepare to go with him against the rebels. He had more details by then. Another formidable ally had joined the conspiracy; for Hotspur had released his captive, the earl of Douglas, and the Scots knights he had held since Homildon, and they had enlisted gladly under his banner to march against the crown of England.

The muster letters were not yet despatched, when a squire in the livery of the earl of Stafford rode in with the most shocking news of all, and was brought in, soiled and sweating as he was, to the king's cabinet.

"My liege lord, the rebel forces are not far north of Stafford. We judge them to be something more than twelve thousand men—and strong in archers. And, my lord, Sir Henry Percy has reinforcements now from another source. It is truth, I swear," panted the young man, trembling, "we sent out a scout who has seen the pennant with his own eyes! The earl of Worcester has drawn off more than half the forces the prince had with him in Shrewsbury, and taken them with him to join his nephew's army. The prince is left abandoned in Shrewsbury with only a small force to hold it—and Sir Henry Percy is marching on the town to secure his Grace as prisoner and hostage!"

The Scottish earl of March found him sitting alone and inert, after the last of his couriers had ridden out, his hands empty on the table before him, the mulled wine they had brought him cooling unnoticed at his elbow. A gust of the outside world came in with the earl, the dust and heat of a long ride, in which he had worn out a whole relay of mounts, and the sudden bracing impact of a powerful and persuasive personality. He had hardly rested on his journey south, and he arrived still vibrant and alight with energy. What was a mortal peril and a shattering shock to Henry was his best opportunity to George Dunbar. He still had his reputation to make on the English side of the border.

He bent his knee almost perfunctorily to the king he had chosen for himself, and was in no position to betray. He had never hesitated where to choose, for with the Percies he would stand no chance of favour; it was stand or fall with this one.

"My liege lord, I quit the siege as soon as I heard the way of it. You have more need of me here." He stooped his red head close over the table, the glitter of his blue eyes narrowed and keen. "My lord, you must move fast, as fast as I've moved since two days gone. And you have not as far to go as I had. As I heard it, Percy's aiming for Shrewsbury. It's a link with Wales, a safe river crossing, a well-victualled town, and left with barely a garrison worth the name. And your son—yon's a bonny hostage to pick up so cheap. The heir to the throne, no less!"

"You tell me what I know," said Henry with bitterness. "Do you think I've not been exerting myself about this business? But it was good in you," he said, softening, "to ride in such haste to join me. Indeed I value it."

"But, my lord, your foot soldiers should be on the march this minute, if you mean to be there before him! You may rest, and ride after, but your slow-moving companies should go night and day, and your supplies. This Percy moves fast, and we must move faster yet. You have three days at the most to be in Shrewsbury."

"It cannot be done," said the king, aghast.

"There's nothing in this world within arm's-length of possibility that cannot be done, when a man must. I could get you there in two, if you'd heed me, but three may do well enough for us—Three he'll not expect of mortal man." But he meant: "of you!" and the criticism, so close a reflection of the king's own thoughts, hurt and goaded, rearing Henry's head indignantly and stiffening his back.

"I know very well I have two choices, and both risky. To strike immediately, and at a disadvantage, or to wait to make up my numbers before I act, and lose Shrewsbury. I was debating the same choice." And indeed all his martial memory had cried out on him to strike at once, before the enemy had time to organise and consolidate; but his limbs were lead, and his very hand moved with the slowness of an overladen cart. For as surely as he felt plain, clean rage mounting in him, and cried out at Hotspur: "Traitor!" like any honest monarch thus confronted, he heard the echo cast back into his own face, and Hotspur's voice answering: "*Traitor to whom?*" Whatever he could urge in his own defence, so could Hotspur urge it in his. Only when he protested: "I never meant to seize the throne, events forced it upon me!"—only then did echo ominously inflect the utterance into a new shape: "I want only to place the true king on the throne and maintain him there." For even at this pass Henry could not make himself believe that Hotspur was greedy for a throne himself. Not because he had not enough pride, but because he had too much; too vast, too singular a pride to contain any ambition. He was already Hotspur, what was there to aim at beyond?

"It's no choice at all, my lord," Dunbar urged vehemently. "Numbers? You have nigh on twice what Percy can muster at this moment. Fourteen thousand men at the most I give him, and you have twenty-five thousand and more. But if he's given three days' grace, he has Shrewsbury, Glendower, Mortimer and all, and the prince for his surety. And Northumberland on his way south by tomorrow to bring up the reserves."

The king's head jerked up abruptly; he stared into the subtle blue eyes, under the thick, sandy brows: "Is that certain? Northumberland, too?"

"If you have Hotspur and Worcester, do you think the earl will be far behind? They hold by their own blood, the Percy clan. I stake you my life the old man's stirring before this!"

They hold by their own blood! The Percy clan—yes. And the Lancaster clan?

He had not thought of it before. Somehow his mind had avoided making that last, logical step, and questioning the inevitability of Hal's loyalty to him. Now suddenly the horrible doubt opened like an unsuspected wound in his spirit, quick with pain. They did not sound him out, no, he knew nothing, they did not dare go so far. *But how if they were mistaken in abstaining*? Then, if they take the town, and he falls into Hotspur's hands, what will he do? Whom will he choose? For he loves Hotspur! It was an admission, abject and agonising, and wrung out of him against his will. And what inevitably followed was worse: *Does he love me*?

He had never understood children, and this child out of all of them he understood not at all. He would not even have known if he was hated instead of loved. But Hotspur—Hotspur could not fail of love wherever he touched. How could an ordinary man compete?

No, he could not let it ever be put to the test, his heart could not bear it. Some men might desire to know, but he desired never to know, never to have to face this defeat of all defeats. Whatever befell him after, he had to get to Shrewsbury first, or at the least place his army in between, and prevent Hotspur from reaching the town. From this moment on, the crown was almost a secondary consideration.

He surged so abruptly to his feet, lifted such a changed, resolute face, that for ever after Dunbar credited himself with instilling a daemon into his king, and prided himself and traded on his influence.

"Come, then let's set this war in motion, and see who lags behind. By the morning of the twentieth I'll have my army in Shrewsbury." He crossed to the door of his private cabinet, and flung it open. "John! Call the earl of Stafford here to me, and send out word for all my captains of companies to muster here on the next hour. Before dawn we move!"

The march to Shrewsbury was one that none who took part in it ever forgot. This was the tireless, hypnotised, stoic marching of the Roman legions, hour after hour even after the will and the mind were asleep. To keep up foot soldiers, supply wagons, re-mounts, armouries and cavalry in planned, methodical progress, separating and re-forming regularly, without stragglers, without casualties and without complaint, was a prodigy of which no one had ever supposed the king capable. They said that he was either possessed of a devil, or inspired by the direct fire of God. But the devil that possessed him was the spectre of his stranger son turned traitor; and to lay that ghost he was willing to sacrifice even the supreme luxury of proving the prince's constancy by putting it to the test. Better never to try an issue so likely to be lost! He trusted neither God, the devil, nor the prince. It was better not to know!

～ ～

The prince stood leaning between the merlons of the town wall, in that same spot where he had leaned with Hotspur barely six weeks previously, and on just such a still, sunlit day, with haze on all the distances, the lush greens of the fields and woods filmed over with delicate smoke-grey and amorphous gold, the river beneath him a soft blue, silvered with light, and gilded with sunshine where the shoals troubled the still surface. At every bend a pool of deeper blue, rimmed with a shimmer of gold. Last summer had been cruel everywhere; this summer was tranquil and kind. The soft, undulating plain of Shropshire seen from the wall of Shrewsbury was inexpressibly fair and benign.

He was looking out from his vantage-point for the first sighting of an army. One of two armies. If he looked to the left, he saw the neck of land opening out beyond the castle foregate, the one dry-foot approach to the town, from which the roads led north-east. If he looked to the right, he saw the suave curve of the river below him, swerving round the foot of the abbot's vineyard to sweep under the arches of the stone bridge. Across that bridge—the drawbridge was raised now, though it was nearly midday—lay the abbey and the abbey foregate, all that enclosure of holy ground, and then the great road going eastward to Lichfield. That was why he had chosen this spot. There was nothing for him to do below, until sunlight on steel, on one of these roads, prophesied the future. All defences were manned, all captains had their orders. When the sign came there might be more to be done; not before.

He had known now for three days what confronted him. At first, when the frightened squire brought him word that all but the castle garrison and the town guard had been quietly withdrawn in the night, and that his governor, the earl of Worcester, was gone with them, he had been unable to understand or believe what had happened to him; only later, when the first news came of the Percy manifesto, passed from lip to lip across the county, did he realise all the implications.

The surprise should not, perhaps, have been absolute, but so it was, a stunning shock. Even when he began to salvage from the disastrous debris of his memory of friendship those dim, significant things that burgeoned out of misunderstanding like the seeds of truth itself, when he remembered their last exchanges, the revelation of Hotspur's knowledge of murder, his own faltering appeal for guidance as to what was forgivable and what could never under any compulsion be justified, and Hotspur's sombre valediction, he was too near to them yet to find any coherent sense in them. It was like being lost in a fantastic forest where words budded like vines winding about him, inhibiting all action, conveying some truth that might help him if he could but interpret it, yet spoken in an unknown language. Only gradually did something valid and expressive begin to come back to him now, here in this spot where they had had their last interview.

"I do what I do because I cannot do otherwise...for what we do we must be answerable...whenever we may be called upon to pay it, there will be a price..." And: "By your judgment I will gladly abide, and whatever dues you charge me with, I will pay with a good grace." And last of all, and clearest: "Nothing I do can change the love and honour in which I bear you!"

"Nothing you do," he said passionately within his own heart, "can change the love and honour in which I bear you!" And of that at least he was sure.

Hotspur had known then what he was about to do. That was why he had come. Perhaps it was even why he would not look into the guardrooms or the armouries, or ask anything about the garrison. He desired to see his charge again before the world turned upside-down, but he would not make use of him, or take advantage of having access to his castle. Yet now, so the scouts reported, he was heading here in arms, to take Shrewsbury and the prince with it. It was a race, and he and this town were the prize. Thank God, he did not have to take any action or make any decision, there was nothing he could do but wait. Nothing, at least, until those sharp terrestrial stars began to glitter on one horizon or the other, and the dim, moving serpent of fine dust marked the approach of the marching men. And then? What was his part then? To post his archers and see every gate fast closed and every portcullis lowered, and have parties standing by to throw down the scaling ladders if entry was attempted? Or to send down orders to open the gates? *And to which of them?*

He had long ago learned to keep his countenance against all comers, even when his heart seemed to him to be riven bodily into two parts, and drawing him two separate and irreconcilable ways. Was that what was meant by a heart breaking? He could not remember that he had ever in his life been so unhappy, not even when Richard died.

"Your Grace..." One of his squires came out from the narrow doorway of the turret above him on the wall. "The lookout reports sighting steel—a mile away yet, but clear! They're coming!"

"On which road?" he said. But he already knew, for the young man offered it as good news. He turned to look beyond the stone bridge, beyond the roofs of the abbey buildings and the great tower of the church; but from where he stood, some twenty feet lower than the sentry, there was nothing yet to be seen.

"On the Roman road, my lord, this side Atcham."

"And on the other road, nothing?" Was he hoping or afraid? For his life he did not know what he wanted. Let God decide! Whatever came, he must accept it as a sign. But his voice, at least, was brisk and calm, like his countenance; no one should find any fault in his bearing.

"Nothing, your grace!"

Joyful news he conceived it. So, no doubt, would the town, for terrible rumours of imminent Welsh attack were running from street to street, and feeling was high and hysterical against the Welsh inhabitants. The king's coming would be a calming influence, if it did not actually lessen the danger. But where had his father found this vein of passionate haste and instant decision, to bring that host of his, in so short a time, almost to the gates of Shrewsbury?

He went up to the top of the watch-turret, and looked out where the sentry pointed him. The sunlight found the tips of lances, and the hanging veil of fine dust, tracing the length of the column. It was truth, then; they were here. This could not be Hotspur's army; such a route would have taken them out of their way with no compensating advantage. They had not been seeking immediate battle, but a base here, and command of the routes into Wales. From Stafford they would come straight. And if they had known how incredibly fast the king would move, they would not have halted to recruit and provision on the way, but come like the wind. Now it was too late.

He turned to look along the road that led away into the countryside from the castle foregate, but there was no moving serpent of dust there, no shimmer of lances, or none close enough to be distinguished from the smoke-blue haze of distance. When he looked again towards the abbey, there were already points of colour to be glimpsed beyond, the brilliance of coat-armour like bright dustmotes sparkling in air. The race was lost and won.

Presently a smaller cloud of dust detached itself from the swaying canopy above the column, and spurred ahead towards the town; and within twenty minutes this advance-guard was lost to sight beyond the abbey, to reappear again as a bright cluster of horsemen emerging at the entrance to the bridge.

"Give them the signal to lower the draw-bridge and open the gate," said the prince.

"My lord, his Grace the king is with the vanguard, I see his guidon clear. And Blount is there with him…and Stafford…Will you go down, your Grace, and welcome your father at the gate?"

"I will," he said, and led the way down from the wall to the inner ward where the horses waited. A dozen of his knights and squires attended him on that ride from the castle, down the steep, curving Wile to the English gate. The barriers were already open wide, the portcullis raised, and the foremost horsemen were clattering over the draw-bridge and across the four nearer arches of the bridge itself. The prince lighted down from his horse and stood in the gateway to receive his father.

"My liege lord, we rejoice to see you. You are come in good time." He held the king's stirrup, standing slender and straight and grave as his father dismounted and embraced him.

Under Henry's brushing lips the boy's cheek was stiff and cold as stone, and his eyes wide and clear and quite inexpressive, though that could have been the blank emptiness of shock followed by relief. If he was loyal, he had passed through an ordeal of waiting which was not to be taken lightly, and he might well be wrung and drained now that it was over. And if he was disloyal…The chill face under the parental kiss, the unspeaking eyes, might cover a disappointment he could not show to the world. All this wild ride had passed in hoping and praying never to have to know on which side this boy's heart inclined, and now that he held him by the shoulders and peered attentively into his face, the king was wracking his heart and tormenting his judgment, after all, to discover the truth. Now he would have given everything but his threatened crown to know for certain what he had devoutly prayed he need never know. Prayers are heard, he thought bitterly, searching in vain the clear brow and impenetrable gaze, from this face I never shall know, not even if he willed me dead.

"My lord, will you now dispose our defences yourself? You know what numbers I am left with here, but I trust you'll find I have looked as well as I might to our most urgent needs. And we are well provisioned. If it please you take over the command, I will deliver you account of all."

"We have other accounting to do," said the king shortly, and took his hands from the boy's shoulders and swung himself back into the saddle. "They cannot be many hours behind us, come, we have to secure the suburbs against them. Why have you not fired the fore-gate? Do you want to leave them an easy approach, and the means of filling in your ditch? See to it! Get the people inside at once, and put torch to the houses. My lord of Stafford, see everything within here, and the gate made fast, and follow us to the castle."

The loyal chivalry of England were clattering in orderly columns across the draw-bridge. It would be an hour before all the foot soldiers and the wagons were within, the armourers and servants and baggage-horses. The prince mounted silently, and followed his father, like a dutiful son, a few paces to his side and rear as they rode back to the castle.

"You have no reports of Glendower close?"

"No, sir. We had scouts out yesterday, but there's no sign, and even if they have turned back from the south already, I think they cannot be here for at least two or three days. I have a good man out now across the river. He will send us word if I prove wrong. But I am sure they will not move so fast." He meant, and he was not alone in marvelling at it: Their plans can never have taken into account that you could move so fast!

And why? Why, or how? What had stung and driven him into so outdoing himself? For me? the boy wondered, but could not believe he mattered so greatly to this dry, harsh, absent man. Yet he could have fought for his crown wherever he chose, he reasoned feverishly, without this breakneck race. He has near twice as many men, surely, as Hotspur can possibly have brought so far in so short a time.

Quietly and passively he rode at his father's elbow, and faithfully he rendered account of his stewardship. That he was already in half-armour had been noted before ever he was kissed, that he knew, having eyes that missed nothing. Upon probation he was accepted as satisfactory. But loved enough to stir that chilly blood into fire? That he doubted.

By his own test, God had chosen. He was not yet sure how Henry, prince of Wales, had chosen.

It was in the early evening of that same day, Friday, the 20th of July, in the year of Our Lord fourteen hundred and three, that Lord Henry Percy brought his host, now some fourteen thousand men in all, to the spot where the road from Newport joined the road from the north, and swung left with it towards the castle foregate of Shrewsbury, the single dry-shod gate of a river-girt town, some mile or more distant. The countryside through which they marched was green and rich and lazy with summer, a land of fields and hamlets and scattered copses, undulating only very gently. North-eastwards it subsided with equal gentleness into the flatter plains of Cheshire, without a break. In this equable landscape they had already remarked, long since, the column of black smoke riding up into the summer sky, billowing darkly in middle air before it dispersed in an evil, russet-grey cloud drifting to westward, and making the declining sun angry and baleful. The flickering glow from beneath lit it only briefly and at long intervals; nevertheless, it was recognisable.

"They'll have fired whatever's beyond the wall," said Douglas, riding easy and tireless at Hotspur's side. "Harry, I doubt you're expected yonder."

"Archie, I doubt I am so!" And he laughed, freely and gladly, to see this evidence of resistance. "Ah, but I had a sweet pupil there, a foe after my own heart! He has no more than a handful to stay him, and he fires the foregate against me, and sets me at defiance. Oh, but I'm glad of him! I set out to have him without a blow, that's the truth, but I'll buy him as dear as I must, and never grudge what he cost me, if I can but put him out of risk and out of the battle. I tell you, I'd rather lose my throw outright than harm a hair of his head. We shall have to tread softly here, softly, or he'll impale himself on our lances, and that I'd never forgive."

They were riding at the head of the long column, the earl of Worcester behind with the rearguard, and only a couple of mounted scouts, one a Shropshire man, out before them, sounding the way ahead and harking back to the marching army ever and again to ensure continual contact. They had measured their pace from Stafford to be sure, so far as certainty is possible in human affairs, of being well ahead of any move the king could make, and yet to allow as much rest as was wise to men who had marched long distances and had good need to conserve their strength for the collision to come. A fair part of the chivalry of Cheshire rode at their backs, Sir Richard Venables, baron of Kinderton, Sir Richard Vernon, baron of Shipbrook, a formidable contingent of Cheshire archers, and knights from both Cheshire and Shropshire. With the Percy levies, and Douglas and his Scottish knights, a very worthy company.

"And did you think to take this prince of yours without resistance?" Douglas asked mildly, watching the mounting column of smoke blacken and blot out the sun.

"This prince of mine is not such a creature as may ever be taken without resistance. But I did think to trim the possibilities so far as to tie his hands out of danger. Short of this," he admitted, and frowned thoughtfully before him where the pulsing fires flashed fitfully under the darkling cloud. "If he resolves on fighting to the death, there's a back door I know of, though I'd meant it only for Owen when he comes. With so thin a garrison as Hal has here, we might get a party inside the wall by night."

"A fair enough risk for a royal hostage," said Douglas.

"He will not be a hostage. There shall no ill use be made of him." Hotspur's face was forbiddingly grave. What was to become of Hal in the new dispensation was more than he had yet considered, but it was God's truth that so far as lay in Hotspur's power, no ill use should ever be made of him.

They were drawing steadily nearer to the outer fringe of the suburb that sprawled outside the castle gate. The first broken shapes of what had been shops and houses showed blackly, billowing acrid smoke across the sullied fields, and glowing dully under the murk that was their only remaining roof. With the coming of the early evening a fresh wind had sprung up from the south-west, and was sweeping the bannerole of smoke crosswise in a long, flaunting streamer, uncovering by brief glimpses the crenellated crest of the wall beyond, and the towers of the castle. Hotspur's eyes narrowed against the shifting, smarting smoke and the delusive light, holding fast to those jagged outlines against the sky. They could hear timber beams bursting like bombards, and the fallen wood of doors and shutters crackling like a fire of thorns.

Hotspur's hand tightened smoothly on the rein, and his horse, instantly responsive, checked and eased to a halt in a few paces, and stood quivering. Hotspur glanced once over his shoulder, and waved the following ranks to a halt.

"Sound the recall," he said to the trumpeter who rode attentive at his back, "and fetch the outriders back to us. Let's hear what they have to say. This is beyond reasonable. I would not have supposed he had even the men to spread his devastation so far. Much less," he said with dark uneasiness, "the will. He does not love destruction, if he has no fear of it."

The trumpeter sent a piercing call before them, bright brazen gold shearing into the smutty blackness. In a few minutes it brought the nearer of the forward scouts cantering back out of the sluggish, wallowing fog that covered the road ahead. He dropped the fold of his cloak that he had been hugging across mouth and nostrils, and wiped his soiled face.

"My lord, it's all but impassable ahead, the whole foregate's burning. John Rowan has ridden forward to see if he can make out more of their dispositions, but the wall's manned, and heavily. I would not have believed the prince could have so strong a force here."

"How long ago do you suppose they put fire to this quarter?" asked Hotspur intently.

"My lord, not above five hours, I swear. And not in one or two places, but a dozen. And, my lord, I have not been so far ahead to be certain, but it seemed to me that all the houses close to the castle ditch had been not merely fired, but razed. There's a clear zone round the gate, clean of smoke."

"It's impossible!" said Hotspur in the softest and bleakest of whispers, to himself rather than to them. "He would have needed thousands of labourers. He had not the men by him for such a task. And if he had, he would have found them better work!"

The earl of Worcester was trotting up to join them from the rear of the column as the second outrider came blundering towards them out of the foul darkness ahead, face-down on his arm, and oozing black tears down his furrowed, sweating face. He was the Shropshireman, and he knew his Shrewsbury.

"My lord, the place swarms! They've razed the houses all along the ditch, and massed more archers than I dreamed they had along the wall. They've marched out a guard of pikemen and bowmen before the gate, in cover of the rubble, and are making shelters there for cover. I've been as close as man can get, and I make them more than two thousand men outside the gate, and at least as many well-placed inside, to pick off any who get through as fast as they come. If they've laid out so many, they have at least as many in reserve, and more resting for the relief. There's not a hope of carrying the gate against such odds."

There was no doubting his report; the evidence of the destructive activities of some thousands of men was there before their eyes. They looked at one another frowningly, incredulous still.

"I left him with barely a thousand to his name," said Worcester positively. "He has got reinforcements from somewhere. But in God's name, where? You cannot whistle up an army out of the ground. You'll not attempt battle now on such terms, Harry? At this hour, and after such a march?"

"No, impossible!" By Monday Glendower would be there on the other side of Severn, and Edmund with him, with all the Mortimer arms. No, there was not so much haste that they could not wait to be certain. And if they could not get in but at too high a price and too great a risk, yet they could prevent young Hal from getting out. For whatever force he had found from some secret resource of his own, it could not be as great as now it showed. The town was mounting an elaborate deceit to ward off attack, or else attract it upon the best available terms. It was too transparent; and Hotspur was not merely holding his own quarrel in his hands now, but his nephew's crown. Risks which might have been acceptable to him, on his own account he could no longer contemplate. "No, we'll wait our own good time to fight. We'll draw off and camp overnight. John, you know this river of yours. Is there a ford within reach where we can hold touch with the Welsh bank, out of range of the town?"

"Yes, my lord, at Shelton, to the north-west, by the Whitchurch road. We shall have to circle the bend of the Severn—half a mile back by the road we came. I'll bring you there."

He had had a bitter check, and he sat silently for some minutes, coming to terms with it. Tonight he had hoped to have a base, well-provisioned, with ample accommodation for his men, excellent communications westwards, and reinforcements on the way from both north and west. And most of all, and his heart grieved and fretted at the shattering of this hope, the prince disarmed, immobilised, out of danger, spared any ordeal of choice between rival affections and conflicting loyalties. That was over. He must deal with things as he found them. But he waited to have the mastery, not only of his face, but of his heart and will, before he turned about and withdrew to a night camp somewhere in the meadows north of the town. Nothing was lost but soft lying, a little indulgence by way of better eating, and a degree of security. But what was security, and who possessed it, in this world?

He sat with his hands lax and open on the rein, his eyes fixed upon the towers of the castle, seen fitfully between the coils of smoke. And as he watched, the wind, freshening boisterously with the changing temperature of the evening, suddenly tightened its hold and drew back the black folds as a hand draws a curtain, sweeping them strongly aside and delivering to view a long segment of the wall, clear against the westward sky. The same gust drew out fully the great banner on the tower, spreading it vauntingly before Hotspur's eyes, every colour and every shape seen clearly for one long moment. He had excellent eyes, keen, long-sighted and tireless, able to pick out detail and stoop upon it like a hawk striking. He reared his head, suddenly rigid from heels to hair, and the horse shuddered under him, and froze to the ground in sympathy.

"No!" he said in a whisper, to himself, not to them. "No, he could not! It's impossible!"

"What is it?" Douglas demanded, stiffening to the same tension. "For God's sake, man, what is it you see?"

"Nothing but a banner on the wall," said Hotspur, and laughed briefly and bitterly. "Dear God, I blame myself! How could I have miscalculated so grossly? I should have known! I should have done him justice—if he could no longer fight for himself with a whole mind, there was one for whom he could!"

"The prince's banner?" said Worcester, with blank incomprehension, peering through haze as the smoke doubled back across their field of vision. "What of it? I see nothing curious in it."

"Uncle, your eyes are less sharp then mine, or you see what you will to see. Watch now—the wind freshens again. There!"

The wind took the heavy silks again, and spread them triumphantly to view, the deep blue with the fleurs de lis of "France moderae," the blood-red of England with the three golden lions, the arms of the royal house. "Do you see any silver label of cadency there?"

The regal colours, distant as they were, streamed clear before them for a long, derisive moment, before they were veiled again in recoiling fronds of smoke. And it was plain to see that there was no silver bar, with three teeth pointing downwards, set across the upper quarters of the device. What they had taken for granted as the arms of the prince was, in truth, the royal banner itself, without any badge of cadency. They caught the truth of it, in all its implications, and sat mute and motionless, staring until the caprice of the wind veiled the phenomenon from their sight.

King Henry, Henry of Lancaster in the new dispensation, had done the impossible. By what frenzy of jealousy or prodigy of anxious paternal love he had achieved it might never be known, but somehow he had conveyed a clumsy, unwieldy, slow-moving army of twenty-five thousand men, with all their baggage and supplies and camp-followers, a quarter of the way across England in less than three days. It was not the prince of Wales with a hapless skeleton force, but the king of England with all his host, who waited to confront them in Shrewsbury.

13

In Shrewsbury there was disorder wherever the soldiers were not, and order of a disorderly kind where the soldiers were, order that meant a systematic looting of all citizen armaments and stores of food, and the billeting of troops wherever there was space for them, in every household and barn and workshop, in every orchard where the summer nights made sleeping in the open air possible. No army is ever popular where it must set to work to feed and partially arm itself at the expense of the citizens. Yet Shrewsbury welcomed this army with gratitude and relief, and grumbled less than usual about its depredations. English feeling here had always been heavily on the king's side, simply because the English here lived so close to the peril of Wales. To trade across the border was one thing; to be threatened by a large Welsh army, reputedly already hammering at the gates, was something very different.

The panic rumours grew after the firing of the castle foregate. Surely the Welsh were coming, in strength, to kill and rape and rob. A half-demented friar preached at the Cross, and laid all the town's sorrows at the door of the Welsh within the gates. Within an hour after the houses outside the wall began to burn, the first house within the wall was burning, too, the house of a Welsh baker. The soldiers quartered on him put out the fire before it set light to a whole district of the town, expelled the raiders, and sent them away with a flea in the ear. But they only acquired a few more enthusiasts

round the next corner, and went on to the next house. By then
every Welshman resident within the walls was a secret agent and
a traitor, waiting to let the enemy in. Doors were broken open,
shutters wrenched away from windows, household furnishings
stolen, and a few people beaten and wounded. Sometimes the king's
soldiers, if they were at hand, intervened to save worse chaos and
injury. Sometimes they let be, and went on indifferently with what
they were doing, for indeed they had more than enough to do.

There were ten of King Henry's men-at-arms quartered on Rhodri
Parry, in the spacious and comfortable lofts above the store-rooms;
but they were not there when the mob reached the house of the
Fleece. There was no one within-doors but Rhodri and Julian, and
the old woman Joanna, deaf but not ill-informed, and shrewd enough
to slip out by the side door and attach herself quickly and compliantly
to the rear ranks of the mob as soon as she grasped what was happening. Even the servant of a Welsh household might be suspected unless
she cried out as loudly and venomously as the neighbours.

Supper was over when the mob reached the house. It was six
o'clock, and Julian had cleared away the dishes and trenchers, and
was at the foot of the stairs, on her way back to the solar. She heard
the first thunderous battering of fists against the cart-door, and froze
where she stood, one foot on a higher stair, one hand on the balus-
ter, listening too intently even to turn her head. She knew that the
gate was bolted and barred, and strong enough to withstand fists and
feet and shoulders, if they stopped at that. But the wall, though high,
was not too high to be climbed, if they brought up a cart, or some
giant lent himself as a ladder.

It was no great surprise to her; in a sense she had been expecting
something of the kind ever since the war in Wales had flared into
violence. But to hear the shuffling pressure of many feet outside in
the alley, and the mindless muttering that broke suddenly in shouts
and rattling blows against the solid wood, chilled her heart with a
revulsion which was more than mere fear. Quickly she turned back

the few paces to the door of the undercroft, and secured it with the three great beams which were seldom used; one more barrier against unreasoning hate. All the ground-floor shutters were kept closed and fastened, but there were second shutters within, and these, also, she made fast before she climbed the stairs.

By then she knew that this was no mere malice of street-boys, for the blows that thundered at the gate and along the timber of the walls were heavy and strong, and the voices were not those of children, but adult and malignant, howling now in the echoing lane: "Welsh traitors…Welsh traitors! Come out! Fetch them out of their holes! Get rid of the Welsh!" There were women among them, too, shrill and vindictive: "Welsh witch, Welsh witch! Traitors—they want to betray the town!"

She went quickly and quietly up the stairs, and Rhodri was standing in the open doorway of the solar, listening. For years she had not seen him look as he looked now, younger, taller, all the lines of his face sharpened into fierce, concentrated attention.

"If we keep quiet within," she said, "they may tire of it and go, thinking there's no one here."

"I doubt," he said, as one making a detached estimate, not at all as a timorous man overtaken by a devil he had provoked. "If they conclude there's no one within, they'll be all the more eager to break a way in and pillage the house."

"The door below is bolted, and all the windows fast. Perhaps I should go and warn Joanna," she said. "So deaf as she is, she may not have heard, and if they feel as it seems about us, even she may not be safe. If it's too late to slip out by the back window from the cart-house, at least she could take refuge with Nicholas and hope to pass unnoticed."

But when she had climbed the little ladder-stair to the attic rooms in the roof, she found them empty. Joanna had removed not only herself, but also the meagre bundle of her belongings. Julian accepted the omen, and went quickly downstairs again and across the yard. The thunder at the cart-door was more than fists now; they had brought the yoke-pole of an ox-cart, or something like it, and were using it as a ram, and she heard the scrabble of toes against the wood, as someone tried to climb high enough to reach the top of the wall. In the store-rooms there was no one, in the loft above, where the journeymen slept, no one. The elder man had been pressed into service loading and unloading for the soldiers, but the younger one had left even the half of his clothes behind, and climbed out by the back window, and down into the narrow lane at the rear. She knew the manner of his going because he had left the shutters standing wide open. She secured them, and went back to her father.

"We're deserted. They've gone to their own, the old woman and Nicholas, too."

"So much the better," he said. "At least there's no one to let them in."

"As they're howling that we intend to let Prince Owen and his Welshmen in," she said. A pity, a great pity! What had possessed a slow-moving king to move so fast on this occasion? Only a few more hours, and Hotspur's army would have been masters of the town. And now where were they, and what could they do, against double their numbers, until Prince Owen came? Nicholas had brought home the rumour that the rebel army was at the gates, intending to invest the town until their reinforcements arrived. There was no one here for the Welsh inhabitants to count on; the soldiers would not interfere with the townspeople's amusements unless they became dangerous to more than the hated Welsh. She was both sorry and glad that Iago Vaughan had slipped away to rejoin his lord three days ago, and could not be expected here again until the prince came in arms; she would have found some bleak comfort in his presence now, but it would have been a pity for him to make one more sacrifice, and all for nothing.

"You'd better give me a dagger," she said, hearing the first splintering of wood below at the gate, and the great roar of triumph, and the heaving and struggling of men as they dragged their ram out of the timber and hauled it back to strike again.

He had been methodically clearing the last personal papers from the press in a corner of the solar, and he turned then and looked at her somewhat strangely, with a look she remembered afterwards, though at this moment it seemed to her detached and grudging as always.

"You'll need no dagger. Here, take these—the last. The rest is all piled there in my private closet—everything that could betray us. I began to burn them. Go and finish the work for me."

"And you?" she said steadily. The noise of the door being gradually battered to pieces tore at her nerves, but physically rather than in any other way. What complaint had she, after all? She had gone into this conflict with her eyes open, and it had given her the first intense purpose of her life, and the one immense joy. If they killed her for a traitress, that was a possibility she had accepted long ago. One man's patriot is another man's traitor.

"Do as I tell you," he said, not petulantly, as once he might have said it, but with an authority she did not even desire to question. "Hurry, get rid of them!"

There was a small withdrawing-room behind the narrow door in the panelling, and beyond that, and opening from it behind one more tapestry-hung door even smaller than the first, the closet where he did his most private work and kept his most perilous records, both of trade and of his activities as an auxiliary of war. And he kept few, to make the whole transaction disposable at short notice. Though she did not think, as she carried his seal and papers into the little room and knelt at the stone hearth with them, that the absence of all proof would save them. But it might buy half an hour, even an hour, long enough for the soldiers quartered on the house to come back from their shift of duty at the wall and the foregate, and intervene in the interests of their own comfort. What use would a sacked or roofless house be to them?

The embers glowed in whitening ash, and there was still flame enough to catch the next fragment she fed into the heat. She worked devoutly, for the first time in her life, perhaps, intent on doing his bidding as quickly and cleanly as she could. As though he had been her general in battle, and she his reliable officer. How strange, to respect and love him whole-heartedly only now, when they were at the last extreme! She fed the flames neatly, quickly, so intent that she felt little. But she heard the sudden terrifying swell of roaring voices and rushing feet as the gate gave way and the mob came hurtling over the creaking fragments into the yard, and across it to thud and hammer at the door of the house. Voices drunken upon fear and anger and hatred, screaming: "Welsh dogs! Welsh dogs! Traitors!" And some screaming without need of words at all, a frightful sound, belling, pursuing, scenting a kill. She had a glimpse of how the hind feels at the end of her strength, with the pack not many yards behind her labouring silver heels.

The house door was strong, but the very weight with which the foremost attackers were hurled into it made the hinges creak and the beams complain. Julian fed her fire, thrust such fragments as rolled aside deeper into the heat, and watched the last traces of her father's activities burn gradually out to black. It was barely over when she heard the door below splinter out of its frame and crash upon the floor of the undercroft, and the shriek of a woman fallen and trampled in the rush for the stair. One more barrier was torn from between her ears and the sound of murder, of ordinary people turned to extraordinary beasts, their cries magnified into a discordant babel by the lofty roof above the staircase.

Now she knew that whoever came to intervene would come too late. They meant killing. If one grovelled, they might spare, out of pleasure and vanity. But who was to grovel here? Not she, and not her father! How had she ever, even for a moment, believed in him as in a narrow, fearful man? She pushed the last shred of parchment into the embers, sprang up from her knees, and ran to the door, to join him where she knew he must be, there at the head of the staircase.

She wrenched at the handle of the door, and it would not give to her. He had locked her in! She had never heard him cross the outer room on her heels, but so he must have done. The door was fast; she wrestled with it, and it resisted all her force. And there was yet one more door between herself and the solar, and both screened with woven hangings. She could not remember that the outer one had any lock or key, but what comfort was there in that, when she could not get through this inner one to reach it? He was alone there, against this half-demented mob.

In her rage and grief she cried out against him, cursing him for making her of less honour than a son, a son whom he would surely have acknowledged beside him, flank to flank, each keeping the other's side and back against all comers. And then she cried out to him in entreaty, begging him to let her through to him for pity's sake, because he was her sire, and she his dear daughter, and his fortune was her fortune, and his death her death. But neither he nor any other heard her. What was one voice against so many?

She tore at the coiled braids of her hair, dragged down all that weight of pale bronze about her shoulders, and plucked out one of her long hair-pins to attack the lock of the door, but still it defied her. And all the while she worked in frantic quietness, she heard what went on beyond two doors, out of her reach.

He was there at the head of the staircase when the door gave way below, and they rushed in over the splintered timbers and over their fallen fellows to mount the first few steps. She heard them check there, suddenly confronted and instantly daunted, except that they were so many, and he was one.

They came on, of course. They could do no other, the pressure behind them being so great; they were thrust upwards whether they would or no. Even in her anguish, she felt their fright and desperation as they were hoisted within Rhodri's reach, and her heart swelled in a kind of wild exultation. Then she heard them shriek in a new way, hewn and hacked, the outcry of men dying.

She dropped the useless hair-pin, and battered on the door with her fists, and called until her voice failed her, but no one heard. Not even Rhodri, who in any case would not have heeded, but now heard nothing but the thunder in his ears, and some distant, triumphant echoes of old harping, and the clamour of his enemies. He stood with his long gown kilted into his belt, and his thick legs straddled across the landing at the head of the staircase, his grizzled hair and beard on end, as if some supernatural lightning had drawn every hair erect; and with great swings of his bull-shoulders he drew vast semicircles before him with the two-handed sword that had belonged to his great-grandsire, a modest captain in the following of Llewelyn ap Griffith, the last of the great princes of Wales before the Lord Owen came. As often as the mob, thrusting senselessly forward, heaved their leaders within his reach, he cut them down, and swept the highest steps of the stair clean again, between his ranging blows, with thrusts of a booted foot, hurling the fallen back into the arms of those below. And as he fought he cried his defiance against them and against all the English in the name and the tongue of Wales, in a great voice that presently fell into a rhythm and measure like a religious chant, and after that into full, roaring song. For there had been bards among his free kin, as well as warriors, and at this hour he was all of them.

Julian forsook her senseless clamour, and darted back to the sunken cupboards in the wall of her father's closet, and there swept everything from the shelves and dragged everything from the chest, to find something with which she might hope to lift the catch of the lock. Pewter cups and dishes, hooks, reliquaries, woollen cloths, tapestry hangings, gowns—at the bottom of the chest there was a long, thin dagger in a figured leather sheath. She fell upon it joyfully, and drew it out; almost a foot long, and very narrow and finely ground. The crevice between door and jamb would admit several inches of it, more than enough.

She worked the point in delicately, felt for the barrier that halted it, and tilted with terrible patience at the hilt, groping her way with eyes closed and fingers quivering with nervous sensitivity. And she heard the great, resplendent voice without, that she hardly recognised for the grudging, grumbling complaint of her father, roaring forth the two-hundred-year-old declaration of Gwalchmai, son of Meilyr, the bard of another Owen, Owen Gwynedd, long ago:

> "'…my name is Gwalchmai, the enemy of all things
>   English…
> Bright is my sword, dazzlingly fashioned,
> Deadly in the day of battle. Golden my shield flashes,
> Multitudes sing my praises that never saw my face.
> My name goes before me…I am the anger of Wales…'"

From the invaders there arose suddenly a shrill, savage cry, soaring even above their fear and venom and pain, and she knew that they had overrun him, though how it happened she never knew. It had been inevitable from the first. One man cannot hold off hundreds even of his inferiors for ever. Someone had clawed him down, someone had had the sheer luck to slide under the stroke of his broadsword and grip him by the garments and pull him down into the whirlpool. And then their weight overpowered him, pinning hands and feet and sword, and there was nothing but a frenzied, animal keening and howling, at once exultant and frightened, jubilant and anguished, and the last subsiding paeans of Gwalchmai's hymn to his own prowess, broken, spasmodic, strangled in blood, until the hacking, battering, ululating voice of the mob triumphant silenced it totally at last.

She crouched trembling and sick against the door, her hands still questing, probing, hoping, feeling iron and steel grate together, but never fruitfully engage. She was hardly aware when the note of the outcry on the staircase changed, when fear and awe, and the panic desire to be held clear of fault, overcame even triumph. Those behind had grasped at last how far those before had gone, and were drawing off, quietly and furtively, to put themselves elsewhere and blameless while there was time. And those before felt themselves deserted, and looked round uneasily for reassurance, and finding none, also thought well to remove themselves from this place of death.

The heavy lock gave at last. The door swung open before her weight, and she fell forward and lay for a moment face-down over the threshold, drawing breath deeply, her eyes closed. Only then did she realise that there was silence all about her, unbroken by any movement or word. They had frightened themselves out of the house, perhaps to slink away home from venturing any more such assaults, perhaps to turn their attention to some easier victim. Numbly she gathered herself up from the floor, and dragged herself across to the door into the solar. It was not locked or barred. Nor had a single one of the attackers got past Rhodri to set foot in either room. Alive, he had held the staircase single-handed in arms, and dead, he had so awed them with fear of the consequences that they had not stayed even to loot.

He lay sprawled over the topmost step of the stairs, his head dangling as he had fallen forward, his body slashed and trampled, and oozing from a dozen wounds. Knives and bludgeons and boots had been used on him at the last in frantic vindictiveness, the fruit of pain and fear. There was no breath in his mouth and no lustre in his eyes. She turned up his face to her between her hands, and it was bloody but not broken, though his head was pulp. The hilt of the great broadsword was still gripped in his hand.

Rhodri Parry was dead, like his forefathers, with his slain heaped before him. There were three of them tumbled like sacks against the wall, and by the smears of blood that trailed away out of the house door more than one wounded man had dragged himself away to end or mend elsewhere. Above them the incredible quietness hung like a spell, causing Julian, too, to hold her breath and move on tiptoe about this house she hardly recognised, and in which she would never live again.

There was nothing for her to do here, and nowhere for her to go in this town. To stay here with her dead might mean her own death, at the hands of the townspeople or the soldiers, did it matter which? And whether her life was of any moment or not, it had a value now for her because her father had covered it deliberately with his own body, and bequeathed it to her as his last legacy. She was, in any case, a lover of life, and hungry still, and she was the only creature left here, until Iago returned, who was in Rhodri's secrets, and knew his plans, the routes he used, where to find his agents, everything that might still be useful to the Lord Owen and to Hotspur.

She could think of only one place where she might find safe refuge until the Welsh came, and that was Walter Hanner's cottage by the Severn, two miles up-river. She had no idea how she was to reach it, but she could not stay here alone. Nor dared she venture into the streets as she was, to be recognised and cornered somewhere where there would be no one to defend her, and no one to pity her.

She remembered then that young Nicholas had left half his belongings in the loft. She made her way down the staircase slippery with blood, and littered with curious debris of cast shoes, and woollen cap, and a torn wimple, edging past the dead bodies and clambering over the wreckage of the door, and crossed to the store-house. Nicholas was barely seventeen, a lanky lad an inch or two taller than herself. He had bundled together his best clothes and taken them with him, but there was an old, dun-coloured tunic of his, and patched chausses, and they fitted well enough, turning her into a willowy peasant boy. Even under a capuchin the mass of her hair betrayed her, and to wear the hood on such a summer evening might mark her out as having something to hide. She went down into the store-room and looked for the great cloth-shears, and taking her hair ruthlessly in handfuls, lopped it off as neatly as she could in such haste, drawing the short strands down on her brow to change the narrow oval symmetry of her face.

There was money in Rhodri's closet. She went back for that. The rebels had need of money, like any other army, and she grudged leaving anything here to be looted by street thieves as soon as they found the broken door, or forfeited to the king's treasury. She took, also, the dagger with which she had forced the lock, buckling it to her belt under her tunic; and with nothing but this and the cloth purse hidden against her body, she slipped out through the deserted alley and away through the town.

There was no hope of using the postern gate at the friary now, with the town full of soldiers, and the towers in the New Work fully manned. She made her way instead to the main street above the castle, where the curious had gathered, hampering the movements of the garrison, and under the murk of smoke from outside the wall faces were as dim and strange as in dusk. It was well to be a boy at this pass, for boys make their way everywhere, and pass for harmlessly inquisitive even when they have other designs. The guard was not making any very serious efforts to keep them from crowding into the gateway, to peer at the burning foregate, and the nearer dispositions of the soldiers deployed outside the town wall. Julian went with the boldest, edging along the wall, until she could see the blackened shells of buildings stretching on either side the road, and parties of townsmen busy piling masonry shelters from the rubble of the razed shops to give cover to the archers. The king's forces were ready to offer battle, but there was much yet to be done to strengthen their positions, and new parties were marching out from the town to help in the work. Julian added herself to one of these ragged troops as it came through the gate, and went with it, unchallenged, out across the castle ditch, and into the smoky turmoil of the foregate.

Getting out had been simple enough in the end, but getting

away was not so easy. She took what chance offered, and chose her moment to drop flat into a clump of bushes behind the smouldering ruins on the left of the road, and there she lay hidden until the dusk came down fully. The preparations had been wasted, at least for today; no one was going to accept battle upon these terms and at this late hour. If she could lie undiscovered until the detachments on guard here were withdrawn into the town and the gate closed, she would have the night to herself, and could make her way round the coil of the river to Walter's holding.

She rose at last in the darkness and quietness of a night still soiled with smoke but already quick with clean stars overhead. She saw the wall of Shrewsbury looming high over her, and the turrets of the castle gate jagged against a faintly luminous sky. Nothing stirred about her. It seemed a world without armies, and almost without life. She stole out through the ruined foregate and away to the riverside path, where her feet could go quickly and silently in the grass, and the silvery movement of the water was her guide.

Not until she had been walking for twenty minutes did her path bring her close to the road at Cross Hill; and in a little while after that she became aware that the heath-land here was trodden flat in a great swathe, and there were horse-droppings, and the ruts of wheels, over a breadth of probably fifty yards. And later she saw, still far before her, and surely no great way from Walter's house, the small, still glimmer of fires, terrestrial stars, spread in a broad belt along the heath.

Then she understood in whose footsteps she was walking. Those sparks were the fires of Hotspur's army, camped here in the night close to a ford of Severn; and those tracks were the marks of his passage hither, horse and baggage-wagon and pack-mule and foot soldier and cavalry and all, and himself at the head. He had not withdrawn from Shrewsbury far.

For the first time since she had turned her back on Rhodri and walked away into the town, her heart rose and quickened into warmth and pain and hope within her, and believed in vengeance, and in joy and freedom, and above all in herself, a woman with much to give and to get and to do before she left this world.

❧ ❧

"Am I to under-rate him a second time?" said Hotspur, frowning into the dying glow of the fire. The night was mild and still; they had not troubled even to erect tents, it was pleasant lying in the open, and there was heather and grass enough to pile rough, fragrant beds. "My knowledge of him, my judgment of him, everything I have trusted before says, with you, that he will fight none but a defensive battle. And yet I say, once I was thus sure of him, and he outdid me and gave me the lie. For love of his son, I grant you, and the more credit to him. And now, as you say, his son is secured, he has a town to stead him, and an heir to keep inviolate, and everything in him must prompt him to hold Shrewsbury and stand me off. And God knows it would suit me well to have him act so. But I have been mistaken in him once, and can be so again. God grant us two more full days, and all is well. Even if he move against me then, I need not avoid, I can hold him until Owen comes."

"If he keeps his time," said Worcester, not doubting Glendower more than he doubted every other man, but never building upon any.

"He'll keep his time. And there's Edmund to double the assurance. He's committed now, like me. We've declared for Roger's boy, and we must make it good."

"We're agreed, then." Douglas lay at his ease in the thick July turf, and in the dying firelight his face showed as an oval of pallor pierced by the black hole that was the patch over his blind eye. The eye was not quite dead, it felt pain from bright daylight still, and distinguished between light and dark, but he was grown so used to the protective shade that he forgot to doff it even in the night. "We hold off as long as he bides within his walls. And if he ventures out, we dog him, but avoid battle until the Welsh allies are here. Though for my part," he said, "I'd rather have at him wherever I may, and whether he stand or run. I mind me I'm still a Scot, and I have issues at stake with this king of yours."

"Not mine," said Hotspur, gently and certainly. "No more my king." He looked towards Shrewsbury, invisible in the night, for even the glow of the foregate had dulled into umber and black by this hour; but he knew where it lay, and for many reasons it drew his eyes and his heart. There were some within there whom he had failed, and not only the prince. "If I had but my own hand to play," he said, "I should be wholly of your mind. I have matters of dispute with Henry of Lancaster myself that grow worse by waiting."

"Oh, I'm with you! You are my general now, Harry, and I'm under your orders. I'll fight as you see fit. For I never yet heard tell," he said blithely, "of Hotspur showing any man fighting that was less than bonny to see and grand to share in."

"I'd liefer show a guest successful fighting, if I can," owned Hotspur with a small, dry smile. "We're not in the lists now, but in good earnest. What bridges he left standing between us, I've burned. There's no going back."

"And would you wish for it?" Worcester asked.

The answer came without hesitation or doubt. "No. I never have wished, nor never can wish, to turn back even by one day. I know no other way but forward."

"And you regret nothing?"

"Nothing." Not even that too precipitate choice I made, he thought, when Henry landed at Ravenspur. What I did, I did with all my will and my might, then as always, believing in it as in the gospel. It is for a man to act as best he knows, and afterwards pay for what was done amiss without grudging and without humility. There is a price upon everything, and I am not a market tradesman, to haggle over the pence.

The fires had died down to glimmers, a hundred such guarded sparks mirroring the stars in the sky. Kinderton and Shipbrook had long since made the rounds of the Cheshire levies, and checked on the line of outposts strung along the riverside to signal any activity from the town. Worcester arose, yawning, to make a similar patrol of the companies to eastward, keeping contact with the road and the field of withdrawal in case of need.

"I'm for sleep, Harry, when I've checked on the landward watches. You'd best get some rest, too. Who knows how much we may hope for tomorrow?"

He had barely withdrawn a few yards from their fire when he turned back. "Here's someone heading for us. But from the river! It's too early yet for Owen to be within call."

Douglas rolled up lazily on one elbow to see, and Hotspur, in a movement as sparing as a cat's, came silently to his feet.

They emerged gradually from the darkness, a close little knot of figures, headed by a thickset Cheshire master-at-arms, and followed distrustfully by two soldiers with hands on their swords. Hotspur recognised three men from the Severnside outposts. And solid but wary between these guards, four men in the common homespun clothes of peasants or small artisans, one elderly and squat, the other three in their strong middle years and powerfully made. And a thin, agile, shabby boy of eighteen or so, who walked before them, and carried himself as one having authority, either over them, or to speak on their behalf. A boy whose movements he knew, even before the flare of a collapsing branch in the fire showed him briefly and blindingly the features of the bright, pale face.

"My lord, here's a young fellow claims to be bringing you four good recruits, and weapons to go with them, and says he's Welsh, and so are they, runaways waiting here to cross over to the Lord Owen. My lord, it's true enough concerning the arms—three good bows, and arrows enough, and swords, too. And this man here does seem to know his business as fletcher and master-bowman. But, with respect, we thought well to bring them to you, as the boy asked. For they could as well be spies sent out here from the town to take note of our defences."

"You did right," said Hotspur, his eyes upon the young man's face, that watched him unwaveringly from great, gaunt eyes that caught the reflection of the firelight, and flared from black to burning red. "But all is as it seems here. I know the boy. He has been my good friend and messenger in these parts many months. Deal with him as with one dearly valued by me, and you will do well."

"Then, my lord, will it please you we bring these men to your lordship's master-bowman, and have him find them place in his companies? The one, my lord, is said to be a first-class swordsman, once in the prince's army, but a Welshman born."

"We'll ask their guide," said Hotspur, "to name them. Friends, you're welcome here. I think I need hardly ask if you know what you do?"

The boy stood among his companions, and named them one by one, with their skills; he spoke for all, offering fealty to the ally of Wales. The men, alert and intent, spoke out agreement.

"Then I, too, pledge you that I will do what I may for the cause which is also your cause. And I trust in God you shall not regret that you entered my service. Go now with my master-at-arms, and he will see you to your proper places among us. Even with some who can speak your own tongue, as, God forgive me, I cannot."

"My Lord," said the old fletcher bluntly, "you speak a language we understand, and that's enough."

"And the boy?" asked the master-at-arms doubtfully.

"The boy stays here with me. He has matter to deliver. Only take note of him, so that if he come again you may know him, and give him instant access to me. He is under my protection. Make it known!" said Hotspur, with emphasis his own men knew how to value.

"My lord, willingly!" He slapped the hilt of his sword, and withdrew with his recruits into the dark.

Hotspur looked from his uncle to the Douglas, who had also come to his feet some moments since, aware of private matters heavy on the air. He was very quick to sense any need or urgency in those he once accepted into his arbitrary grace.

"Leave us alone," said Hotspur, very gently and low.

"I'm gone," said Douglas, and clapped his friend on the shoulder in going. Worcester had already turned and vanished into the night. The two of them were left alone in this hollow of heather and turf and broom-bushes, as he had desired, looking fixedly at each other across the narrow, fading zone of firelight.

"Julian!" he said in a whisper, when he was sure that there was no third left within hearing; and he reached out to take her by the hands and draw her close to the fire, the better to search and devour her face. "For God's sake, girl, do you know what risks you take, coming thus into a military camp? What brings you here? What has happened to you? Sit down here with me, and tell me! For I see by your face that whatever it may be, it is terrible, and I fear that I am the guilty cause of it. I pray God it may not be worse even than I have deserved, and more than you can bear."

She sat with him beside the dying fire, still at last after so long of being in flight, and told him everything. And now, with his hands gripping her hands, and his face confronting her with fierce, dismayed eyes, she felt that a place of arrival at least had survived for her, and from there it was but a step to a place from which she could again set out, if need be alone.

"This death is at my door," he said, in hushed and grieving certainty. "I have killed him, and ruined you. Better for you if you had never seen me!"

"No!" she said. "It is not true!"

"It is true. I failed to make good what I set out to do. By my own error, by rating my enemy too low, I failed of occupying Shrewsbury, and left you to the mercy of a disordered mob." And it was in his mind then, for the first time, that the omen meant yet more than the loss of Shrewsbury and this death that accused him now. For if the stars turn against a man, neither courage nor wit can avail him.

"Even if you had come those few hours earlier," she said, "so would the mob have taken to killing in their terror a few hours earlier. If we had never known you, he would still be dead, and I should still be homeless. But if I had never known you, I should be poor and wretched also, and alone, and that I am not. And he would have died in doubt of his lord's triumph, at the least in fear for it, and that was not his case, dying. He felt himself glorious in glorious company, and his cause invincible. Is that reproach to you?"

"It is a heavy burden," he said. For he was learning new and grave things concerning himself. Never had his own life, or even the fortunes of his house, weighed so sombrely upon his spirit in the day of battle as did this supreme issue in hand now, which drew into itself the lives and destinies of so many others. Such a terrible responsibility, he thought, kings must bear; and the first sudden tremor of understanding and sympathy troubled him for Henry's sake, but troubled him too late. Happy the man who travels light, with nothing to weigh him down but his own honour and his own life. Nothing worse can happen to him than death, what has he to be afraid of? But I, he thought, passionately studying Julian's soiled and weary face, have been the cause of death to others, and shall be so again. "I doubt not," he said, "that you forgive me, but I do not forgive myself. And even you cannot absolve me."

"I have done better, for I've trusted myself to you, to bring you help and to get help from you." She meant only the help she already received, in his touch and his nearness and the enlargement of her spirit to reach the last extremes of the love she felt for him; but she saw the spark of pleasure and consolation spring eagerly into his overshadowed face, taking her in another way. And she was glad beyond measure that even mistakenly he should be comforted.

"Yes, we must take thought what is to be done for you now, until I am free. You are on my conscience and on my heart, Julian, for now the Lord Owen and I between us are all the family you have, and the Lord Owen is still some way from us. But I am here, and I am the kinsman whose pleasure and privilege it is to provide for you and care for you as best I may. You cannot go back to Shrewsbury until it falls to us. And you cannot stay here among us after tonight. How do we know what tomorrow will bring? And though I dare swear my men are as good fellows as any, and better than most, yet they are not saints, and in the night you may pass for a youth at arm's length, perhaps, but by daylight not at a hundred paces, my sweet comrade. What like of man is this Walter Hanner? Can you trust him fully? You have brought me four stout men," he said, grieved, "who could better have been standing guard over you in the toft until all's over."

"There was one of them, the youngest," she said bluntly, "that I would not have trusted with any woman short of fifty years old, and ugly into the bargain. But Walter is elderly, and has been my father's man for a long time, and known me from a child. In any case, you need not fear for me. I have a dagger."

"I had seen the hilt of it," he said, with respect and affection, and even a little mockery. "But I trust you may never have to use it. Then surely you may lie quiet at this riverside holding for a few days, until our issue comes to the proof. But I cannot let you go back there tonight alone, I cannot go with you now, and I would not trust you to any of my men in the dark. Sleep here in my charge through the night, and in the dawn I'll bring you to the edge of the camp and see you safe on your way. If Iago comes looking for you before I am free, it's at the toft he'll look. Wait there in shelter until either he or I come for you. And if he is the first to come, leave me word there where to find you."

He took her by the chin in his right hand, and lifted her face to him, and studied her earnestly. She had never yet seen his countenance so close, or so moved. From straining to see her intimately by starlight his always wide, wide-set and candid eyes had dilated into great dark-brown peat-pools full of reflected light. Very faintly she saw her own image there.

"Julian, you and I know each other now too well for any pretence.

If the day goes well for us, then it will be my joy to provide fitly for
you, and you of your goodness will not deny me joy. But I must
take thought honestly for the chances of battle, for they cannot be
long delayed. No man can take his victory for granted—and no man,
even victorious, can take his life for granted. And therefore I long
to make you some endowment now, while I may. Not many even
of the generous can take as generously as they give, but you I know
now as I know my own soul. Better, for when I remember to think
on my soul it bewilders me sadly, and I choose rather to leave it to
God. But in you I find no bewilderment. Do me this kindness!...
suffer me to give, for once, instead of getting! Turn your head!"

In all her life she had never heard herself addressed in a voice so
charged with eloquent tenderness, or ever felt hands touch her as
his touched her now, the proudest hands, the most accomplished
in arms, the most feared by his enemies and revered by his friends,
of any in England. They smoothed down the folds of her capuchin,
and passed about her throat the golden collar of heavy links he had
just unclasped from about his own neck. His warmth was still quick
in it. And as he shot the clasp home, he suddenly set the tip of his
right forefinger in the top of the delicate groove at the nape of her
neck, where the mangled dark-gold hair was cropped short, and
stroked gently down to the hasp of the golden collar; and there was
such grief in his touch, in this one intimate caress she ever had from
him, that she said in a soft, distressful cry: "I've made myself ugly
to you!"

"No! You are to me beautiful and fearless and true, even more
than ever before. This is not repayment, for I can never repay you,
it is a grace and a blessing to me, and in some sort an offering to salve
my soul. And will you give me something in return?" He smiled
suddenly, and opening his palm before her, showed her a shorn tress
of her own hair. "It was caught inside your hood. It might have
betrayed you—it can only be a talisman and a blessing to me."

"I pray to God it may," she said, and watched him blow gently upon the curl in the bowl of his hand, to make it quiver and stir with life, and then roll it round his finger and put it carefully away in the breast of his cotte. "On this exchange at least will you call quits with me?"

"With all my heart," she said, and drew the collar of her tunic and the folds of her capuchin over his gift. She did not say to him that as long as she lived she would never part with it for any price that could be offered her, and whatever need she might suffer; but she thought that in his heart, which was very subtle in its simplicity, he knew it.

"At least it could provide you a dowry, should I fail to come for you."

"God forbid!" she said, understanding him too well; for no man may take for granted his victory or his life.

"If I live, I shall not fail. And if I cannot come, go with Iago to the Lord Owen, and he will surely stand to you in a father's place."

"You will come," she said; but for herself she made no promise.

"Now you must get some rest. Sleep here in my cloak. You may in safety, I shall not leave you, and there's enough dry grass piled here in the heather for two."

He brought her wine in his own drinking-horn, and offered meat and bread, too, but she would not eat. Then he shaped the bed of grass for her, and spread his great cloak, with his saddle-roll under her head for a pillow, and for a moment stood looking down at her thoughtfully, and sniffing the chilling air of the night, for it was close to midnight, and the scattered fires over the heath had all burned down into black as the great camp fell silent. He went away briefly into the darkness, and came back with a sheathed sword in his hands. He met her watching eyes, already faintly filmed over with sleep, and smiled.

"This was my talisman and my luck in the old days, and many a time served me for a cross when there was little time for priests and prayers before a fight. It was my grandsire's before me, I'm never parted from it. Now, with your goodwill, it may well serve us as swords were wont to serve noble friends in old time, or so the singers tell us. For it will be cold here in the small hours, and you're but thinly clad, and I would give you my warmth. Open a fold of your cloak to my priest and me, and let us in."

She stretched out her arm and spread the thick frieze wide to make room for him, and he lay down beside her, and drew the hem close about them both, with the sword laid between them. Suddenly moved by an awareness of great danger and great blessing, she clasped her hands upon the cross of the hilt, and prayed her usual nightly prayers, knowing with all her heart that this night was matter for thanksgiving even though it had begun in death and might well end in death. After a moment of hesitation he laid his own hand over hers, and so held her; and when she had said to the end, he answered: "Amen!"

Then they were silent, and he lay beside her with all forbearance and consideration, not so much as touching, but listening constantly to her soft breathing until from very exhaustion it lengthened into the ease of sleep. Fitfully he slept, too. But in the small hours she dreamed of terror, and stirred and moaned in distress, and then he drew the sword from between them, for fear of hurting or waking her, and laid it aside from them in the heather, and gathered her into his arms. She drew deep, relaxing breath, turned to him, and ceased to dream; or if she dreamed thereafter, it was not of horrors. She had marvellously slender, delicate bones, like a bird, and her cropped hair against his cheek was smooth and soft like a bird's breast-feathers. Filled with heavy, dark tenderness, he sank into deep sleep with her.

❧

Together they fell asleep, and they awoke together, before the first hint of dawn. There were few words then. He went with her through the camp, already beginning to stir, until they sighted the roof of the holding and the clump of trees that screened it. There he kissed her hand, and stood to watch her walk steadily away from him. She did not look back, and for that he was grateful; and when she was already growing small and lonely across the fields he turned back into the camp.

14

In Shrewsbury castle the king held council of war until nearly midnight.

"Percy's first aim is already frustrated," he said, "which was to secure a strong base close to Wales, and to capture the person of our son. He has refused immediate battle. I am not without hope that we may yet avoid so great a disaster as this strife and bloodshed would be to our land, and I am loath to carry the issue to extremes if there is still a chance of an accommodation. If they will bring their grievances to discussion, I am disposed to hear them. Yet we must be prepared to put the matter to the test of battle if all else fails, and in circumstances to our advantage. My lords, let me have your counsel as to what our course now should be."

They spoke according to their age and experience, and the temperament born in them, the young earl of Stafford for instant action, Blount and some of his elder colleagues for caution, for holding this almost impregnable town, garrisoned and manned thus formidably as it was, and bringing up more levies from the south for reinforcement before attempting to dictate the conditions of a battle which nevertheless seemed inevitable sooner or later. Delay would give time for wiser counsels to prevail among the rebels, for the Cheshire nobility to think better of their defection and make their peace, and for some of the Northumbrian soldiers to grow discontented and desert in order to head for home. Two days might even cool the tempers and the ardour of their leaders, and make a reasonable approach possible.

"Two days, my liege," said Dunbar bluntly, grown impatient with this wise folly, "will do nothing for you, and all for Percy! Two days, and you'll have Glendower here with all his host to keep his troth with Hotspur, and Northumberland on his way south to join them, and what advantage you have this day will all be gone. You *may* get reinforcements, ay, but so for certain will they. And if you're fond enough to suppose that one man from the north will run and leave Hotspur, whatever the odds, whether he's paid or no, you know nothing of the hold he has on his own. If you leave it to him to come to you, you leave all in his hands, and he'll come when he's ready, and on his own terms. You have but one chance, to go to him, and this coming day or never, for even a day later may be too late. You've struck one fast blow, and gained by it, now strike another and clinch your victory. Give no time to Glendower or to the earl to come to Percy's aid. Hunt him out of his burrow the morn, and make an end."

They argued back and forth over it, the king as yet saying nothing. Dunbar spread his freckled hands across the table, and leaned his weather-beaten face and red head earnestly close.

"My lord, you may still make your fair bid for an honest peace, but only from a warlike station. He denies you for a king—go out to him and pin him fast, and show most like a king, and you may most surely bide one. For, credit me, this fire he's lit will not die out of itself, it can but grow unless you douse it. It's now or never, your Grace, if you will to save your kingdom."

The prince, sitting silent and watchful, almost admired him for the tone, as well as for the logic. Not many men would have taken that tone to his father, even for the best and most urgent of motives, unless in privilege and privacy. Dunbar at least has understood enough, he thought, to be desperately afraid for his own future if my father aims astray now, or he would not so risk the favour he has

worked so hard to gain. Surely he means it in all earnest. For him
and for us it's now or never.

"Our son has not yet spoken his mind," said the king, mild of eye
and voice, but with that oblique manner of address which caused a
prickle of warning to tighten the boy's skin. He gazed back unsmil-
ingly, even coldly, into his father's probing eyes, and answered with
all the truth he could see clearly:

"There's nothing for me to add to what the earl has said. He is
right in every word. To delay now is to throw away everything your
Grace has gained by your exertions of the past days. If you hesitate
here, you had far better have hesitated in Lichfield, before you were
isolated here so close to Wales."

His voice could bite, too, when he was perplexed and sore; and
always keeping its filial respect and its formal grace. But it seemed
that his prompt reply had pleased and reassured. The king sat back
and squared his heavy shoulders against the carved back of his chair.

"Very well, so be it. I judge as you do. We have at this moment
nearly double the resources the rebels can muster, and surely it
would be folly to sit idle, if safe, while they bring their numbers
level with ours. Very well! We muster in the morning, one hour past
the dawn, as soon as we have heard mass. And now let us consider
the ground."

The prince's castellan had already sketched out for them on the
scrubbed wood of a table trestle the lie of the land between them
and Hotspur's camp, making use of all the reports brought in by his
own spies, by military scouts, and by one or two frightened peasants
who had thought it safer to take refuge in the town. They pored
over it intently, and made their plans.

"The ground where he's camped," said Dunbar, drawing his
sandy brows together over the sketch, "is none so ill for a defensive
battle, with this great scarp ayont his rear, and the river on front and
flank. If you throw all your force against him there, my reading goes,
he'll stand and fight, and may do right well, too. If you want him at

disadvantage, and room to use your numbers, you must flush him out of there."

"He's not the man to be tempted or tricked out of a good position by a token force too small to be taken seriously," said the prince with disdain. "He'd sit and laugh, prick off any who were fools enough to get within range, and let the rest break their heads to no purpose, and go home empty-handed."

"He shall have reason enough to take us seriously," said the king grimly, "if his intent is to avoid battle until his allies come to his aid. What I propose is that we shall march out with all our forces by the castle gate, and there divide our army, a strong detachment taking the road west and north round the riverside, to come up with their camp as close as may be, while the main force will go with me north-east through the foregate and by the Hadnall road. By this means, even if he stand and choose to fight, with allies or with none, my main army shall be in close touch, and can turn to westward and be in the field within the hour. But if he choose to avoid, as I maintain he will, there is but one way he can retreat with any speed, and that is eastward into my arms, and our two forces can close him between them on the march, and deny him any stay to plan his battle."

"Good!" said Dunbar, rubbing his hands. "Good! Since his main aim is against your Grace's person and life, he'll surely draw off from wasting his force on another. And who's to have the command of this probing force?"

"Our son, the prince of Wales, will lead it," said the king with deliberation, his eyes on the boy's face, which moved not a muscle, and told him nothing at all, merely accepting the order with impenetrable calm. "You have understood your part?"

"I have. Clearly I am to keep, as well as I may, between Sir Henry Percy's army and the river, and to set him in motion towards the east. And as I understand it," he said, staring his father full in the eyes, "if he stand and fight, then I accept battle, and send you the signal to come to my aid." In the closed fortress of his mind he was thinking feverishly: He gives me an army and sends me to Hotspur! Is he tempting me to my undoing? Sending me to my death? Or to the treason he half expects from me? Is this distrust so sore a torment to him that he must put it to the test and know the answer before he can let me or himself rest? "And if he strikes camp and takes his force eastwards," he said calmly, "as we hope, my part will be to dog his steps, keeping always a little behind, and between him and Shrewsbury. Until you intercept him and bring him to bay," he concluded with an expressionless face.

"You have grasped it." King Henry began to fill in details for his captains, to appoint places and times. Nor did he elect to send with his son either George Dunbar or any other of his most experienced officers, or deprive him of the following that knew him best. He was to be free to do his office faithfully, or turn traitor if he would. How easy it would be, once a mile away from the walls of Shrewsbury, to send a courier ahead to Hotspur, and offer him reinforcements instead of enemies, to bring him every detail of the king's plans, and every shadow of uncertainty and weakness in the king's mind!

But he knew by then that he neither would nor could do it. Out of the isolation and loneliness where he stood there was no easy way; but some ways were impossible.

He was dismissed to his bed like a child when the conference ended, and did not know whether this disrespect towards his acknowledged maturity was the anxious carefulness of a loving father or the displeasure of an angry one. It might well be both, if the king had indeed been in desperate anxiety about him during that forced march on the town, for anger tends to gather about the object of love when fear has bitten too deep.

But he found no rest in his bed, and long before dawn he arose and made his preparations, and went up on to the tower to watch out the end of the night. There was nothing as yet to be seen but the hushed and windless dark, mysteriously divided between the levelled, lowly, lightless darkness of the earth and the luminous, soft darkness of the sky, powdered with stars. The quarter under the castle still stank of smoke, but the air was clear and transparent there above the ruins. In this expansive plain to north and east there were few ridges or hills, and even those not great: the wedge-shape of Haughmond hill to the east, the abrupt but shallow escarpment of Leaton Shelf to the north. Only to westward and south-westward did the Breiddens and the Stretton hills heave their loftier heads out of the earth. Now all was invisible, nothing but a tiny gleam here and there from some house; but he knew this landscape as he knew his own palm, and when he leaned between the merlons on the wall and looked out to northwards, he could people the hidden plain with the ordered bivouacs of Hotspur's army, hardly two miles away.

He had learned a great deal about himself in the past twelve hours, he knew who and what he was, and what he was going to do. He even knew why, if this was a choice, he had made that choice; but it seemed to him that he had had no choice at all. Nor had the pain ceased when he chose, if indeed he had chosen.

He would go with his blood, and against his friend. Not because love and loyalty to a father are things to be taken for granted; far from it, he was in no doubt as to where he loved. Not because the king expected and demanded it. Not even because the thread of that blood in him linked him, far back, with men to whom he felt closer than to his father, and would flow into the veins of his children some day, and carry his imprint into the future. He had utterly discarded the idea that he must make his decision in accordance with his father's will. For a while it had seemed to him, in fact, that he was making it because it was what Hotspur would have expected of him unquestioningly, cheerfully, without grudging; there was a being who went with his family as a matter of glorious course, and would applaud his friend and pupil for doing the same. That helped and warmed him, but it was not his reason.

No, the decision was and had to be his own. He had not even expressly confided it to God, though he had prayed his routine prayers with an added fervour and consciousness, asking nothing new, only trying more devoutly even than usual to align himself with the will of God, and so choose. His reason lay all within himself. He was the heir of England, the next king of this land. He had not coveted it, he had not schemed for it, it had been laid upon him like a burden and an opportunity, something to which he was called with an unmistakable calling. He had not coveted it, but when it was visited upon him he had, with all his hungry heart, embraced and espoused it. His mind was strongly set, how strongly only he knew, to be a king. He accepted his fate with joy and awe and pride, he knew himself equal to it, and he would not suffer it to be taken from him. He could not; it would be a dereliction of a duty more sacred than any filial loyalty.

He had now only one comfort, but one so great and grateful that it filled his heart to the exclusion of all fear and regret. To Harry, battle was a natural state, governed by generous rules as absolute as life and death, and altogether free from malice or hatred. There they could meet without shame or constraint, and without fear of misunderstanding. To kill each other would be a minor thing, a human grief to be endured; to fail in chivalry or mutual respect would be an alienation for ever. But from that they were safe, now and always, living or dying.

The remembered voice was always with him now, all the more clearly heard in the night's stillness and his own loneliness, saying for him all that needed to be said: "We have both things to do that we must do. What I do, I do because I cannot do otherwise...Nothing I do can change the love and honour in which I bear you."

In the first light of dawn they heard mass in the chapel, and then they mustered their men by companies, the whole unwieldy army but for a strong castle garrison, and marched them out by the barbican, the king's sixteen thousand leading, to make a good advance to the north-east before the prince's probing force was reported to Hotspur in his camp; then the remaining nine thousand or so, wheeling to the left in the foregate, to circle the curves of the river by the closest way, and come upon the quarry from the south-west. It was a glorious morning, the grass moist with dew, the meadow-sweet along the water-fields heady with fragrance, and such singing of birds that even the marching of an army twenty-five-thousand-strong was drowned in the ecstatic din.

The chaplain and furnishings of the king's chapel went with him to the fight. So did Thomas Prestbury, abbot of Shrewsbury, praying heartily for a compounded peace, and John Prophet, dean of St. Chad's, the king's secretary, sometime a clerk of the privy seal, and some day to be keeper of that same invaluable symbol of office. He prayed single-heartedly for his master's victory, for he was one of those who, throughout a long life of service, never fell away from the house of Lancaster.

Once they were well launched into that methodical advance through the summer fields of Severn, the prince set his standard well forward to be seen from afar, so that his friend, who was now formally his enemy, might be assured upon sight that the foe who came to confront him came with no deception and no unchivalrous proposals, but challenging openly to a clean collision upon the field of honour.

He believed then that he might well be going to his death at Hotspur's hands, and that he did not grudge. But he knew with certainty that if God designed that he should survive, it was to be king of England, both serviceable and glorious.

The sentries who had been posted on the most remote edge of the camp territory, still within clear sight of the town gate, and with their horses grazing close by ready for action, saw the bright, pin-cushion glitter of lances and pennants and standards burst out of the gates, and as soon as they had assured themselves of the magnitude of this exodus, mounted and rode in to the next line of outposts, to pass the word on through the perimeter of the camp to the centre, and the general himself. They lighted down again there to watch for the next sighting, and thence relayed news of the arms they first observed, chief among them those of the prince of Wales.

Hotspur had barely walked back into the camp from the river meadows when they came running to him with the news.

"Not Lancaster?" he said sharply.

"No, my lord! The prince's standard leads all. He is in command."

He thought for no more than seconds, braced and still.

"Ah, no, my sweet Hal!" he said. "Not today, and not with you!" And he laughed, quite softly, and the next moment sprang into the violent life to which they were accustomed in him. "We move out! Eastwards out of reach, as far as we must, but no farther! Uncle, you know the route, get your vanguard moving. Sound the muster! Let's have no man in doubt, and camp struck as fast as may be." Worcester had the eastern approaches, and that way they must go to avoid being pinned down to an encounter before it suited them. "Archie, I leave you the rearguard. But hold off unless he prick you home, for I doubt this is no more than a probe to test how wide-awake we are. I'll not touch a man of them on those terms. They must withdraw. They have nowhere to go but back into Shrewsbury. And if they quit it, by God, I'll pick it up and be glad. I have scores to pay there, and once Owen is with us, we'll find Lancaster wherever he may go."

"And if he come first to you?" said Douglas, looking back over his shoulder.

"Then I'll meet him the more gladly, for he's more than I thought him."

And he was away at a striding run, like an athlete of eighteen, easy of breath and sure of foot, to where he had slept the night with the Welsh girl in his arms. Julian was gone, pray God, into relative safety. He never so much as glanced at the nest of grass from which he had lifted his cloak at dawn, and shaken it free from clinging seeds, for the grasses were ripe and in fruit. He was met on the spot by one of his squires with his horse ready in hand, and was in the saddle and weaving away among the scattered stations of the camp in a moment, checking on the loading here, issuing an order there, running a practised eye over all, and ending in a long ride along the southern perimeter as the whole camp broke into ordered motion. The sun was just picking out the distant points of lance and pennon, like exotic flowers flaunting out of the long grass.

"No, not today, not if I may avoid. Two days more, and please God I shall be done with waiting. But forehead to forehead with you, my heart—no, never, God forbid!"

Julian watched them go, from the hatch of the loft above Walter's holding. She saw the full light come, and the camp swarm suddenly like an ant heap disturbed, as fiercely and as purposefully. There was no disorder. Men moved as though thrust into motion by a spirit beyond their own impulses, assembling everything they had disposed about them, scouring the heath clean of their presence, cohering into their fore-ordained masses, and withdrawing from the river flats towards the east. Only the trampled and flattened grass and heather, the bruised harebells, the rutted turf, showed where they had been. They had created a desolation; but only when they were gone was it seen to be desolate. And in a few days, and especially after the first rain, the grass would have sprung upright again, the flattened heather have revived, and new flowers burst out of the earth to supply the loss. In a week no one would know there had ever been some fourteen thousand men encamped here, unless by chance he still came on the faded traces of their fires, or the trimmings of feathers where the fletchers had re-flighted arrows, or thought to wonder at the number of horse-droppings disintegrating into the turf. When they were all gone, she caught, distantly and fleetingly, the glitter of lances and banners approaching from Shrewsbury, though they did not come near, and remained for a while as a shimmer and a dazzle in the air, before they, too, moved away eastwards.

After that, everything was quiet. She came down from her loft, and walked slowly back across the deserted fields, and through the abandoned camp, until she found the place where her bed of heather and grass was made. The cloak that had wrapped them was gone with the man who had spread it for her, the circle of the fire's ashes was white within and black without, but not yet quite cold. There was a little clump of starry centaury flattened under the place where they had lain together. She stooped to pluck it, faintly sticky to her fingers, and fragrant, and the sun flashed a little spike of light in her eyes from the hilt of Hotspur's sword, laid gently aside in the roots of the heather, and hidden by the clustering, wiry stems.

She took it up in both hands and held it before her. His talisman and his luck he had called it, and summoned it to serve them as a charm in the night; and here he had let it lie forgotten in the haste of his withdrawal, leaving it to his baggage squire to gather up everything he left behind him. But God had willed rather that it should lie here until she came to find it.

She accepted the omen with a surge of confidence and joy, for it seemed that after all there was a role for her, and she was permitted a share in whatever this day held for Hotspur. She had been the means of the sword's loss, and she must be the means of its restoration.

She turned her face to the east, towards the sun, and began to cross the deserted camp-ground, following the tracks the army had left in their withdrawal. And as she went she became aware that on her right, between her and Shrewsbury, the shimmer of lances and standards kept pace with her, step for step, all the way.

15

Throughout the two miles of that march they had been well
aware that the force from Shrewsbury was shadowing them
on a parallel course, and at some little distance behind, out of
reach, and unable to reach them, but holding station there on their
quarter with obstinate precision. Between them and Shrewsbury,
between them and the river now, but never pressing to close the
distance, though with the town as their base they travelled lighter
than their opponents.

"I mislike this," said Worcester, in the van, and sent a squire on a
fast horse far ahead even of the out-riders he already had in station.
They were crossing the broad, rich, open fields of the plain, with only
minor undulations to break its level, but ahead there was a low rise
from which a somewhat wider view ahead might be possible. The
young man spurred eagerly, overtook his fellow who scouted before
them on the left flank, and the two rode on together to patrol the
crest and view the ground beyond it. Worcester waved the column
to a halt, and presently Hotspur rode up from the centre to join him.

"This is not to my liking, either. They cling to us, yet not close.
They have a part to play, but I think, by God, not alone."

The squire wheeled his horse, and came back to them at a gallop,
staring consternation.

"My lord, they're between us and the road—the king's whole
host. Less than a mile beyond the crest! I guess at some fifteen

thousand men or more. There are riders keeping liaison between them and the prince's force…"

Uncle and nephew looked at each other with the same thought in both minds. "He reads too fluently," said Hotspur, without anger or resentment. "He knew how to move me out of too secure a station. If he had come himself I would have had at him there by the Severn, Owen or no Owen."

"So we may here," said Worcester grimly. "So we must if we cannot reach the road. North we could turn, and still avoid, but to what end?"

To what end indeed! I am sick at running even so far, and I'll run no farther. Henry I wanted, and here he is before me, why should I go elsewhere? If I must fight at disadvantage, I'll choose my ground and stake out my defences, and not be hunted in flight, like a hare. Follow on slowly, while I go and look over what choice of ground I have."

He spurred ahead, and before the column came up with him he had ridden the ridge from end to end. It was no more than a mole-hill in the lush green and striped gold and silver of the fields, but it afforded him all the view that was possible here, and it was enough. Deployed along the summer land, far beyond arrow range but clear and sparkling in the morning air and the early sunlight, the chivalry and men-at-arms and bowmen of the royal army barred all approaches to the roads drawing off to the north-east. The plain glittered and fluttered with their lances and standards. Between him and them there were a few scattered trees, a hamlet lying away to the left, and a shallow glint of water, three little, linked ponds in a hollow under this gradual slope, the drainage of the fields that ringed it. Along the headlands between the fields, which were large and ripening here in pied and generous crops, poppies flaunted, and the grass was high, with some scrub trees and bushes here and there. He thought coolly, we might do worse. There's cover for archers, and rising ground, if the rise is but small, and the mud of the pools to clog the hooves of his cavalry. Having brought me here, he must attack now, he has no choice if he is to keep his face, and his face, so often bruised, is nonetheless dear to him.

On the near side of the bowl where the ponds lay like three small mirrors, the slope carried a great field of peas, well-grown after the earlier rains, standing high and paling into ripeness. On either side of it the headlands were banked high, good barriers, and crowned here and there with bushes. He marked it, and knew that it would serve.

He rode back the little way he had to go to meet his army, and halted them there, still out of sight of the king's forces, though no doubt somewhere a hovering scout took note of all he did. These men who had followed him from the north or rallied to him in Cheshire had a right to know what was asked of them now, and against what odds they contended. He stood up in his stirrups and told them truth as he knew it, hurling his voice like a lance; and those within earshot passed back what he said to those who caught but the half. Never, in such a case, did the impediment in his throat dare to trip him; that same constricted instrument became a brazen trumpet.

"Here we must let fall all thought of avoidance, and stand to meet in arms those who come against us. Even if we so wished, there is no time left us to take passage from this fight. The royal banner is there before us—we make that our aim! Stand your ground here like heroes, as I know you will, and this day shall see us the conquerors, and glorious, or delivered from the sway of this usurper if we fall. Better to die in battle for a cause we believe in, than after battle at our enemy's pleasure. As for me, I have come this far, and now I will go on to the end, whatever that end be, and I will carry it as far as I may, God helping me. If you are with me, say it, and I'm content!"

The roar that answered him came like a gathering wave, first from close before him, then the lingering surges from far back along the column came swooping in like the force of a driving tide, washing about him in eddy after eddy. He was never given to long talking or much ceremony in appealing to those who followed him. He sat

back in the saddle, wheeled his horse, and waved them after him
to the site he had chosen; and they followed him in high heart.
That blithe acceptance wrung his spirit and troubled his conscience
momentarily, but he had no time to indulge even that sensitivity.

He was well aware that as soon as his foremost line rose clear of
the mild curve of the crest, he was seen and his every move noted.
It seemed to him that a curious, rippling shiver passed along the line
of lances below, and the whole host wavered, between eagerness
and tension, a few paces closer, before the ranks again halted and
dressed their array. This was the strangest moment in any pitched
battle, when the two armies deployed in full view of each other,
achingly watched, and in this crystal air blindingly seen, but out of
range of voice or arrow, like a page at exercise in front of a mirror
for want of a partner. Hotspur had lived the same ghostly experience many times. This courtly, methodical, formalised preparation
for execution in the sight of the condemned was more wonderful
and terrible than any surprise assault. When he led his men down
into the orderly husbandry of the pease-field and the headlands, the
scrub bushes at the near edge of the drainage bowl, and the scattered
clumps of trees at the corners of the long field, it was like a dance,
elaborate, civilised and aloof.

"Buy a little time," counselled Worcester in his ear. "Send a pair
of your squires to deliver him our manifesto in person, that he may
not be able to say he never had any formal complaint or gage from
you. It will hardly soften him, but it may distract others—and who
knows, it may even upset his judgment and make him cast astray
when it comes to the assault."

"Well thought of, so we will."

The document was, in substance, the same they had issued abroad
in their journey south, with the whole catalogue of their charges
against Henry furiously set forth therein. Its content the king already
knew; but the manner of its wording was here particularly judged
to offend and scarify, fuller of implacable anger than of grievance

seeking redress. Worcester had compiled it, yet rather as looking through his nephew's eyes. It could not have come from either of them, composing alone; but from the one striking hard for love of the other it had issued like an effusion of blood. And it spoke, for the first time openly and savagely, of murder.

"Also we set, say and intend to prove, that whereas thou didst swear at that same time and place, that King Richard, our lord and thine, should reign during his life in his royal prerogative, thou didst the same our and thy lord and king traitorously, in thy castle of Pontefract, without his consent or the judgment of the lords of the realm, for fifteen days and nights, which is horrible to be heard among Christian men, by hunger, thirst and cold, cause to be slain and murdered: whereupon thou art perjured and false."

All the other charges against the king were there expressed just as forcibly, the levying of unlawful taxation, the manipulation of the constitution of parliament, the malignant desertion of Mortimer; but this was the kernel of all. Let it be said, formally to his face. Hotspur knew, better than any, that it contained the final rupture between them; once it was delivered, those two could not both continue to live in the realm of England. But he said, "Well thought of, so we will."

Two of his squires, young, trusted and well-schooled, Knayton and Salvayn, carried the cartel. They set forth round the headland, skirting the ponds, riding stirrup to stirrup at a decorous, dancing walk, to prolong the respite and make it clear to the enemy force they approached that they came as envoys, with a right to be respected. The horses and the boys who rode them were matched as if for a pageant. Hotspur watched them until they dwindled into figures in the foreground of a green, spangled tapestry. Then he turned to work.

The formidable Cheshire bowmen of Venables and Vernon had claim to all the positions with forward cover, notably along the wings and up the slope, where they could shoot over the heads of

their fellows; and the men-at-arms were massed behind the stout
headlands on either wing, and behind the scrub bushes and the
watery bowl and ripening peas in the centre. The chivalry of the
north poised in formation, two companies aligned with the hard
ground either side the centre, where their downhill rush could not
be impeded by crops or water, and the headlands would give them
firm running if they carried through; two more set in reserve, one
on either flank, to the rear of the archers, and to be used only when
the archers had done their part, and themselves were in need of
reinforcement. He did not make the mistake of spreading his limited
forces too widely, for the weight of numbers was hugely against him,
and they had need of a solid central mass that could not be shifted.
He held what pikemen he had well back, so that if any cavalry broke
round the flanks to the rear they could still be confronted with a
solid wall of steel, able to turn and hold them off from any angle.

"Hugh Brow commands the left wing. You, uncle, the right. My
lord of Douglas, I would have you with me in the centre. Take the
right company here, and keep your Scots about you." He cast a
critical eye over his dispositions, and could see no immediate way of
bettering them. Across the green expanse of fields before them the
two squires were riding back from their errand. "We'd best begin to
arm," he said. "We shall at least get some word of their state soon."

They went to work, the squires coming running with their
knights' mail and plate and helms. Revolving under the hands of
his servitors, Hotspur watched his two emissaries ride in along the
headland at the edge of the field.

"Well, what said the duke of Lancaster?"

"Hardly a word, my lord, but the common coin of greeting and
thanks. But he read it, beginning to end! In dismissing us he said he
would make reply when he had considered and taken counsel. At
least," said young Salvayn, "he gave us time to look about us. He's
busy making his dispositions for attack, and the prince's companies
are just moving up on his left to join with him." He gave a detailed

account of such arrangements as he had seen, and his companion added his own observations. "My lord, most likely they've already reviewed this ground before we occupied it, but if not, you may trap their centre when they reach the edge of the bowl here, for the ponds can hardly be seen until a man is very close. In such soft land even a little slope like ours here is a hill, and even a ditch full of water is a valley. And if they separate and turn aside to go round, the archers will have a fine target at an easy range."

"They'll have seen you turn aside," said Hotspur drily. "Henry is no fool, he can read the signs as well as any."

"My lord, we took good care to set a direct course for the headland. No one will think that unusual in field country, where men ride round the crops out of pure habit—even when they may be charging through the same crops within the hour."

Hotspur smiled and approved him. The boy was from yeoman stock, and thought as a farmer thinks, and none the worse for that. And he reflected for a moment, ruefully, on the farmer who had planted this field of peas, and what good he would ever get out of his labour.

"I thank you for your errand and your news. Better go and get into steel now. If we may doff again without dinting it, so much the better, but we'll be ready for whatever comes. Though for my part I think his reply will be the trumpet sounding."

But in that he was wrong. Douglas, tall and glistening in steel, but as yet bare-headed, stood peering out from the shadow of a clump of trees, and suddenly turned his head sharply to bring his good eye to bear upon his friend. "Harry, you're to have visitors in your turn! Look here, at yon venerable gentlemen! We shall have priests enough to bless us or bury us!"

Others had heard his words, and turned to gaze where he pointed, and a gradual hush of surprise and wonder passed like a shudder along the lines. Out of the king's camp two sedate, unmartial figures had advanced, and were ambling slowly towards

Hotspur's lines, mounted on two white riding-mules. The sober clerical robes were easily recognisable, but not until they had covered more than half the distance between the two armies could face and bearing be distinguished.

One was a big, vigorous, well-fleshed man in his prime, with a commanding face and an upright carriage; the other half a head shorter, half his companion's bulk, and some ten years older, lean, agile and grey. Both were known to Hotspur, and by the hush that attended their approach, to many of those who followed him. Whatever Henry had to say, he had chosen the most venerated and pacific figures in his following to be his voice, for he had sent to Hotspur as emissaries Thomas Prestbury, abbot of Shrewsbury, and his own secretary, John Prophet, dean of St. Chad's.

They were brought into camp with all reverence and ceremony, and delivered their message.

"His Grace the king is desirous of avoiding, even at this late hour, the bloodshed that must result to many of his subjects if this quarrel come to trial in battle. He offers you, my lord, and your adherents pardon and peace, and promises redress of all those grievances of which you can justly complain, if you will disperse this force quietly and forbear such gatherings hereafter. If your will is as good as his, then an agreement can be negotiated. Or his Grace asks, if you prefer, that you will come yourself to speak with him, or send another in your place."

Hotspur stood bare-headed before the abbot, and fixed his wide brown stare intently upon the face of this man, patently honest, who offered him pardon and peace in Henry's name. The sound of the words was infinitely sweet, and tugged at him unexpectedly with all the old memories of companionship and rivalry. Henry, absent, and speaking through this anxious, kindly man, was again the Henry he had known from childhood. But he could not forget the stranger who had peered out at him through the known mask no long time ago. And there was matter to be pardoned upon both sides, and he was not sure that he could pardon, or that he had any right to do so, or that there would be peace for him ever again if he did.

"Father abbot," he said, "I am obliged to you for the pains you have taken in this matter, and for the grace of your visit. Will you hold me excused if I leave you for a moment to speak with my uncle and counsellor?"

"Don't go," said Worcester shortly, when they had drawn apart among the scattered trees. "I know you too well. He still has some power to disarm you. And trust me, it is useless. The peace he designs for you is not of this world."

"I have no thought of going. There are grievances he's too late to redress by two years and more, and the redress not due to me or mine." But there was more in it than that; he did not want to see Henry now at the end, and start again every treacherous doubt that had ever harboured in his heart. And above all, he would not for any consideration have set eyes at this pass upon the boy, to Hal's bitter distress and his own. "But for the due appearance of our right, we ought to fall in with even the apparent offer of discussion. Will you go with them and see him? It may even be," he said, tormented, for he had the lives of many men upon his heart, "that he means peace honestly."

"Do not believe it. But if you want me to go, go I will."

"Yes, go. And judge for me. I trust your wisdom more than my own. Listen to what he has to say, but read his eyes, too, and if they speak a different language from his tongue, answer as you see fit. Give him the last defiance, if need be," he said, "and let's have done. Yet if you can with good assurance speak peace with him, do. I trust the decision to you. You will not go beyond the bounds of honour."

Only when Worcester had ridden out with the two clerics, and was dwindling into an embroidered knight-errant upon a green field, did he suddenly realise how much time had been eaten away by these to-ings and fro-ings across what must soon be a battlefield. For the sun was in the zenith, and the hour past noon. He realised, too, how foolish it had been in him to suppose, even for a moment, that any return was possible from this precipice over which both he and Henry were sliding irresistibly with all their host, as though the earth had opened under their feet. And curiously, he found this certainty calming and comforting, for irresolution itself was the rarest and bitterest pain he knew. He turned to finish his arming, his mind no longer divided. There would still be time for shriving when his uncle returned. The chaplain was among the archers, doing his principal office with as much fervour as he would presently undertake his secondary one among the ranks, with a pike in his hands.

"We waste the day," complained Douglas, fully-armed, and passing his unsheathed sword from hand to hand in many varying throws to exercise his quickness of vision with his one good eye, that saw as much and as clearly as most men's two, and the agility of the left hand he had been practising to use freely ever since his injury at Homildon. "I have a great hunger in me to meet with this Henry of Bolingbroke."

"Be content,' said Hotspur sombrely, "there is still time for a deal of dying before the sun sets." He looked round for the page who ran his errands, and the boy sprang eagerly to meet even his unexpressed wishes. "Martin, bring my sword." The page ran for it, and made to buckle it on. "No, not that. My luck—the old one. Knayton knows."

This time the boy came back empty-handed and distressed, not out of any fear, but chagrined by his failure to satisfy his lord's wishes. "Sir, they say it's not to be found. It was in your baggage yesterday, of that they're sure, but now no one can lay hand on it anywhere. My lord, they're afraid it may have been left behind overnight."

There was dismay in his voice, for the squires were more disturbed by the loss than he cared to remember. An ill omen, they said, considering how the Lord Henry always loved to have it about him, and called it his talisman. "My lord, they say, all of them, that they never touched it last night, that it cannot have been lost by fair means. Is it witchcraft? How could it go astray?"

Hotspur remembered then what he himself had done with his favourite, and laughed, though softly and privately, to think of it still lying beside Julian's secret bed. No wonder his squire had not missed it, it had gone to earth like a fox. How she came back to him at the very thought of it, fragile flesh and yielding bones and steely spirit in his arms all the night through.

"Never give it a thought, child, there's nothing sinister here. No ill omens! Tell them this is not yet my death-field—I was promised long ago by a soothsayer in Northumbria that I should die, when my time came, hard by Berwick, and that's two hundred and fifty miles from here, and so close on my own doorstep I doubt I shall die an old man in my bed. I have remembered now what I did with the sword. It was lost in a good cause, I don't repent it. Very well, let me have the other."

The boy hastened to serve, proud to be allowed to help in his lord's arming, instead of merely carrying his messages; for his seniors in this jealous service were themselves getting into steel, and marshalling their master's lances and their own. Many of the archers and men-at-arms, satisfied of their readiness, had sat down at their stolid ease in the turf, and were gnawing at the bread and meat they had carried with them, for the day was past its crest, and a man fights better with food in his belly. Their faces were dour and calm; they were professionals who fought for pay, and gave value for money, and yet in their own fashion they fought for more than pay, since so few of them ever quit their lord to go after a wealthier or an easier service. Some of their parents and kin were new and ambitious tenant farmers, like many who had rented land in these parts, once worked for the manor by heavy, grudging feudal labour. Some of them looked with compunction at the ripe crop before them, and wondered what poor soul its loss was going to ruin, and whether this day would sell him back into the serfdom from which he had

escaped by his own efforts. Or whether so many more local land-
lords would die here that a dozen other poor souls now serfs would
climb out of their servitude over the corpses and this field of pease.

"Father," said Hotspur, "do your good office also for me, for I am
a sinner, and all too sure of penance due."

He made his brief confession—he had never a mind for brood-
ing in retrospect on detail, even in his sins—kneeling, but never
thinking to bend his head or cover his eyes either from God or his
confessor. He so seldom looked back, and so seldom regretted anything, that he had difficulty in thinking of many sins, and concluded
simply: "What I have else done amiss, God He knows, and when the
time is fit He will remind me after His own fashion."

His chaplain was tall and spare, and burned like a votive candle,
and in his youth he had been a soldier before he took orders; but in
his heart, and in this one lifelong service, he was a soldier still, and
though he wore a cilice of hair next the skin, he wore a coat of mail
over it, beneath his gown. He was growing old as a tree grows old,
dourly, strongly and stubbornly; and whether he believed more in
the cross he carried or in the rightness of all that Hotspur did, was
matter for doubt. That he believed devoutly in both was past doubt.
Yet he was no courtier, and had not been chosen for his pliability.
Fanatical love had grown upon him unawares; and Hotspur had
never observed it.

"Son, in this hour I bid you lay aside all hate from your heart. For
he who fights in hate is in deadly sin."

"Father, I am without hate, but not without anger. Our Lord
himself knew what anger is, and himself felt its power. I will well
to this land, and to all good men within it, even those in whom I
am mistaken, and cannot see the good. For there are more men
mistaken than evil. God sees all, and will divide and assign according
to right and justice. I do not ask more or better."

The chaplain shrived him clean, and he drew aside, and walked
again the length of his lines, to leave Douglas free to make his

confession in privacy, though dearly he wondered, being human, about that dark matter of Rothesay's death. From the crest he looked out over the Fields towards the king's station, studying the formation there, and picking out by their colours the standards he could identify at that distance. Henry had drawn up his whole army now in two main divisions, it seemed, with a third and smaller one as a vanguard before them. The attacker must needs use his cavalry to try to break through the cover set up by the archers, before ever he could get to grips; and to do that he must be ready to see great slaughter done among his knights and squires, however skillfully he used them. A great many of those gay banners and pennants would fall before night. But he had nearly double the number his opponent could muster, and in the end weight tells, and even archers can be killed.

Hotspur knew both the exultation and the guilt of this hour before the battle, but they balanced within him, and his mind was at rest in that hushed equilibrium, like a hawk riding the air all but motionless. He was still there watching from the crest when he saw the solitary figure of his uncle draw clear of the lines and set course for his own camp. It was nearly time now; for in his heart he knew how that encounter had gone, and almost he knew why. He turned back, and went lightly down the slope to his own division.

He had almost reached it, when one of the older squires from the pickets along the rear came running after him.

"My lord!…My lord, here's a local lad come asking for you. He says he's brought your sword…"

She came down the green slope between the companies of archers, heads turning to stare at her with more than usual curiosity, for any strange comer filled up this heavy waiting, and for a youngster of the countryside to venture near instead of removing himself hurriedly from the path of an army was a rare enough happening. Her face had a strained and brittle serenity, but her eyes were glad, and shone when she saw the astonished pleasure in his. If he felt any anger that she should again walk so hardily and stubbornly into danger for his sake, it left him almost before he knew it for anger. How dared he attempt to limit her right to do what she chose, to throw away what she did not value, and hold fast to what she did? He knew her by now too well to suppose that she did anything with her eyes closed, or was more likely to repent her actions than he. All the same, he must send her away quickly, before the trumpets sounded.

"My lord," she said, "I could not reach you sooner, there were some outposts of the prince's army covering their march as they rejoined the king's host, I had to wait in cover until the last withdrew. But I have made what haste I could to bring you back what I know you prize."

She looked full into his eyes and smiled, holding out the sword to him on her two spread hands, like an offering. "You left it behind," she said "in the camp by Berwick."

❧❧

He had put out his hand to take the sword by the hilt, smiling back at her no less gladly. The hand halted on air, a stone hand; the smile remained, but frozen into intense stillness. He was gold and bronze and steel in the sun, and could not turn pale, but some motion of joy in him had died abruptly. He put forth all the force that was in him to contain and overcome the moment, and at all costs to be to her reassurance and comfort. The hand came to life again, gripping strongly and affectionately on the hilt of his old favourite. The smile warmed and moved and spoke. He got command of his voice, and it came brisk and cheerful, without impediment:

"Is that the name of the place where we slept the night—Berwick? It seems I was nearer home than I knew."

"The village is half a mile from where you lay, my lord. What is it? I thought you started at the name."

"Nothing! I was startled to hear it here. I am to be always in your debt, it seems. I can but thank you now, and bid you go. As you must, for my peace. But tomorrow, if God please, there shall be better thanks."

"I could not let you go to such a venture without your talisman," she said. He had stripped off his gauntlet to unbuckle the sword he wore at his belt, for her pleasure, and put his favourite in its place, but she swooped to her knees suddenly, and was before him at the thongs. "Let me do the service of squire to you this once, my lord, before I go."

He looked down at the crown of her dark-gold head as she bent earnestly to the straps, and there were eyes upon them from every quarter, a little wondering and inquisitive but for those who had seen this same boy in the night, and heard him presented as a good and valued servant of their lord in these parts. It mattered not at all now whether they wondered or no. But once he looked up over her head, and found himself gazing into the single dark, alert eye of Archibald Douglas. It was the only time he had ever seen that audacious face fully conscious and also desperately grave.

He reached down and took her hand as she finished the last strap, and raised her gently to her feet.

"Julian, the time is close now, and I would have you in safety, for my own sake, for I am guilty who caused you to come here. Go back now, quickly, to the toft, and wait there. Ask my men at the crest there, in my name, to give you a horse, for time may be short. God willing, I shall come for you. And if God will otherwise, then Iago will do my part for me, and bring you to the Lord Owen. I shall go into battle the happier if I know that you are out of danger."

She said: "I will go." But for his peace she did not say how reluctantly, or how short a way.

"And, Julian, pray for me!"

"My lord, without ceasing. That God keep you!"

He was searching her face with an intensity that she felt almost as a caress, but did not fully understand; for she knew only that this might be the last time they would touch and confront each other so, but he in his heart knew that it would indeed be the last in this world. He saw the rounded line of his golden collar, a barely perceptible weal under the thin, soft stuff of her tunic, and wished that he had had by him some better gift to give her, for her future was dark, uncertain and lonely, and he had come by this ambiguous daughter-son too late to make proper provision for her in any formal way. Moreover, the possessions of traitors are forfeit! No, he checked himself, strongly rejecting this fatal acceptance of fate, a man's death does not always imply his defeat. Think of the old Douglas at Otterburn, who died but won his battle!

It was the first time he had ever looked so deep into these eyes, black shot through with red, like the embers of camp-fires; there was nothing they kept from him now. Daughter she might be to him, and by their ages well could have been, for she was still only twenty years old. But father he was not to her, nor lord, nor brother, nor friend. As what would she remember him? She was not dependent upon love and lovers as women are wont to be. She had married, and sickened of marriage, and chosen of her own will to look towards other satisfactions, this being soiled and spoiled for her, though not, please God, eternally. You cannot die of disillusion at twenty, not with such a spirit in you. And some day, he thought, her body will awake to joy, all the more fiercely for this waiting.

And for this bereavement, he thought, with humility, and gratitude, and desperate, loving sorrow. For I have been the supreme cause of joy to her, and I shall be her grief; but because of me she will keep some faith, and it will not always go unfulfilled.

At this last moment he thought only of her. He took her face between his hands, one bare and one in its steel gauntlet, and stooped and kissed her with formal gentleness first on one cheek, then on the other, the kiss of kinship with which he would have greeted or parted from his own youngest brother, if that brother had not died so long ago.

"And God go with you, now and always!"

She turned, as soon as he took his hands from her, without another word or another look, her face pale and bright and remote, like a star, and walked rapidly away from him up the slope, past the curious men-at-arms who watched her in silence, over the crest and out of his sight.

He turned his back on her as she vanished, and went to stand beside Douglas in the shade of the squat hawthorn trees that had rooted in the broken ground above the field. They were silent together for some minutes, watching the earl of Worcester draw close on the other side of the hollow where the ponds glowed in pewter stillness.

"A soothsayer is not God," said Douglas at last, abruptly. "He can lie, and he can be mistaken."

"So he can. But not she, who came as the innocent messenger of God." He took no account now of what he said to this man; he knew how much the single piercing eye had seen, the delicacy of those austere bones, the slight swell of her breasts under the faded, dun-coloured cloth. "I have had my summons, Archie, from lips that never dealt in anything but truth for me. She does not know what she has told me, and it cannot but be truth. If she had known, she would have held her peace. And was there any need to speak the name, if it had not been meant that she should do me this holy service, and give me warning of my end?"

"Every man's death is treading hard on his heels every day of his life," said Douglas stoutly. "Yet it will not overtake until he flags. And as for you, my friend, you will outrun him many years yet."

Hotspur smiled, looking at him warmly along his shoulder; and after a moment of silence he said: "Archie, there is not a man in the world, not even my uncle, I would rather have by me now, and in my secrets, than you. If I should not run fast enough, and you come out of this day alive and free, will you make my last loving compliments to Elizabeth? And kiss my son for me?"

"And your little lass, too," said Douglas heartily. "But all this you shall do for yourself, and I'll be your echo."

"Very well so, and you may yet be right. But remember what I asked of you."

And still later he said, his eyes narrowed to watch the look of his uncle's familiar, and to him expressive, face, as he rode along the headland and into the lines: "Well, if my plough is drawing to its last furrow, let's make it wide and deep, something for men to remember, and broad enough for two. For, God helping me, I'll take Henry down with me into the earth."

16

W e had best stand to," said Worcester, "for I have committed us."
They had already grasped as much who were near enough
to see his face. The men-at-arms had risen silently from the turf,
and marshalled their lines. The archers took the cue, and each tested
stance and bow, and hitched his quiver to bring his arrows readily
to hand. A deep breath and a purposeful stir passed wordlessly along
the ranks.

"So he was implacable!"

"On the face of it, no. He spoke us very soft and fair. Too soft!
Too fair! He was not speaking only for me. He had the prince at
his knee."

"Ah!" said Hotspur, drawing understanding breath. "And how did
Hal take him?"

"Unreadably, by Henry or by me. Yet the sweet reason was all for
him. Having no faith in it, I put our liege lord to the test. I spoke
out all that we hold against him, without stint, and in the hearing of
more than merely his son. There is not an honest man in England,
so bearded, who would not have blazed out in his turn and had his
say at me. And he continued mild as a maid, and repeated his offers
of pardon and consultation between us, if we disperse in peace. All
his words are fair, all are rehearsed, all are hollow. And his eyes
speak vengeance."

"I hope," said Hotspur, "you answered the eyes."

"He said: I would that you would accept of grace. And I replied to him: I do not trust your grace. For I tell you truly, Harry, what I see in him, rightly or wrongly, of life and death. Me, perhaps, being old, not of his own generation, not fore-fated to go through life stride for stride with him, at every day's beginning a challenge and a gall to him, at every day's end out-shining him, he might forgive. Your father also, for the same reasons, he might let live. But you—you, Harry, too close, too much praised, too dear to his boy, too gloriously his overmatch, you he cannot now leave live in this world. If we dispersed he would hold to terms for this time, but I do not believe it would be long before he would find another occasion, more favourable to his hand, and more secret. I chose to have open combat now."

"You chose rightly," his nephew said. "And I tell you now, I never looked for any other." He looked along his lines, and the knights were getting to horse, and the squires handing up lances, every man fixing his eyes upon the tight array in the distance. It had grown very quiet; men moved about the final business without words, even the birds had fallen silent.

"We made this day," he said, "and we'll abide it. Let's mount now and to our places."

They had barely reviewed each his own division, and taken station, when the royal trumpets sounded for the onset across the languid noonday fields.

∾ ⌣ ∾

The whole of that glittering mass before them began to move in immaculate order forward across the green, slowly yet, for they had to bring forward their bowmen and their unmounted men-at-arms with them to the edge of shooting range before launching an attack which they knew, from the condition of the ground and the known skill of the Cheshire archers, must be costly. Hotspur sat his horse at the head of his cavalry, and watched them come, and his heart lifted and sang in him dangerously, forgetful of both Berwick and death, waiting for the moment when that splendid line of steel and banners would burst forward and gather speed. There was a great formal beauty about the discipline and unanimity of this forward surge, more like a festival procession than the opening of a battle. Here there was nothing to do as yet but wait and watch. Every man had his orders. Every captain knew his own time, and every master-bowman his range.

They were well aware when the opposing vanguard was drawing almost within their reach, for they fitted their shafts, and levelled, and began without haste to draw, waiting for the order to loose. And now the colours and coat-armour began to take on significance, and they saw that Humphrey, earl of Stafford, had the perilous honour of leading the van, and of the two great divisions supporting him the prince had the left, and Henry himself the right. Sunlight danced in a dazzle of pin-pricks from the raised lances. When they came down, as superbly drilled as the steady advance, the spurs would drive in and the reins shake out, and the whole great formation sweep forward together, battering and tearing the green earth.

Up went the royal banner in the midst, down went the lances, and the line leaped forward. The trumpet-call, and the roars of: "St. George...St. George!" that had launched them were left behind by their rush, and came in late and strangely through the still air to the watchers on the slope.

"Not yet! said the master-bowman, crooning to himself as he calculated their progress yard by yard. "A little nearer yet—a little nearer...Now! *Loose*!"

The volley took wing with a sound like a vast flight of wild geese lifting, and the air shook. All the practised hands, without haste and in spare, synchronised movement, plucked and fitted the second arrow, and again waited. In the royal line, now in full and thunderous career and every second gathering impetus, sudden gaps were torn, and round each a small whirlpool of confusion and delay sprang into being; but the balance of the line came on, and those following circled the fallen and the plunging, squealing horses, and dressed their ranks, and spurred forward afresh.

The second volley took them to more deadly effect, the range being less, though the front ranks of the vanguard were still short of the edge of the bowl, and in the next few seconds must wheel either way to go round it. Evidently, thought Hotspur, watching motion-less in his place, Henry's venerable clerics were less use as observers than my squires, or else he thought it unbecoming to question them on anything but their office. For the centre, with Stafford's banner high, was hurtling straight for the slight drop into the ponds. They might, after all, choose to drive through rather than go round, and risk the mud for the sake of the impetus they might lose by circling the obstacle.

In the end they had little choice, for their speed was such that by the time they were fully aware of the difficulty they could not check without being thrust over the edge by those behind. One or two horses baulked, but the rest came plunging down and in, labouring in flurries of shallow green water, and floundering deeper into soft, clinging layers of mud. And volley upon volley of arrows drove into them there and cut them down, bringing the centre to a halt in a tangle of panicking horses and wounded and fallen men. Any who picked themselves out of that chaos and made at the slope beyond were picked off at leisure by the archers. By that route not a man or a horse came through.

Those on the right and left had fared better, having the firm ground of the headlands to help them. And now their own archers had advanced into range and taken possession of what cover they could, mainly on the flanks, to avoid shooting into their own cavalry; and there were the first casualties among the defenders, and it became a matter for caution even to lean out from cover for a fair shot. But still the slope held intact. Those few of the king's knights who reached its foot found themselves isolated, and drew off in haste to regroup before trying the assault again.

For more than an hour the archers had the battle in their hands. The king's bowmen closed in to new cover wherever they could find it, and shot each man for himself, selecting targets as they offered, and did some execution among the men-at-arms, waiting haplessly with no enemy within their reach.

This was always the stage that troubled Hotspur most, this new warfare to which he could not adapt himself without fretting, where the knight who had been the focal point and the transcendent weapon of war hung helplessly aloof, while the archers won and lost for him, and owed him nothing. He would rather have been constrained to an attacking battle, as Henry was now. There a knight could still come into his own. Archers might break a way into a square for him, but only he could go into the cleft and demolish the formation. Foot soldiers had not the mobility and speed and force, archers were helpless at close quarters. But in defence they held everything in their hands.

He detached himself briefly from his division to ride along the rear to the right wing. Richard Vernon's archers were immovable as yet, less pressed by the king's bowmen than on the other flank.

"If you can keep this battle defensive long enough," said Worcester, staring down, "you will have won it."

It was in his mind then, as he rode back, that this was the same counsel Dunbar had urged on him at Homildon, and he knew now, as he had known then, that there was a limit to the killing he could stand at this remove. Where was Dunbar now? Somewhere down there close to Henry's royal person, surely, for everything he had was staked upon Henry, and if Henry died, Dunbar was a lost man. His hands itched and his heart ached to be away down the slope and into that knot of chosen men that massed about the royal banner.

Then he heard, away before him in the centre, the sudden roar of voices shouting: "Espérance Percy!" and picked up the cry and hurled it back to them on the gallop aware of the wild shifting of air and thudding of hooves where he had left Douglas. His own division on the left of the centre stood fast as he had left it, but Douglas and all his knights and squires were away down the slope, and into the labouring ranks of horsemen who came surging to meet them. He heard lances shiver and blows fall, and the two forces collide and start below him like bones breaking. Tossing above the ranks of the king's knights he glimpsed the royal arms with a silver, three-pronged label of cadency, bravely afloat over a tangle of hewing, weaving, bellowing horses and men. He laughed aloud with a crazy, vindicated pride. The only leader who had carried that slope was the prince of Wales, the little, ruthless, whole-hearted paladin of Chester and Shrewsbury.

This was more to his mind. Since the pressure had reached so close, he had cause enough to thrust in his own hand now. And by the grace of God he had chosen the left, and could let fly at Henry himself, and leave the boy to God's care. He wheeled his horse again, and leaned down to the master-bowman.

"Break me a way into the ranks on the left there! Have your men cut me a line between me and the royal banner. Salvayn, go give the same order to my lord of Shipbrook on the flank. His men have the better view there."

His own mounted division shivered forward a foot or so in response, feeling their liberation near, and pricked up the points of their lances experimentally, peering keenly down towards the headland and the confused field beyond.

He watched the shots of both companies of archers converge steadily, and with merciless accuracy, upon the channel he had indicated, directing volley on volley into the royal ranks. He watched the concentrated shooting gouge into the mass like a knife, minute by minute widening the alley into Henry's flesh. He could not bear it long.

"Enough, hold your hand now! We're going in!" His runners carried the word. He spurred to the head of his knights without waiting for the shooting to cease, for he had some distance to go to reach the breach in the line, and he trusted the judgment of his bowmen to read his moves and act upon their own initiative. Where he rode they would leave the way open for him, and tear a channel for his passage if they could. He stood up in his stirrups, and bayed aloud to the ranks behind him: "Espérance Percy!" and hurled himself forwards towards the causeway below.

Down went the horses, headlong in their own madness, stretching their mailed necks and starting nostrils. And at the point where the gradient levelled out at the headland, down went the lances in a flutter of pennants and a glitter of steel, the sunlight splintering from their points. The king's archers had no time to do any great destruction during that onslaught, for their target streamed down the slope at such mad speed and at such an angle that they had difficulty in holding a mark, and the scattering of the prince's knights, driven some yards downhill again by Douglas's swoop, complicated the field and hampered their aim. Such hits as they made were made by blind chance, and Hotspur and his company plunged almost unscathed along the headland to the field beyond, and sheared accurately into the breach the bowmen had made in the massed ranks of the king's guard, like an axe into a wound.

The king's knights closed in to defend the standard, and Humphrey of Stafford flung himself and his red chevron deliberately in Hotspur's path. He was young, exalted, commander of the vanguard, and since that morning constable of England in Northumberland's forfeited place. His white horse was mired and wearied after struggling out of the mud of the ponds, and almost Hotspur regretted both the man and his mount, but they came between him and Henry, and he drove at them without relenting. His lance struck with precision just above the rim of the raised shield, and pierced through the steel gorget into flesh. The earl's body went somersaulting out of the saddle, and the horse was battered back on to its haunches, shocked and squealing, and flinched away sidelong from the weight of mount and rider bearing down upon him. The impetus of those following enlarged the opening. As one iron shaft the division slashed towards the standard.

Once thus entangled, all perspective was lost, for it was close cut and thrust, and nothing to see, and no time to see anything, but the enemy at grips. After the first impact the king's greater numbers told; and even the initial success of the assault created its own perils, for the knights of Henry's escort closed in on either side the wedge of their opponents, and set to work with grim determination to cut it into small, isolated groups which could be demolished separately. The knights of Cheshire broadened their line and drove in on either flank to enlarge the gap, and avert the danger that their leaders might be cut off. For some time the two armies were locked in one confused mass, and recognition of coat-armour became a game of life and death. The rider flung suddenly against a man in the press might be friend or enemy; only a quick eye and a good memory could determine and strike in time.

Hotspur's lance had shivered in that first thrust. Here in this tangle it was in any case useless to him; he hurled it from him, forward over the heads of those nearest, to fall among the royal guard and entangle the feet of the horses, and took to the sword instead. He rose in his stirrups to lengthen his already formidable reach, with great sweeps to right and left enlarging the alley he had cut in his enemies; and having stamped out room to look round him for an instant, fixed his eyes upon the standard, now being hastily withdrawn to a slight rise where the king's knights could rally to it in force, and having found it, never let it out of his sight again. Where it went, he pursued it implacably, and his division drove in doggedly after him. "Espérance Percy!" bellowed at his back, treading on his heels all the way.

On his right, though he had no time to observe it, Douglas's charge had swept the prince's knights out into the open field, leaving only a knot of stragglers fighting confusedly in the flattened pease. Douglas, finding himself with room to draw breath and muster afresh, gathered a small company of his closest companions and abandoned the prince, to set out after the quarry he most desired. Two columns converged ferociously upon the standard, and swept to its very foot.

The gold and scarlet and blue heaved and dipped in the air, and suddenly folded upon itself, its stem slashed through, and disappeared among the struggling bodies of men and horses. A great cry of triumph and delight went up at its fall, and a wild shout of dismay from its defenders. Douglas had felled it, Hotspur grasped a corner of it as it dropped, but it was torn out of his hold, leaving some ravelled threads of gold in his steel fingers. Desperate bodies closed in between to save it, at the sacrifice of their own lives. Sir Walter Blount went down before Hotspur's sword, and died among the hooves of the horses, so pressed together about the standard that they could not avoid trampling him. The standard-bearer himself fell dead beneath his broken banner, his head half-sheared from his body by Douglas. What hands snatched the silk away they never detected. It was passed back and back from them and vanished out of their sight, and with it, for a time, the focus of their quest.

They had enough to do, at this moment, keeping themselves alive and their followers still welded into a tight, indestructible wedge, for they had penetrated far into the royal ranks, and their contact with their own main body was tenuous. Hotspur and Douglas found themselves fighting elbow to elbow in the press, and edging their way out by cautious degrees, each keeping the other's flank and back as they extricated themselves. Only by fleeting, sidelong glances had they recognised and acknowledged each other, and yet there was delight in this harmony of feeling and temperament, the joyous trust they shared, and the absolute security that at every need the other would tread right and strike truly, as though they had been two bodies animated by a single soul, or twin brothers with a more than human understanding between them. When they drew out successfully at last from the circle of their enemies, and wheeled with slashing hooves to enlarge their ground, they ended face to face in laughter and love. Knee to knee they trotted aside, and breathed their horses for a few borrowed moments. There were no words, not yet. None would have been heard, nor was there leisure to raise a visor and let in clean air, or let out any word but the battle-cry that was a rallying-point at need.

Hotspur took a moment to view the field, and look for the close knot that marked where Henry was. He counted the picked men he had close about him, and made the number thirty. He lifted his visor, and gulped the cool, sweet air greedily.

"Archie, are you with me? There goes Lancaster untouched!"

"At your side, Harry! Where you go, I'll match you!

He waved them after him round an arc of open ground, clear of the roar and tangle of the fight, choosing a vulnerable blister in the circle where he could best break in. The archers, swarming lower among the wreckage of crops wherever there was cover, followed his movements, and hung upon the bowstring lovingly, ready to open a way for him.

The king's arms glimmered in the air again, a standard improvised by lashing the broken remnant to a lance. They fixed their sights upon it, dressing their ranks into an arrow-head, and at the raising of Hotspur's hand broke into measured motion, a trot, a canter, a gallop. Wandering wounded marked them and got out of their way in haste. Scattered members of the royal forces, washed aside by the shifting tides of battle, avoided as discreetly, seeing the blue lion fluttering over this advancing company. A few from the north, also cast up by the wash of war, girded themselves and joined the rear ranks. With clear ground still before them, Hotspur shook the reins and drove in the spur, and they leaped into the charge.

"Espérance Percy!"

"St. George! St. George!"

Cry and counter-cry came in time to help open the way in for them, for the confused personal combats weaving about the fringes of the fight gave way hurriedly before Hotspur's onslaught. For the second time their tight formation drove deep into the quick of Henry's army, and hurtled towards the broken standard. The entire mass of horse-flesh and man-flesh shook with their impact, and was carried bodily forward; and before the single, straining eye of the Douglas blazed suddenly the lions and lilies of the king's shield. He rose in his stirrups with a bellow of exultation, and struck a great, ranging blow with the mace which was his favourite weapon, caving in tardily-lifted shield, helmet and head together. The bulky body was swept sidewise out of the saddle, to hang a moment by one foot before the stirrup-leather tore free and dropped him like a flung sack into the trampled grass.

Douglas leaned in the saddle, arched over his fallen foe, and uttered a yell of triumph that sheared even through the babel of steel and terror.

"Here's your king! Here lies Lancaster dead!"

Hotspur looked down from the other side. The force of the blow had burst the joints of the helmet, and before his eyes the body, trodden by a frantic horse, rolled over, and the shattered remnants of visor and gorget fell away. Half the face remained unbroken, still with the colour of life in it; but it was not Henry's face.

"Not he! A counterfeit!—This is Sir John Calverley, I know him!"

Douglas heard the shouted words, and turned from his prey like a disgusted hound that has coursed a stag and cornered only a rat, to look ahead for more kings. It was no new device, where the survival of a leader meant life or death to many of his followers, but it was not in Henry's style, whatever might be said of him, to hide his own golden branch in a forest of gilding. Dunbar's counsel? Dunbar had everything to lose if he lost Lancaster, life, living, freedom, family, everything he had. There might be more such pseudo-kings before they brought the one they hunted to bay.

Grimly knee to knee, hewing their way by laborious inches deeper into the royal host, they pursued the standard and its master. They were part of one unwieldy mass that reeled now east, now west as the weight and the impetus of struggle carried it; and in one lurching movement the ranks before them broke apart, and opened an alley towards a second royal shield. This time Hotspur knew the very bearing, the seat in the saddle, the manner of sword-play; this one was no counterfeit. There was room for only one to drive into the gap that opened before them; and Douglas had also seen the quarry, and was before him into the narrow lane. The two horses were flung together and reared breast to breast with lashing hooves, but Douglas wheeled his mount aside on its hind legs, and struck hard as he drew clear. Down went the king's horse on its crupper, and his rider was thrown clear and lay half-stunned on the ground.

A great cry of anger and dismay burst about them, and a surge of devoted bodies hid the fallen king as though a curtain had been drawn over him. Now they would die where they stood rather than let an enemy come so near to him again. A trumpet blared alarm, and from half a mile around the stragglers rallied to make a wall of men about King Henry and withdraw him out of danger.

Dunbar had dragged, persuaded, and hustled him some way towards the rear while he was still dazed from his fall, and Hal had sent him a young knight with a fresh horse for his use. As soon as his head cleared he turned again towards the thickest press of men and horses, so tightly interlaced now that men might as easily die of suffocation in there as from wounds, and horses were going crazy with terror. Dunbar's hand was urgent upon his bridle, trying still to lead him away, and hide him in a place of comparative safety.

"My liege, think on your worth to us all, and take some count of your life! If you're lost, we've lost more than a man! Take thought for your own son's crown, and be ruled. We may give our lives, you may not!"

It was true, and he knew it; if he went courting his death he lost everything he was fighting to protect, and lost it for his children's children no less than for himself. He had not only to win his battle, but to survive it.

Knights and squires made passage for him out of the press, and closed their ranks after his passing. Here the lines held firm, a channel of something approaching calm gave him room to raise his visor for a few moments, and gulp in air. His breastplate was dinted and stained, but not with his own blood. He looked at the prince, who rode for these few yards between his father and harm. The boy had also uncovered his face, which was streaked with sweat and grime.

"You're hurt! Your cheek bleeds!"

The boy put up a hand in surprise, and felt at his right cheek, astonished to find a jagged slash and a constant trickle of blood there, "It's nothing! A narrow...I knew the plate was pierced, but not that I was grazed."

It was more than a graze; the steel, driven inward by the shaft, had marked him with two irregular scratches beaded with blood, and let the point of the arrow drive in between.

"Go back to the rear camp, and let them dress it. You've done enough!"

The boy looked over his shoulder. The force of Hotspur's attack suddenly swept the centre towards them afresh. He saw the familiar plume rise tall above the mêlée as Harry stood up in his stirrups to search for his enemy.

"No!" said the prince flatly. "I turn not my back at this pass. I have taken the field, and I will not quit it."

Over the tossing sea of heads and fumbling arms and flailing weapons, Hotspur marked the slight swirl of movement that was the only orderly thing in sight, the parting and closing in again of the lines as someone withdrew from him. He followed its course and found its reason.

He dropped back into his saddle just in time to escape the arrow loosed at him by one of the prince's archers, who had found himself a vantage-point in a clump of low trees on one of the headlands, and for the past hour had been waiting and hoping for a clear shot

at the king's arch-enemy. But always there were king's men screen-
ing him, or so entwined with him that the marksman had held his
hand, for fear of killing a friend rather than a foe. Others he had
already picked off successfully, but a man who was always at the tip
of a lance probing deep among the king's defenders was a hopeless
target. That reckless moment of standing clear above his neighbours
had provided the first real chance. But Hotspur dropped back too
soon, having found his own mark. The hand that gripped the reins
shook them out and knuckled his charger's streaming neck, his knees
urged, and the horse answered.

"Espérance Percy!"

They roared it back to him, and came plunging after. He set his
course straight for the place where the little whirlpool of motion
conveyed his enemy steadily away out of his reach, and turned aside
for nothing. Horseman after horseman barred his way and was cut
down, ridden over or swept aside. Some reined out of his path and
ran from him, for the terror his presence inspired had swollen into a
superstition, and the manifest madness of his proceedings confirmed
some in suspecting him to be a demon and not a man like other
men, with the sensible fear of death in him.

He was gaining, yard by yard; the same dread that opened a way
for him now confused and paralysed those who stood inadvertently
in Henry's way. And thrusting hard behind came Douglas, and a
dozen knights from Scotland and the north.

"Espérance Percy! Espérance Percy!"

And louder still, sudden and shrill as lightning, came a single
brazen north-country voice behind the leaders, hallooing jubilantly:
"Henry Percy, king!"

It sprang from nowhere, unprompted, unprophesied, and it was
taken up in a huge shout of acclamation: "Henry Percy, king! Henry
Percy, king!"

Hotspur heard but never understood it. It was a sweet thunder
in his ears, like horns at a hunt, but nothing more. He saw nothing

but the figure of Henry of Lancaster on his fresh horse, urged away by Dunbar, urged back to the fight by his own conscience and will, torn every way, and looking back over his shoulder towards this nemesis that bored through men and horses to reach him, shieldless now, with a stained and dinted sword in its hand.

All the shouting had fallen behind him; he hacked and spurred his way forward through a private silence. For if this was his death-field, then he was resolved that it should be a double death, for there was no other just ending. He did not know, nor would he have cared, that he had outdistanced all his companions, that even Douglas was cut off from him, and he stormed through the royal ranks alone.

Not ten yards between them now—barely seven! Henry was thrusting off Dunbar, and turning, sword in hand, to face his end.

The mindless currents of movement that convulsed the battlefield cast up a violent wave at that moment, and sent a succession of men and coat-armour reeling across Hotspur's path. When the wave receded, marvellously baring some yards of open turf, a single figure was flung into his way, face to face at sword-point in the middle of this accidental arena. A slender, light body—the big horse carried him as daintily as a lady; but a fine seat, and a practised grip on the hilt and the reins. There was a deep, jagged dint in the right side of his visor, and blood on his gorget beneath the tear. But he spurred eagerly forward, freeing his right arm for combat, and leaned with alacrity to the encounter, all the more proudly for knowing whom he faced.

Hotspur in mid-career checked abruptly, and leaning hard back, wheeled aside from the meeting, dropping his sword-arm so suddenly and resolutely that it was like a salute in passing. He had swung to the left, and for that one moment there was no obstacle between him and the archer among the thorn trees, who had followed his progress with so much patience and persistence.

The passage of the arrow was like the flight of a bird, a strong vibration of wings and a vehement alighting. It pierced dinted breastplate and fine mail hauberk under, and drove clean into the heart he had deliberately exposed to assault. The sword slipped almost silently out of his relaxing hand, while he still sat erect and immovable, turned away from the combat he would not accept upon any terms. Then slowly, as it seemed, he leaned backwards towards the crupper of his horse, stiffly and solidly as a tree falls, and heeling to the right, perhaps drawn by the mere remaining impulse of the weight of his fallen sword, crashed from his saddle at the prince's feet.

The shifting tide of battle, ungovernable as the sea, had hung in balance only for an instant. It swayed again strongly, casting men lurching one against another. It caught up the king's raw, exultant shout of: "Henry Percy, slain! Henry Percy, slain!" and flung it echoing across the twilit, long-shadowed field, to be taken up and echoed as far as Haughmond hill, for a warning to all rebels:

"Henry Percy, slain! Henry Percy, slain!"

And it caught up in its ebb Henry, prince of Wales, nearly sixteen years old, sword in hand and poised and ready to take or give death without quarter or grudge, and swept him helplessly away into the meaningless aftermath of slaughter, though he struggled and fought to get back to the fallen hero, weeping like a heartbroken child within the privacy of his helmet, blinded and choked with blood and tears.

17

When he was dead, without whom there could be no victory, they fought on dourly into the fall of the night, and into the darkness, driven and scattered as they were across three square miles of the plain, and hunted like hares; fought to kill, as long as there was anything within their reach to kill, but not to save, for now there was nothing to be saved. Hotspur had died in the belief that they, like himself, were fighting for a right and for a rightful king, temporarily and shamefully dispossessed, and for the rights and dignities of the king's magnates under him and in despite of him. But those who followed him knew that they were fighting for Hotspur, and for no other man, nor king, nor child, nor right that existed in this realm, and if he was lost to them, all was lost.

So though they fought on, they fought every man in a circle, to destroy whatever foe came within reach, no longer as an army with an end in view. They fought with weapons, and hands, and teeth, but no longer with heart or mind. And when the darkness came down, and no man could distinguish friend from enemy, they broke away and took to flight. Some had kin close by who hid them and helped them away, some trusted and were betrayed, some made their own way back to the north, having discarded their arms, and came safely to bereaved Northumbria at last. They would have been secure enough as prisoners, since theirs was not a case of treason, their fealty being to their lord. But they preferred to adventure their lives still in freedom.

As long as there was light to see by, the pursuit went on, in every corner of the field, until Henry withdrew into the town with his battered host, his silent son, his noble dead and wounded, and his prisoners. Worcester had brought his cavalry down to his nephew's aid in time to see him die, and after that, so said those who had surrounded, disarmed and captured him, had fought like a man dazed, weighted down by the languor of dreadful dreams. Sir Richard Venables and Sir Richard Vernon had fought with their knights and pikemen until they were broken and overrun by sheer numbers. Douglas in his reckless battle fit had done great slaughter until in the failing light he chose rather to absent himself than to run, and his horse had been brought down by a wounded man-at-arms of the king's company, and the earl himself surrounded by some half-dozen mounted knights, of whom he slew two and wounded a third before they stunned and secured him. But Douglas was not, like his friends, in peril of a charge of treason, for Douglas was a Scot in justifiable arms against the English king, and owed allegiance to none but his own king in Scotland. He was an honourable prisoner of war; at Henry's disposal at last, over Hotspur's dead body.

The night came, incredibly lofty and mild and starry above, and hideous in wreckage and waste below, three miles and more of once flourishing fields trampled and harrowed and littered with dead and dying, cast weapons and bloodied armour and the rags of horses and men. A field where the past had just received another mortal blow in its drawn-out death, and the future had cast its forward shadow long and stark, the chilling image of battle after battle, treason after treason, change piled upon change, interminably reeling to and fro across the ruined crops and desolated hopes of peasant cultivators and tenant farmers, stamping their ripening peas and small human aspirations into the ground.

With the night, after the fragments of armies had limped away into the shelter of the town, the small and secret people came out from their hiding-places, and shadows began to roam the darkness, searching among the fallen. Some stole out from the holes where outlaws and cutpurses lurk by day, to rob the dead and carry away what loot they could find, clothes, armour, weapons, rings, even an occasional wretched, wandering horse, dazed but undamaged. They said afterwards that sixteen hundred good fighting men died in that field, on both parts, and some three thousand more were left badly wounded to lie overnight, and there died even more miserably of their wounds, or at the hands of cut-throats too cautious to leave alive the helpless victims they robbed. And some of the local peasant farmers crept out to lament over the despoiling of all their year's labour, and avenge themselves by picking up something of value from the spoilers to compensate. They, too, put a knife into a throat here and there, where they happened upon some local lordling to whom they owed a grudge. So death did as brisk a business in the night as in the day.

And some of the silent shadows supping from corpse to corpse in the starlight had come out, from both village and town, searching for the bodies of their kinsfolk, to take them away for decent burial. The dead were so many, and scattered wantonly over so vast a ground, that it was a search that went on until morning, and found no surcease.

Julian came out; like the other shadows, with the dusk. For a while she hovered in the clump of thorn bushes where she had waited out the day, until the confused alarms and desultory slaughters had faded into the terrible silence. Though why she should hide or take thought, who had nothing now but a life to lose, was more than she could determine. Ask for a horse, he had told her, and one shall be found for you. But she had not asked for anything, nor promised him obedience, nor gone farther from him than the closest cover she could find. If she had had any skills that could have been profitable to him she would not have withdrawn from him even so far; but she was a charge upon his mind if she stayed, and all her will had been to lift every weight from him, so this weight she had lifted in her own despite.

Nevertheless, he was gone, he the brightness and the savour and the sense, the whole valour and value of living was gone. She came out of her thorny solitude, and at the very edge of the headland the endless dying began; for there was a leather-clad archer dangling in the branches of the best-grown thorn tree, with his bow idly swaying across his breast, and another man's shaft through his throat. She had flattened herself in the grass all that day, like a hare in her form, beneath many such shafts flying loose at any mark. She had heard this man shifting in his prickly perch, and from the time that he had made his stealthy way to this tree, she had crept as far from him as she might without being detected, for he was the enemy. Now she looked upon him, mute and inoffensive in the faint starlight, and felt pity, for he was young and comely, and wasted like the rest, like the best.

She did not know, as she passed him by and went down the slope of the headland into the field, that he had been Hotspur's death before he himself died, and that this death had been his pride and hope of advancement. No one was ever going to identify, praise and reward the man who had won the battle for the king; a king he had never even seen but as a casque beneath a banner in the far distance.

Julian had fixed her sights by headland, tree and copse before the light died in the death of all things here. She walked forward steadily, not even knowing, not even wondering, what she was going to do when she found what she was seeking. How could she get him hence? She had neither horse nor litter, no means of carrying him away. She knew only that she must find him, and do what service she might for him, if need be keep watch through the night until God saw fit to send her help in his honour, since not even God could choose but do him honour. And as she went, first walking freely, unafraid of darkness or of those who skulked in the dark, she addressed him silently, with moving lips, like a pilgrim in ecstasy advancing upon her saint:

"My sweet lord, my loved lord, my phoenix of most worship, my prince, my companion, my most dear friend, you who did me such honour and whom I honour so much, you my life's crown, my love's laurel…"

Then she came among the spoils and the spoilers, and the dead who cared for neither, and felt her way step by step, her eyes still fixed ahead to maintain her course midway between tree and copse, where she had seen that everlasting fall, and heard that terrible cry of grief. And she spoke to him no more in words, even silently, but only within, while she kept one hand ready with her dagger in it, and her eyes upon her mark, and went without fear, like a ghost who cannot be halted by mortal means.

Distant Shrewsbury lay beyond her mark, a faint glow upon the darkness. The bells would be rung in the churches there tomorrow for this victory, the priests would offer thanks for deliverance, and yet there would be many hearts, perhaps most, that would turn in revolt to take the opposing side, and remember rather the dead man than the living, and deny a triumph to the victor, in favour of passionate lament for the vanquished. But silently, like her, in the fortress of the heart. Even those who had run wild in the town killing and despoiling the Welsh. Even they! Men are strange creatures. They spurn the careful, deserving, husbanding victors, and remember always, with epic songs and legends, the heroic dead who spent everything to buy a future, and bought instead an eternal reputation.

She came to the place she had noted, and halted there to breathe the night, and get her bearings among so many dead. For here had been the centre of that struggle for the standard and the king. She looked to the right and to the left, turning her head slowly, scenting the air like an animal. Somewhere within a circle of a dozen yards from her he must be, and at this close remove she could not be unaware of him.

Something shadowy and deformed started up before her out of the ground, and hovered, uncertain whether to menace or avoid.

She tilted the long dagger in her hand, faint light flowing down it to the point, and said without fear or animosity: "Get out of my way!" and the furtive thing slid sidelong and scuttled away from her. There were dogs, too, among the discarded bodies, snuffling and licking inquisitively at blood, for it was summer, and they were well-fed, feeling no compelling hunger. To them she paid no attention, but began to search in a narrow circle about the approximate spot she had marked out as the place of her irremediable loss. And not ten yards from this centre she found him.

He lay as he had fallen, never trampled nor troubled since, half on his back and half on his right side, his cheek against the turf, his limbs spread abroad like a man large and easy in sleep. She went on her knees beside him, cut off the shaft of the arrow close to his breast, and with careful hands began to attempt the straightening of those discarded members into the order of death, but his stiffening arms resisted her. She would have to watch with him until the rigour passed. Yet she might still do him service, in easing him of the weight of part of this harness that pinned him to the earth. She drew off, with some trouble but infinite patience, the gauntlets that cased his hands, and by touch in the darkness unfastened his plumed salade from the mentonnière of steel cupping his chin, and laid bare to the cool of the night the proud and passionate face, unmarked and unastonished, confronting death with the wide, fearless stare of a princely equal. His head yielded to her hands a little, allowing itself to be turned up to the starlight. Reverently she closed the arched eyelids, and with her fingers held them closed until they consented to this formal sleep. And finding under his side the fallen sword that had lain between them in the night, she drew it forth, and unbuckling the scabbard from his belt, restored the blade to it, and laid it like a cross along his body. Rigidly held by the chin-piece of his helm, his jaw had not fallen, and his lips were closed and calm, firmly folded for ever upon the utterance that sometimes, in most need, played him false. He had the eloquence of eternity now.

She stooped to him gently, and kissed him upon the cold, smooth brow and the silent lips. Her mouth was on his when she heard the two voices drawing near out of the night, a mere murmur, yet not so furtive as the movements of thieves and scavengers. Silently she sank into the grass beside her lord, and for the second time lay with him in the night, her lips against his hair, her arm spread over him to hold the sword in place, and the dagger ready in her hand. She held her breath, listening, waiting for the searchers to pass by. Doubtless they had dead here, too. The voices were low, constrained and sad.

"Somewhere here...I do remember those trees in line with the place."

"Here is plate-armour like his...No, this is not he. This is a Massey by his arms."

"Then we must be close. Sir John Massey was among the guard then, and I know he was not with us when we drew off."

"My lord, you're shivering. You should not have come, hurt as you are, it's too easy to take fever. At dawn we shall have light enough..."

"Dawn might be too late," said the first voice, with still, contained bitterness. "Who knows what jackals might be at him before then? And my father could change his mind and withdraw his grace as suddenly as he gave it. No, we must find him and have him away now!"

Then she knew this one for the prince, and knew beyond doubt for whose body he was searching, and for what purpose. With his father's leave, but expecting that leave to be as capriciously cancelled if tonight was lost. She raised her head, and saw that they had passed by at some yards' distance, and were moving slowly away from her. Softly she rose out of the grass, and called after them clearly: "Your Grace is looking for Sir Henry Percy? You have found him. He is here."

To whom else could she confide him, and to whom better? Exhausted as he was, and wounded, or so this second man said, the boy had cared enough to beg respect for the dead, and come out in the night to see his rest assured. He would not baulk at having the prince for his priest.

They had both whipped round upon her, startled, and came peering doubtfully through the dark. She stood to be examined, an unkempt country boy with a thin, beautiful face silvered into stillness under the stars. He would not know her; he had good eyes, but they were not Hotspur's eyes. He was very young, greatly torn and troubled, and so tired and sick that he went with exaggerated care on his long legs, like a man too full of wine. No, he would not know her.

"He is here," she said again, faintly smiling to see them both lay hand to hilt, though both of them relaxed and loosed the grip as quickly. They looked down at the figure on the ground, blessed from the riven breast downwards by the cross of his own sword, and drew breath in a deep sigh before they looked again at her, and intently.

"You know me?" said the prince.

"Who does not?"

"You have so served, so laid him? Why? For what cause?" But his voice was gentle and warm in its bewilderment.

"Sir, for he was my lord, and I was his man, and I had good cause to love him."

"You do well," he said, "and for his sake I thank you. But will you now yield him to us to care for? For this is his kinsman, Lord Furnival, and there is a chapel of his kin at Whitchurch where Sir Henry Percy can lie in peace and honour, with all the rites due him."

"I will," she said, "with gratitude, for I could not get him hence alone, and I have no one to help me. But to you, your Grace, I trust him with all my heart."

They had horses hobbled close to the copse which had been their landmark. They took up the body between them to carry it to the place, and the sword making their task difficult, she took it and bore it after them. So it came that she was still holding it when they had swathed the dead in a cloak and bound him carefully on the back of the third horse they had brought for him, and turned, still in some awe and wonder at her composure and fearlessness in this deathly place, to say their farewell.

"No!" she said, when the prince would have taken the sword from her. "Let me keep it for my peace through this world and into the grave."

"You did indeed love him," he said slowly, and let his hand fall empty at his side. She saw him lean closer, searching her face.

"Have you not been in his retinue in Chester or Shrewsbury once, boy? For it seems to me that I should know your face, and yet I cannot place you."

"You may well have seen me before, your Grace. I have been sometime in Shrewsbury."

"Come back there with me now," said the prince earnestly, "and I will see you are not molested. Come into my service. There is a place near me for any man who served Sir Henry Percy faithfully, and now is left bereaved."

"There are many who will say yes to that, and thank your Grace, and so would I if I could. But I shall never have another lord to my life's end."

He drew back from her then, not understanding, but asking no further questions. She watched him mount, and look back yet once more, one hand stretched to the bridle of the third horse.

"God be with you, boy, wheresoever you go, and keep you from harm."

"And with your Grace, for this great goodness in you." She watched them go, the three horses picking their way fastidiously until they vanished into the dark. And that was her last glimpse of the prince of Wales and of Hotspur.

✦✦✦

Once in the night, wandering without purpose, almost without awareness, she drew the sword, and set the hilt between her feet and steadied the point with both hands against her breast, and so leaned, wondering why it should seem hard to do, when she felt no

fear, and expected no joy. Yet she knew that she could not do it.
She despised it as he would have despised it, as a trivial course in a
world made for great courses. Nor would she for any cause have so
misused his sword.

She was walking away from the field towards the west, turning by
instinct to the river, when the first pale grey of dawn lightened the
sky behind her, and after a while, for she took no account of time,
she began to cast a long shadow, and realised that the sun was rising.
Thus with eyes fixed on the darkened part of her spirit gliding before
her, she saw it meet and blend with the darkness under a holly tree,
and through this darkness a man burst suddenly to be gilded by the
sun. She raised her eyes to him, and looked into the narrow, burning
face and frantic sapphire eyes of Iago Vaughan.

He had ridden without rest most of the night and all the previous
day, to bring word that came too late. By the dawn of Monday the
Lord Owen would be here on the border in accordance with his
pledged word, only to find the battle fought and lost. Iago knew it.
He had been in the town, he had seen the dead lying, he saw now
this calm, chill stranger walking away from the end of her world with
a sword in her hands for a remembrance of things lost. She saw the
dust and weariness upon him, and the blanched intensity of his face.

"I have been looking for you," he said, his voice low and wary.
"In Shrewsbury, and at the holding."

"You have found me," she said. "And I am all you will find. He
is dead." She did not mean her father.

"I know it." He was gone who had linked them rather than separating them, and yet had been always immense and impenetrable
between them. Armed as she was, she could have died if she had
been so minded, but she had not died, and she would not die. And
he could wait for his hour. "I heard it in the town. Your part is
done. There is nothing now to keep you here."

She was studying his face with fixed, attentive eyes, as though she
saw him now all the more clearly because Hotspur had commended

her to him in his farewell. As the prince in his misery reached a hand rashly to every liegeman who had served Hotspur loyally, so she remembered the many journeys, the messages carried, even the music of the little harp that hung behind Iago's shoulder. Every creature who had been in that service shared in its lustre, and confided a little of its warmth. Until he came she had been cold as death, even in the dawn.

He looked her over in silence, from her patched chausses and shabby tunic to her shorn hair and broad, pale brow, and she was strange and dangerous, but to him beautiful. She did not come empty-handed from this last encounter; something had been given, and something taken, and in his heart he thought that she had been the gainer, at whatever cost, and whoever was man enough to win her and her winnings would be the gainer, too. Also, she was inexpressibly alone, though he dared not therefore suppose that she was lonely, or felt the need of him that he had long felt for her. No untimely word must be said here of love.

"The Lord Owen kept his time faithfully," he said. "This is no fault of his. And I must ride back to meet him, and tell him we are forestalled, and he comes too late. Come with me! Come with me now to Walter's cottage, and we'll cross there, and ride to Montgomery before night. There is no place for you now but the place that always waited for you, with us in Wales."

She looked at him long and gravely, the sheathed sword clasped jealously to her side, and said neither yes nor no to him; but when he held out his hand to her in silence, she put her left hand into it, and went with him, their two long shadows straining and beckoning before them, towards the west.

18

On Sunday there were services of thanksgiving in all the churches of Shrewsbury, the bells pealed, and the king heard mass after mass to his comfort and consolation. The rest of the day was given to the pious duty of burying the dead, of whom by now there were some four thousand, besides those of birth and coatamour whose kin had already conveyed them to the grave. Citizens, peasants, and soldiers were all recruited to the sacred labour, and the summer being so high, and time so short for so many obsequies, there was no alternative but to make one great mass grave upon the battlefield, and there lay all the slain of both parties together, to wait for judgment day,

So they did. And so they wait still.

Those three noble prisoners who owed direct fealty to the king were brought to trial, without overmuch ceremony, on the Monday. There was little room for much trying of any issue, since they were taken in arms against King Henry, to whom they had once sworn allegiance, and King Henry, through his council, was their judge. The two barons of Cheshire made blunt avowal of their unending loyalty to Richard, and to the child who was Richard's acknowledged heir. They knew they were dead men. So was their only desired liege lord. They made no complaint of their fortune, they asked no clemency, as none would have been granted.

The earl of Worcester came to his trial composed, distant, and
stern, as judge rather than judged. He stood before King Henry with
bound hands but free eyes and free tongue, though the eyes were
wept half-blind for his dearly-loved nephew, and the tongue was dry
with thirst, for they had kept him close, and forgotten the heat of his
cell. He, too, was a dead man, but already past one death, and the
second is a nothing, a desired oblivion. But he had somewhat to say
before he completed his dying.

"My lord of Lancaster, there is nothing now your vengeance can
do to me, nothing you can take from me that I will not gladly part
with. But I tell you to your face, you do ill to use such words as
traitor and treason to me, or to him that's dead in his splendour.
What have we done that you have not taught us before? We took
arms for our rights against wrongs inflicted by an unjust king. So did
you! We did our endeavour to curb his actions and take from him
his crown. So did you! If we are traitors, so were you when you
struck against Richard. Did we go back on an oath of allegiance?
So did you! There is nothing we have now done against the crown
that you did not yourself commit against it four years ago. Hold
up the mirror of treason before you, and see your own face! And
more—for you did things we have not done, nor never thought to
do. It was in fair fight in the field, and far outnumbered, that Harry
Percy set out to take your life, Henry of Lancaster, man to man, not
by proxy in a prison cell, fifteen days starving to death!"

He had not raised his voice at all, nor was there need, for the
silence in the stone chamber within the castle was profound; and
when one made to silence him or hustle him away before he had
done, the king made a faint gesture of his hand, and held them still.

"Let him speak! It is his right." His own face, heavy and greyish-
white, looked like the face of a dead man not yet decently composed
for burial. This was a part of his penance, and he could not avoid it.
Even vengeance was sour and stale, and showed him always a new
vengeance waiting at the door to make answer to the old.

"It was Richard's right, also, but it was denied him. But let me speak, for after this day you'll hear my voice no more, that was never backward in your council, and willed well to this kingdom. And you will do well to remember what Worcester said at his departing, for you have no long time left, and you will be old before your time, and before your time you will make an end. This is not the last battle of a war, my lord, but the first, and your sons and grandsons will reap what you have sowed, for a hundred years yet. For this is truth—the one treason my house ever committed was committed against Richard in your favour, not against you, and though we began in all good intent, not meaning such usurpation as came of our act, yet we cannot escape the penalty. What we have now done was not treason, but penance for treason, and this ending is just, but it is not your justice, Lancaster. And your turn is yet to come."

"I abide," said the king, in a voice as hollow as if he spoke from a tomb, "the judgment and the mercy of my maker. I will answer, and not stint."

"You will answer your fellow-men also, though you live out your reign almost in peace. For he is gone, that was the pattern of chivalry, and valour, and noblesse in all this realm, and make no doubt but that he shall be missed as long as men have memories and singers make ballads. Whenever our grandchildren speak of this battle of Shrewsbury, never think they will talk of your triumph, but only of his death, never look for any celebration, but only laments. He will be Hotspur still when your name is forgotten and you have no face, as all the glory of Troy clings to the name of Hector, and not of his killer, and to Hector's nobility, not to ignoble Achilles. He was the first of my brother's sons," said Worcester softly, "and the last. And I am not sorry to go after him out of this world."

And so he turned, not waiting to be taken, and went out with a firm and masterful step to bend his neck to the sword, he who had been high admiral of England, and governor of the household of the prince of Wales, besides many lesser offices. And the king, as he signed the order committing the earl's head to be set up on London Bridge, knew to his abysmal grief and frustration that within every traitor to him, as long as he lived, there would exist such a man of parts and quality, disaffected beyond cure or redress.

It was harder to face them, dead, than alive. After death they grew, like legends passed from lip to lip. The future was swollen with the ghostly offspring of this almost denuded house.

On this same day the earl of Northumberland, moving south with a force in arms, heard of his son's death and of the battle lost and won, and drew back before the levies of the earl of Westmorland, his nephew and bitter rival, to his castle of Warkworth, there to contemplate his bereavement, and his inevitable submission to the king.

And on this same day, while the prince lay retired in solitude and silence, nursing his wound, the mysterious, sourceless word began to be passed furtively through Shrewsbury, over market stalls, over counters, in the settles of inns and the backyards of houses, that Hotspur was not dead at all, but spirited away living from that bitter field by those who loved him exceedingly, and that he was now safely away into Wales with Mortimer and Glendower, and would come again with a new and terrible army to avenge his uncle's death and his own passing defeat.

There was also the small, strange matter of what could have happened to the earl of Worcester's body, which had been left neglected for a while after the head was taken away, and now was nowhere to be found. Only the stain of his blood remained after the head had been despatched to London. And everyone knew that Glendower was a wizard, and Hotspur, perhaps, more than mortal.

It was John Norbury, the only man to be trusted with bad news, who brought the ghostly word to the king. Henry sat with tired, sagging eyelids, and jaw set like a man braced against nausea, and leaned his head upon his hand for a long time in silence. It was more than he could bear. Let there be no more dead men eternally climbing out of their graves and dogging his steps in their shrouds wherever he turned. Shrewsbury should learn by its own senses, England should learn by the stench and the putrefaction, that death could overtake even Hotspur. There was no other way with these defiers of the grave but to deprive them of a grave.

He lifted his head, and looked up with sick, savage eyes into Norbury's face.

"John, take six men with you, and a horse litter, and ride to Whitchurch. In the vault of Furnival's kinsfolk there you'll find Percy's body. Bring it back here and set it up under strong guard at the Cross. He shall never again set an ambush for me out of his tomb. Not Shrewsbury only, but the whole realm shall see how even Percy flesh can rot."

The prince got out of his bed when he heard it, burning with fever, a bright, rose-coloured blotch of heat on one cheek, the bloated dressing of his wound on the other, wrapped his gown about him with shaky hands, and went down to plead with his father. It was the first time he had approached him since his appeal on Furnival's behalf on the night following the battle, and but for this extreme distress he might have kept his bed and his privacy a week or so longer. Already he had stirred himself once that day, to give orders to some whom he trusted utterly to be his men and not his father's, to have Worcester's corpse quietly conveyed to certain cousins of the house, and to ask no questions as to how they meant to dispose of it, for what is not known cannot be told. But this was a dearer need. He went himself, thin and bright, and dropped to his knees beside the king's chair, and would not be lifted up.

"This you cannot do, upon grounds so trivial! You gave me your good word, now you take it back as though it weighed nothing. If you be not as light as you seem, send after, call them back! Do not so shame yourself and me, for I, too, gave my word."

"Child, what are you about?" Henry took him by the wrists and tried to lift him, aghast at his burning intensity. "You should not be out of your bed. Get up! This is foolish!"

"Let him rest! Let rumour run its course, as it will. Fools will always make up stories, what hurt can they do you? Have you not enough advantage over him, seeing he is dead? The whispers of the whole world cannot bring him back. Let him rest in the grave!"

"Fool boy, he will not rest! There's no other way but this to lay him. They must see, they must be made to see, that he was mortal, and is gone to a mortal end."

It was on the boy's tongue then to say outright: "They saw Richard, and yet they still believe him living, and you will still be haunted by him all the days of your life." But he did not say it; there was too great a distance between them, and no bridge across the void capable of sustaining so much truth. Instead he said, with practical and chilling certainty: "If you do it, you undo any good you have gained, for they will hate you for it, and pity him, and you had best set a strong cordon about him, or they will have him away in spite of you, and give him clean burial."

The king in his despair forgot his son's wound, his fever, and his youth, and took him roughly by the chin, jerking up his hectic face to the light. "*You* will see to it, I suppose? This is your intent, so to defy me? Is that your meaning?"

"No," said the boy, coldly and steadily. "God forbid I should force salvation upon you, if you will not be saved." And he rose from his knees, knowing that argument and pleading were alike vain, and plucked his face from between his father's hands so fiercely that the dressing was torn aside, and his wound bled again. He turned to leave the chamber, asking no permission and making no farewell, and fell like a felled sapling in the doorway, and was carried back to his bed.

The wound is healing well enough," said the surgeon, anxiously questioned, "if his Grace can be made to rest. But he'll carry the scar of Shrewsbury to the day of his death."

In the Trinity chapel of St. Mary's church, by night, certain good friends to the earl of Worcester opened the tomb of the Leybourne family, once lords of Berwick, a family now extinct in the county, reverently lifted out the bones of two men and a child interred there, and laid beneath them, at the bottom of the grave, a rough wooden coffin hurriedly nailed together. Inside it, swathed in leather, lay the earl's headless body. The Leybourne bones they carefully replaced above him, and closed the tomb. Nor was there wanting a priest to say the office over him. On the stone lid a Leybourne knight lay cross-legged and calm in his armour, a hundred years and more out of fashion. The iron crow with which they had opened the tomb had done some slight damage to the stonework at his feet; but if anyone ever noticed, he took care to say nothing. Worcester slept with strangers, but in dignity and peace.

After two days the prince rose from his bed, his fever gone. He had asked nothing and confided nothing; the last interview with his father might never have taken place. He was cool, courteous and apart.

When he was ready—and by what strange and terrible process of thought and prayer and will he made himself ready no one knew— he went out and rode the short way up to the Cross from the castle gatehouse, and sat his horse there for many minutes, gazing earnestly at the spectacle the king had provided for the inhabitants of Shrewsbury.

There were others standing gazing as well as himself, though it had already been there some days; and all of them were silent, and secret, keeping their thoughts close behind the masks of their faces as he did. There was no triumphing over this carrion exposed here between two millstones, and ringed by a dour-faced and formidable guard; rather a strong distaste, a large, inarticulate pity, and a deep and obstinate resentment, not against the dead enemy, but against the author of his defilement. And stranger still, infinitely strange, the body itself in its dusty decay, the ruin of nobility and valour and generosity, was not defiled. Everything that had been done to him his very corpse parried and returned triumphantly upon his conqueror. It was not the man to whom this thing had been done who stood humiliated and contemptible, but the man who had done this abominable thing to him.

In the night there was a double guard set, so afraid were they of rescue. If the king felt insecure when he had that resplendent enemy enclosed in lead and stone, how much more did he dread him now that he had enlarged him, and how much more cause he had for dread now that he had himself turned all the sympathy he had enjoyed in this town into burning animosity, and all their earlier terror of Hotspur into awe-struck sympathy. A dead eagle he might have buried, but he had chosen rather to light a fire for a phoenix.

For the first time the prince despised his father; and that was merciful, for if he had not, he would have had no choice but to hate him. But now he was liberated from hating, and if he could never love, at least he might some day be able to pity.

He took his eyes at last from the poor relic that was not Hotspur, that could not touch the legend of Hotspur at any point, or by its slow corruption dim by so much as a breath his hectic glory. He rode back slowly with the sunlight on his face, and there were birds wheeling and soaring above his head, so high that they dwindled to silver sparks and vanished into the blue.

The quarters of that dead wonder would soon be disseminated to all the regions of the realm as a warning to traitors, to vanish utterly at last into air, without need of obsequies or tomb, as though his fiery spirit had never had a body.

Epilogue

MARCH 1413

I

The king opened his eyes in a room in the abbot's lodging, where they had carried him after he had fallen senseless against the stone of St. Edward's shrine in the abbey. He saw, but in a blurred double vision because his eyes were affected, a tapestry-hung chamber, and two faces close to him, on the right his confessor bending solicitously over him, on the left the prince, erect, observant, dutiful and chill, as he had been all these past ten years, through all the vicissitudes and aggravations of their relationship, the alternate suspicion and affection, the terms of favour and the terms of disfavour. Always consistent, always loyal. But loyal to what? To some image of kingship, perhaps, kept private from other men.

He asked, in a thread of a voice that hardly reached his own ears: "Joan?"

"We have sent word to the queen, my liege," said the priest gently. "She will come."

"What is this place?"

"They call it the Jerusalem chamber. We carried you here from the church, to bring you to a place of rest."

A place of rest! No question but he was in need of such a place, and very near to it now. There had been little rest in his life since he first put on the crown. He turned his head in sudden disquiet, looking for it, for he had come in state to make his offering at St. Edward's shrine. But it was there, on a cushion beside his pillow, where his eyes, however dim, could find it. Jerusalem! Yes, how fitting an allegory for a life of such early promise, long since dwindled into anticlimax and discouragement. He had been promised that he should die in Jerusalem, and he had dreamed of a glorious pilgrimage, a crusade to crown his achievement. And here he lay dying in the Jerusalem chamber in the abbot's lodging at Westminster, in his bed—no, in a borrowed bed, like a beggar and a stray.

What was that story they had of Hotspur, long ago, that he was to die at Berwick? Berwick by Shrewsbury, a hamlet no man from north of the Humber had ever heard of! The wrong Berwick, the wrong Jerusalem! Why should he remember those linked destinies now, when he was bond, and the other was free? Freer than any man who lay sepulchred in the earth, for where he lay who could say, and the blowing abroad of his dust who could measure or control? A few bones had been conveyed to his widow at last, the fragments still tangible; but the rest of him was where? Not even the church and chantry chapel the king had founded over the mass grave on the battlefield, to pray for the souls of the dead, could lay for him the ghost of the man who had no grave. And those eyes that stared so straight and wide-set, and whose regard he could not sustain…

"My lord," said the confessor, with silken urgency, "you will rest the better if you make an act of contrition now, and then sleep."

He did not want to flagellate his memory, but he tried, whispering his shortcomings wearily, his eyes now upon the cross his confessor held before him, now upon the crown, now upon the young, mature, unsmiling, unfrowning, utterly detached face that regarded him across the cushion where the crown lay.

"I have sinned—in impatience, ingratitude, despondency—I have complained…"

"My liege, think on your end, and repent your share in the death of Archbishop Scrope—and your usurpation of the crown."

"As to the first, I have already received absolution from the Holy Father himself…"

Yet he had killed an archbishop, brought him to a traitor's death, along with other, lesser souls, for one more conspiracy only two years after Shrewsbury, one more attempt to spirit away the Mortimer children and set the elder on the throne. And absolution from the pope, though it might hold good in heaven, was distant, and York was near, and there had been miracles at Scrope's tomb, and fingers pointed at the king who had killed a man of God. The sudden ugly rash that had broken again on his face they had called leprosy, the chastisement of God. One conspiracy after another, one rebellion after another, Scrope dead, Northumberland dead, Bardolf dead, the earl Marshal dead, Mortimer dead of a wasting sickness during the siege of Harlech—one long litany of deaths, ending now in mine! Only the old Welsh wizard, he thought, though his wife and daughters and grandchildren may be taken and his chief strongholds razed painfully one by one, still goes free and hale, and however many of his branches we lop off still he grows new. He will never die, only vanish.

"As to the second," he said, labouring, "as to the crown, my sons will never permit me to make that restitution." And he smiled, if that contortion of the querulous, neurotic mouth was indeed a smile, however laced with wormwood, and not a new disability of the muscles. For his face was fallen and flabby, and every movement of tongue or throat was hard exertion. He made his act of contrition patiently and humbly, and was blessed to God.

The king closed his eyes, desirous not of sleep but of respite from all company, from the exhaustion of justifying himself and the empty labour of being regal. He heard the door close softly upon John Tille, his confessor. The two of them were left together, the worn-out wreck of a man, old at forty-six, and the cold, capable, guarded young man of twenty-five, fully awake to his own powers, and well aware that for some years now the populace had looked to him as king rather than to his father. The house at Coldharbour had become a court in every sense, the order of England went better when it reverted to his hands by reason of his father's ill-health; and his father's recovery regularly meant the prince's relegation to the background, a banishment jealously decreed and coldly accepted, where he amused himself after his own imperious fashion, asking no man's leave, caring nothing for any man's disapprobation, but always ready to emerge again when the need arose. Need? Or opportunity? Do him justice, he had never shown any sign of impatience with the long duration of his apprenticeship. Yet surely his wings were aching and his heart fretted, like a hawk mewed too long.

The king opened his eyes, and the young hazel eyes were upon him, and did not avoid. On its cushion between them the crown lay dulled in shadow. It was the 20th day of March, and a dim and dismal afternoon, on the edge of frost.

Only too clear, the tired man thought, for which of these two brows that circlet is more fitly designed. No wonder he watches it, between his moments of watching me, as a lover watches the bride.

"How can you assert any right to it," he asked clearly, "seeing I had none?"

The prince was not disconcerted by any sudden flight of thought, now or ever. His face did not change, and his voice was mild and low. There was no way in to him, circle him as you would.

"Sir, what you took with the sword I may very well make shift to keep with the sword, and will, as long as I live."

"I know," said his father, "that you always desired it."

"Yes, since I was taught that it was my inheritance."

"As it was not mine!" said the dying man bitterly. "You think to escape with the prize and slough the guilt upon me. You think to have no blame. But in truth you will have no choice—no more than I had when first I came to it."

He wasted his time, he knew, for he was speaking to a stern, decisive creature who found a choice everywhere, and took his course fearlessly and ruthlessly, rigid in honour but absolute of will, despising the feeble excuse that there could be any situation in which a man had no choice. Yet there can be no restoration of a crown to a deposed king, or of life to a dead man—no restoration of a dismembered and rotted body to its wholeness in a quiet grave. He knew well who the two men were who stood invisibly but implacably between his son and himself. And he knew, even as his vision began to fail and his son's face to fade, that they were still there, watching him through those hazel eyes that burned upon him like two green flames.

"Do me this justice," he said in a whisper, "it cannot all have been ill-done…"

It was not the sudden descent into entreaty that shook the prince out of his ten-years frost, but the unexpected echo of another voice. He leaned forward, and caught and clasped his father's wandering hand between both his own, the first spontaneous motion of warmth, and the last. "Some of us," said the voice in his pricked and quivering memory, "will stand in great need of advocates before we come to our life's end. By your judgment I will gladly abide, and whatever dues you charge me with, I will pay with a good grace." Even this one impulse of pity and affection had to be Hotspur's gift.

He found some words of his own to say, unfamiliar, not even completely true, hard to formulate and harder to utter, and yet they eased him. For his life, too, would end some day, that was just gloriously coming to flower; and in his life, too, not all would be done well, and there would be need of advocates. Of late he had become a stranger to humility, but he rediscovered it now within his heart, and was astonished and chastened. So much so, that he sat gently cradling his father's hand for a long time, even after he had run out of words.

Only when the silence began to seem greater than natural did he realise that the hand in his was already growing a little colder than life, and the king had ceased to breathe. And even then he remained quiet in his place until they came again to enquire, and could not for his life determine whether it was the vanquished who had spoken up for the victor, or the victor for the vanquished.

ABOUT THE AUTHOR

Edith Pargeter (1913–1995) has gained worldwide praise and recognition for her historical fiction and historical mysteries, including *The Brothers of Gwynedd* and *A Bloody Field by Shrewsbury*. She also wrote several novels of crime fiction as Ellis Peters. She was awarded an OBE (Order of the British Empire).

A Burning Desire For
One Country, One Love, and One Legacy
That Will Last Forever.

L lewelyn, prince of Gwynedd, dreams of a Wales united against the English,
but first he must combat enemies nearer home. Llewelyn and his brothers—
Owen Goch, Rhodri, and David—vie for power among themselves and with
the English king, Henry III. Despite the support of his beloved wife, Eleanor,
Llewelyn finds himself trapped in a situation where the only solution could be his
very downfall...

Originally published in England as four individual novels, *The Brothers of Gwynedd*
transports you to a world of chivalry, gallant heroes, and imprisoned damsels; to
star-crossed lovers and glorious battle scenes; and is Edith Pargeter's absorbing tale
of tragedy, traitors, and triumph of the heart.

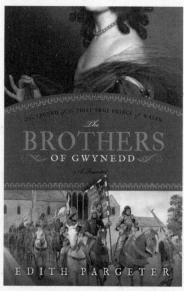

"A lively evocation of life on the Welsh
borders in the Middle Ages, coupled
with an ingenious plot, and the whole
narrated with elegant crispness."
— *Times Literary Supplement*

"Strong in atmosphere and plot, grim
and yet hopeful...carved in weathered
stone rather than in the sands of current fashion."
— *Daily Telegraph*

"A richly textured tapestry of medieval
Wales."
— *Sunday Telegraph*

"Those who fancy historical fiction
with an emphasis on the history will
savor this convincing tale."
— *Publishers Weekly*

978-1-4022-3760-7 • $16.99 U.S./$19.99 CAN